the Pleasure Quartet: *Summer*

the Pleasure Quartet: *Summer*

VINA JACKSON

**SIMON &
SCHUSTER**

London · New York · Sydney · Toronto · New Delhi

A CBS COMPANY

First published in Great Britain by Simon & Schuster UK Ltd, 2015
A CBS COMPANY

1 3 5 7 9 10 8 6 4 2

Simon & Schuster UK Ltd
1st Floor
222 Gray's Inn Road
London WC1X 8HB

www.simonandschuster.co.uk

Simon & Schuster Australia, Sydney
Simon & Schuster India, New Delhi

A CIP catalogue record for this book is available from the British Library

PB ISBN: 978-1-4711-4157-7
EBOOK ISBN: 978-1-4711-4158-4

Typeset by Hewer text UK Ltd, Edinburgh
Printed and bound in Great Britain by CPI Group (UK) Ltd, Croydon, CR0 4YY

the Pleasure
Quartet: *Summer*

1

It's Not You, It's Me

It was the squirrel's fault.

Following a late brunch in the West Village, close by Greenwich Avenue, Noah and April headed for Washington Square Park. The Sunday warm-weather crowds were out in force. A pianist had wheeled his large ambulatory instrument close to the afternoon shadow of the arch and was playing an improvisation on a melody from a Rachmaninov concerto with loud flourish. The hordes of guitar players spread across the park strummed away in total discordance, echoes of their songs clashing indifferently against each other in the sultry air, and the resident pigeon lady sat further south against her usual railing, busy knitting. Around the fountain, children and adults dipped their toes in the water while tourists snapped photos on their sleek mobile phones. A street fair filled the side roads on the other side of the park by the tall university buildings, stalls alternately offering aromatic bites, handcrafted jewellery and other items Noah would never have contemplated gifting even to his worst enemies. Not that he believed he had any genuine enemies.

April had suggested eating at a vegetarian gourmet on Sixth Avenue that she had developed a strong liking for and, just under an hour later, Noah still felt hungry, his taste buds and appetite barely tickled by the somewhat tasteless food they had been served, and now the combined smells of barbecued meat and grilled onions floating across towards them from the fair seemed to swirl around him and make his mouth water. He now regretted not having talked April into visiting Toto's sushi joint on Thompson Street.

They held hands, strolled lazily along the pathways, turning right after the fountain to avoid the dog enclosure, April's shoulder-length hair gently animated by the breeze.

She wore a simple floral print summer dress that reached to just under her knees, her tanned legs straight and sporty, her movement relaxed above the tread of her flat, pale-pink thin-soled shoes.

Rushing around a corner, two children on scooters sped towards them, weaving their way through the crowds. The boy, blond-haired in blue shorts and a yellow T-shirt, must have been six or thereabouts, and his hardy sidekick was a tiny girl with a massive green helmet that dwarfed her features, round-faced and dark-eyed and with a look of utter determination, as if intent on colliding with them if they didn't steer clear of her path.

Noah couldn't help chuckling at the sight. April gripped his hand tighter. They slowed down, anticipating the accidental collision but, just inches away from their feet, the two speeding kids veered away with practised grace and rushed by, oblivious, as if they owned the park, never slowing down.

'That little one was so cute,' April remarked.

Noah smiled.

'There's space over there,' April said, indicating a wooden bench a stone's throw away which was just being vacated by an elderly couple and was shielded from the sun by the shadow of a nearby tree with low-lying branches. 'Let's go and sit.'

They had no plans for the afternoon. Noah thought that maybe later, towards evening, they might catch the new Michael Mann movie at the Union Square multiplex, but until then there was nothing on the cards. All he wanted to do was relax, slob, what with the rush of meetings he had scheduled at the office the following day. Similarly, he knew that April's following forty-eight hours would be frantic and involving as the monthly magazine where she worked as a production assistant had to go to press. They regularly relaxed this way at the end of the weekends, their Sunday routine.

Noah remained silent as they sat. April did not interrupt

his reverie. She took a sip from her bottle of water and offered it to him. He declined it.

Usually content to sit alongside him in silence, she seemed unnaturally restless today. Even after almost two years together, she often complained that she couldn't read him properly, interpret his changing moods with any degree of accuracy. She was upset by his impassivity.

She finally broke the silence.

'Something worrying you? You seem . . . distant.'

'Not at all. Just daydreaming.'

There was something on his mind, but he couldn't put a finger on it, define it, isolate it. It burrowed away in silence, unsettling him.

He looked around at April, sketched a silent kiss on his lips and directed it towards her. Her mid-length hair was shaken by flutters of gold as the sun snaked its way between the branches that mostly shielded it. Her bare shoulders were a similar shade of warmth, the tan they had both acquired that summer in Cancun persisting.

He couldn't help but find her beautiful. Always had. His golden girl.

'I love you,' April announced.

'And I you,' he responded.

He had spoken the words automatically, not for the first time in answer to the same phrase, he knew. As if not actually responding in kind was not lying.

Other couples walked by, young and old, trailed by dogs or children on occasion, many hand in hand, their faces blank, their body language a mystery to him.

Noah's throat tightened.

April lowered her hand to his right knee and squeezed it.

Noah watched her slender fingers as they gripped the material of his jeans.

'Oh . . .'

She let go of his knee.

She was no longer gazing at him but was looking at the tree behind the bench that faced them, on the opposite side of the pathway. He could hear her holding her breath.

He peered ahead. There was nothing out of the ordinary.

April eyes widened.

'Wow . . .'

Noah blinked, and finally noticed what was catching her attention.

A bushy-tailed grey squirrel was peering at them through the railing, sashaying its way from the tree across the sparse grass, its slow but steady straight-line movement like a clockwork toy's, its eyes round and dark and fixed on April.

She hesitantly extended her hand, bidding it welcome.

Noting her invitation, the hardy squirrel ventured past the wide opening of the railing and took a foothold on the busy path, in blissful ignorance of the passers-by, unafraid of being kicked or run over, and inched its way towards the bench where April and Noah sat.

'It can see me . . . it's coming towards me,' April whispered.

'It's that come-hither smile of yours. Bet you it's a male squirrel . . . Or maybe it thinks you have some food for it . . .'

The small animal had finally made its way across the path and faced them, actually looking up at April, whose happy grin was broadening by the second.

What was it expecting? For her to stroke it, feed it?

April dug her fingers into her small handbag, searching for some food she could offer the squirrel, but came up with nothing.

She glanced at Noah, hoping he could help.

He shook his head.

The diminutive animal sat facing her like a supplicant.

April slowly extended her hand downwards in its direction.

Her palm was just a hand's length away from the squirrel's face when the speeding duo on the scooters returned and the squirrel raced back across the path and onto the safety of the lawn to avoid them.

April straightened.

Noah could sense her disappointment.

Silence fell.

Had she been expecting the squirrel to lick her, kiss her?

A thin smile appeared on her face, as she reflected on what had happened, wry, lonely.

Noah finally recognised her mood. It wasn't the first time in the past months that he had witnessed it. She was getting broody, not so much distant but restless, as if something was missing from her life, their relationship.

And although he would never admit it to her face, he knew she was right.

And his feelings were not dissimilar, although they expressed themselves in different ways.

She wanted more.

He wanted more, or at any rate something different. But where April was no doubt aware, deep inside, of what she sought, Noah was not, aside from the fact that their paths were imperceptibly diverging.

A family, each respective member greedily enjoying ice cream cones in a variety of pastel colours, walked by, two small dogs on leashes trailing them, tails wagging.

'Want one?' Noah asked.

'What?'

'An ice cream?'

April didn't answer.

'Do you have any gigs this week?' she asked instead.

'A couple. The Nevsky Prospekt are playing at the

Bowery Ballroom, and the Holy Criminals are doing an unpublicised appearance as support at the Knitting Factory.'

Viggo Franck, who'd fronted the Criminals for years, had allegedly retired or, alternatively, gone solo, although in the latter case he was not contractually committed to Noah's record company should he come up with new product. The group had found themselves a new singer and were hoping to bed him in away from the attentions of the press and fans.

'Cool,' April said. 'Can I come along?'

'No problem.'

The spectacle of the squirrel, and the kids with the scooters, had triggered maternal thoughts, he was certain of it. Yet again.

After their time in Washington Square Park, April had expressed the wish to walk more and they'd strolled over to the High Line and ambled along its length twice, mostly absorbed in the flow of their private thoughts.

'Make love to me,' April asked as they closed the door to the apartment behind them.

Noah turned towards her, blissfully enjoying the sight of her beauty. After so many hours spent walking in the sun, her freckles were breaking through, delicately scattered across the bridge of her nose and the sharp ridge of her cheekbones. The golden sheen of her hair was now burnished with warm shades of bronze, the pale emerald hue of her eyes now matching the paint she had used to decorate the narrow corridor that led to their white bedroom. Noah had never been much of a visual person and had allowed April total control over the apartment's configuration, shades and furnishings when they'd moved in together a year previously, his only proviso the integrity of the wall of CD shelves in his study. She'd initially argued he could transfer them all to digital – it would take less space – but Noah had insisted on keeping them, arguing that music was his job and he was allowed this idiosyncrasy.

He kissed her, the plush softness of her lips an experience that renewed his faith in their closeness every time he did so, warm silk cushions with the sweet aftertaste of her fading lipstick.

Holding her tight, he could feel the beat of her heart through the thin fabric of her dress as she hugged him, her hands circling his back, pulling his body against hers as the kiss lengthened, tips of tongues touching each other in an unpredictable dance, breaths growing short, almost a battle of wills as to who would disengage first and both refusing to be the one who did so.

The rhythm of her heart was growing more frantic, like a distant drum, settling into a regular, steady pattern, like a song taking flight, unformed tides of desire spreading through her bloodstream.

Noah's hand moved towards her waist, their lips still

locked, took a firm hold of her dress, twisting the material between two fingers to get a grip on it and began pulling the garment upwards, baring her thighs and then her white lace panties. The back of his hand brushing against her stomach, he pulled aside the elastic of her knickers and delved deeper until his nails grazed the forest of curls shielding her intimacy. The heat radiating from her crux immediately washed across his intruding fingers. He slipped inside.

'You're so wet . . .'

'Yes.'

Their lips parted. April moved. He pulled his hand out of her panties and raised it to her hair, running his fingers through her silken curtain, parting its smooth waves, relishing the sensation. He swivelled slightly and gently bit the lobe of her ear. April shivered, a faint shudder animating her body, endangering her balance and almost causing her to stumble. Noah's hand on her shoulder steadied her.

'Come,' Noah said.

They walked to the bedroom, fingers interlocked, throwing off their shoes as they passed its threshold.

Out of instinct, April moved to the window and pulled the net curtains tidily together. Noah couldn't help feeling a touch of irritation. She always did that. Just couldn't let caution go to the wind, even though they were on a high floor and there was no taller building across the street towards Battery Park and anyone wishing to spy on them from below would require strong binoculars, a camera drone or supernatural voyeur powers. Even about to trip into sex, April always thought of other things, unnecessary precautions. Yet again the magic of the moment had been spoiled. A spell had been broken.

April turned back towards him, an enigmatic smile drawn across her lips. And began to undress.

Noah was taken aback; he had expected, hoped to undress her himself. Slowly, stretching time, baring, revealing her an inch or so at a time, lingering, fingers wandering lazily across her skin, building his desire in infinite increments, each breath a sigh, teasing, playing with the minutes.

April looked up at him. With a note of reproach, seeing him standing motionless and in no rush to disrobe.

'Why are you waiting?' she asked, her hands stretching behind her back to unhook her bra.

She had no sense of ritual, he realised.

For her, sex was just another element of life, one to enjoy and indulge in, like you did a good meal or a pleasant conversation. A condiment like salt and pepper or sweet words of endearment whispered in one's ear at the right moment, even if neither partner actually believed in them. An ingredient that would serve to enhance the quiet pleasure of a long-term relationship, smoothing its rough edges, filling the unspoken gaps of intimacy, nothing more.

Noah was beckoned by roughness. Not in bed; April always bristled slightly whenever he deviated from the well-worn path of their embraces. But in life he found an unexpressed thrill in danger, magic.

Which was probably what made him so receptive to music and good at his job in spotting bands and singers who could prove innovative and with whom he could work to mine their unpredictability, leave the surface of things behind and reach a new level.

April set her bra to the side and revealed her breasts.

She bent over to pull her panties down to her ankles and then imperceptibly shimmied and allowed them to slip all the way to the bedroom floor where she stepped out of them.

Her pubic hair was a darker shade of blonde, tightly woven, but so soft to the touch, Noah knew. She had never allowed him to shave it or responded to his suggestions.

Rooted to the spot and unwilling to do anything quite yet, he kept on gazing at her. Fuck, she was beautiful. It was as if every time he saw her nude anew was the first time again. A revelation. Even her minute flaws seemed to serve as a frame for her perfection. An ever so slightly crooked top tooth only visible when she laughed aloud, a thin scar across her right eyebrow, a slight discoloration of the skin on the inside of her right thigh in the shape of an island on a map of the world, just a nail's length across. April was terribly self-conscious about the stain, and Noah had once been in the habit of annoying her when he insisted that the mark was shaped like Sardinia, or it could have been Sicily or Malta or Tuvalu for all he knew. Geographical accuracy had not been the object of the exercise. And then there was the dark, harmless mole on her back, equidistant from each shoulder.

All these made her real.

And even more attractive to him.

April, now fully nude, walked over to their bed and pulled the cream cover away and dived under it.

Noah finally set to and pulled his grey T-shirt above his head, disturbing the even cushion of his dark curls, and began to unbuckle his jeans, tugging on the worn leather belt.

As he joined April between the covers, her body warm and soft against his, he found that she had placed herself at the centre of the bed, so he had no choice but to position himself above her. She had already opened her legs wide. Her wetness greeted him. He nestled his lips in the crook of her neck and breathed in the barely fragrant aftersmell of the perfume she had sprayed on before lunch and their walk through Greenwich Village, L'Eau by Issey Miyake. He knew because she had asked him to buy it for her for last year's Christmas gift. They rarely surprised each other.

He slid inside her.

With ease.

Comfortable weekend sex.

Predictable. Pleasant. Silent.

He was hard, but tender and attuned to April's inner rhythms, riding her with care and energy, expertly surfing across the inner waves of her lust, ever trying to match his movements to the currents of their respective desires, equalising the ebb and flow and intensity of the hidden seas that controlled their sexuality.

Soon, April was beginning to gasp and he knew she was close to coming and he accelerated his thrusts.

'Jeeezussss . . .'

Her triumphant cry punctured the room's peace.

Noah closed his eyes, now fixed on releasing his own pleasure. She was one of the few women he had known who came easily. There was no challenge in it.

A thought intruded in his mind as he kept on burying himself inside her pliant softness: the next time they fucked, he wanted to play loud music as an accompaniment. Whoever had said that you shouldn't mix work and pleasure?

He had met April just a few months after he arrived in the city. The now ex-girlfriend he had initially followed from London to New York, Bridget, had quickly failed in her attempt to conquer the Big Apple, and had soon come to the conclusion that she didn't have it in her to navigate the course. Bridget had enjoyed a modicum of success on the university and club circuit back in England as a folk singer with a dusky voice and clever phrasing, but on Bleecker Street, she was just one of a handful of moderately talented singers and, despite a few gigs at Kenny's Castaways and The Bitter End, she did not get enough favourable reviews or repeat bookings.

He'd been freelancing for a handful of music magazines, which was how they'd met. He'd championed Bridget with a positive review, in a successful attempt to bed her, and with a laptop reckoned he could work from anywhere, so following her to Manhattan had not been too much of a dilemma.

When a discouraged Bridget summarily gave up on her dream and decided to return to the UK to complete her law studies, Noah had opted to stay put. He'd always loved the excitement of New York and, half-American by birth, he didn't need to worry about obtaining a work visa. Thanks to a book advance he had pocketed to write a warts and all biography of a popular boy band with whose manager he had been to university, he had found himself an affordable rental in Brooklyn where the rock scene was burgeoning.

Within half a year, he had been offered an A&R job by a mainstream record company with a brief to nurture further local bands. He had a good ear, a distinctive taste for the original, and a British no-bullshit attitude which quickly made him popular with the musicians with whom he had to work and seduce into the corporate fold without any of them feeling they were compromising their ideals and principles in the process. Unlike other record business types, he would not pretend to be their friend and was careful not to interfere too openly with their music, opting for gentle hints and subtle production recommendations once he had managed to get the bands into the studios, an attitude they and their often inexperienced and wary managers appreciated.

Noah had found a life he enjoyed. Although not essentially creative himself, he was nevertheless involved in the creation of powerful music. It was the best of all possible worlds and yet something was missing. Sex, women.

A string of harmless one-night stands around the networks of clubs and venues he now haunted for his job had proved unfulfilling, and then he met April.

A photo session had been set up for one of his groups, a trip hop trio from Philadelphia, whose female singer's deep, sensual tones always managed to move him inside from the moment she began to sing, although her everyday non-performing voice was a bit strident and oh so American. She was part of a long-standing couple with the bass player in the group, but despite that, the temptation to get to know her more had, against Noah's best judgement, skirted his thoughts more than once.

The record company's art department had signed up a fairly well-known fashion photographer whose studio was on the Lower East Side and Noah had agreed to meet up with the guys there after the shoot, to pick up some test recordings of a couple of new songs they were working on. He was waiting in the studio's anteroom for the session to end. Leafing through a fashion magazine left open on a low glass table, he was smiling at the incongruous thought that he could just as well have been sitting in a dentist's waiting room when a young woman, a blonde with short hair, walked through, a pile of cellophane-wrapped clothes on hangers looped over her arm.

Their eyes met.

She noticed the ironic smile on his lips.

'What's so funny?' she asked him.

'Not you, I assure you. Just something that was passing through my mind before you entered.'

'You're English.'

'Indeed.'

She smiled back at him.

By then he'd been in America long enough to recognise her own accent was also not local. He took a guess.

'You're Canadian?'

She nodded and laid out her cumbersome bundle of clothes onto a nearby sofa.

'I'm April.'

'Noah.'

'Are you waiting for Hutch, or are you one of his assistants?'

'Neither. He's finishing a shoot.' He indicated the door that separated the waiting room from the loft studio where the work was taking place. 'I'm with the group, musicians being shot. The band.'

'Their manager? Minder? You don't look like the rock type.'

Noah appreciated her attitude. And he wasn't ashamed to admit it, her looks, too. She had a quality of self-assurance that appealed to him greatly, as if she knew what she wanted and nothing would change her aim or direction.

'Is there a typical rock type?'

'I don't know. You look normal . . .' Her sentence halted in full flow, as if she thought she had said something wrong, was maybe insulting him. She lowered her eyes.

'I don't mind in the slightest being normal,' Noah countered. 'Feel no need to conform to popular expectations.'

'It's not what I meant,' April said. 'I expressed myself badly. I do that sometimes.'

'It's fine. What about you?'

'Me?'

'What brings you here, April? Do you work for a dry cleaner, maybe?'

She laughed. 'No.'

He laughed along with her.

'So what's all the clothes about?'

'They're for a fashion shoot tomorrow. I brought them ahead of time. I work for a magazine.' She looked down at the one he had dropped back on the glass table. 'Actually, the same one you were reading.'

'How fortuitous.'

'Wow, big words!' Her eyes were a pale shade of green and he couldn't help but stare at them. Not that the rest of April didn't call for much closer attention, but you could only admire a woman one step at a time, he reckoned. His attention was drawn to a thin, almost invisible line, a scar, he realised, that partly bisected one of her eyebrows. A terribly minor imperfection that made her seem less plastic, he felt. He liked the girl. A lot.

'No one's perfect. Even more so with a British university education.'

'So I see.'

'And what about Canada? Where do you come from?'

'Vancouver.'

'Never been,' Noah said, 'but got close. I was visiting Seattle a couple of years ago, and was tempted to hire a car and drive up. Never got round to it, though.'

'You should have. Gastown is a gas.'

'Would you have been there, or already in New York?'

'If I'd known you were coming, maybe I would have stayed on . . .'

He enjoyed the way she could playfully sustain a conversation, spar with him, tease, seduce him already.

Right then, the studio door opened and the band poured out, all in an ebullient mood, still high from the photo shoot.

Noah and April exchanged phone numbers.

She'd arrived in the city at almost the same time he had, they later discovered, leaving a small local publishing house where she'd found a placement following art school studies, and now worked in Manhattan as a production assistant for a mid-level magazine group. She wasn't actually involved with the fashion department, and the errand at the photographer Hutch Lea's studio, had been a favour she was doing for a colleague whose child was down with flu. Normally, she wouldn't ever have set foot there. Her job was assisting the art department to complete their layouts in readiness for the printers.

Noah pondered at length where to invite her for a first date and how long to wait until he actually called her and suggested they meet. He had the intuition she wouldn't be impressed merely being a 'plus one' on a guest list, however prestigious the gig was, and actually suggested they visit the Metropolitan, where a new exhibition transferred from London's Royal Academy was enjoying rave reviews and tickets were at a premium, but available to him against musical favours. He chose right.

They were lovers within a week.

Noah knew his feelings on the subject were profoundly irrational, but soon after April moved in with him, she took the decision to grow her hair longer, and even though all their individual and common friends loved her new look, he felt cheated; as if acquiring a new partner he had been given a wrong bill of goods.

Thus were seeds sown.

Outwardly, things were just fine. They seldom argued, the sex was good if at times predictable, they looked good together and enjoyed each other's company, and New York was vibrant. What could go wrong?

April was untidy, relished in the chaos of mess, her clothes scattered across their bedroom or further afield if Noah indulged her, while he was meticulous and precise, over-organised apart from the piles of cassettes and CDs that spilled over from his desk into even the kitchen, which he always blamed on the nature of his work and which she never reproached him for or used as an excuse for her own state of domestic wildness. She even approved of the way he dressed, conservative and unimaginative and somewhat repetitive in combinations of black, blue and grey, whereas she generously mined every colour of the rainbow and, miraculously, wore them equally well, avoiding clashes, gaudiness or fantasies of outmoded psychedelia.

'Are all Canadian women like you?'

'Like what?'

'So easy to live with?'

'Am I?'

'Absolutely.'

'Would you want me to be more complicated?'

'Like a messed-up maiden with a tenebrous past in a Victorian novel?'

'Or any period you can think of . . .'

He wanted to answer in the affirmative, hint that there was too much brightness, normalcy even, about her, but Noah knew she wouldn't understand. He pecked her on the cheek. They lay together in bed. She was reading a magazine; she seldom read books – another mild if occasional bone of contention – and he was halfway through a compelling thriller while listening to a series of remixes one of the bands he was overseeing had sent along that day following a week of arduous recordings with a local producer Noah had suggested. There was no improvement in their sound. The material, the songs were great, but the textures were still wrong. Although not a musician himself – he couldn't read music, let alone play either piano or guitar or any instrument whatsoever – his intuition had always served him well even if on occasions like this he couldn't properly express the way forward with just the excuse of emotional intelligence. It sometimes proved frustrating. His mind half on the book he was holding in his left hand catching the light from the bedside table, and half on the music and wandering through its melodic meanders in an attempt to blindly create new aural paths that would lift it to another level, Noah didn't realise that his right hand had disappeared under the covers and that he was distractedly stroking himself. They both always slept naked.

Her voice reached him, like a dream emerging from a cloud just as Noah simultaneously felt her fingers pinch his left forearm hard. He pulled the earphones off.

'What the fuck are you doing?' she complained.

He had no clue what she was on about.

His eyes must have betrayed his incomprehension.

'What?'

'Your hands are all over your cock . . .'

He looked down. She was right. He was playing with himself, his fingers moving between his cock and his balls. He was only half hard, the contact between hand and genitals barely there, no more than a pleasant feather's touch.

'Oh, I'm sorry.' He withdrew his fingers.

A veil of annoyance passed across April's eyes.

'How could you?'

'It just happened. I didn't realise. Doesn't mean anything.'

Didn't she ever unconsciously touch herself? Surely everyone did.

'I feel . . . offended . . .' She was visibly struggling for the right word. 'Insulted . . .' she continued.

'You shouldn't.' Noah tried to reassure her. 'It means nothing. Really.'

'Don't I please you enough?' Her lips downturned, her face child-like in sulk.

'You do, truly.' He set the book down and his hand brushed her cheek.

April shrugged him off with a look of disgust.

'You've just been playing with your cock with that hand . . .'

'It was the other hand,' he retorted.

She turned away from him.

In silence, she switched off her own reading light and pulled her side of the quilt over her shoulders, ignoring him. Noah did likewise, settling with his back to her, their arses cheek to cheek. He knew that by morning the cloud would have passed and the subject be unlikely to be mentioned again.

But he couldn't sleep, his thoughts now focused on her earlier question. It bounced around in his mind: 'Don't I please you enough?' Round and round it went.

And every time the answer came back positive.

Making him angry with himself in the process.

Maybe he wasn't cut out for a simple, unassuming state of happiness, of domesticity. He was aware of the fact that in crowds, at parties, functions or elsewhere, he was always looking over his shoulder for others, for new conversation, for distractions. Ever trying to escape boring company, hoping for something better on the other side of the room, in another room, elsewhere. It was the same with women. The thrill was in the chase, the initial exploration, the early days of passion and sexual intemperance and excess.

He wanted more.

But didn't know what that might consist of. Could he have recognised it even if it presented itself?

He thought of April, by his side, her body warm and soft, almost perfect, the velvet heat when he moved inside her, the faint night smell of her breath, the musky fragrance of her cunt, the way she breathed when they fucked, haltingly, gasping for air as if she was hanging on to a cliff and was playing a game and unsure whether she wished to let go or not.

But she never let go, did she?

Sometimes he dreamed of more.

Of waking in the small hours of morning, his mind still shrouded with fog, to feel her silken lips wrapped around his cock, sucking him slowly, engineering his rise, conducting the blood arousal like an orchestra conductor. Swallowing him whole and literally. Not a thing she would ever willingly do, he knew.

He evoked the pale orb of her arse cheeks when he moved inside her as she kneeled on all fours and allowed him to thrust away and he couldn't help but wonder how tight her other hole would be. On a couple of occasions, he had been tempted to move just that vital inch or so and try to penetrate her anally but she had always made it clear it was not on the menu. Not that he had a particular fetish for anal sex, although he had enjoyed the few times women had allowed him to practise or suggest the supposedly twisted art, but there was a dirtiness, a taboo about the act that drew him strongly towards the idea of it.

April was normal.

And nigh perfect.

And transparent.

And boring.

She fucked because that's what girlfriends did with boyfriends. Women did with men. He didn't even know if she enjoyed it. She came so easily, he often wondered if she faked her orgasms. She expected him to take her, to enter her, to possess her, seemed to believe that her sex was a gift he (or other men) would be grateful for, an offering, but she seldom initiated the act. Had it not been a healthy exercise, a sanitary flexing of their body hydraulics, he reckoned she would have been totally indifferent to the act. Seen it as just another function, like eating, running or conversation.

More.

He wanted more.

He dreamed of a dark sexual power that would move him like music did, like magic.

Shortly after, for her job, April had to fly off for a few days to the magazine printer's plant in Illinois to overlook a new production process. Her trip had been planned for some time, and had nothing to do with that awkward evening. Noah found himself alone in Manhattan for a series of nights and, although he would never have admitted so to her, he felt a sense of relief and a quiet sense of excitement. Opportunities? The chance to reconsider their relationship? His thoughts were still vague on the subject.

He'd detoured past Electric Ladyland studios to pick up the masters for some new material by a West Coast middle-of-the-road balladeer who had been signed to the label long before he had become involved, and walking out into the midday sun had decided he had no wish to continue to his office on Perry Street. His company hours were flexible and, anyway, he could always be contacted on his mobile. He was in no rush to listen to the recordings. He knew they would be bland but efficient, tailored for the radio market, every beat in place, superficial but perfect for the dance floor.

In truth, the frosty exchange with April that other evening had left a seed of doubt in his mind.

Why had he begun to touch himself, rather than reach out to her nude body at his side? He tried to remember if he had been daydreaming, fantasising, drumming up past girl-friends or mental caches of pornography that might have caused him to absentmindedly stroke his cock rather than his girlfriend. He could not recall anything particularly erotic passing through his mind right then. Was he actually seeking arousal, just a Pavlovian reflex buried deep inside his male senses responding to a primeval bell? The thought that he might no longer be attracted to April, despite her beauty, burrowed in the back of his brain like a termite, quiet, insistent, small but definitely there, nibbling away at the mental banks of his relationship.

He sat at the outside table of a café on Sullivan Street, sipping a coffee and watching the passers-by. A petite long-haired dark blonde walked by. She looked foreign, in the way she was dressed, with both elegance and simplicity, and the way she carried her head straight, assured in the knowl-edge that she was attractive, chin to the fore, snub nose raised, kissable heavy lips free of lipstick, cushioned, inviting.

She caught Noah staring at her and hesitated a brief moment when he thought she might even stop, begin con-versing with him, maybe even come and sit with him. A faint smile emerged across her lips and she continued past, supremely self-confident, reassured by the power she knew she had over men. His eyes followed her arse. The skirt was

28

short and tight, her legs straight and sinewy, the thin material of the cotton skirt adhering to her skin like a thin veil. As she reached the corner with Bleecker the sun exploded behind her, exposing the shape of her body through the flimsy material. Somehow Noah was convinced she was wearing nothing underneath. He grew hard in an instant at the thought that this foreign girl, in her mid-twenties but looking dangerously younger, was absolutely the type of woman who would, without hesitation, suck his cock between the sheets in the morning to wake him up and confound him with wonderful obscenities should he fuck her in the arse.

She disappeared around the corner, her ostentatious sexuality carrying her along to her destination where an unknown lover was no doubt already caressing his cock awaiting her arrival.

For a brief moment, Noah felt like jumping out of his chair, dropping a few dollar bills on the table for the coffee and rushing off to follow her. But he didn't. He was aware he presented well, looking neither like Brad Pitt nor like Frankenstein's monster, could hold a conversation with a modicum of wit, but he had never mastered impromptu pick-up techniques, he knew. 'Sorry, Miss, do you happen to be French?' And if she did, what to say next? And if she wasn't?

Damn, sometimes, he wished he was more decisive. He

was when it came to work and business, so why not in his private life?

The waitress came along to ask if he wanted a refill, which he turned down. She had a pronounced Mid-West accent and wore tight black jeans with a thin red plastic belt, wedge-heel canvas shoes and a white T-shirt advertising the logo of the café. She wore a visibly sheer bra, her nipples hard and sharply delineated behind the stretched material. She looked down at him and he was certain could not avoid seeing how his trousers were deformed by an obvious erection. Her face was pleasant but inexpressive, and Noah felt a wave of shame when he realised that it was not unlike April's, somehow devoid of emotions, of depth. Adequate for the majority of onlookers but not for the seekers of truths, for whom mere simplicity was not enough. He held her gaze one instant, as if challenging her to object to his ever so inescapable hardness. He paid up and left.

Walking home, he found himself captivated by the spectacle of women. Old and young, walking alone or with others. Thin and voluptuous. The variety of ways they dressed, revealed degrees of flesh, hints of their personality, their likes and dislikes. Their posture, ramrod straight and slouching, waltzing along the streets, tiptoeing as if through water across the busy pavements, eyes peering right ahead or avoiding his incoming stare with false modesty. Each one distinctive. Unique.

And, with every vision, a million scenarios began hatching in his febrile mind. Of undressing them, fucking them, loving them, hurting them, having them beg, making them come, manipulating the underground rise of their lust, bringing their basic truth to the surface.

Would that skinny woman in her late forties with the pastel cashmere coat enjoy having her hair pulled while he rode her? Would that teenager in a Harvard rowing team sweatshirt and jeans torn at the knees enjoy being pinned down with brute force while he lowered himself into her? Would those two Scandinavian-like waifs speaking in a language he couldn't recognise as they crossed the street in a different direction consent to take turns sucking him off, both on their knees in front of him?

No wonder he couldn't lose his erection.

Greenwich Village was becoming a world of possibilities. A city symphony of female faces and bodies. Each one as clear and defined in his overworked imagination as a wide screen porno movie. Noah couldn't recall how long it had been since he had enjoyed such thoughts. He imagined with a strong tinge of self-consciousness that the eyes of every woman he passed and fantasised about in the process was fixed on his unyieldingly hard crotch. He really had to get indoors and relieve himself.

At last, Noah reached home.

The airy, well-lit lounge. The Eames chair he had paid an

outrageous price for, despite its age. His cluttered desk, a warren of piles of tape boxes, CDs, papers, folders, elastic bands and paper clips. The laptop booting up, its screen shifting from sky blue to pale grey. Slowly. Too slowly.

It had been ages since he had surfed any sex sites, but the computer's predictive ability locked on them after just a few strokes of the keyboard.

He unbuttoned his jeans and pulled out his cock. He had gone soft again, waiting for the website to load. He shrugged at the timing.

Had every woman in the world, at one time or another, performed in pornographic acts in the eye of a lens? It felt that way. Racing through clips, sites where the activities in question were carefully categorised: colour of hair, age, body shape, position, settings urban and bucolic and wilder, openings used solo or in unison, nationalities, even scenarios ranging from pretend lost hitchhikers to interception by border guards, casting auditions, medical examinations, school encounters, orgies, weddings, all the life sexual was present and on display and available to him and whoever else was seeking relief right now, and the choice of faces on offer was infinite. He knew he was only seeing the tip of the iceberg, and his mind felt dizzy at the thought of how many women had espoused sex on camera. The clips travelled the ages, from teased sixties hairdos and clothes and bushy genitalia to a maelstrom of smooth, exposed cunts and more modern furniture in the irrelevant backgrounds in front of which they all performed. Rarely did he recognise a woman from clip to clip, film to film. Always a new one, a fresh face. Because it wasn't the act, the position or the combination of participants that stopped his fingers in their tracks, it was the women's faces. There was something anonymous about the men, just an incessant parade of steadily performing cocks. Despite their obvious necessity, they were interchangeable and forgettable.

Here, the faint smile of a young girl with a strained air of dramatised innocence at the instant of feigned violation by her supposed teacher that unconscionably gripped his heart, the emotion immediately transferring down to his cock which hardened and pulsed in his hand.

There, the panicked look in a Czech would-be model's eyes as she auditioned in a hotel room, was asked to strip and examined from every close-up angle by the camera and the interviewer, when the unlikely agent promising her modelling gigs makes it clear she has to suck him on camera to determine her talents.

His cock hardens again towards the end of a lengthy sequence in which another young woman has been used repeatedly in all openings by two tattooed studs, the resigned fall of the shoulders as she is dragged towards a bath tub to be urinated on as a final insult in the story of her degradation.

He felt ashamed at the way some images or situations could arouse him even further as he stroked away, his cock now at full length and hard in his grip, moving up and down across the ridges of his glans, his veins at bursting point, trying to hold the orgasm back just a little longer, until he reached the image, the woman, the act that would make the explosion inevitable and even painful in its intensity.

Noah flew from clip to clip, sometimes just a few seconds here, seeking the ideal face, the right emotion.

Still dissatisfied, he noticed a provenance link for a brief GIF of a faceless girl whose 'master' was tracing clumsy letters from the alphabet across her offered rump, with the letter O strategically placed to advertise the availability and popularity of her anal aperture. It was not an uncommon image, but the shape of the woman's pale arse intrigued him and Noah clicked on the link to a Tumblr page he couldn't recall encountering before.

The screen went blank for a few seconds and he reckoned the link had expired, the account been closed.

The page opened slowly, the buffering agonisingly halting as the screen filled up. He scrolled downwards to hurry it, but it was no help.

He was edging his cock, tiptoeing on the precipice of his own sought-after eruption, anxious to come, to lift the burden from his mind and body, impatient to reach an image that would form the perfect trigger to his orgasm.

Noah held on, waited for a quartet of images to finally come to life on his laptop screen.

The photos were of poor quality. An amateur production. They were sequential.

The first one was just a repeat of the one he had linked onwards from, reposted on a BDSM site about reputedly beautiful slaves. The apple-shaped pale arse, its opening red and distended, the back of the young woman's thighs, tense, sinews on alert, the fall of her back an exquisite curve expanding to an unknown horizon, a promise of further forbidden delights.

The second image repeated the initial one but was shot from the side so you could trace the sketch of a breast, small, its curve an exquisite geometry, and beyond the bent-over body the legs of a group of men. Onlookers, previous users or users still to come? The blurry background was a white wall. Some form of cellar, a dungeon? He peered closer, seeking out details. A tile caught his attention. A sauna, he decided.

The penultimate photograph appeared to have been taken later, following the inevitable excess and plundering of the victim. It was clear to Noah that what had occurred on the occasion of these photographs was real, not a set-up with professional participants. This had happened in real life, wasn't a scenario elaborated for a porn clip. The photographs taken had been incidental, and maybe the young woman at the centre of attention had not even been aware they were being taken. Might not have allowed them had she known. Her body was splayed, as if stretched on an invisible cross, drenched in sweat and the assorted men's cum, as if broken, but there was a pride in her abandon, the looseness of her limbs, attitude. The photograph was cropped so you couldn't see her face, ending at her neck, a delicate extension to the ravaged body that lay fully exposed, betraying all the indignities she had just suffered.

Noah swallowed hard. His cock hurt. His chest felt tight.

With his free hand he rapidly scrolled down the page to the final image.

It was similar to the previous one but the crop was different. The image was slightly out of focus, a garden of shadows, taken by a cheap device in badly lit circumstances. You could distinguish the woman's chin and her mouth. It was half-open, a horizon of white teeth profiled beyond the dry lips (how many cocks had she sucked? how many times?), but there appeared to be an ambiguous grin there. No sadness or resignation, or shame, or a reflection of hypothetical tears flowing from her eyes. No. There was something oddly triumphant about the downturn of her lips, as if in her degradation there was some form of victory achieved, that the pleasure she had extracted from the men still surrounding her was her own accomplishment, a measure of her will. A caricature of insubordination. Which added to the sheer obscenity of the series of images, screamed a mighty defiance. Damn, he wanted to see her whole face, her eyes. To witness how the pleasure in her gaze combined with the unavoidable pain.

Noah's throat felt terribly dry.

He highlighted the final photograph and tried to lighten the image better with the software he stored on his laptop.

Yes.

That was a bit better.

And from the murky depths of the image he finally noticed the young woman's hair, laid out behind her, a darkness against darkness, untidy, unkempt, wet from her exertions and the ocean of fluids released earlier.

It was red.

Gorgon-like.

Striking. Like a beacon being lit up in his soul.

His heart stopped.

He groaned.

He came.

His cock shuddering out of his control, spilling his seed across the desk and even the keyboard before he could control its terrible and powerful flow.

By the time his orgasm had faded, he was exhausted, his mind running around in circles trying to interpret what had happened and why it had proved so strong. There was much similar porn on the internet, he knew, but this had been different. Not the scenario, to be sure, but an unholy combination of elements: the pallor of the woman's skin, the allied grace of her curves, some hint of the intensity of her submission, the curl of her lips, and in his imagination, the look he knew he would have witnessed in her eyes had the photograph been more informative.

That red hair, like a stain in the night sky!

It began to haunt his own nights.

'Is there something wrong?'

'No. Why?'

'You were a bit rough last night, Noah. When we were in bed. It's just not like you. Are you angry at me?'

'And expressing it physically? Not at all. Surely you know I wouldn't do that?'

'I didn't like it. It felt almost as if you wanted to hurt me. Or like you wanted me to be someone else. Maybe that's even worse.' She was buttoning her blouse, and paused as she spoke, pinching a button tightly between her fingers as she stared at him.

'You're imagining things, April.'

'I don't think so.' She fastened her top button and turned away from him to straighten her collar in the mirror.

'What does that mean?'

'I'm not sure . . .'

'Maybe things have become a bit routine, and I was subconsciously trying to add a bit of spice. I hadn't noticed I was doing anything differently. Perhaps it was both of us, trying something new? In bed, together, things come naturally, don't they?'

'Not when you scare me. I like familiarity, the Noah I first met and wanted.'

'Nothing remains the same forever in life . . .'

'Don't give me that crap. You're starting to sound like a self-help book. That's not you, either.'

'That's not what I meant. You know my feelings on pseudo psychology.'

'What is it, then? Are you happy with me, Noah? With us?'

'I am.'

'Are you?'

'Yes.'

'When was the last time you said you love me, and meant it?'

'That's a trick question.'

'Maybe.'

'Quite unfair.'

'I'm not going to let this drop, Noah. Why don't we go out later, try that new place in Nolita you mentioned, that the *Village Voice* reviewed last week? We can talk. It's been ages since we've been on a proper date, just the two of us, no music, no movie or anything to do with our jobs.'

'Sure.' He was relieved to be granted some form of respite from the conversation, albeit temporary.

She leant up to kiss him.

Her lips were soft, tremulous, her body vibrating slowly in his embrace. Winter was nearing, and she slipped on her faux fur vintage Balmain coat which she had left draped over the sofa. Noah seized his brown leather jacket and they left the apartment together. The cold winds wrapped themselves around the Manhattan avenues and there was a chill in the air. They parted and April made her way down Broadway to catch the subway near Canal Street. Noah continued straight ahead to the record company's offices. He watched her walk, her slim calves encased in nude stockings, impractically high-heeled shoes on her feet. She looked deep in thought.

After the weekly strategy meeting in the glass-panelled boardroom, Jake took Noah to one side and asked him to stay on. Apart from this vast room, the company's offices were mostly open plan, everyone working around an enormous oak table, designed accordingly, almost thirty metres in length and five metres wide, with desktops and laptops delineating their individual areas. A few soundproofed booths with curtains and doors had been set up at the back of the central room for individual meetings with visitors and artists when it proved necessary.

Their colleagues filed out.

Jake, although nominally Vice-President of Marketing, was effectively in charge of the label. Wignall, the CEO, had based himself on the West Coast, and mostly overlooked the financials and the dynamic between the record company and its multinational owners.

'That mix you selected for the Rumble crew was just right,' Jake said.

The band and its management had been fiercely opposed to Noah's decision to go with that particular version of the song, but he'd won the day following an exhausting series of meetings and arguments. Now, the track was breaking fast with radio and the downloads were increasing exponentially with every passing day. They had a sure-fire hit on their hands.

'It was obvious from the start,' Noah said. 'The other takes were predictable. Safe. Sometimes you just have to gamble and try something different. We would have done well enough with the version they preferred, but not great. It was an okay song but it needed the right arrangements and sound.'

'I'm glad you held your ground.'

Noah smiled. 'I'm pleased it worked.'

Jake gave him a high five. His outmoded version of hip. Noah stifled a laugh.

'Listen,' Jake said.

'Yes?'

'This is another mighty notch on your bedpost, you know. I was talking to Wignall last night. He's over the moon. We'd like to make you a proposal.'

'Tell me.'

'Some of the best sounds of the past year or so have been coming out of England. But all the best talent seems to be ending up on other labels. Which is a bummer seeing that we have an office in London that's already costing us a fortune to run.'

Noah remained silent, curious to see where this was leading, although he had a premonition and felt a tinge of excitement run through his fingers. He'd never had much contact with their British offshoot, which was run by a flamboyant entrepreneur with a flair for self-publicising, but a patchy track record in discovering new artists or appointing the right people to do so.

'We'd like you to take over. Give the place a kick in the ass. Bring it into the current century. You'd have carte blanche. Interested?'

The company were about to give the London boss his marching orders this afternoon, coinciding with the office closing in the UK to avoid complications. Lawyers were already in place to do the dirty work and avoid too much of a mess. They wanted Noah to be in place within a week.

He had no hesitation in accepting.

It wasn't just the job and the opportunities it offered. The posting would be open-ended and, naturally, dependent on him making a success of it, but it would provide an escape from New York and the unease he was now in the grip of.

Noah and April met up at the restaurant.

She'd been back to their apartment to change first and wore a little black dress and another pair of perilous heels, her long, elegant legs uncovered from mid thigh, taut, agile, a picture of sleek sexual remoteness. He'd stayed on late at the office, already planning the London trip, and came directly from there.

They ordered.

The cuisine was inspired by New Orleans. He had the andouillette gumbo, followed by half a dozen oysters and a small lobster salad, and April went for the shrimp remoulade and a duck jambalaya.

He watched her eating, admiring the delicacy with which she chewed her food, and imagined, remembered those lips so often tasting his cock and the barely there traces of red blush that often spread across her cheeks as she did so, as she realised time and again that she enjoyed it but was also a touch ashamed of her lurid actions. Once he had loved that dichotomy. It had moved him, excited him.

Coffee came.

'I'm going to London.'

'How long for?'

'For good. I've been asked to run the London office of the label.'

There was a strange look on her face. It was neither excitement nor disappointment. Almost one of relief. Noah was about to ask April if she would be willing to leave her job and follow him to London, even though he was fearful of the answer she would give him.

She lowered her eyes, set her coffee cup down, took a deep breath.

'I won't be coming with you,' she said, in a low voice, as if whispering.

'I see.'

'It's not you, it's me.'

And there he was, thinking he would have to say the words. Because he knew it was him. Because of him.

2

On the Beach

The rain falls differently here. Not the constant drizzle of a New Zealand spring, or the umbrella-defeating sideways spray of a British winter, but in great sheets that erupt so swiftly from the heavens that droplets bounce up from the steaming tarmac and soak my knees in the same instant that I am drenched from above.

I sprinted the last two blocks to Zaza, the café near the seafront in Ipanema where I was scheduled to meet Aurelia for a late lunch. My sandals slapped against the footpath, flicking more rain up my calves with each step. My white short-shorts bunched up uncomfortably between my thighs, perilously close to exposing the lace hem of my underwear. I felt infinitely thankful that, for once, I was wearing a proper bra beneath my singlet, and not one of the drawerful of flimsy bikini tops that I had accumulated since my arrival in Rio de Janeiro six months ago.

On my right, a wide expanse of sand stretched for miles, all the way from Leblon, where my apartment was situated, close to the famed Copacabana. Those beachgoers who hadn't already sought shelter in the neighbouring bars and restaurants were hurriedly gathering up umbrellas, deck-chairs and sports equipment, and shaking out brightly coloured towels that formed streamers of blue, green, yellow and red against the darkening sky. Tropical storms were so full of life, clouds brewing mighty occult movements with an underlying magic that always delighted me.

On my left, tourists hurried into hotel lobbies, pink-skinned and paunchy alongside the chiselled perfection of local beach bodies. The plastic tables they previously occu-pied now stood abandoned outside, cigarette stubs still glowing in ashtrays. A fat man dressed in a pair of black and white horizontally striped jocks held the hand of his kaf-tan-covered wife and stared at two young brunette women strolling ahead of him, their unfeasibly firm and round but-tocks delineated by the thin straps of their thong bikini bottoms. The girls sipped from respective cans of diet guarana soda and walked slowly along, indifferent to the rain. Their tanning lotion mixed with the water beating over their skin and pooled into shining pearls that ran in rivulets over their curves.

I kept running. Another block, and the hotels and cafés drifted further apart; isolated islands of commerce separating high-rise apartment buildings sheltered behind security gates, their plain exterior shells painted in bland hues of cream and grey giving little indication of the wealth that lay within the homes of Rio's richest residents, anonymous despite the enormous sheets of glass that offered broad views over the ocean but sat too high up to allow outsiders a glimpse in.

Raoul, who worked behind the counter of the juice bar on the corner of Rua Garcia d'Avila and Avenida Viera Souto, called out after me as I passed.

'Olá bonita! Did I scare you away?'

I turned my head towards him and smiled instinctively in response to the sound of his voice. He was broad-shouldered, shirtless and ripped. He wore his dark hair long, and it shone as though he had laboriously blow-waved and straightened it. His front teeth were a little crooked, a flaw that did not discourage him from grinning widely when I stopped by most mornings to order a maracujá juice or suco de caju, for the first time in my life breaking my perennial daily caffeine habit.

'Come see me later,' he cried out, and began to laugh, secure in the knowledge I was unlikely to do so.

I had never even seriously thought of having sex with Raoul. I hadn't seen or spoken to him outside of our morning commercial banter. But the undercurrent was always there; his questioning look when he stared at me, shoulders back, spine straight, flicking back the hair that fell over his face without breaking eye contact as I stuttered my order in halting Portuguese, made me think that he sensed it too. There was a natural sense of physical chemistry between us, and if I had felt at liberty to behave like an animal, devoid of any inward sense of morality or social pressure, I would have met his questioning gaze with action and stepped around the chest-high, red laminate booth that separated us, bent over it and encouraged him to fuck me from behind. But I was too frozen by the constraints of public expectation to do anything more than admire his firm arse as he turned away from me to prepare my fruit juice in the giant silver blender that sat like a sleek behemoth on the opposite counter.

Two men leaning against the counter, sipping from tall, lime-green-coloured takeaway cups, turned and looked at me. One of them wolf-whistled.

I turned left up Rua Joana Angélica and the rain came to a halt. I was already too wet to bother avoiding the puddles that had gathered on the pavement so just traipsed through them until I reached the restaurant perched two steps up from the pavement at the far corner, its bright blue and white exterior a tropical blot on the otherwise bland street. A waiter dressed in a white shirt with a black waistcoat over the top was hastily rearranging a stack of yellow, pink and orange cushions on the low picnic seat that lined the verandah out front, while patrons standing and huddling under umbrellas stood wrapped in a babble of conversation while they waited for a table to become free.

Aurelia spotted me and waved. She was standing on the front deck outside the main doors, waiting for the tables that had been pushed towards the wall during the rainstorm to be returned to their usual places. Her short-sleeved shirt-dress was typically modest, the collar buttoned almost all the way up to the base of her neck, partially concealing the living labyrinth of her tattoos, the sheer, flowing, sky-blue fabric falling to just above her knees, several inches longer than the Rio average. In stark contrast to me, she was a woman of few curves and the boxy shape of her outfit hid her small breasts and waist entirely. If it were not for a sweep of bright red, glossy lipstick covering her full mouth, and a pair of high platform cork wedges, she would have looked quite androgynous. Her pale blonde hair was pulled into a messy knot on the top of her head, besides a few loose strands that framed her face.

Every person who passed her as they entered or departed the restaurant either openly stared or surreptitiously glanced at Aurelia. She refrained from making eye contact with any of them, and appeared quite unaware of the attention she received. It could have been her natural blonde hair, which was rare in Rio, her many tattoos, her height, or her particular brand of beauty which seemed even cooler and more distant than usual in this sultry city. She had the poise of an ice statue, all cool chiselled perfection and reserve in stark contrast with the tanned beach bodies clad in sheer bright chiffon mini-dresses or tight vest tops and short-shorts that populated the city.

The hostess hovering over her voluminous reservation book on its wooden podium caught my eye and I paused before I approached her, running my fingers through my hair in a futile attempt to break up the damp strands that I could feel sticking together like dreadlocks on my head. She smiled at me broadly. She was young and tiny, her pocket-sized frame balanced precariously on pincer-sharp heeled ankle boots. Her shorts were wide cut, black with grey pin stripes and cropped at the very tops of her thighs. Her breasts loomed uncomfortably large for her small frame and were held high with a push-up bra, its rich purple-blue tone clearly visible through the pastel peach blouse she wore over it. When she leaned forward to check my name in the book, the fabric fell open, revealing the firm mounds of her bosom almost all the way to her nipples. She peered at me again.

'Sorry,' I said. 'I got caught in the rain. I'm with Aurelia. Aurelia Carter. Over there.' I nodded in Aurelia's direction.

'No problem,' she replied. Her smile didn't reach her eyes.

'Summer,' Aurelia called out, stepping past the hostess and kissing me lightly on each cheek. 'So good to see you.'

'And you.'

She was bone dry. Regally impervious to the elements.

'Sorry I'm late,' I said, although a quick glance at the Dali-style melting clock on the far interior wall indicated that I was exactly on time.

Aurelia bent down, picked up a cream duffel bag and handed it to me. Her dress rode up her thigh as she did so and revealed the tail and body of a peacock, rendered stylistically in deep indigo and green tones across her flesh. It didn't look new, and yet I was sure that the last time I saw her, she had displayed the body of a whale etched in plain black on that particular part of her leg. The landscape of her skin seemingly ebbed and flowed with the seasons and her moods, just another of Aurelia's many mysteries. Merely a trick of the light, she claimed. I no longer believed her insistence that the intricate map which I knew was etched into every inch of her flesh, including her most intimate parts, was mere illusion. I had resigned myself to the existence of magic since I had been in Aurelia's employ.

'I was sunbathing before the rain started – there's a few spare dry things in there. If you want to change?'

The hostess straightened her posture, an action that I felt certain was directed at me.

'Oh, thank you.' I took the bag and headed towards the

restrooms, weaving my way through the tables to get there, careful not to bump into anyone in my bedraggled state.

I stepped into one of the cubicles, peeled off my wet clothes and scrubbed the water from my skin with Aurelia's beach towel, which was clean and dry, and not littered with so much as a speck of sand. Her bag contained a high-waisted, fire-engine-red bikini bottom and matching top, both designed to cover the wearer's parts in full, totally unlike the Brazilian string-style that was ever in fashion around here. I disregarded the bikini, presuming that it would be too small for my more pronounced curves, and instead pulled on a loose white long-sleeved sun-dress. The baroque framed mirror above the sink indicated that it did absolutely nothing for my figure, but at least it wasn't see-through, so while my shape might make onlookers guess that I was not wearing anything underneath, my breasts weren't actually visible through the thin material. God only knew that I was not shy with my body and had lost count of how many had seen it in all its glory or otherwise, but sometimes discretion was the better part of valour.

I dug through the duffel bag's pockets and located a small toiletry bag with a comb inside, next to an old paperback romance novel. A woman wearing a tight corset and full skirt adorned the front cover. I flicked through the pages, stalling for time. It was the most unlikely book for Aurelia to carry. I just didn't think of her as a die-hard romantic somehow.

We'd had this meeting planned for weeks, and yet I still wasn't sure what I was going to say to her.

I was confident that she was going to ask me to continue working with the Network, the organisation that I had been ultimately employed by for the past two years. Initially in New Orleans, running The Place, an upmarket erotic dance bar, and more recently here in Brazil, organising the latest Ball, an erotic, circus-style festival of the senses behind which Aurelia pulled the strings with almost supernatural intuition.

In many respects, my gig with the Network was a dream job, and working behind the scenes rather than on the stage meant that I didn't need to bare my body or even engage in any of the sex acts that most of the guests came to watch or enjoy if I wasn't in the mood for it. Instead I had all the perks – the salary, the international travel, collaborating with some of the most unique and talented performers I had ever met – without any of the drawbacks. And, more importantly, it had allowed me to retreat from music, and its often pernicious influence on my own senses.

But in spite of all that, I wasn't sure if I wanted to continue. I felt tired of it all. Perhaps I was ungrateful, unaware of how lucky I was. Or maybe I was just growing old.

I thought back to the last time that I had seen Aurelia. The Ball on the Amazon.

It had taken me the better part of eighteen months to organise. The Ball's guests had come from all corners of the globe, as they always did. I felt a surge of pride as I saw them gather at the Port of Manaus in the North of Brazil, on the Rio Negro. To any outsiders, we must have looked like a large party of tourists about to embark on a river cruise identical to so many others. In fact, we had bribed port staff and a small number of other tour operators with significant sums to keep the river to ourselves for a full three days, time for the crew to set up, the Ball itself to occur and the Ball's guests to embark and disembark unnoticed.

Attendees had been advised to arrive in normal dress to avoid drawing undue attention or upsetting the citizens of Manaus. Room and time for them to change into their party wear would be provided on board. But the Ball's guests were by nature not a tribe of people that blended into the background. They possessed a palpable type of energy, not unlike that of the populace in Rio. As if their desire to reach realms of pleasure that existed outside even the imaginations of ordinary people made them seem more alive.

I watched as a young man of about twenty with his white-blond hair gelled into a Mohawk bent down to pick up a rock and tossed it over the rickety wooden barrier that separated the footpath from a sheer six-foot drop into the water below. It traced a neat arc through the air and was swallowed up by the river without a sound, the inevitable splash drowned out by the lapping of waves. Near him, a pair of women who appeared to be in their mid-seventies stood shoulder to shoulder, holding hands, their fingers threaded together tightly. They each sported long grey hair that flowed over their shoulders and wore long coats, despite the incessant afternoon heat. I speculated on what they might be wearing underneath. Latex? Leather catsuits? Lingerie? Neither of them looked the type to wear any of the typical outfits favoured by sex-party regulars.

I had deliberately avoided outlining a theme for this year's proceedings. I had explained to Aurelia that I wanted this to be a Ball of individuality, an environment that would give each guest the opportunity to truly be themselves and not concealed under a compulsory costume. Besides which, I knew that previous Balls had covered every possibility from under-the-sea themes, where all the guests had been painted as marine creatures, to the zodiac, with a myriad of men as bulls and women in sequins representing galaxies, and I had no hope of coming up with anything original.

Our boat approached. At first just a white blot on the horizon, like a low-hanging cloud, gradually morphing into a ship as she floated towards us, cutting a sharp V through the water. The Ball's engineers had crafted her specially for this event, since there was none large enough, nor of the right dimensions, available to hire. I had nothing to do with the mechanics, but oversaw the layout of the cabins and performance rooms. I knew that the dungeon lay at the bottom and spanned the full length of the ship, a vast space fitted with all manner of props.

There were several St Andrew's crosses: X-shaped, padded standing frames that subs could be strapped to, crucifixion-style, and whipped. Spanking benches which fitted the same purpose, but with the sub bending over at the hip, arse in the air. There were ornate thrones that dominatrices could sit on while being pleasured orally by a sub lying beneath, and faux walls complete with glory holes for anonymous pegging. Trolleys were located at intervals and set up with bottles of lube and glass sweet trays filled with condoms and latex gloves, along with trays of various implements. Paddles, a range of whips and floggers, pinwheels, anal plugs and dildos. Staff would be on hand to refresh and monitor the equipment, and professional doms and dominatrices were available to train amateur attendees in any practice they deigned to learn, and to dish out pain and pleasure to a few lucky volunteers.

The lighting was soft and low, and the space perfumed with a very mild spicy fragrance, akin to toasted chocolate and cardamom. Pots of lilies in water were situated in safe corners, away from the sharp end of a whiplash that might break the glass. Along the walls, low cushioned seats and beds were stationed, where onlookers could relax and watch the proceedings, or subs could curl up after a scene and be nurtured by their dominant.

The dungeon was my pièce de résistance.

Perhaps because it had been so long since I had been truly dominated, in any formal or deliberate way. Dominik, the man I still thought of as 'my dom', the man who had widened my eyes and my imagination to the wonders of sex and proven the love of my life, had been dead now for over three years. Long enough for me to grieve, and to move on, although he would always take up a space in my heart. Since then, I had no shortage of lovers. Most of them mere fucks, and some of them I no doubt would have been better off without, and had taken them or let them take me only as an attempt to blot Dominik out of my mind, to dull my pain. Others had been simple physical connections, men and sometimes women that I had met when I was horny and fallen into bed with, the same way that a hungry person might stop by the nearest fast-food joint. Convenience and filling a need, nothing more. Then there had been Antony, the playwright and theatre director whom I had fallen in with, my first proper relationship since Dominik's death. He now worked with the Ball also, although he was working on the next Ball's incarnation, scheduled to take place in Iceland in the future, so I had seen little of him recently despite our shared employer.

But Antony was not a dominant by nature. We had fooled around with rope, silk scarves and the like, as lovers do, but he had never taken me to that brutal and blissful edge that I still longed for in my dreams. He was good in bed – great, even – but he did not want to hurt me, or to control me. And I had wanted him to want to hurt me. I had wanted to surrender to him, to feel the overwhelming sense of letting go and freedom that I found with Dominik, when I allowed him to do whatever he would with my mind and my body and I knew that he would keep me safe, despite the sometimes dangerous activities that we engaged in, because he knew me so well. Every iota of my thoughts, every inch of my body had been mapped against his heart. Since his death, no one had come close to freeing that part of me, that kernel of doubt and fear and lust and shame that I kept curled up tight in the deepest reaches of my soul, like a dark stone in a river bed, buried deep.

That was what I wanted to give the Ball's guests. A place to let their demons come out to play.

Our vessel pulled into port with Aurelia at the helm. She was dressed all in white, a long flowing sheer dress that flew back in the wind, revealing every straight line and curve of her body. She was barefoot, and when she shifted her stance, squaring her shoulders with her arms outstretched, and held firmly onto the rail ahead of her, a gust blew the fabric of her dress firmly between her legs, highlighting the long length of her thighs and calves and the valley of her cunt. She spotted me watching her as the port auxiliaries grabbed hold of the prow and threw up ropes to the sailing hands on board to secure the ship to the mooring point. With her arm raised in a wave, palm outstretched, she looked like arriving royalty.

The crowd turned into an orderly queue, and filed on board, almost in silence. Occasional whispers in languages that I guessed at but could not identify with any certainty reached my ears, but few people spoke in tones louder than a hush. We were like a congregation filing into a church hall. Reverent, awed by our surroundings and what we knew would come.

I bathed slowly, deep in thought. As one of the organisers, I was assigned to the main dressing room and bathing area set aside for the higher echelons of the Ball's crew, and the performers. The painted walls and plush carpets were a rich purple. Chandeliers hung from the ceiling. Long mirrors were set up at various intervals along the walls and sweeping wardrobes were packed with costumes and accessories. I was soaking in one of the many Jacuzzis, filled with warm, mineral-salted water. With me in the pool were half a dozen others, none of whom I recognised. Selecting and training the dancers, aerialists, gymnasts and those whose expertise lay in the sexual arts was not part of my remit.

The six who shared the pool with me were near mirror

images of each other. All medium in height, with bright red hair, an even truer shade of ginger than mine. Their skin was deathly pale and every inch of it covered in freckles, so they looked as though they had been dusted with specks of cinnamon. They had entered the pool after me, so I had been able to witness them saunter across the black slate tiles towards me and lower themselves into the steaming water. Their nude bodies were worthy of art. Slender and lithe, none of them older than twenty-five, unless they partook of Botox or drank the blood of virgins or had some other trick to keep them so firm and supple. Their legs were endless in relation to their torsos, and so slim and toned that they might have belonged to racehorses. Their stomachs were flat, abdominal muscles just visible in the right light. None of them were shaved. They each sported a thatch of ginger pubic hair that covered their slits fully. As far as I could tell without running my fingers through the curls, their bushes were soft and fine, not thick and coarse like dark hair often was. I was disappointed, I realised, that their hair prevented me from getting a proper look at their pussies, and my disappointment surprised me. I considered myself straight, although I had occasionally toyed with women. It was rare that the female form aroused me as much as these six did, with their lanky limbs and locks of fire. They did not appear to be wearing any make-up, but their lips were full and pouting. Their breasts were larger than mine. Each of them possessed a more than generous handful, and their nipples were small, pert and hard, pink nubs balanced upon the dark pink circles of their areola. They were pierced. A thick gold hoop was affixed to each of their nipples, and another to their clits. Each of the hoops was joined to a thin gold chain that ran from their cunts to the centre of their breastbone and then to each breast.

They were not alone.

A man had led them into the room. A thick gold ring circled his wrist, and from it a length of gold branched off into six, each length attached at the navel to the chains that bound the women. They were rigged together in the manner that a dog-walker might join a bunch of canines, for ease of handling, and managed to avoid getting tangled up together or having their parts pulled too hard by walking in perfect formation, the rhythm and length of their steps perfectly synchronised.

He reached the steps that led up to the platform of Jacuzzi pools, paused, and stared at me openly. I recognised his gaze. It was arrogant, the look of a man who is accustomed to ownership. There was a question in his eyes, too. One that he thought he knew the answer to, but couldn't be certain of, although he might pretend to. Would I submit to him, become one of his chained women?

I leaned back, squaring my shoulders, and raising my elbows out of the water to rest on the Jacuzzi's lip, boosting my body up and displaying my bare breasts to him. I met his look with a hard stare of my own. Neither yes, nor no. I would not run to a man like that the moment he snapped his fingers; not anymore. But I was glad to be sitting down, because the rush of desire that raced through my veins and tugged at my heart as well as my clit was so strong that it left me feeling faint. I was too proud to remove myself from the hot water and seek some relief in the comparatively cool air outside of the bath.

'Here,' he instructed the redheads, inclining his head towards the pool that I was in, rather than one of the other five. They remained still, frozen in place, and he released them one by one, pressing his mouth to the lips of each as he did so. Once freed, they entered the pool. Watching their bodies slide into the water's embrace, I felt my temperature rise even further.

There was a dull thud near me, the sound of glass on slate, as he placed a tall tumbler of liquid down within my reach.

'Drink this,' he said. 'It will make you feel better.'

I reached for the drink. It was ice-cold and tasted of lime and sugar, like a caipirinha without any alcohol. I gulped it down and my faintness passed. Clarity returned to my thoughts.

'I'm Vincent,' he said. 'Pleased to meet you here.'

'Summer,' I replied. 'And nice to meet you too.'

'Your expression suggests you're attending the Ball for the first time. But I am guessing that isn't the case, or you wouldn't be in this dressing room.'

'It's my first time as an organiser. I helped with the logistics. Not my first time as a guest, or a performer.'

'Really? You performed? I would like to have seen that.'

'Perhaps you did,' I told him. 'I played violin, at the last Ball, in Nevada. The desert.'

'Ah,' he said. 'I remember now. You were quite wonderful. I looked for you afterwards, you know, but you were nowhere to be found. I was told that you were otherwise engaged, with one of the lighting crew.'

'Antony directed some of the major performances.'

'Director, then. I apologise.'

'But we're no longer an item.'

'Sorry to hear it.'

His tone indicated that he was nothing of the sort.

'Mind if I join you?'

Before I could respond, he undid the tie on his silk robe and dropped it to the floor, then began to ease himself into the water. His movements were almost comically slow, as though he knew that I was watching him, and he was giving me every opportunity to admire his body. His calves and thighs were thick with muscle, and his chest broad and meaty. He had straight blond hair that fell to his shoulders, like a Viking warrior. A small silver piercing decorated his left nostril. He was younger than me, perhaps about twenty-five. His cock and balls hung low in the warm room. I resisted the urge to reach up and grab his package as he lowered himself into the pool.

We bathed together in relative silence, and then retreated to opposite ends of the dressing room to ready ourselves for the night ahead. My eyes stayed fixed on his reflection in the mirror in front of me as he covered the bodies of his six acolytes in oil until their skin shone. His hands worked slowly, massaging their body parts with reverence. When he was finished polishing their limbs, he fixed their hair, brushing it out over their shoulders and smoothing their frizz with hair balm. They stood frozen, accepting his ministrations like mannequins in a shop window. He bent down onto his haunches and slipped their feet into high-heeled, peep-toe shoes with a buckle at the ankle. Then stood back and admired his handiwork. Satisfied, he clipped each of the women back onto his leash, and turned to depart.

'See you later,' he said to me as they trooped out of the door. His tone suggested that he would make sure that he did.

It was my first Ball as one of the staff, and I did not allow myself to relax until it was almost over. I stayed upstairs to watch the ceremony, and then, relieved that all of my plans had passed without a hitch I headed downstairs to the dungeon.

Aurelia was there with her partner, Andrei. She had changed into a canary-yellow lace slip, low-cut at the front and back, just barely reaching down to the tops of her thighs. With her hair flowing loose and her energy palpable after the earlier ritual, she looked like a sunbeam that had been trapped from the sky and brought to earth. Her quilt of tattoos quivered and shimmered over her body, a plethora of fauna and flora that mysteriously came to life in circumstances like this. I saw the peacock etched on the back of her calf fan open its tail feathers and strut.

Andrei took hold of her each time that she turned. Touching his palm to her waist, grasping her hand, or curling a lock of her hair in between his fingers. He could not bear to be apart from her even for a moment. They had an apparently open relationship, since it was part of Aurelia's traditional duty as the Mistress of the Ball to take the starring role in a sexual ceremony that occurred each year and required her to fuck the men chosen by the Ball for the purpose, inevitably young, fit bucks – sometimes up to a dozen of them at a time. She certainly didn't seem to mind. In fact, during and after these occasions she lit up like a firework, as though the sex brought her truly into herself. But I never saw Andrei with anyone else. He stuck faithfully to her side, always. They made a striking couple, his tall, lean body, the broad shoulders and ginger hair a good match for her cooler tones and long, lithe form.

'Summer,' she called out, when she spotted me lingering at the door. She lifted her arm into the air along with the scanty fabric that covered her arse, coming narrowly close to flashing me the smooth valley of her genitals. A pair of plain gold bracelets decorated her wrists.

I walked over to them, threading my way carefully through couples who were using the various pieces of BDSM equipment, each of them occupying their own private universe, seeking that elusive high I knew of so well.

She drew me into her arms as I approached and kissed me on each cheek, and then on my lips. Andrei kept his hand on the small of her back as she did so.

'It was magnificent,' she said. 'You did a wonderful job. Truly wonderful. Not a jot out of place.'

If I hadn't known that she avoided all alcohol and drugs at these events, I would have assumed that she was drunk or high. Her pupils were dilated and her eyes appeared enormous, like great wells of blue that didn't seem able to focus on anything.

'Thank you,' I replied.

'Not at all . . . I wanted to speak with you. There's someone who wants to meet you.'

She raised her arm again and gesticulated towards the corner of the room. When her skirt lifted as she raised her hand in the air, her thigh brushed against mine. Her skin was soft and cool. I felt my muscles tense in response, and

66

instinctively looked away, catching Andrei's eye as I did so. There was both sadness and pride in his expression, as though he was aware of the effect that Aurelia had on others. I knew well enough that the ability to provoke desire in others could be a double-edged sword.

Vincent was threading his way towards us in response to Aurelia's signal, a large grin spread across his face.

He nodded a greeting to Andrei, kissed Aurelia on the cheek and then turned to me.

'Hope you don't mind my tracking you down, water nymph. I didn't want to leave it to chance this time,' he said.

'Oh,' Aurelia interjected, 'you two have met already?'

'We bumped into each other earlier,' I told her, 'in the dressing rooms.'

'Good,' she replied. 'I was hoping that you would meet.'

She paused, and I waited for her to elucidate.

'Vincent has certain skills that I think you might enjoy,' she explained.

'Darling . . .' Andrei intervened. 'Maybe we shouldn't spring it on her. Might be best to talk it through first, in a different environment.' He stared pointedly at the scene continuing alongside us, a domme dressed in a shining khaki and black governess's get-up and caning a man who was bent over in front of her, weeping.

It was Andrei's tentative attempts at protecting me that encouraged me to throw caution to the wind.

'I'm game,' I announced, although I wasn't at all sure what I might be agreeing to. Vincent's eyes gleamed, and he pushed up the sleeves of his black silk robe, exposing his thick forearms. He looked like a magician of the dark arts, which I supposed, in a way he was. A tattoo was carved in white ink on the inside of each of his wrists. I squinted to make them out – infinity symbols, like figures of eight lying sideways.

'I was hoping that you would say that,' Vincent replied. His head was cocked to one side and he was staring at me, smiling, with a satisfied look in his expression that suggested I had confirmed whatever guesses he had previously made about my character and desires.

Aurelia picked up a flogger from the nearest rack of accoutrements; walnut handled with long, soft hide falls. She turned it over in her hand and swept the leather over the inside of her wrist, learning the whip's particular feel and peculiarities as a musician might come to grips with a new instrument.

Vincent undressed me, without paying the slightest heed to the ritual of baring my flesh. He simply unzipped the black lace playsuit that I was wearing so that it dropped down to my ankles and then he hunched down, helped me step out of it, and tossed the garment to one side. He unbuckled the towering heels that I had been bravely tee-tering on all night, and set them aside, gripping my ankles

68

firmly as he did so to assist my balance. When he began to push himself up again, his mouth was only inches from my crotch. How pleasant it would be, I thought, to feel his tongue inside me. Instinctively I threaded my hands through his hair. He took hold of my wrists and pulled himself to his feet.

'Another time,' he whispered into my ear. His lips brushed against my ear lobe. My nerve endings began to tingle with excitement. Vincent had a way about him that all of the dominant men I had encountered possessed. An aura of confidence that transcended any wealth, education or other positive qualities he might possess, including his good looks. I had found even short, dumpy dominants that were absolute bastards attractive in the past. There was no rhyme or reason to it. The sense of power that ebbed out of him affected me in a deep, visceral sense. If I allowed myself to be swept away by it then he would have me wrapped around his little finger like another member of his chained harem.

It began and ended with rope.

I noticed, vaguely, that a space had appeared around us. The steady flow of noise in the room emanating from couples and groups engaged in BDSM play had muted to a low rumour of whispers as we became the central focus in the dungeon. Even Andrei had stepped back into the crowd. Aurelia seemed to have grown an extra foot tall. She was terrible in a regal sort of a sense, her limbs taut and her legs spread apart with her weight on her heels, a coil of energy inside her like a red-hot snake ready to strike.

There was a noise above me, and I glanced upwards and saw a panel in the ceiling move back on invisible hinges. A rigger kit appeared; a length of thick black rope attached at the top end to sturdy iron hoops. The trap door and rig was not part of my design, and I had been over each inch of the plans for the dungeon, and signed off on every last whip and paddle. Aurelia must have planned all this.

The rope dropped down and Vincent caught it easily in his palm.

His robe was now untied, revealing the centre length of his torso, his inner thighs and calves and the dangling spectacle of his ball sack. His cock was fully erect and swung as he moved. Aurelia was circling around us, still toying with the flogger she held, waiting for her chance to smack the leather hide against my skin.

Music began to play. The lush tones of Lana del Rey rose up around us. It was a record that Dominik had often listened to, one that I knew he favoured when he was writing a bittersweet scene, something that required a deep layer of melancholy. Sadness began to well up inside me as I remembered the games that we had played together, the elaborate lengths to which Dominik had gone to tease my senses and bring my body, heart, soul and mind right to the edge of reason. Anything else would never be the same, I realised then. Vincent only had access to my body, and perhaps a portion of my mind. Whatever pain or pleasure he and Aurelia could inflict on me would only ever be surface level. To reach the depths, I needed more. I needed love. And that was not something that I could ever get from the Ball, these manifestations of sexuality that crossed and even celebrated every boundary and taboo in existence and yet could not bind people together. Few of the Ball's guests knew each other outside of these annual or bi-annual festivals. They barely spoke during the events themselves, they just fucked.

I was growing tired of it all.

I wanted something different, something more than sex.

My body was getting by well enough, but without music, and without Dominik, I had nothing and no one to nourish my soul.

The rope pressed against my skin. Soft, at first, but as Vincent expanded his web the bonds became tighter. My breasts had been bound into a corset that squeezed them until they were unnaturally prominent, jutting out from my chest, my nipples hard, pink and proud. My waist and thighs were circled in a harness and my arms pulled behind me, my wrists tied behind my back. He methodically bound my calves to my thighs, with my knees bent and my heels pressed against my buttocks. By the time that he had finished I was tied like

71

a spider's fly, ready for eating. My mind floated in a state of deep relaxation so it took me a few moments to notice that I was slowly moving, winched up inch by inch on the rig. Several points held me steady; a network of ropes linked to the bonds at my hips, shoulders, and each ankle, splaying my bent legs apart. I was flying, belly down.

I felt the whip, then. Not lashing against my limbs but rather softly caressing the parts of my skin that remained uncovered, from the soles of my feet to the tips of my nipples and down again to my bare cunt. When the rope stopped, fingers took its place. Two sets of hands. Aurelia and Vincent; squeezing, probing. I had begun responding bodily to their ministrations long ago and my pussy was soaking wet. Was she using the whip's handle to penetrate me? My breath rasped. My throat was dry and I longed for a glass of water. I licked my lips. Something wet was pushed against my mouth and I sucked, greedily. Fingers coated with wine. Then another pair of lips pressed against mine. They were full and firm, the kiss too rough to be Aurelia's. It was Vincent. I kissed him back.

Another rope was looped over my head and rested around my throat. It began to tighten. I shifted my shoulders, instinctively trying to bring my hands up to protect my neck but I couldn't, my wrists were secured firmly behind my back. Dominik's image and voice appeared again in my head. My lingering ghost. He had always teased me about playing so near the edge, but I knew that he was only half teasing. Part of him had worried about me, venturing too close to danger.

'One day we'll go too far,' he'd say.

'I hope so,' I'd quip back.

My heart beat faster. I was dizzy. The music roared in my ears and the lyrics blurred, Lana del Rey turned into the rush of the sea on the shore heard through the trumpet of a shell held close to my ear.

I felt myself falling.

A sound escaped my lips. A croak? A scream?

For a few seconds, there was nothing, only the blackness in my mind and the echo of the music playing.

Then I heard Andrei's voice, cutting through the noise.

'Bring her down.' His tone roused me.

He said nothing more. My bonds were removed rapidly and a glass of water pressed to my lips. Someone handed me a bar of chocolate. Aurelia was kneeling on the floor behind me, ready to cover me with a blanket when the ropes were pulled away.

It was nearly morning.

I slept through the day, until we returned again to port. Dreamlessly.

I glanced in the mirror one last time, tried in vain to smooth the fly-away frizz from my drying curls, packed the remaining items back into Aurelia's beach bag, set my shoulders back, sucked in my stomach and returned to the table.

'You look exquisite with that on,' Aurelia murmured, eyeing me with undisguised appetite, the way she did most people, both predatory and with admiration.

Our waitress was already hovering around the table, visibly irritated by our presence, jealous of our appearance maybe. She was almost a carbon copy of the woman in charge of the reservation book, young and pert with a set of breasts that seemed unfeasibly large above her small waist, slim legs and wide hips, dark hair cropped around pointed ears and a face that settled naturally into a scowl.

We quickly ordered. Pork ribs with sweet and sour pineapple for me and marinated tuna served with mashed potatoes for Aurelia. It was not my first visit to Zaza, and I had already sampled nearly all of the cocktail flavours on the menu. I opted for a lime caipirinha.

'Sugar?' purred the waitress. 'Or sweetener?' Her tone suggested that I should choose the latter.

'Sugar,' I replied, and hoped as she walked away that she wouldn't spit into our drinks.

Aurelia turned and watched her saunter towards the kitchen.

'Nice arse,' she observed.

'Shame the same isn't true for her personality.'

74

'True,' she shrugged. 'Most people only need one or the other to get through life, I suppose.'

She may have disliked us, but to her credit, she wasn't slow with our order. Our drinks arrived in minutes, along with a basket of warm crusty bread and fresh butter, and a bright blue ceramic bowl filled with plump green olives.

Aurelia popped an olive between her lips.

'Cheers,' she said, with her mouth still full.

'Cheers,' I responded, cautiously knocking my short, thick tumbler against the far more fragile looking white and black chocolate-coated rim of her long-stemmed martini glass filled with icy pink liquid. A strawberry bobbed precariously close to the top. I took a large gulp of my caipirinha, She downed her dubious strawberry, hot pepper and basil concoction nearly in one.

'Now,' she said, as soon as we had set our glasses back on the table, 'let's get down to it. There's just a year to the Ball in Iceland, and much of the work has been put in motion. We need you now, for the finer details. Not right away, but within the next few weeks. I suppose the cold will be a shock,' she added, looking around at the other patrons sitting near us, all of them in skimpy outfits, 'but I'm sure you'll enjoy it there. It's a beautiful place. Stark, bleak. We'll leave this to you, of course, but I expect that the performances will be very different from the last, to suit the atmosphere.'

I picked up a piece of bread, smeared it with a thick coating of butter and bit into it, stalling for time so I could gather my thoughts.

'Summer?' she said after a pause, filling the silence between us. 'Is something wrong?'

She looked at me again, with a concerned, searching expression on her face.

'Is it Antony? I know there's something going on between you two and if that's bothering you, we can sort out a way to keep you apart. Send him back to London, maybe.'

'No, no,' I said. 'It's not Antony.'

'What happened with Vincent, on the boat? The rope? I'm so sorry about that. I got carried away. Andrei was furious with me . . .' Her face flushed, and she twirled her empty glass in between her fingers.

The waitress materialised alongside the table. 'More drinks?' she asked.

I was about to say no, thank you, we would wait for the food, but Aurelia ordered another round of the same. At this rate, I would be stumbling back to my apartment later.

Our main courses arrived. I quickly abandoned my knife and fork and picked up a pork chop with my fingers, sucking the sweet and sour sauce from each digit greedily once I had finished gnawing every scrap of meat off the bone.

'Tell me,' she said, putting her knife and fork down. 'Whatever it is that you need, I am sure we can work it out.'

The waitress appeared again to check if we had finished and Aurelia waved her away. 'Not yet,' she said, hovering a protective hand over the remainder of her mashed potatoes.

'The truth is,' I told her, 'I'm not sure what I want to do anymore. I've loved my time with the Ball, I really have. And I'll be forever grateful to you and the Network for the opportunity,'

'You can spare me the platitudes, Summer, and just tell me how you feel. I know you're grateful, and all that.'

She reminded me of Lauralynn, in that moment. My oldest friend, and never one for beating about the bush. I hadn't been in touch with her or her partner Viggo since arriving in Rio, not even to let them know where I was. I felt a stab of guilt, thinking about it.

'I think I need a break,' I blurted out at last. 'From everything.'

She nodded.

The waitress came back and cleared our plates away. We had both finished every last mouthful, even mopped up all of our respective sauces with bread.

'Will you return to London, then? Or some other part of Europe? Another tour, perhaps?'

I had deliberately put my music career on hold since joining the Ball. Hadn't been in contact with my agent or even picked up an instrument in months. I was even considering selling my Bailly, the violin that I loved most, for sentimental as well as practical reasons. It just wasn't necessary to have that kind of money sitting in something that I wasn't going to play. I would rather see it used by someone who would love it as much as I had than sitting in storage until it deteriorated for want of proper care.

'No,' I told her, 'I don't think I will. Go back to Europe or my music career, that is. I think I need a break from that as well.'

'I thought joining the Ball was your break from music?' she interrupted, a smile playing on her lips.

I sighed. 'I know it doesn't make a lot of sense,' I said, 'and maybe I'm just being contrary. But it's all tied up together for me. Music, playing the violin, bleak climates . . . the sort of sex that makes me lose my mind, like the erotica the Ball specialises in. I can't have one without the other.'

'What's next for you then, sweet, contrary Summer?'

I watched a young boy of about ten in bright orange-and-green swimming shorts walking down the street with a beach ball under his arm. His eyes were obscured by a pair of dark sunglasses that were far too big for him. He was barefoot, and sauntered along past the restaurant as though he hadn't a care in the world.

'Nothing. I think I'm just going to sit on the beach and do nothing.' I would probably have to leave Rio, because life here would eat through my savings. But I had enough in the bank, and a diminishing stream of royalties coming through from my old albums which were ticking over, so I wouldn't have to worry about working for a few months at least. And then I would figure something out. Maybe I could learn Portuguese and work in a local juice bar.

'The Network is willing to continue to take care of you, financially,' she said.

'Oh no,' I insisted, putting my hand up. 'You've done enough for me. I appreciate it, but it's not necessary. Really.'

'I'm not doing you a favour,' she said. 'We do the same for everyone. It's pretty straightforward. Once a Ball employee, always a Ball employee. The Network is buying your discretion. Not quite to the level that you're used to, perhaps, since you're no longer being reimbursed for work, or working expenses. But you'll continue to receive an annual stipend. And there's no point arguing about that, as I have your bank details and will be making the deposits whether you like it or not. You can stay in the apartment here, so long as you look after the place. The rent was paid up front and there's another few months on the lease. We won't be needing it for other staff any time soon.'

'Thank you,' I told her. 'You've been so good to me.'

'It's been a pleasure.' She reached over the table and squeezed my hand. 'Don't fall out of touch. I mean it. And any time that you want to come back, there will always be a place for you. Travelling with the Ball, or staying put, in any city that you like, we'll find something for you to do.'

We ordered dessert, and one last round of drinks. I opted for a simple lemon sorbet, which came served with orange-flavoured, paper-thin crisps, and Aurelia chose the far more decadent devil's food cake, a rich chocolate fondant with a firm exterior and glossy, melting-soft pudding within. She leant across the table and fed me a spoonful.

The sun was setting by the time we finished and the sky was streaked with vivid stripes of red, purple and gold. Aurelia paid the bill and we gathered our things.

'Your dress!' I exclaimed. 'I'll change back into my own stuff.' My damp shorts, vest and bikini top were stuffed inside the towel in Aurelia's beach bag, and probably still wet.

'Keep it,' she said. 'We're flying out tomorrow, and I won't be needing a kaftan in Iceland. Besides, it suits you better than it ever did me.'

She asked for a plastic bag so I could carry my clothing home.

We embraced on the steps, and turned in opposite directions to walk to our respective lodgings. I wheeled back again, one last time to wave goodbye. Aurelia was still standing there on the step, flirting with the waitress. She had a white card in her hand, probably like the one she'd given me the first time we met, with her Network contact details written on it. Probably recruiting another dancer, I thought. Trust Aurelia to make the most of every opportunity. The Ball wouldn't miss me. Of that I was sure. I was by no means indispensable.

She looked up and noticed me watching her, and raised her arm in a final gesture of farewell.

I carried on walking. I felt light, as though a load had been lifted from my shoulders. If I had been wearing proper shoes, and had a bra on, I would have lifted my feet quicker and run all the way home, just for the pure joy of it.

What would I do now? I could do anything that I liked. I would start to explore South America, I decided. I'd been too busy working to see any but the closest sights. I hadn't even been up to see the statue of the Christ that overlooked the city. I was too off-put by the big crowds of tourists that swarmed there during the day, and had been too lazy to get up and go first thing in the morning when it would be quieter. I noticed a paraglider sailing past on the winds above me, coming down to land on the beach. Maybe I would hang-glide over the statue instead, see it from the air.

It was time I started taking more risks in life, the way that I used to when I was younger. I resolved to be bolder, more spontaneous, to not waste the time that I had left. I would start by walking past the juice bar and asking Raoul out on a date.

His booth was closed, the green shutters pulled down and padlocked.

Raoul could wait until tomorrow. I had all the time in the world to make the most of Brazil.

I rose uncharacteristically early and spent the day exploring the Tijuca National Park on foot.

'Don't wander from the trails,' the taxi driver told me as he dropped me by the main gates. He threw his arms open wide. 'There is a favela inside. You walk in the wrong place, you get shot. You should not go alone. Take a tour.'

'I'll be careful. Thank you.'

I tipped him and began walking up the tar-sealed road until I found a likely looking path that veered off to the side and then followed that, hoping it wouldn't lead me to the centre of a coca plantation or a gang headquarters. Within minutes, I was surrounded by forest, lush and green. The raucous bird calls and the density of the trees blocked out any sign that I was in the middle of a city. I strained my ears for the sound of passing cars but heard nothing.

The further I walked, the rougher the path became, until I had to duck and dive through overgrown bushes to continue and was certain that wherever I was headed hadn't seen human contact in months. My forearms were covered in long red scratches and my mouth was dry. I had only brought with me a small bottle of water that was already perilously close to empty and a packet of dehydrated bananas to snack on. But the uphill walk was stretching my legs and taxing my heart, lungs and muscles in a way that I hadn't experienced for ages and so I ignored the danger and carried on walking.

Finally I reached the summit, and looked out. I was on the top of a mountain, and surrounded by a handful of other curious-shaped granite peaks, like a handful of worn teeth in the mouth of a giant. I thought I recognised Pedra da Gávea and Pedra Bonita, and saw humans moving across the tops like crawling insects, then swooping down as the hang-gliders took off from the summit. My blood pumped in my ears in empathy with them. The risk-taker in me loved the thought of being airborne, but in truth I had never been great with heights, and stood well back from the edge, one hand clutched onto the face of a nearby rock for support.

I made my way down again, and rushed to the café at the base of the park's entrance to buy a can of lemonade from the overpriced and limited selection aimed at the tourists who arrived in hordes to view the park from the safety of convertible jeeps. A young waiter with a diamante stud pierced through one ear pointed me in the direction of the bus stop. 'That way,' he said in clear, accentless English in response to my halting guidebook Portuguese. The heat had dulled my appetite, which was fortunate, since it had also turned my dried bananas into an unappealing ball of mush.

I peeled one away from the rest and gnawed at the end of it cautiously, before tossing the remainder of the packet into my backpack and rummaging around at the bottom for the rest of my real, tucked into the fraying seam of my bikini top.

The first bus to arrive was of the cheaper, non-air-conditioned variety, which I had been warned not to use as they were allegedly often flagged down and the occupants subjected to armed robbery. I got on it anyway. The bus took a less scenic route than my taxi driver had, driving down motorways and past characterless shopping malls that seemed so out of place in comparison to the sea, mountains and forest that made up the rest of Rio. It was as though they had been dropped from the sky like concrete asteroids and never moved.

I changed buses at an anonymous junction and got on an even busier coach headed for Ipanema. This one too was full of locals, most standing like I was and jostling against one another in the packed aisle, abs tightened and arms loose and relaxed, manoeuvring their bodies like surfers as the vehicle screeched and jolted, tossing the bus's occupants backward and forward with each sharp acceleration.

By the time I finally arrived at Ipanema beach, I was hot and sweaty and could not have cared less about the crowds sitting en masse on their sun loungers or worried in the slightest about finding a private place to change into my bathing suit. I deposited my backpack on the sand and stripped off in full public view, pulling my singlet over my head, quickly removing my bra and then stepping out of my shorts and knickers. I had my bikini on in a flash, but not quickly enough to avoid hearing a few wolf-whistles aimed in my direction. I ignored them, and ran to the sea.

The water was blissfully cool lapping against my parched skin. I waded in through the breakers and dived under, wetting my hair and washing the dust and grime from my face and then flipped over onto my back and floated, aimlessly making pictures from the white clouds that streamed through the blue sky overhead.

The burning, dry heat of the day had dissipated, replaced by a humid, sultry afternoon. I hadn't eaten properly since the fruit that I had snacked on at breakfast, and was probably dehydrated from my earlier walk. So when the strains of violin music reached my ears, I first thought that thirst and hunger had sent me into a trance, and I must be dreaming. But the sound continued. The chords of a pop song, I thought, although I couldn't put a name to it. The musician was doing a reasonable job of the piece, but their instrument needed a tune. I ducked under the waves, trying to block out the sound. It brought back too many memories. But in the end, curiosity got the better of me. I opened my eyes and searched the shoreline for a violin player among the darting volleyball athletes and stretched-out tanning bodies, but couldn't distinguish anyone with an instrument. Whoever was playing wasn't following any partition, so had some degree of talent, although evidently unschooled. I paddled back to shore, wrapped myself in my towel and followed the stream of notes, annoyed that my reverie had been broken.

She was standing on the roadside, next to the cycle and running lane, beneath a palm tree. A young girl in a sheer floral-patterned sundress over a turquoise blue bikini. She was thirteen or fourteen, I guessed; that perilous age when your body is morphing into that of a woman, but you are still slightly behind. I bought a fresh coconut drink from a nearby stand with a few plastic chairs and tables scattered outside and watched her play. She wasn't bad. Not bad at all. And she clearly found some joy in her music. She played with her eyes closed. Her lithe body swayed slightly as she moved the bow. I winced when she hit a bum note, and a string screeched. Probably, one of the pegs was loose, or needed lubricating. She didn't notice me watching her until the song came to an end, and I put the coconut shell down and clapped.

'Muito bem!' I called out, then blushed as I realised I had probably used the wrong words, and embarrassed myself. She smiled at me and came over.

'Are you American?' she asked, pulling up a chair next to me. She laid the violin and bow down gently on the table. 'Do you play?'

The owner of the stall called out to her in their native

language, and she yelled back, then stood up and bought a can of guarana soda and a packet of crisps, fishing the real coin from the inside of her bikini top.

'He said I had to buy something if I wanted to sit down,' she explained when she returned.

Her English was totally fluent, which wasn't common here, I had found, unless in the more expensive restaurants.

'I'm from New Zealand,' I told her, 'but I lived in London before I moved here. And yes, I do play. At least I used to.'

I was about to ask her where she learned to play, and to speak English so fluently, but she carried on talking before I had a chance. Her face was animated as she spoke. Her dark curls bounced when she moved, and her eyes flashed, an uncanny shade of purple. She was vivacious, like a tropical bird that had alighted alongside me and wouldn't shut up. I was still uncertain about her age. She had an unusual naivety about her that suggested youth.

'My father speaks English,' she said. 'He has business meetings in the city this week, and we live near here. I came with him so I could go to the beach, but I knew I'd get bored of swimming, so I brought my violin.'

'Do you take lessons?'

'I did, at my school, but the violin teacher moved away and so far there's no replacement. I've been learning songs from YouTube, mostly.'

'You're doing good. It's not easy to play well without following music.'

She shrugged.

'I don't have much else to do.'

It occurred to me that I didn't have much else to do either, and no one to do it with.

'Will you come back here to swim tomorrow?' I asked her.

I was hungry now, and tired, and wanted to eat in peace and then go back to my apartment and nap.

'Sure,' she said.

'Why don't you meet me here?' I told her. 'Around lunchtime, maybe. I can give you a violin lesson, and you can teach me some Portuguese.'

She laughed.

'Okay then, violin teacher.'

'You can call me Summer,' I told her.

'I'm Astrid,' she said.

The Devil's Fiddle

There was a familiarity to London that soothed Noah.

Always one to follow through in full once he made a decision, he had not been back, even for a holiday, since moving to New York. But now as he stared out the back window of the taxi cab that he had flagged down at Heathrow, he had to admit there was something homely about the red-brick terraced houses rushing by outside and the grey blanket of sky overhead that promised to punish him for failing to pack a pocket-sized umbrella into his hand luggage.

Noah tipped the cab driver and wrestled his suitcase out of the vehicle and up to the front door that led to his new apartment, a reasonably priced – by London and Brooklyn standards, at any rate – one-bedroom flat with generous living space and access to a private roof terrace arranged over the ground and first floors of a period conversion near Little Venice, off Maida Vale. Or at least, that was what the estate agent, a smarmy type with a public-schoolboy voice and a glossy-brochure photo that prominently displayed his full head of bottle-blond, gelled-back hair, had assured him.

Light drops of rain began to fall. Noah stood his wheely case up and fumbled for the keys in the battered laptop bag that he wore slung over one shoulder. He cursed when the door refused to budge. Tried turning the bottom lock once more, and then the top, before reversing the two again, but without success. He reached for the tan Moleskine note-book he always carried in his shoulderbag's side pocket, holding it close to his chest to protect the pages from the elements, and double-checked the address, in case he had got it wrong or the cab driver had mistaken one street for another since all the houses around here were virtually indistinguishable from one another. There was no number on the front door to indicate which house he had arrived at, or whether he was outside flat A or flat B. He turned back and looked around, searching for information from the let-terbox or even the digits scrawled on the blue-green recycling bins that decorated the footpath.

His eyes alighted on a woman striding towards him. She wore a large, but evidently not heavy, long black tube-like case balanced on her back, the strap crossing over her body diagonally between her breasts. An instrument, perhaps?

She was tall and voluptuous, with wide hips and equally broad shoulders. Her dark green and red plaid skirt was short and pleated like the bottom half of a stereotypical schoolgirl's uniform that might be found in any chainstore sex shop alongside a rack of pink rabbit-eared dildos or furry handcuffs. Below it, her thick legs were encased in opaque tights, visible from her thighs to her knees, where they slipped into a pair of long boots with a high flat platform heel. Tucked into her skirt she wore a tight black top made from stretch fabric with sleeves that reached to her wrists and a wide boat-cut neckline that exposed her throat and her collar bones but was not low enough to provide any hint of cleavage. A jet-black, dead-straight pony tail hung from the back of her skull and swung when she walked. She carried neither jacket nor umbrella and ignored the rain, apparently daring even the weather to defy her.

'Excuse me,' Noah called out, as she turned off the pavement onto the steps that led down to the basement flat below the one he still assumed was his.

'Yes?' she said, glancing at him with a scowl spread across her unlined face. The only sign of make-up highlighting her features was a sweep of lipstick in a deep red, femme-fatale shade. Noah couldn't guess her age. She might have been anywhere from 27 to 45. Not his type, but attractive nonetheless.

'Is this Tevington Street?' he asked. 'Flat 36B? I'm

moving in,' Noah explained, in case she suspected him of breaking and entering. 'At least that's if I haven't arrived at the wrong place. The lock doesn't seem to work and I've just got off a long-haul flight from New York . . .'

'Hold the top key to the left as you push. Works for me,' she interrupted, and then immediately turned away and continued down without making any kind of neighbourly introduction. Typical Londoner, Noah thought, as he watched her disappear into her apartment. Not that New Yorkers were known for their friendliness either. Ever attentive, now, to the sight of any potentially classical musical instrument, he tried to make out what it was that she carried on her back. A half-dozen or so long slim implements poking out of an open top cylindrical case. Paint brushes? Arrows? Or canes, or riding whips? His neighbour could be an artist, an archer, or a dominatrix, he thought. He continued to ponder the unknowable and curious private lives of others as he stepped inside, finally out of the rain, and examined his new residence.

He had expected something sleek and inhospitable, the type of acceptable yet anonymous décor that adorned corporate hotels across the world, but it was cosier than that. The place had personality, albeit not his own. An open-plan kitchen with a deep-purple laminate breakfast bar backed onto the living room, with expansive wooden floors and a wide bay window that looked out onto the street. Net curtains had been fixed permanently into place for privacy. A worn cream sofa suggested that a previous tenant had ignored the landlord's regulations and owned a dog. The walls were painted a dirty-looking variant of cream, probably labelled 'eggshell' on some interior design colour chart. A rug might have improved things, but Noah knew that home decorating was something he was unlikely to ever get around to.

For a brief moment, he missed April, who would have had the place looking elegantly lived-in in a jiffy, re-painting the walls in apple or indigo and replacing the tired sofa and generic flat-pack shelving units with something comfortable, leather and chic, recycled vintage bookcases, colourful throws and art that managed to walk the fine line between pretentious and generic.

The estate agent had at least lived up to his word and ensured that all of the rooms were fully furnished. Noah filled and switched on the kettle, then rifled through the kitchen cupboards until he found a mug and a cafetière, pausing when he realised that he was bereft of coffee. In his rush to escape the airport, he hadn't thought to stop and pick up a loaf of bread, or even a single tea bag.

He checked the time. It was nearly 7 p.m., but he was nowhere close to tired, besides the usual long-flight weariness. An evening of television didn't appeal, and neither did further reading, since he had already finished one throw-away paperback spy thriller purchased along with a packet of sweets moments before his flight had closed for check-in at JFK. His laptop was sitting on the kitchen counter. He recalled the last time that he had spent an evening alone in front of his computer screen and shivered. Felt he needed to take his mind off things, seek out some kind of distraction and human contact. A shower, some fresh clothes and a trip into the city would do the trick. On his way back, he planned to recce the nearest supermarkets, takeaway joints and Tube stations, to get to know the lay-out of his new environment.

The streets were more homogenous than he remembered. Old-fashioned boozers he had stumbled out of years ago had been replaced by conglomerate bars with glossy, glass exteriors. A clothing store selling cheap leather jackets now stood in place of the second-hand bookshop where he had enjoyed browsing and had picked up occasional bargains from the small vinyl record collection the owner had kept alongside the racks of dusty, battered paperbacks. Later, there was the reassuring presence of the Thames as he walked the long way from Monument station to the foot of London Bridge and then along the Thames Path towards the National Gallery, not as vast as the Metropolitan but confident in its own quiet grandeur. Noah had always found the Trafalgar Square lions somewhat mawkish, although it might have been the presence of flocking tourists

94

clambering up to sit astride their smooth backs and have their pictures taken that reduced the animals' dignified repose in his mind.

He studiously avoided the coffee shop and health food empires that had popped up a dozen to a block in the streets around Charing Cross, and headed instead for the subterranean comfort of Gordon's Wine Bar on Villiers Street, which he was glad to see remained open and apparently unchanged. Once he had taken a date here, and abandoning any hope of finding a table amid the queuing Friday-night hordes they had attempted to gain access to the gated gardens next door, and, denied that too, Noah had ended up fingering her behind a bush as cars raced by along the Embankment, aware that the patchy vegetation behind which they sought cover afforded them very little, if any privacy. He had been faintly embarrassed by the whole affair. Later, he had realised that canoodling in full public view was not an inconvenience, but rather the very thing that had encouraged her to bend over in front of him and shamelessly grasp his wrist and manoeuver his hand beneath her short skirt, directing his fingers to her panties. She had been thoroughly lubricated and the ease with which he had slid into her cunt had caused an immediate erection that he had subsequently relieved in private, after she had confessed that she was already married and refused to come home with him. He recalled that she shared her name, Victoria, with the street on which these sordid events had occurred, and the fact had struck him as more funny than serendipitous at the time.

Now, mulling on it, Noah was convinced that Victoria was the kind of woman who would let herself be used like the redhead in the photographs he had viewed that New York night on his laptop screen, even the sort of woman who would ask for it. He wondered how many other women existed like that, who actively enjoyed being defiled by men. His cock twitched in his trousers. He had never previously thought of himself as the kind of man who would enjoy doing the defiling. Thinking of hurting or humiliating someone, a woman, had never even remotely aroused him. Noah had often encountered it in pornography, and always trained his focus away from the would-be abusers and onto the willing models and their evident provocation, the expressions on their faces, feeling vaguely ashamed at times of the sentiments that such clips stirred up in him, but he had never pictured himself in the driving seat. Until now.

A space at the bar opened, finally, and he paid the weary bartender for a mixed plate of cheeses, bread, olives and cold cuts, and ordered a red wine that the menu board described as full-bodied, round, and ample in the mouth with a lingering finish. Coincidentally not unlike the woman next to him, who interrupted him as Noah's entrenched habit of economy directed that he buy a full bottle although he was unlikely to consume it, since the value was far greater than the same wine sold in smaller measures.

'If you're not going to drink all of that,' she said, when he notified the bartender that he would only need one glass, 'you might as well share mine instead. I won't finish it.'

He agreed, and followed her through an archway to an empty table in a room reminiscent of an ancient dungeon, with close stone walls and only thick, melting candles for light. No music played, but conversation was nonetheless difficult over the hubbub of chatter emanating from the other patrons crammed in around them.

Her name was Clarice, and she was an insurance broker who originally hailed from Sussex but lived in Leeds and was spending a few days in London visiting clients on business. She was totally unlike April, who would have delighted in engaging Clarice at a party, as a cat might engage a mouse, and then later profess to be bored by her in that way she had of categorising anyone who happened to be employed outside of the arts as utterly dull.

They drained the last drop from what was left of her bottle, and Noah began to shift out from behind the table to fetch another.

'My hotel isn't far from here,' she remarked. 'You could join me for another glass there, instead?' Her expression was neutral, but her meaning could not have been clearer.

If he agreed, Clarice would be his first post-April fuck, and the two could not have been more polar opposites. Perhaps the change would be good for him. She was a large woman, with a round arse, wide hips and shoulders, and heavy breasts. Dark brown hair cut into a bob that framed a paradoxically pixie-like face and sharp chin. Teeth that struck him as chemically whitened, a stark contrast to the crimson streak of her lipsticked mouth. She reminded him of his new next-door neighbour, the tall woman with the pale skin, sleek black pony tail and carry-case of unidentifiable accoutrements. Maybe he would fuck Clarice and picture his neighbour, punish her by proxy in the safe confines of his imagination for her earlier rudeness.

Clarice was staying at the Amba Hotel, barely a five-minute walk from Gordon's, in a deluxe bedroom decorated in shades of beige with a view overlooking the Strand. He placed his hand on her rump as she searched in the mini-bar for a suitable obligatory nightcap. Unzipped her pencil skirt and pulled it down to her knees, exposing the lace tops of her hosiery and the pale expanse of her upper thighs. Her g-string was emerald green, the minuscule waistband and thong a thin band of colour delineating the firm orbs of her buttocks. He ran his finger inside the elastic, pulled it back gently so the thong snapped against her. She moved her feet backwards and apart, her stance inviting his further exploration. She was still wearing her high-heels, a delight-fully prim pair of Mary Jane-style court shoes.

'Wait,' she whispered, turning her head towards him. Her hair was mussed, her pupils dilated and her red lips slightly open, a picture of titillation. She was gripping the corniced wooden edge of the drinks cabinet tightly.

'Yes?' he asked. He was rock hard. Hoping she would not back out now, or he might have to venture into the hotel's guest bathroom and relieve himself before returning home to save the embarrassment of standing on the street with a tent in his trousers.

She indicated that they should move to the bed and began to remove her skirt, wiggling her legs so that the bunched fabric slipped down to her ankles where she could step out of it.

'No,' he said. 'Leave it there.'

An image sprung into his mind; Clarice on her back, knotted up in her clothes, struggling, unable to move as he fucked her.

Noah led her, stumbling, to the bed's edge and she sat down. He knelt at her feet and removed her shoes and each of her stockings, then slipped her heels back onto her feet and buckled them up again. The sheer, stretch nylon was gos-samer light in his hands. He paused, unsure of what to do next. Should he simply bind her? Or should he first ask her permission? He was acutely aware of how different pornography and his mental fantasies were from real life. Noah's mental cinemascope might indicate otherwise at times, but he had no wish to assault an unwilling participant.

'Lie back,' he instructed her. 'I'm going to tie you.'

'Ooh,' she replied. 'Sexy.'

He instantly wished that he hadn't spoken, that they could read each other's thoughts on the matter somehow. The vision he had earlier conjured had lost its lustre in the few moments between his imagining and the execution. He pulled her hands up and used one stocking to bind her wrists together, then fixed the other around the base of her skull and through her mouth like a horse's bit, checking both restraints were neither too tight nor too loose.

Next time he tried this with a woman, he would plan it out first. The hose made for awkward fetters – lengths of rope would have been better, and some kind of fixing to attach them to. All hotel headboards seemed to be one solid piece these days, poorly suited to bondage.

Clarice squirmed, a gesture, he felt, of encouragement rather than struggle.

He pulled a lock of her hair back.

'Can you breathe?'

She nodded.

He kissed her. Her lips were sticky, with a waxy taste from her lipstick.

She tried to kiss him back, squirming to escape the barrier

of her gag. Her bonds prevented her from touching or undressing him and she was barely able to murmur her assent. He unbuttoned her blouse, regretting again that he had not thought this through properly; her bound wrists prevented him from removing her top entirely. Unhooked her bra and revealed her breasts. They were huge, bigger than any he had seen before, two plump pillows with comparatively tiny, pink nipples. He bent his mouth to suck one, and then the other, and she groaned; a glottal sound muffled behind her gag.

Noah was by turns aroused and deflated by their situation. Both aggressor and benefactor. He could gift her pleasure, or force her to perform inescapable acts of perversion. He wanted both, at the same time, but did not know how to achieve such a thing. Perhaps Clarice was the wrong woman. Was she actively enjoying, or just tolerating his ministrations? He felt his cock going soft. Too much thinking, not enough action. He resolved to get the whole thing over with.

'Do you have condoms?' he asked her. April was on the pill, and they hadn't used protection since they had both been tested in the early days of their relationship. It had not even crossed Noah's mind that he might end up having sex tonight. Literally straight off the plane. Was it something about London that beckoned wantonness? He briefly pulled the fabric back from Clarice's mouth so that she could speak properly.

'Bathroom,' she murmured. 'My toiletry bag.'

Half a dozen Durex were slotted into the side pocket of a blue zip-up case containing a lily-of-the-valley perfumed liquid soap, a myriad of cosmetics and three gold-wrapped Magnums, advertising their XL size. He chose a condom. And stood in front of the wide, chrome framed mirror, searching for an image to bring his arousal back to life so that he could roll on the rubber and return to Clarice, and then his own bed. His urge had passed, but he could not bring himself to simply untie her, explain things, and leave. It seemed rude.

A flash of red hair. The outline of a woman's body cast in shadow, small breasts obscured by clouds of steam. A glimpse of red-lip, an upturned, triumphant smile.

He was hard again immediately.

It was over in minutes.

'Sorry,' he said, rolling off her and releasing her bonds. 'The wine . . .'

He didn't stay the night.

A few weeks before leaving New York, Noah had attended a gig in Brooklyn featuring Viggo Franck's old band the Holy Criminals blooding a possible new lead singer. Both the music and the dynamics had proven underwhelming. Without their charismatic front man they were reduced to a humdrum band, professional and slick but lacking that undefinable magic that makes for a great group. The absence of Viggo's swagger and fantasy created a void that could not be filled, Noah reckoned, and one of the first decisions he had to reach now in his new position of power would be to assess whether the musicians' contract should be renewed. Their management were hinting heavily that, should he decline, another rival label was ready to sign them up in a flash. Noah was hesitant. A one-year extension could cover one album and maybe in the studio a spark would fire, and if the budget was held on a tight leash, the profitability break-even point would not be astronomical, and the new product would inevitably have a healthy influence on back catalogue sales. He also knew the guys in the band well and they happened to be particularly nice people, not that it should influence what was strictly a business decision.

The company's headquarters were situated at the top end of Portobello Road, just a minute's walk from Notting Hill Gate, and unlike their Manhattan counterpart were not open plan. Noah had the privilege of a large office that occupied the whole top floor, with wide bay windows that opened up overlooking a set of gardens at the back of the building.

He'd been considering the dilemma for some days now and had cleared the afternoon of meetings to contemplate quietly and try to reach a decision. He sat listening to the band's past albums in strict chronological succession in order to catch any thread of musical progression that could not automatically be attributed to Viggo, who often only supplied lyrics for the songs.

He knew the records well already, had to a certain extent grown up with them. As he listened to each, his desktop screen called up the respective Profit and Loss accounts for the individual recordings. The trend was downwards. He knew what logic dictated.

Then he noticed a jewelled CD box still lingering on his desk. He'd asked his PA, Rhonda, to bring in the band's entire catalogue. Maybe another album altogether had slipped into the pile by error? Unlike Rhonda.

He picked up the record. He'd never even heard of it, even though it sported the label's logo.

'Rhonda?' She sat just outside his office.

'Yes?'

'There's a CD here I'm not familiar with.' Noah handed it to her. The cover art was generic, an image of the sea at sunset and a handwritten title 'Christiansen', with no name of artist.

Rhonda, a prim, tall woman in her early forties who had been with the label longer than anyone in the building and kept all non-musical matters running with a sergeant major's cold efficiency, peered at the CD.

'Ah yes, that. It was something of a favour to Viggo. Some experimental stuff he did with a classical violin artist who was a friend of his.'

Noah's memory clicked.

It had happened just as he was about to move to New York with Bridget and seeking a way to finance the move, and courting editors to get a book contract. Viggo had performed a series of European gigs with some violin player and had then gone into the studio with her and later other talent from the classical world. A vanity deal.

'I didn't realise we'd actually released it.'

'We did, albeit with little marketing support. Your esteemed predecessor felt it wise not to advertise Viggo and the band's involvement in it, so it never made waves. Still gets played on Classic FM, though.' The expression on Rhonda's face betrayed what she thought of the executive who'd previously sat in his chair. 'It's actually quite nice,' she added. 'Although not very commercial . . .'

She returned to her desk.

Noah slotted the CD into the player.

Strumming acoustic guitars forming a wave of gentle sound, the familiar underpinning of a bass guitar ordering the beat into place before Viggo's voice would no doubt surge from the depths in customary fashion, as the echoing drums joined in. But as the group's instruments all met on the upbeat, smoothly clicking into space, there was just a deep hum, the shadow of a voice in the distance. Viggo double-tracked, it felt like. And then, the sharp sound of a violin punctuating the cloud of the nascent melody, pure, crystalline in its clarity, dragging a parade of emotions in its wake and building the emerging foundations of a melody. The tune had a slight familiarity.

Noah picked up the box and peered at the track listing.

'Fingal's Cave.'

It had been ages since he had listened closely to classical music.

The violin soared, its tone mixed up front, dominant but gentle, fierce but tender. Noah closed his eyes. Listened. Abandoned himself to the sounds pouring from the two small speakers arranged at opposite ends of his desk. Surrendering. This was certainly not what he had expected to hear.

The music painted scenes in his mind, like a brush magically conjuring landscapes built on feelings and primal instincts. A raging sea, the cavernous abysses where sunken boats lay, a sky in turmoil, clouds battling above like mythological titans. He recalled vaguely that the orchestral version as originally composed by Mendelssohn was in no way so affecting. Or had he misheard it back in the day?

The way the violin merged with the more modern sounds of the band and its jerky rhythms and electric sensibility was eerie. Opened up new dimensions in the music, like the Northern Lights parting to reveal some dark, enticing, uncommon vision.

He caught his breath.

What the hell was this? How had he not even heard of the album before?

Time flew by and the piece ended, not with a loud climax but with a delicate whimper, the sound of the violin fading ever so delicately until there was just silence floating.

The next track evoked idyllic fields, naked bodies frolicking, an improvisation on one of Vivaldi's Seasons; he was unsure which. Sensual. Albeit slightly spoiled by Viggo's spoken words soaring across the sharp tone of the violin. Words were unnecessary. The piece would have been so much better without the slightly pretentious recitation.

Rhonda knocked on his door. He was lost in the music still two hours later, the CD on repeat, playing on and on inside his head. Office hours had come to an end and she was returning home.

'I'm staying on,' Noah told her.

She reminded him of tomorrow's schedule of meetings.

The brightness outside began to fade. He did not switch on the lights. Remained in the dark, alone with the music. Aimlessly watching the sky darken above the neighbouring gardens.

He had never come across such an exquisite blend of classical and rock before. Indeed, it was a collaboration which had always been fraught with peril and which no one had to his knowledge properly mastered.

Why in hell had they not given this album some promotional support and decent marketing? It was bloody wonderful. Parts of it, even when the melodies were familiar, had left him breathless. Whoever played the violin on the record had managed to not just blend in seamlessly with the other instruments but was actually leading the dance in a merry and clever way, imposing his or her will on the others without them noticing it, using Viggo's group as a foundation for a skyscraper of improvised sound that communicated its passion with so much more power than he ever remembered classical music doing for him before.

'Fingal's Cave' was about to play again for the fifth or sixth time and Noah switched the system off with his remote as he leaned back in the black leather chair and swivelled round to face the desk again. He picked up the CD box and pulled out the liner notes. They were succinct. Just credits.

He had to look twice to learn the name of the violin player.

A woman.

Summer Zahova.

The name rang a faint bell, but he had never followed the classical scene closely.

Someone who'd had her hour of fame some years back, he thought.

He delved into the old files, buried somewhere in his computer's memory, those concerning this set of recordings. Damn, she wasn't signed to the label! Had been a free agent at the time, allowed by her own record label, an essentially classical outfit owned by a rival corporation, to play with Viggo and the guys as a one-off against a minor participation in any of the recording's profits. Which, of course, had not been forthcoming.

Was she still signed with them, he wondered?

He returned home to his Maida Vale flat. Called for a takeaway sashimi. The music he had been listening to still reverberated inside his head, in turn full of languor or aggressive and savage. Mad thoughts ran in conflicting streams through his mind. Reissue the album with some serious money behind it? Contact the artist and lure her to his label, work with her on something new and equally powerful?

He pulled out his laptop. Searched for her. Found hundreds of hits. Rather than open up random links, which mostly appeared to be reviews of concerts, Noah called up images. Expecting a staid-looking matron in evening dress, he felt his throat tighten when a page full of photographs of Summer Zahova materialised. Each image featured a striking splash of red. The Medusa-like curls of her long hair always the centre of gravity, often matching the russet colour of the violins she was holding or playing.

She was no middle-aged typical classical artist. She was young and marketable. Undoubtedly. In most of the images of Summer playing on stage, she was wearing short black dresses, barely reaching her knees. Long legs tense, body captured in trance, her gaze distant as she played. Even when she was wearing demure evening gowns, her provocative playing stance was unmistakably sexual.

Noah felt his throat go dry.

That flaming hair.

Those eyes, so full of craving and, he also felt, unnameable sadness.

The way that, in every picture, she stood taut, unsmiling, remote, every invisible nerve in her system on alert, in quiet provocation, her body lacking in self-consciousness, screaming out its availability, a willing captive of the music she was playing.

Just as he had felt listening to her on the CD earlier.

A further search established that she had issued a handful of albums, all purely classical. It had been some years since the last, though. Why?

He quickly proceeded to download them all.

Noah managed to make contact with Summer's label and discovered she was, as he hoped, no longer under contract to them. She had, it appeared, not been willing to renew beyond the initial number of albums she had committed to.

'Any particular reason?'

'Wanted a break from recording. A difficult young woman, she was.'

'I can't find any trace of any public concert appearances since, either,' Noah continued. 'Just retired?'

'I think she got involved in some experimental theatre, a play that enjoyed a short run. But it was all a bit hush-hush,' his interlocutor added. 'Nothing was recorded, to the best of my knowledge. I heard there was something a bit off about the whole thing, though. She was part of the play as well as its musical director. There was a whiff of scandal in the papers, some reviewers thought it sordid. Tell you what, we were a bit relieved that she went her own way. Always felt there was something of an unexploded bomb about the girl. Like that collaboration with Viggo Franck she was so adamant about. Rock and classical just don't mix well, do they?'

'Did she have representation?' Noah had no wish to argue with the other executive and his conservative attitude.

'Let me look it up. I wasn't directly involved with her . . .' A moment passed. 'Ah, here we go: her agent is Susan Gabaldon. A good woman.'

Noah arranged a meeting with Susan.

'She just disappeared. Haven't heard from her in ages. Had a private gig with some organisation I'd never come across before, but who made an offer she couldn't refuse, Summer told me. But when that engagement came to an end, she said she needed time off, turned down all further touring offers and just buzzed off somewhere without a word of warning. Sad,' the business-suited woman who had once managed Summer Zahova's musical activities informed Noah.

'So you have no idea how to contact her?'

'No. Not even had a postcard, let alone a courtesy phone call to say how she is getting on, wherever she might be. Could be she returned to New Zealand. It's where she came from. And in the meantime, what's left of her career is going downhill fast. People forget so quickly, you know.'

'Sometimes, there's a mystique in being invisible,' Noah mused. 'Could be a deliberate move. Absence makes the heart grow fonder and all that . . .'

'Not with Summer,' Susan said. 'She was never a planner. Her emotions ruled her. A somewhat tempestuous private life, if I might be indiscreet.'

'Tell me more,' Noah said.

'I'd rather not, but I'm sure you'll come across many rumours. I wouldn't even disbelieve all of them,' the agent remarked with a wry, resigned smile.

'Artists live in their own world, different standards. In the rock 'n' roll world a touch of madness has always proven productive, I've found.'

'Depends what your standards are. Anyway, your label has never been into the classical business, Noah, so why the sudden interest?'

'Just curious. Had a listen to the album she recorded with Viggo Franck and his band. Found it unexpectedly moving . . .'

'Maybe you should be in touch with him. He might have heard from Summer?'

'You're right. Although maybe a bit awkward as he's also taking a break from music. Could there be a connection?'

That night, Noah kept perusing the images of Summer he had found on the internet.

She captivated him. There was no denying the fact.

The way her face now fitted the sounds of her music.

And the fire splash of her hair.

All of a sudden, he recalled again with terrible sharpness those crude photographs of the gangbang in the sauna he had stumbled across on his screen that night in New York.

The same unforgettable shade of hair.

The same pale skin.

The similarity in the shape of the woman's chin, from the little he could now remember of it.

Noah shivered.

'Why all the curiosity over our red-haired friend, Noah?' Viggo's live-in partner asked.

Viggo had been happy enough to discuss his musical dealings and friendship with Summer Zahova, but Lauralynn, who was stomping towards Noah to refill his cup from the filter jug she held in one hand, was obviously suspicious. 'Is there something that you haven't told us?'

Her fingernails were filed long and sharp, and painted a glossy blue-black. Noah found himself practically cowering back in the profusely cushioned bucket seat that he was ensconced in as she gazed at him, her Amazonian form cased in a pair of high-cut, wet-look leggings with a long, industrial-style exposed zip that ran provocatively from the top of her waistband down to the base of her crotch and a plain white, cropped T-shirt that exposed an inch of her flat torso and was tight enough to indicate that she was not wearing a bra. She was pure rock chick; he'd seen the style often enough on young groupies at concerts, or new front-of-band singers, usually still struggling to define their branding through their wardrobes and evince a suitable degree of sex appeal and fuck-you attitude in a Debbie Harry way that few managed to pull off.

Lauralynn was undeniably both sexy and sexual, and her sharp, calculating stare made Noah feel as though he'd gone back in time fifteen years or so and was being interrogated for teenage misdemeanours by his erstwhile headmistress, a domineering woman named Ms Abbott, whose no-nonsense attitude was made all the more terrifying by the nipped-in pencil dresses that she wore, which made no secret of her long, shapely legs and ample cleavage and gave every boy in the school a hard-on when she called him into her office to be simultaneously aroused and berated.

Noah squirmed in his chair, hoping that Viggo would return quickly from the errand that Lauralynn had sent him on, to search for any further demo tapes that might never have been passed along to his management and were likely to be tucked away in his studio from the occasions on which he and Summer had jammed together.

The lanky rock star had meekly acquiesced to Lauralynn's suggestion without so much as a sigh of irritation, even though he had already mentioned that all of his files had been put away into storage since he had decided to take a break from recording, while he worked on getting his mojo back and figured out what direction to move in next. Making Noah wonder what exactly was the status of Lauralynn and Viggo's relationship. Viggo wasn't what he knew some would crudely term 'pussy whipped', and neither did his blonde girlfriend have that tired and resigned attitude about her that he recognised in women who proclaimed to be exhausted from browbeating their other halves. They were playful with each other and seemed to revel in their respective roles.

Noah had been engaged in conversation with the two of them at the gated mansion they shared in Belsize Park for the past hour, sipping coffee and snacking on a plate of peanut brittle that Viggo had prepared, after proudly

115

informing him that baking patisserie had become a new hobby over the past few months during his sabbatical away from music. The fact didn't show on either of their figures. Viggo was as thin as a rake, and Lauralynn certainly voluptuous in shape but not even close to Rubenesque. Over-indulging on the bowl full of sweet confection had caused Noah to feel faintly sick. He had still not managed to glean any particularly useful information from either of them about Summer, since Lauralynn kept cutting Viggo off short before he had a chance to reveal any interesting nuggets of gossip, leading Noah to suspect that the whole trip to meet them would prove to be a waste of time. Then Lauralynn ordered Viggo out of the room, an orchestrated move to speak with Noah alone, he was certain.

'I assure you,' Noah repeated, 'it's just about the music.'

Lauralynn paused. Assessed him with that shrewd stare of hers, as if she was absorbing every inch of him and then formulating a judgement on his character.

'Well,' she said at last, filling his mug to the top and stepping away, 'I don't believe you in the slightest, frankly, but that aside, you seem like a decent enough person.'

Noah was unsure whether or not she meant him to be flattered. He wished that she would sit down.

'You'll forgive my reticence,' she continued, 'to provide you with much in the way of details. Summer is my friend.

One of my closest friends.' A wave of sadness swept over her features.

'Of course,' he agreed. 'I fully understand. And you must know, my position being entirely mercantile, that I have absolutely no interest in harming her reputation in any way, or god forbid, actually harming her. I run a record label, and just investigating left-of-field possibilities.'

Lauralynn nodded. An affirmation of some modicum of trust in him, at last.

'Oh,' she said, 'the damage to her reputation was done long ago, but I'm sure you know that already. You cannot have come this far in researching Summer Zahova without stumbling across some of the rumours. Mind you, any publicity is good publicity, as they say. I'm not sure that any of the stories circulating ever did her career any harm. Probably quite the opposite. Perhaps even part of her appeal.'

Noah remained impassive, politely waiting for her to continue.

'I really don't know where she is,' Lauralynn explained. 'And if I did, I wouldn't tell you. Summer has had a hard time over the past few years, she lost someone close to her . . .'

'Oh. I'm sorry to hear that.' He waited for her to elaborate on the circumstances, but she didn't.

'She's always had a tendency to be self-destructive, passionate. You must have seen it before, working in the industry.'

Noah nodded. 'Stereotypes about creative sorts and musicians abound,' he agreed, 'but there's some truth to them.'

'Well, Summer's wild side always led her to seek out men. She found some solace in sex in the way that others drink or take drugs. Not an addict as such. At least, I don't think so, but she always had very specific cravings in that regard that some would consider unsavoury.'

Lauralynn's features had now taken on a definite leer. She almost winked at him.

'Go on,' he encouraged.

'She attracts others to her who seek out the same extremes, albeit on the opposite end of the spectrum. Always has done. Now, there's no shame in any of that; I'm partial myself to the sort of activities that would make some people faint in shock, probably, but the problem with Summer was that she never had the sense to exercise her demons in the confines of a healthy, mutually enjoyable kinky relationship. Or a one-nighter, whatever. There's plenty of clubs around, groups, where people indulge, you know.'

Noah was aware of such places, of course, but had never considered attending one or entertained any thought about the goings on there in a serious kind of way.

'No, Summer liked to take things one step further. To play with risk more than she ought to. Especially when she was feeling down. I had hoped she'd grow out of this kind of behaviour, but I suspect she hasn't and maybe she never will. We all have shadows,' Lauralynn explained, 'some of them are more powerful than others, I guess.'

Again, that calculating stare, as if she could see right through him, read his thoughts, knew exactly the kind of things he fantasised about. Understood his desire and his shame.

'And you think she's on some kind of . . . sex binge?' he asked. 'Now? That's what has led her to disappear?'

'No,' Lauralynn said. 'I think that she's battling with staying away from going down that road again, and that's why she's taking some time out, particularly from music.'

'Her playing caused this? That's a bit of a stretch, don't you think?'

'You've heard her music. Felt the extreme level of emotion, the fire that she puts into her bow, how she lets it take over her whole psyche and how that comes through on the recordings. You wouldn't be here, otherwise.'

'Yes, yes, that's true I suppose.' He had to agree that there was an element of fire in her recordings that intrigued even him – no particular fan of classical music – to the point of a minor obsession.

'She used to tell me sometimes that she couldn't separate the two things. Her ability to play like that and her desire for rough sex. I've seen her channel it, both, in a positive way. But she needs an outlet. A safe place to let go. She lost her safe place. Now, I think she's disappeared to try to find that again somehow, and she's possibly hung up her violin as a way of avoiding temptation. I can't say, honestly, that I think it's a bad thing.'

He nodded. The woman that Lauralynn spoke of fascinated him more and more, but he wished that all of this wasn't so vague. He was a practical kind of person, a doer, and wanted concrete details. The person he had spoken to at her label who had given him Susan's contact details had mentioned a play that Summer was involved in right before she disappeared, and some controversy surrounding the reviews.

Noah cut in. 'She was the musical director, I believe, on a theatre piece. I found some sparse reviews online, and heard mention of it through her former record company, but I can't find any indication of the play's backers, as if the whole thing was organised by ghosts. Very unusual. Do you know anything about that?'

Viggo waltzed through the doorway and approached them with his customary swagger. His hands were empty.

'Couldn't find a thing, sorry mate,' he said. He refrained from telling Lauralynn 'I told you so'. 'That play . . .' he added. 'More of an orgy, really. Good fun though.' His mouth spread into a wide grin which quickly vanished when Lauralynn shot him a 'shut up' glare.

'No, we can't tell you anything more about the play,' Lauralynn responded firmly. 'We were there, sure, but just as ignorant as you of the origins of the whole thing.'

Noah was convinced that she was lying.

Lauralynn made it clear that she had imparted as much information as she was prepared to, and that whatever other knowledge Viggo might possess, she would not allow the rocker to share it.

He thanked them for their time, made his excuses and left, promising to keep in touch with Viggo about any further move he might decide to make to return to the music industry. 'Any time. Just call me.'

The repercussions of the new information about Summer Zahova, those heavy hints of a world beyond his ken and how little one could fathom of other people, strangers, women beyond the familiar but deceptive veil of normalcy, bothered Noah more than he wished.

He'd attempted in vain to retrieve the link where he had initially located the photographs he now increasingly suspected featured her in some sordid gangbang in a sauna, but it was like hunting for a needle in a haystack, artfully concealed behind the billion layers of porn that populated the interweb. The impact had proven so shuddering he hadn't had the presence of mind to bookmark it and it now seemed forever lost. Could have been anyone with red hair, he reasoned. A coincidence, surely.

In his mind, he could picture Summer. At odd times of day, waking mid-night, his mouth biting into a sandwich at lunchtime while working at his desk and countersigning contracts, more often caught in daydreaming. Summer in a distant, exotic city, like a ghost passing through a bustling market, her face always studiously out of focus, unseizable, unfocused, walking along a beach, palm trees fluttering in the breeze, fleeing from him around the next corner.

He had printed out all the images he had found of her on Google, and in each photograph he could see something new, something different, as if the essence of Summer Zahova was teasing him, refusing to conform to any expectation, malleable, impossible to pin down.

The constant, her red hair, loose, flowing, wild. Like a stain on snow or a flower obscuring a distant sun. Taking root on a perpetually lit screen across the back of his vision.

Where in the world could she be?

How can one just disappear off the face of the earth, Noah wondered.

Rhonda marched into his office to pick up the paperwork he'd been working on for a few hours now; not his favourite part of the job. She was wearing a pinstriped trouser suit with a white silk blouse, a shiny amber broach pinned to her left lapel. Her light brown hair was tightened into a chignon.

'I have a courier waiting in reception. Are the contracts for the option renewals of the Holy Criminals all fully executed? Their management would like to have everything ticked off by the weekend.'

Noah had finally come to a decision to give the Viggo-less band a new contract, in view of Viggo's hints that he might eventually go back to recording with them, an opportunity he couldn't afford to ignore.

'Yes, all done. Have signed my life and the company's away. In triplicate and again. Not that I always understand all the legalese, but if the contracts boffins are happy, so am I . . .'

He handed the blue and purple folders over to his PA. She turned on her heels and prepared to walk out when she suddenly stopped.

'Oh . . . by the way . . . you know that violin player you've been looking into so much. Summer something . . . There was a small piece in today's *Metro* about her . . .'

'Really?'

'One of her instruments is being auctioned, it seems.'

'Can I see the newspaper? Do you still have it?' It was a freebie given out at every Tube station. But Noah normally walked from Maida Vale to Portobello Road or took the bus or a cab if the weather was unfavourable.

'Of course. Let me put all the contracts in a jiffy bag and I'll retrieve it from the bin.'

'I'll come and get it.' Noah left his chair.

But the newspaper had little information; barely a few paragraphs. A violin known as the 'Christiansen' was being auctioned tomorrow. Once owned by famed classical ace Summer Zahova, it had a fabled history, it appeared, and had once been featured heavily in a bestselling novel he hadn't heard of.

He rang Susan.

'Did you know about this?' he asked her.

'Yes,' she confirmed.

'Why didn't you bother to inform me?'

'I didn't think it would interest you. She's not planning to return to performing, you know . . .'

'She's been in touch with you? Since we met?'

'Yes.'

'Where is she?'

'No idea,' the agent answered. 'She sent me an email and we arranged to Skype. She gave me access to her things in storage and requested I put the violin on sale and then transfer the proceeds to her bank account. She needs the funds, she said. She could have been anywhere in the world.'

Noah's mind was racing with questions.

'Did you inform her I was interested in making contact with her?'

'I did.'

'And?'

'She didn't react, I fear.' From the tone of the agent's voice, Noah was convinced she hadn't even mentioned his enquiry, or at least not with any enthusiasm.

'Anything else I should know?'

'I'm afraid not, Noah. Summer is my client and I have to respect her wishes as well as her privacy.'

'I understand.'

At least he now knew she was still alive.

He fell asleep that night with his headphones still on, Summer's fiery escapade through Vivaldi's music echoing through his head. Her violin sounded like the devil's fiddle, leading him a merry dance.

The walls of the New Bond Street auction house's main room were wood-panelled in soothing but sturdy shades of light brown and Noah felt out of place.

Sitting at the back, he had to wait for a whole hour until the violin came up. By which time Noah was beginning to wonder why he had even come along. It was just an old instrument Summer had once played. She was not likely to be present, surely? To pass the time, he had begun to read the novel which was said to be about the violin. He'd found a copy online as it was out of print and he'd paid extra for overnight delivery. It made for uncomfortable reading, gave him a sense of unease, its story's opening pages like an overture to something both horrible and overwhelming, as if, as he rushed along, he was about to meet Summer and her spirit on the page at some stage. He'd not previously heard of the author, who had only written a couple of books and had since passed away.

He had a vague irrational idea he might bid for the instrument, but the opening offer, which came over the internet, was already way beyond what he could have afforded and, within minutes, the violin had reached a price that even a massive mortgage and his income for years to come would never reach.

There were only a handful of bidders, from his perspective at the back of the auction room.

The auction ended. The price reached totally extravagant heights. Even with the likely commission, Summer Zahova would now be able to afford much in the way of luxury wherever she might be, Noah reckoned. He had no idea who had triumphed among the bidders, or if whoever had won was even present.

The auction continued, now focused on furniture and jewellery from a titled estate.

Part of the sparse crowd moved to the front while a few individuals began their retreat towards the door, with no interest in the treasures now featuring in the auction.

Noah wanted to finish the page of the book he had set aside before the violin had come up for sale before departing.

'Ah, you know the book, I see . . .' A man's voice, educated, basso profundo. Noah looked up.

Charcoal-coloured Savile Row suit, old school tie, in his late sixties, pepper-and-salt hair and carefully trimmed beard. His frail posture sustained by a wooden cane he held

126

for support. Noah's gaze travelled up and down the stranger's silhouette; his brogues were polished to within an inch of mirrors.

There was a hint of mirth in the stranger's eyes.

For a moment, Noah was bemused and then realised that his interlocutor was referring to the book he held in his hands and its relevance to the now completed auction.

'Yes,' Noah said.

'He was her lover, you know . . .' the man added, almost grinning now.

'Who?'

'Dominik, the book's author. Summer Zahova's lover.'

This was news to Noah. He knew so little about Summer's life beyond her musical résumé. There had seemed to be a conspiracy of silence around Summer's life prior to her absence.

'You weren't aware?'

'No. I only knew about the violin connection.' Noah was beginning to understand why he was finding the book's tone and undercurrents so unsettling.

The man extended his hand. He wore thin black leather gloves, which he kept on. 'I'm Nikolas Mieville.'

'Noah Ballard. I work in music, albeit in other areas, and only recently came across Summer Zahova. Discovered her past albums by accident – just rather curious.'

'She was indeed fascinating,' Mieville remarked.

'Was?'

'Retired, it appears.'

'Oh yes.'

'So you're a fan too?'

'Of the music? Enormously.' Noah hesitated. 'But I gather there are interesting secrets surrounding her,' he added. Mieville appeared to be the sort of man who might know more about the violinist.

'Absolutely. So many stories . . . You could say she has a strong following. People like me – you? – who follow her with keen interest.'

'I'm fascinated. By the way, do you know who won the auction for the instrument?'

'Another rich collector, I think.'

'Also a fan.'

'Could well be. The bid came over the telephone.' Mieville's grin was beaming. 'In a hurry? Care for a coffee?'

'I wouldn't say no.'

Mieville had a car waiting for him outside with a chauffeur who drove them to a private club in the Mall. He was greeted with reverence by the doorman who almost sneered at Noah's more casual attire and silently ushered them to a large, sparsely populated reading room whose windows looked out onto Hyde Park.

'I saw her. Three times,' Mieville revealed.

'Tell me?'

'She was magnificent. The first time was at a concert at Wigmore Hall, in the early days of her career. Just her and a string quartet. That fiery mane of hair, that aggressive stance that was so characteristic of her. The musical choices were safe, but it was obvious she had an inner streak of wonderful madness – the way she launched into the music, as if nothing else mattered. She transported you . . .'

'You can feel it in the music on the albums,' Noah agreed. 'I'm no classical expert, but you can feel she's . . . different . . . from others. Comes from the gut.'

'The second time was at a concert hall in Brighton, a huge soulless auditorium on the seafront. A few years later. She'd matured, but what was new was, how can I explain it, the weight of life, experience, that extra layer that now coloured the way she played, the sounds she could extract from her violin. There was still abandon, but also both a form of anger and sadness present. By then, of course, some of the rumours were already circulating. Nothing that could be printed in newspapers, of course, but there could have been no smoke without fire . . .'

'What sort of stories?'

'Her private life was something of a mess.'

'Alcohol? Drugs? I thought that only happened in the world of rock.'

'Oddly enough, no. Sex. Odd behaviour, in private but also in public. Tales of a red-haired violin player who sounded just like her at rather exclusive gatherings of a strange nature, sex parties. Also another which at first was hard to believe, but reached me from diverse sources, about a woman playing violin in the nude in a remote corner of Hampstead Heath who, according to the reports, bore a strong similarity to Zahova . . .'

Mieville paused, his eyes now distant, as if he was searching his memory.

'And the third time?' Noah asked him, setting his empty cup of coffee down.

'Ah, the third time,' Mieville said, with a deep sigh.

'Yes?'

'Her last appearance in public, it turned out to be. Some time later. By then the rumours were more than that. After the death of her lover, the writer, some mad play, a theatrical happening that was by invitation only, in a Spiegeltent on Hackney Downs, an interpretation or improvisation on one of the books. She played violin, but also acted, if you could call what she did acting. It's an evening I will always remember. It felt like a dream, a fever dream of excess, an atmosphere I just can't explain. She had us all, the audience, in a trance. I myself doing things I would never do in public. And so was she, deep in a trance. Madness, I tell you. But a beauty beyond compare.'

A veil of regret passed across Mieville's eyes. Noah held his silence.

Finally, the older man continued. 'Shortly after that, she disappeared totally from the scene. It was said she had retired from performing, from recording. There was no longer any trace of her.'

Noah sat. He wanted so desperately to hear more.

'I wish I could have seen her play live. There or before,' he said.

'Like me,' Mieville said, 'you would have immediately become a great fan, a follower of Summer Zahova . . . No sane man could resist coming under her spell. But there won't be any further opportunities for me, I fear. I'm ill, you see. A question of months.' He mentioned this with a complete sense of acceptance. He was retired now, but had been an opera impresario, which explained his interest in classical music. 'There's so little to do, after you stop work,' he explained. 'With the pretty Miss Zahova, it began with the music, then became an amusing sort of side project, collecting the rumours. An old man's folly . . .'

'I think I've just joined the club,' Noah said.

4

Wild is the Wind

I woke up.

Rolled over on my front, eyes still closed, stretching my arm across the bed in search of another's body next to mine. Old habits died hard. Who did I think I might find: Dominik, Antony, Simon, Viggo, some anonymous face from the revels at the Ball?

I found nothing.

Vaguely remembered where I was.

I was alone.

My pale, pink skin wrapped between the crisp, white sheets I had slept in.

The lace curtain by the window fluttered in a gentle breeze, animating the room, pink stucco walls absorbing the heavy heat already building up outside the house. I felt sensations flooding back into my limbs, found my bearings.

There was a knock on the door.

My mouth was dry. How long had I slept? The cushion on which my head lay was soft as feathers and was temptingly drawing me back to dreamland.

I failed to respond on time and again there was the tentative rap of knuckles on the sturdy oak of the door.

'H-hmmm . . .'

The door opened.

A beaming face appeared on the threshold, backlit with an explosion of sun, dark hair in ringlets, generously tanned features, eyes violet and laughing. It was Astrid. In a pristine T-shirt and jeans torn at the knees.

And I remembered where I was.

'Hi.'

'Did you sleep well?'

The bed held me in the clutch of its plush comfort and I felt no compulsion to get up. I sketched a smile.

'Wonderfully,' I had to confess. My first night without dreams for as long as I could remember, as if all the lassitude stored away in my bones and mind had finally been held at bay. I felt blissfully light-headed.

'I'm glad you decided to stay,' she said, tiptoeing towards the bed. She was barefoot. She reached me and leaned over and gave me a peck on the forehead. She smelled of citrus. A deep, warm tang left hanging around her by whatever soap or shampoo she had just used.

'So am I.' My mouth felt pasty.

As if guessing how I was feeling, Astrid picked up the earthenware jar on the bedside table and poured out a glass of water which she handed to me.

I swallowed it greedily, washing my mouth, refreshing my throat.

I gulped, as the cool liquid rushed down into my body, reviving me.

'Oh, I needed that. Thank you.'

I pulled myself up and the top sheet slid down and uncovered my breasts. Astrid kept her gaze fixed on me, her eyes unflinching.

'Your . . . what do you call them in English . . . tips . . . they are so pink,' she remarked.

'Nipples.' I corrected her.

'They're beautiful, delicate,' she said. 'Mine are brown and so much darker, as are most women's here,' she stated frankly. I almost blushed. I still hadn't asked her age but was sure she couldn't have been more than fourteen. At least she didn't offer to show me. I manipulated the sheet upwards and covered myself again, although there was an innocence in the way she had gazed at my body.

'We're having breakfast by the patio,' Astrid said. 'Would you join us, please?' She always spoke formally, perhaps a result of learning English as a second language in a mostly academic setting.

She ran out, fleet of foot and with all the insouciance of youth.

I looked around. My halter-neck dress was where I had left it, draped around a chair. As was the discarded black-and-white polka-dot bikini I had been wearing when Astrid accosted me on Ipanema. We'd spent a few hours together every day for the past week, me giving her violin lessons and her trying in vain to improve my abysmal Portuguese. But yesterday afternoon I had been swimming alone and hadn't expected a date. When she found me sunbathing on Ipanema beach and insisted that I return with her to her home in Jardim Botânico for dinner since her father was out for business until late and she was alone besides the servants, I could think of no polite way to refuse.

She had told me on our second meet that her mother had died when she was very young. I hadn't pried for the details, but I guessed her father had not remarried since she never mentioned a stepmother, or other siblings. Now, I felt sorry for her, and I was curious. Jardim Botânico was one of the wealthiest parts of Rio, known for sprawling celebrity homes with lush gardens and swimming pools. Astrid was clearly from a reasonably well-off family, but she hadn't struck me as a celebrity child. She had promised me that it would be casual, and my beach dress would suffice, so I needn't worry about making a trip home to change.

After staying up late watching Portuguese films and eating

popcorn in the basement cinema room, I had agreed to sleep in one of the spare bedrooms and head home in the morning. I hadn't been expecting a meet and greet with any of Astrid's family or other visitors, and I had nothing else to wear. She'd mentioned others, and the pool. Should I slip on the costume or just the dress? Both together would feel and look odd, straps showing and all that. But so would wearing the dress and nothing under.

I settled for the latter. After turning back and forth in front of a full-length mirror to check that my dress wasn't too revealing, I poured some further water from the jar into the palm of my hands and passed my fingers over my face to wipe the sleep away. Astrid had pointed out the nearest bathroom to me when she showed me to my room the previous night, but it felt rude to now delay heading to breakfast so that I could shower.

The nearby sound of clinking glasses and gentle laughter led me towards the patio at the back of the house, where Astrid wallowed lazily in the hollow centre of a mountain of multi-coloured cushions of all shapes and sizes facing the chair on which a dark-haired older man sat, presumably her father, who was leaning back with his long legs crossed at the ankles, sipping from a tall glass of orange juice. She was voraciously biting into a dark-red apple.

Her eyes widened as she saw me emerge from the house and into the heat of the sun. I blinked at its intensity, barely getting a look at her dad. He was dressed all in white. His open-necked short-sleeved shirt revealed a hairy, tanned chest and above it a granite-like square chin and the same violet eyes that Astrid owned. They looked terribly alike, with the same swimmer's build, strong shoulders and the relaxed look of people who are accustomed to living outdoors.

'There you are.' Astrid pulled herself up. Behind her, the turquoise shimmer of the pool glimmered in the sun. 'This is my father, Joao. Dad, this is Summer. She pointed at him and back at me. He did not get up but extended his hand towards me. I shook it. His grip was firm and masculine.

'Welcome. I'm glad you are joining us,' he said.

Astrid dragged a lightweight plastic chair towards me and I sat myself between the two of them. Within seconds, the furtive step of a young male servant crept up besides me and poured me water and juice in different coloured glasses and asked me whether I wanted coffee or tea, or required anything that wasn't already on display on the small table. I mumbled some sort of answer in my rudimentary Portuguese, trying to hide my embarrassment. I found it hard to bear being waited on in a hotel, let alone a private home.

'It was kind of you to assist my daughter with her violin playing,' Joao stated. He spoke in English to my great relief, his vocabulary as formal as his daughter's.

'It was nothing really,' I answered. 'She was just holding

137

her instrument incorrectly some of the time. A common mistake. We've been working on her posture together, and improving her technique. With a solid basic foundation the rest becomes easier. And, of course, reminding her how to tune the instrument properly; a chore so many beginners tend to ignore as they don't realise how fragile the instrument is.'

'It's true,' Astrid agreed. 'My playing now feels so much more natural.'

'I'm away in São Paulo for part of each week,' Joao said. 'Where I have my plantations. So, I'm always keen for Astrid to make new friends, too. Since her classes ended, most of her high-school friends have travelled to Europe but she wanted to stay, and leaving her in this vast house with just the staff is not ideal.'

'What do you grow on your lands?' I asked.

'Coffee,' he replied. 'For export.'

I felt a weight lift from my mind. With his white suit, vast home and swimming pool, I had briefly feared that he was some sort of drug baron, although I also supposed that if he was, it was unlikely that he would have let me in on the secret over breakfast.

Astrid had studiously peeled and cut half a mango and handed it to me. I bit into it with relish and felt the juices explode in my mouth and coat my tongue with blissful sweetness.

'So what brings you to Brazil?' Joao asked.

'The weather, the sights, the life . . .'

'Have you been here long?'

No way was I as tanned as Astrid and he; with my complexion I had to be wary of staying in the sun too long, and always slathered myself in sun cream, but neither did I display the pallor of a newcomer to South America.

'Several months. Relaxing, just taking things one day at a time. A sort of indefinite holiday.' I couldn't tell them about the Ball and the circumstances that had brought me to their country. I hoped he would not ask me what I did for work. Fortunately, Joao quickly changed the topic of the conversation.

'You're not English or American, are you?'

'No. I'm originally from New Zealand.'

'That's far.'

'Very far.'

'Is that where you learned to play the violin?'

'Yes.'

The sun was rising fast in the sky and I was beginning to sweat. Neither Joao nor Astrid seemed as affected by the heat.

'I would love to hear you play,' he said. 'But later maybe. I think it's time for a swim, no?' He rose from his chair. I must have looked hesitant. Both Astrid and he slipped out of their casual clothing and were already wearing costumes, his a tight Speedo-like pair of striped grey and ultramarine trunks that left absolutely nothing to the imagination and she the blue bikini in which I had first set eyes on her at the beach, her lithe body all sinuous and tanned from head to toe like a young colt. He looked to be in his forties, but showed none of the signs of middle-age; legs thick and muscled, butt still firm and pert, and his waist narrow below a broad chest and shoulders. Evidently, whatever his work involved, he didn't spend all of his hours sitting down behind a desk. I instinctively glanced down at the bulge of his package and looked away quickly, before either he or Astrid caught me gazing at him.

I remembered I had nothing on under my thin summer dress and excused myself to return to the bedroom where I had slept and retrieve my bathing suit.

Towards midday, Joao apologised. He had to spend time at his city office but insisted I should dine with him and his daughter that same evening. I gladly accepted the invitation but pointed out that I'd been wearing the same dress for over a day now and would wish to change, and he arranged for a car to pick me up from my own place after Astrid and I spent some lazy time on the beach.

'Do bring your violin,' he asked.

'It's back in London,' I told him, reluctant to play for anyone again.

'You can use Astrid's,' he suggested, on his way out of the house. 'Can't you?'

I was in two minds about performing for them. Aside from helping Astrid out with her posture and scales, I hadn't touched an instrument for ages, it felt.

I hadn't known what to wear for dinner at Joao and Astrid's villa. The wardrobe that had followed me from London to the Ball had been minimal, for obvious reasons, and all I had now were a few flimsy well-worn summer dresses, a handful of T-shirts and assorted casual wear. Burrowing through my belongings, I selected a high-waisted pair of black jeans which I paired with a thin red patent leather belt which accentuated my waist, flat ballet shoes and a simple cream-coloured silk shirt I'd picked up in the local market a few days earlier.

I shouldn't have worried. Neither Joao nor Astrid had dressed up for the occasion. He was again all in immaculate white, albeit with a long-sleeved shirt this time and dark loafers, and Astrid in her customary torn-at-the-knees Levis and a Pink Floyd Dark Side of the Moon T-shirt. I was surprised she'd even heard of them. Maybe I should have slipped on one of my surviving Holy Criminal tees instead. But Joao gallantly complimented me for the way I looked and the cream silk blouse through which, I was aware, my red bra discreetly showed.

We ate in a conservatory on the far side of the villa, a

night full of stars reigning above us, and the lights of the city and its procession of tall edifices facing the long arc of the beaches below us twinkling away madly.

The meal was delightful, served by a cadre of silent servants. The meat was succulent and spiced to subtle perfection, the greens crisp and metal-sharp, and the choice of sorbets we feasted on to cleanse our palates singularly refreshing.

Joao summoned a helper, who brought Astrid's violin along, and he requested she play. I wondered how many servants a household of two could possibly need, and tried to push the thought away. Such attention was not the way that I liked to live, but it wasn't my place to judge Joao's lifestyle.

'Let's see how much influence Summer has had on you,' Joao suggested.

Astrid was a little bit self-conscious as she played, and her version of Kreisler's Liebesleid was at times halting and clumsy. We applauded nonetheless. Coffee arrived.

'Summer,' Joao looked over to me. 'We'd love to hear from you. Will you?'

'Maybe another time?' I said. 'It's getting a bit late. I think the wine might have been a bad idea. I wouldn't be at my best . . .'

'Is that a promise? You'll come back and play for us another day? And we'll be less generous with the wine, maybe . . .' He grinned.

Astrid took that as a cue to excuse herself, similarly pre-texting tiredness and the effect of the heavy red wine we had generously been drinking.

I made to rise as she moved away into the villa, but Joao waved his hand.

'You can stay tonight,' he said. 'I've had the room pre-pared. You're absolutely welcome. But I can have the driver take you back, if you prefer.'

I was hesitant.

Staying in and the comforts of the villa had an undeniable attraction, and tipsy as I was, I couldn't face the drive home and then venturing alone into my apartment. I sat down again.

'Good,' Joao said. 'A nightcap? A vintage brandy?'

He had a kind smile.

A good-looking older man. With violet eyes. Cultured, self-confident, unpushy.

I missed the hands of men. The soft and hard touch of their lips. The way they could play me.

I did not sleep in my room that night.

We'd talked for hours. Or rather he'd done most of the talking, and I'd barely listened, neglectfully watching the curl of his lips, the sensuous droop of his eyelids, the elegant lines of age forming around his mouth, his long fingers and the solid bulk of his body housed with quiet ease under the flimsy white curtain of his shirt.

There was a lull in the conversation. A silence. That found me daydreaming.

He took my hand in his.

'Come with me.'

I felt distant, not quite there.

Looked back at him.

Saw him plead.

'Sleep with me tonight.'

'Yes.'

He led me to his bedroom.

You couldn't say he was a bad lover. He returned me to the way things were before I met Dominik and that indelible fire inside was awakened and had kept on burning ever since. Making love by numbers so to speak, the job done properly and attentively, with enough tenderness and application to soothe the hunger inside but no more. I supposed this was what real life was all about.

Steady.

Loving.

Studious in his attempts to share the pleasure equally with me, even clumsy at times for a man of his age and, I presumed, his experience. Skimming the surface of my lust with practised touches, fingers, mouth, tongue, teeth and inevitably drawing some form of automatic response.

But it felt uneventful.

Not enough.

He even offered me a post-coital cigarette, which I turned down.

The next morning his driver returned me to my small, rudimentary beach flat and I had agreed to become his daughter's violin teacher. Astrid must have guessed he had taken me to his bed, and the expression on her face was one of both jealousy and wariness, but she soon warmed to me again. I just hoped she wouldn't see me as a substitute mother.

The waiter refilled my champagne flute.

'Would you like a strawberry in that, Miss?' he asked, his voice a low, rough drawl that I imagined would enunciate dirty words perfectly, but maybe it was just the wine talking. He had jet-black hair, dark eyes and a close-cropped, designer beard that bordered a pair of full, sensual lips, curled in a sardonic expression. He knew that I was drunk, and found him attractive, I was sure of it.

Joao touched my arm and I turned my attention back to the group, studiously avoiding following the waiter's arse with my eyes as he walked away.

'. . . but what else can we do, Matheus?' Joao was saying to the man next to him. 'All the wealth in the world cannot control the weather . . .'

We were standing on the wide balcony outside one of the penthouse suites at the Belmond Copacabana Palace hotel, visiting a cohort of Joao's business acquaintances and their mistresses. The men had been speaking in Portuguese and Joao had switched to English, for my benefit I knew, but I was only partially grateful since I had nothing in particular to contribute to a conversation about crops or drought conditions. Matheus had a face like a bread roll – pale, round and shining – with a thin sheen of sweat that layered his features. When he spoke, his thin lips curled back and exposed a row of crooked teeth. Saliva hovered at the edges of his gums and a spray of spittle burst forth with each word he uttered.

I forced my mouth to lift into a smile that I hoped conveyed polite interest. The sound of the sea lapping against the sand below was a welcome antidote, and I concentrated on that instead, and let the talk of crops, machinery and the price of holiday homes wash over me. I turned my head and looked out at the wide expanse of ocean stretched out like a dark ribbon beyond the shore and the people below us crawling like ants across the sand. City lights glimmered in the distance.

'Joao, we are being very rude I think, and boring your lovely guest.'

I swung back again. It was Matheus, with a dreadful smirk spread across his face, delighted to make a point of my infraction. I barely knew the man and I hated him already.

'Oh no,' I insisted. 'Forgive me. I could not help admiring

your beautiful city. I never grow tired of looking out at the sea.'

That much at least, was true.

'And what better place to see it from, eh?' Matheus gestured towards the room. His Piaget watch artfully caught the glare from a lamp overhead and caused flashes of light to bounce off the wide glass doors that separated us from the rest of the suite. His wrist was fat and hairy and totally at odds with the effulgent watchstrap that shone when he moved, advertising both his wealth and his terrible taste in jewellery.

Joao had told me as we strode through the chandelier-lined lobby towards the lift that he had offered to host tonight's gathering, but Matheus had suggested that each of the couples in attendance book one of the Belmond's penthouse suites instead. The wide living area alone was larger than my whole apartment, wooden floors polished to mirror shine and dotted with soft, thick rugs. Abstract art pieces were hung on the walls at regular intervals, each of them subtly elevated by the gallery-style lighting that made the colours and textures seem so alive. The long, pale mint-coloured sofa and matching armchairs sat as if someone had arranged them using a ruler and a feng shui guide to achieve the perfect combination of elegance and casual comfort. They probably had. Glass-topped coffee tables with geometric-style chrome legs were decorated with fresh-cut lilies floating in bowls of water. The scent that emanated from them was so heady it made me dizzy.

'It's lovely,' I replied weakly. I would have far preferred to watch the waves roll in from one of the cheap but excellent cafés by the sea side, with a hearty plate of paella in front of me and a glass of cold beer, or barefoot on the beach sipping a caipirinha prepared by one of the beachfront drink stalls, but I couldn't admit that to Joao.

'Perhaps we could make our excuses to Matheus, let them have their fun at the Belmond and catch up with them for lunch tomorrow? We could see a show instead, the three of us?' I had suggested when I saw Astrid's face fall as she had caught sight of me earlier that afternoon trying on the gown that her father had bought me to wear for the occasion.

Joao was immovable. 'Matheus and his friends have travelled all the way from São Paulo to enjoy Rio. It would be impolite of me to refuse his invitation to join them tonight. Besides, why waste such beauty as yours on sitting in an audience with us two? I want to show you off.'

Astrid was sitting alone on the couch in the living room, playing computer games on the widescreen TV, nearly swallowed up by the plush cream leather cushions that were piled on either side of her. She looked even younger than usual, and small, as though she might slip down between the cracks in the sofa like a lost coin and be forgotten about.

148

On the screen in front of her, an animated mushroom was driving a blue Ferrari. The car twisted and spun, navigating hairpin turns and avoiding shooting flames and banana skins as Astrid pressed the buttons on the controller with alarming dexterity. She looked up when her father spoke, and the blue Ferrari ploughed straight off the side of the road and dropped into a jagged crevice. 'Game Over' flashed up on the screen, layered over the face of a laughing dragon. Astrid thumped the controller down, picked up the copy of *Todateen* that lay on the low wooden table in front of her and began idly thumbing through the magazine without stopping on any page long enough to read it.

Her father hadn't noticed. He was choosing between two sets of earrings that he had bought for me to wear, one a pair of long, draping silver tassels that reached all the way to my shoulders, and the other, subtler gold hoops with a single diamond inset into the base.

I stood stock still as he threaded one of each through my lobes to compare them, decorating me as if I were a Christmas tree.

It wasn't the first such evening, or the first gown. The previous weekend Joao had taken me to the opening of a new sushi restaurant in Leblon, where the sashimi was the best I had ever tasted and the prices on the menu had made my eyes water. Before that, there had been an exclusive charity ball in yet another waterfront hotel, where the cost

149

of the buffet alone could probably have filled the charity's coffers for a whole year.

By default, too flattered or dazed to ever say 'no', I was becoming a kept woman.

Tonight he had wanted me all in black.

'You're so pale,' he said. 'So unlike other women here. I love it.'

Fortunately, I had been sunbathing topless often enough that I could wear the dress that he had bought me without revealing any tan marks. The neck and back were cut in a wide, long V, revealing my throat all the way to my belly button, and my shoulders down to the curve of my rump. I couldn't wear a bra with it. A fact that I was sure Matheus was fully aware of. Joao's corpulent business partner had been staring at my breasts all night. I was vaguely irritated that Joao had exhibited no discomfort at all over Matheus eyeing me up so lustily that he might as well have reached over and planted a territorial flag between my tits. I did not expect him to engage the man in an old-fashioned round of fisticuffs, but he might have at least been a little bit jealous.

What was I to Joao? A selling point of some sort? Had he brought me here because he knew that he would do better in his business relationships if he had me hanging from his arm?

Matheus placed a cigarette between his lips and lit it.

Smoke curled from the cigarette's end and around his fingers, which jutted like sausages from the doughy ball of his hand. He stared at me and took a long drag, then licked his lips. I took another sip of my champagne in a bid to suppress a coughing fit. Matheus's mannerisms were so overtly sexual that I could not help but imagine him in the act, nude and on all fours, the paunch of his hairy belly hanging down and obscuring his short, stumpy cock and shrivelled ball sack bouncing between his legs.

Would he be the sort who liked hurting women, or did he secretly harbour a desire to be dominated? By women, or by other men? The possibilities multiplied in my mind along with a cinemascope-worthy screen of disturbing, pornographic visuals. Did others have these thoughts about strangers, or was it just me? I often found myself imagining what men's cocks looked like, whether or not I found the men in question attractive. Sometimes I imagined what they would taste like too, or how they would feel inside me. Just the sort of thing that my mind threw up, often at the most inconvenient moments.

'Excuse me, please,' I said, and whispered to Joao that I needed the bathroom. I held my shoulders back and concentrated on keeping my balance in my high heels as I walked past the huddle of women who were draped over the soft furniture in the lounge area, chatting to one another in Portuguese. None of them looked to be older than twenty-five, probably half the age of their respective significant others camped out on the balcony. They were ensconced on the corner sofa, five pairs of long, lean legs stretched out and sharing the same large ottoman in front of them. Each of them wore a variation on the same outfit. Skin-tight, brightly coloured mini-dresses in vivid shades of red and purple that highlighted their brown skin and voluptuous bodies, curved and firm without an ounce of superfluous fat.

I knew that Joao, with his good looks and money, could have been dating another woman like them. Younger, better looking than me. Certainly slimmer and with fewer wrinkles. Perhaps I ought to have been flattered, then, by his and his business partner's obvious attraction to me, but I wasn't. I was familiar with the minds of men like that. They wanted something different, and here in Rio, with my pale skin and red hair, it just happened to be me. I was a fetish to them and not a person. Another type that they could notch on some metaphorical bedpost.

I darted into the bathroom. It was twice the size of my bedroom. The Jacuzzi-style bath and heated tiles were marble, surrounded by sleek black fittings. A long wide mirror lined one wall, over the vanity unit. I took a clean glass from the tray on the side and filled it with water from the tap and swiftly drank it to wash away some of the champagne that I had imbibed, then sat down on the bath's edge and pulled off my shoes. My toes were red and pinched and the balls of my feet ached.

Astrid would be in bed now, or maybe if she had rail-roaded her nanny into letting her stay up late she might still be awake playing computer games. I wished that I was there with her, eating popcorn on the sofa and racing fast cars. I enjoyed her company more than her father's, and yet, I knew that it would never be the same between us again, now that I was sleeping with him. I was her teacher, and her father's girlfriend, not her friend, and I never would be again. I had ruined everything.

There was a soft rap at the door.

'Yes?' I said, quickly squishing my feet back into my shoes and smoothing down my dress, assuming that it would be Joao.

It was the dark-haired, bearded waiter.

'Pardon me, madam,' he said. 'I noticed you rush in here, and thought you might not be feeling well. I brought some iced peppermint tea.'

He was balancing a tray on one hand that supported a tall glass filled with pale green liquid and mint leaves. In the other hand, he held a pair of tongs and was using them to collect ice cubes from a silver bowl and drop them into the drink.

'Oh,' I said, 'that's very kind of you.' I stood up and took the iced tea from the tray and gulped it down. It was wonderfully refreshing. 'Thank you,' I told him.

He smiled at me and I was briefly tempted to give him my phone number, or even to kick the door closed behind him and lock it, and take him right there in the bath tub. Imagining the waiter naked and in bed was the perfect antidote to my visions of Matheus, and I let my mind run wild, thinking of how his long, elegant fingers would feel inside me, three or four at a time. His lips were deep red and his mouth was wide, and I pictured myself leaning over the tray and kissing him as I fondled his cock through the fabric of his formal, neatly pressed black work trousers.

'Can I get you anything else?' he asked me, interrupting my train of thought and bringing me back into the real world.

'Ah, no, I'm fine. I had better get back to the party.'

I checked myself in the mirror quickly, thankful that my inner secrets did not show on my face, and walked back towards the terrace. Nobody had moved an inch during my departure. The women were still gossiping on the sofa, their voices a degree shriller, as the champagne bottles in buckets scattered around them emptied. Joao, Matheus and the other black-suited men were now smoking cigars, leaning over the white-pillared barrier that separated the suite's outdoor area from the drop down to the hotel gardens below.

Joao looked up as I approached, and swept me against his broad chest with the arc of his arm.

'Are you okay, darling?' he asked me.

'Yes of course,' I told him. 'Just getting some water.'

'You should have just called out to the waiter,' he said. 'That's what he's there for.'

I shrugged. His hand slipped down inside the back of my dress, along the seam of my underwear, and cupped my arse. I was grateful that he didn't venture further, as he would have discovered that beneath the thin covering of my plain black thong I was wet and undeniably horny. But I didn't want Joao tonight. I didn't want to make love, or even to have sex, like any other two ordinary people would. I wanted to have someone who knew me and understood what I was thinking and who even liked to grab me by the hair and throw me down onto the bed and fuck me hard and relentlessly until every thought in my head disappeared and I was left with nothing but a few precious moments of being totally alive.

Later that night, after we finally made our excuses and left the Palace, I asked Joao to drop me off at my apartment.

'Shall I come up with you?' he asked.

'Another time perhaps,' I told him, and explained that I was just tired, and wanted to get up early tomorrow and visit the beach.

He acquiesced without much argument, and kissed me goodnight, a quick peck on the lips.

Inside, I threw off my dress, crawled into bed and touched

myself until I came, visions of past and imagined lovers flooding my brain in a stream of pornography.

I did not think of Joao once.

The heat was rising.

I woke layered in a film of sweat. And realised immediately that I had overslept. My apartment was deathly quiet, and the thick silence made me feel even hotter. Not so much as a single breath of fresh air ruffled the white sheet wrapped around my naked body. I had begun switching off my air-conditioning unit to save costs, and to avoid the low hum that kept me awake at night-time.

Outside, the only breeze that interrupted the stifling humidity against my sticky skin came from the rush of passing cars and motorcycles speeding by on the Avenida Vieira Souto. If only Ipanema Beach were a nudist colony, I would have discarded my clothing right there in the street and continued walking naked. Why had I chosen today to wear the all-over black-patterned floral dress, instead of the thin, white barely-there kaftan that I had borrowed from Aurelia and which was still stuffed into one of my overflowing wardrobe drawers? The halter-neck style I was wearing enabled me to get away with going braless, but instead of leaving my breasts bare and cool as I had imagined, the cotton fabric pulled tight against my chest and around my throat and made me just as uncomfortable as an underwire would have done.

An interactive billboard set up in the middle of the road flashing the current temperature in large orange lettering against a black background advised me that it was 43 degrees. At only ten in the morning. Joggers raced by one after another, ripped bodies glowing with exertion, smiles painted on their faces as though they were impervious to the heat. One, clad only in a pair of short, navy-blue shorts secured low on his hips with a loose white drawstring, reached his arm out poker-straight in front of him with his mobile phone gripped tight in his hand, grinned and snapped a picture. His apparent dedication to health and fitness made me crave a cold milkshake and a burger. I hadn't yet had breakfast.

I continued to wander aimlessly, thinking of what I could do that day. It was now too hot to hike Pedra Bonita as I had planned, a task that would have necessitated rising around 5 a.m. and catching a taxi to the Tijuca National Park before the sun rose. I would be at the top now, if I hadn't rolled over lazily and pressed the snooze button when my alarm went off. There was the National Museum of Brazil, housed in the Imperial Palace, that had been on my to-do list for ages, but my guidebook informed me that it was closed today. I had no money for clothes shopping, and my closet was already jam-packed with more evening dresses and high-heeled shoes than I had ever owned in all of my years living in London or New York combined. The cinema would at least be air-conditioned, but my brain was in too much of a heat-dazed fug to be bothered concentrating on following a film in Portuguese.

My stomach rumbled. What I really wanted was a Salty Pimp from Big Gay Ice Cream in the West Village – vanilla ice cream on a crunchy waffle cone with caramel and sea salt – or a peanut butter banana soft serve from Momofuku in Brooklyn. Even a tub of Ben and Jerry's would have sufficed. America really knew how to do dessert. Not refined and elegant like the French did, but big and cold and sweet and satisfying. Zaza wasn't open yet and I really needed to stop spending money in fancy restaurants and start economising, and besides, their lemon sorbet wasn't nearly fattening enough for what I fancied right now. Beachside Rio, with all its vanity and focus on appearance, was overrun by health foods; low-fat yoghurts, fruit smoothies and juices abounded.

I would have to settle for a plastic tub of frozen açai, a deep purple-red berry mixed with ice and sometimes sugar, the latest superfood trend and consequently available nearly everywhere.

Raoul's juice bar was the nearest. I had broken my habit of visiting there most mornings since I met Astrid and then fell into dating Joao and waking up in my own bed on fewer and fewer occasions. I never had asked Raoul out on a date as I had once planned to.

The tall, broad-shouldered Brazilian was wearing a baggy T-shirt with a V neck which revealed a small thatch of his thick black chest curls and the gleam of a gold chain around his neck. His shining black hair was loose around his shoulders. He was making a drink for another customer and turned away from me as I approached the counter, leaving me free to remind myself of the pert, round shape of his hard buttocks, his tight glutes prominent beneath a pair of white-and-black board shorts. Raoul was one of the few men I had seen here who preferred to wear loose clothing instead of muscle tees or vests and swimming trunks even smaller than my briefest knickers. There was something deeply masculine about him that appealed to me. The brutish way that he moved, his big hands slamming the plastic body of the blender into place and gripping the lid with little care for finesse or the longevity of the equipment. I bet that his cock was long and thick and his balls heavy. He would have a musky smell and a bush of unkempt pubic hair that I would delight in burrowing my face into.

'Hey, bonita,' he said when he noticed me standing there. 'Haven't seen you for a long time. Thought you'd left town.'

I was flattered that he'd noticed.

I ordered a cup of frozen açai, and settled onto the tall bar stool that sat closest to the buzzing fan on the counter.

The other customers, a young white couple, obviously

tourists with their matching lightweight khaki trousers, pockets bulging with real, sun hats straight out of a camping catalogue and expensive cameras fixed tightly around their necks, wandered off, leaving the two of us alone.

Raoul flicked the cloth that he had been wiping down the drink machine with over his shoulder and leaned down to meet my eyes, resting his elbows on the counter in front of me.

'Not taking away today? Heading for a swim maybe? Or just tanning that lovely body of yours?'

Brazilian men flattered women openly here. I did not fool myself for a moment into thinking that Raoul's words meant that he saw something special about me in particular.

'Too hot for the beach today, I think. Can't face the crowds.' I knew that the shore would be littered with deck-chairs, umbrellas and volleyball players as far as the eye could see in both directions.

He nodded. 'You should get out of the city. So many people come here and just see the Copacabana boardwalk, and Ipanema. Sing the famous song, take a few photos and drink a few bad caipirinhas, and leave again.'

'Where would you suggest?'

'I can do better than suggest,' he told me. 'I'll show you. There's Ilha Grande, Lopes Mendes, the other places that are in all the guidebooks, but we can skip those. I'll take you to places where you won't need a bathing suit, because we'll be the only two on the beach.'

He must have noticed my wry expression; just another pick-up line, I was thinking.

'I mean it,' he said. 'I'm also a tour guide. When I'm not working here, behind the bar.'

'Oh.' That explained why he spoke English like a native.

'I could come on one of your actual tours.'

'If you want to drive around slowly with tourists in matching pale beige outfits snapping photos of every cocada stand they pass in the road, sure. Half of them can't walk fifty yards without wanting to sit down and rest.'

I laughed.

His eyes twinkled when he smiled, animating his whole face. It had been a long time since I'd met a man who made me laugh. Not since Dominik. Joao was serious by nature, and even Antony, my ex-lover and theatre director, had been too much of an arty sort to spend a lot of time joking around.

'Besides,' he said, 'if it's just the two of us, we can take the bike.' He nodded towards the road and I followed his gaze in the direction of a sleek yellow Ducati motorcycle.

'Is that yours?'

'My pride and joy, although she's getting old now. Bought her off a British guy a few years ago, who rode her all over Brazil. Reconditioned the engine, bit of body work and a friend did the paint job, and she's good as new. You ever ridden a bike?'

'Only traveling pillion. Not for a long time though.' In my late teens in New Zealand, I had dated a half-Japanese man who rode a red Suzuki and we had spent a week touring the Queen Charlotte Sounds on his bike. I still remembered keenly how badly my buttocks ached after spending long hours in the saddle, and how much I enjoyed wrapping my arms around my boyfriend sitting in front of me, and pressing my breasts against his back.

'Good. It's settled then. I have a spare helmet. We can go tomorrow if you're free, it's my day off.'

'I'm free,' I said. Actually, I was supposed to be teaching Astrid violin in the afternoon, but I decided then and there to give her a call and pretext a headache.

A lanky teenage boy clad in just a pair of trainers and neon-orange speedos appeared alongside me and asked Raoul for an abacaxi and mint juice, one of my favourite combinations.

Raoul seemed openly annoyed by the interruption.

'Tell you what,' he said, keeping the tall youngster on my right waiting for his drink, 'meet me tonight at Academia da Cachaca in Leblon, and we can plan where to go. Do you know it?'

'Yeah, I know it. Best caipirinha I've tasted here so far.'

'You've been spoiled, they make the best in Rio. Eight o'clock?'

I agreed, and left him to serve his customers. A queue had mounted.

We didn't make it to any of the deserted beaches that he had promised to show me. We didn't leave my apartment until dinner time the following day. I couldn't blame it on the cachaca. I'd only had two, one the original limao, and the other a sweeter, creamier version flavoured with coconut, along with a large meal of feijoada served with perfectly cooked farofa and succulent orange slices. The waiter sat us outside in the still-humid night air, on two rickety chairs either side of a round table top that was so tiny Raoul was able to reach under it easily and place his hand on my thigh, a fact that he took advantage of almost as soon as we arrived.

His grip was strong and persuasive, not that I needed to be persuaded. Unwelcome thoughts of Joao and Astrid caused pinpricks of guilt to pop into my brain, which I quickly disregarded.

'Oh,' I said, as he put his other arm under the table after the waiter delivered our second round of drinks, and brazenly pushed my knees apart, oblivious to our public surroundings or just impervious to the reactions of other diners nearby.

'What would you like to eat?' Raoul asked me, as he

163

leaned further forward and grazed his knuckles all the way up my bare thigh to the seam of my panties. I responded to his touch without consciously thinking about it, my body disconnected from my brain – or perhaps the two were perfectly in sync in a way that the moralistic part of me didn't want to admit – by slinking down in my seat to give him easier access. I had changed into a cap-sleeved navy lace top tucked into a short red skater skirt, and for one shameful moment I felt pleased that I had picked the flared number and not the black satin shorts that had been my second choice.

'Good girl,' he whispered, and slid two fingers inside my knickers. He kept them there and continued to lightly brush over my now wet slit as the waiter returned to take our food order.

'We'll have the large plate to share,' Raoul interjected for me, when it became apparent that I was unable to speak.

If the uniformed attendant had noticed the reason for my reticence, he didn't remark upon it.

'You'll make a lot more noise than this when I get you home,' Raoul teased, when we were alone again. 'I'll make sure of it.'

His presumption and his cockiness horrified and annoyed me in equal measure, but also undeniably turned me on.

Some things never changed.

★　　★　　★

I knew juggling two lovers was not a feat I could sustain indefinitely.

I was right.

I was no good at lying and coming up with new excuses. Pretending to Joao that I needed some space and time on my own when I happened to be with Raoul. On every occasion I visited Astrid's father or spent time with him after days of rage and sex with Raoul, I thought he would immediately notice the obvious signs of dissipation across my face, in the depths of my eyes, let alone all over my body. I was ever rehearsing explanations for the small bruises, the pleasurable tiredness that surrounded me like a cloud after rough sex. But if Joao ever noticed anything, he carefully avoided questioning me, retaining his innate elegance and discretion. Or maybe he knew from experience how complicated it was to keep a younger woman on an imaginary leash or happy, and he feared upsetting the apple cart. If there was an affray, I guessed it wouldn't be of his making.

As for Raoul, I had to come up with a different set of answers. And ask he did. Repeatedly. Which meant grossly exaggerating the number of violin lessons I was giving Astrid, to attain some level of plausibility. I sensed his jealousy and possessiveness.

And then there were the nights when both insisted they wanted to see me, and I had to make a choice between them, the smooth and the rough, the slow waltz of love and hovering over the precipice. Never an obvious choice.

Raoul loosening the rope that bound my wrists to the bed's metal headboard, my breath still halting, still half afloat in that envious zone where I was both spectator, victim and sacrificial offering to the gods of lust, and a shameless form of desire through which I navigated as if naturally born to it. His perspiring body, dark and linear, strong thighs taut, thick cock still at half mast, hovering above me.

Rubbing life back into my wrists, noting in passing the marks the rope had left, the momentary imprint of the sweet madness on my skin. Experiencing parcels of pain in parts of my body I didn't know I had. Listening to the life outside filter through, one sound at a time, the air stir, the whoosh of the ceiling fan, this wonderful and terrible man's sweat pearl down from his hairy chest onto my bare skin, pooling around my navel and in the valley between my breasts. Coming down. No longer flying through the holy spheres. Floating. Falling. Becoming myself again. Summer.

He bent over. Kissed me. His hand tight around my throat, immobilising me into position. The pressure in my lungs. The buzz racing across my skin like a web still holding me captive. I couldn't move. Didn't want to move. As if he was testing me, keeping me under observation to see how far I would allow him to go on dominating me. Checking my resolve, my limits. And, out of pride and obstinacy I knew I would not be the first to flinch, to cry out 'no'.

He released me.

My cunt felt abominably raw, so much more exposed, open, ravaged, wetter than wet. He initially refused to wear a condom. During our very first encounter. Unlike Joao. Assuming in his macho way that I was the one who should be taking precautions, not him, and thinking only of children that might come, as if he were invincible to other risks. I insisted from the outset we use protection, but he never stopped making me pay for it. Pointedly spitting on my slit to keep it lubricated. Once bringing a condom filled with his semen to my face and making me lap from it like a dog drinking from a cup. It both disgusted me, this attitude, but also fired a light inside me, the radiance of the moth attracted by the glare of the fire.

His lips abandoned me just as I was about to cry out, gasp for air. His hands moved away from my throat. He was still squatting over me, his knees pinning me down, widening the angle of my thighs. His hand passed through my legs, wallowing inside my juices, brought a finger to his lips, then mine.

'Taste,' he ordered me.

I licked his fingers clean.

'You're like an animal,' he told me later. 'A beautiful beast . . .' Admiration and desire juggling for space in his eyes.

167

He gazed at me, a million thoughts apparently bustling in his mind.

I remained impassive. I didn't love this man, never could. But I craved the way he wanted me and the brutal form of his desire.

'I'm hungry,' I said.

He rose, turned his back on me, walked to the nearby kitchen counter, his naked arse solid as rock, like a throne of stone presiding above the straight towers of his muscled legs, his movements swift and proud. Returned holding a plate. His dark cock had now shrunk but was still visibly wet from our exertions, shone like a warped diamond, reminding me of its relentless journeys inside me, the way it pushed its way down my throat earlier, almost had me gag, and the way he slapped my cheeks and pinched my nose in reaction as I resisted, forcing his authority on me, controlling me, enjoying me.

I was unwilling to move, spread obscenely across the faded white sheets of his narrow bed, my body broken, still relishing the ebb and flow of fading lust that kept animating my mind as I lay on the bottom of the mental ocean. He held a thin strip of beef carpaccio above my mouth. My lips parted.

'Raw meat for an animal,' Raoul said, with an undisguised smirk of satisfaction.

I gulped the meat down with relish, chewing it avidly and sucking out the taste before swallowing it.

'It's not very flattering to be compared to an animal, you know?' I remarked.

'Maybe a thoroughbred would be a more appropriate description,' Raoul said.

'I think I prefer that.'

'A thoroughbred whore,' he continued. 'A pleasure animal.'

'Hmm . . . Animals can sometimes be dangerous, unpredictable,' I pointed out.

'They can also be trained,' he added. Oh yes, he had cruel lips.

'Do I really need further training?' I asked.

'There can never be enough training.'

I was due later that afternoon at Joao's villa, for a lesson with Astrid. Her violin skills were developing nicely, even though I knew I was something of an impatient tutor. I would be expected to stay the night, I knew. I just didn't think I was in a state to do so. My body would betray me. The marks on my skin might not fade in time.

I felt drained right now.

'I need to sleep, Raoul. Can I stay?'

He had a tour booked, I knew. Would be away until late in the evening.

'Sure.'

I switched off, allowing the waves of lassitude to breach the dams of my consciousness. I was about to go under when I heard him.

'I want to show you off, Summer. I feel others should witness how beautiful you are when unleashed, bridled. Even, see you with another man. Oh, that would be quite a sight . . . One day . . .' he promised.

I was too tired to respond and welcomed the dark.

I missed the violin tutorial with Astrid. And was too weary to even phone and warn her.

My explanations and excuses might not have proved convincing, or maybe I was betrayed by invisible signs of my activities with Raoul, but on the next occasion I met the businessman at his villa, I found out that Joao's suspicions had been raised. He'd had me followed by someone, his driver maybe, and he had been made aware of the fact I had spent the night away from my own place and instead at Raoul's. How much more he knew, I could only guess.

He asked me to choose. Between his anchor and the deep blue deep sea that Raoul represented. I told him I was unable to do so. Begged for time. Somehow Astrid knew some of what was going on and became more distant, suspended our tutorials of her own accord and no longer wanted to spend time at the beach with me.

Which left me with just Raoul.

And I knew all too well where the relationship with him might be leading me. It was a combustible path I was all too familiar with and was unwilling to tramp through yet again. God only knew that I wasn't good at learning lessons, but some had made indelible marks and left me badly scarred in the process.

I was also running out of funds.

Aurelia, or the Network, had made a payment into my account as she promised that they would, but I refused to spend it. I wanted to be free of their hold over me, unencumbered by the ties of that world which I had chosen to walk away from. Neither could I bring myself to rely on Joao's generosity, although I knew that given even half a chance he would happily install me in his Jardim Botânico villa permanently, or pay the lease on a new apartment. The Ball had paid up front for my rental for one year only, and my twelve months were nearly at a close. If I wanted to remain in the city by the sea, I would need to find alternative accommodation. My once frugal habits had taken a hit when, ironically, as a result of some of Joao's generous gifts of dresses and outfits, I had felt obliged to accessorise and complete them with added jewellery and, principally, shoes. He had bought me shoes and earrings as well, but I was too vain to wear the same ones over and over, and too proud to insinuate that I needed or wanted more. And I'd always had expensive taste in shoes! What with my loss of income from the Ball, and the fact that I had not undertaken any musical engagements for more than two years now and my old record royalties were dwindling, I calculated that I only had six months' worth of cash ahead of me. I hadn't waited tables since I was a teenager, and I knew that sort of work paid terribly here. My Portuguese wasn't anywhere near strong enough for an office job, even if I could fake a résumé. I had no other skills but music. And I knew I was not ready to return to playing the violin for a living. My soul wasn't ready. Would it ever be?

I wasn't even sure that I wanted to stay in Rio now. It seemed that a simple life of beach and sun was not enough for me.

My foolishness with men had spoiled things. Again.

I rang Susan, my erstwhile agent back in London. She was surprised to hear from me. Had probably written me off completely.

I didn't tell her exactly where in the world I was.

Or explain the true reasons for my call.

Before departing for the Ball, I had left her a power of attorney over my business dealings. I asked her to sell some of my violins, whose storage she had access to, and transfer the proceeds to me via PayPal.

'Any particular violin?' Susan asked.

'Whichever will fetch the best value,' I said.

She agreed, and we postponed any other discussion to a future occasion, although she did insist on advising me that another record label appeared to be strongly interested in signing me up. Some new executive she found rather interesting. I informed her that I was anything but ready to return to music, though. I heard her sigh on the other end of the line.

After I'd set the mobile phone down on my kitchen counter, I felt a momentary spell of dizziness and I gripped the bench and stared out through the window. A compact herd of low-lying clouds was drifting above the golden sands of the beach. Rain was on its way.

The only violin of substantial value was the Bailly Dominik had bought me, I knew.

I wasn't even sure any longer why I had held on to it so long.

Now it would be gone forever.

And with it, its history and personal associations.

I began crying.

5

A Magnificent Obsession

Noah sat at the bar of the Ivy Club, sipping the last dregs of a potent double espresso, his second of the day. He felt both energised and aimless. A meeting with a couple of journalists had ended a half-hour ago. The label kept them on retainer to report on interesting new prospects in the North of England and Scotland, and they'd handed over a handful of demo discs and memory sticks they thought he might turn out to be interested in. He still had an hour to kill before attending a gig in Camden Town in a subterranean club where the sweat poured down the walls and archaeological layers of grime and dried beer coated the floors defying any cleaner's attempt to attack them. Far from his favourite venue.

One of the journalists, a Manchester-based freelancer called Barbara, had caught his eye at first sight. Bubbly and highly convivial, she was championing a local band she had come across and was effusive with her praise for their still-unformed talent. She'd not been part of the company's network of A&R stringers-along, recruited by his ill-fated predecessor just before Noah's return to Britain.

Noah had the feeling the music she was praising so loudly would not prove to his taste, if only by the way she described the group, but he politely heard her out and pocketed the demo disc. The moment she had walked into the bar, he had been struck by her initial appearance. A tiny pocket Venus, curvy, a buzzing ball of energy and all too self-aware of her physical attraction, vertiginous cleavage peering out from her colourful turquoise top and a black denim skirt that adhered to her skin with industrial precision.

She also had red hair.

And a built-in radar that immediately registered his undisguised curiosity. Must have been the way he looked at her, he knew, anything but indifferent, a possible twinkle in his eye as the words poured out of her. She took it as an open invitation to flirt. Totally ignoring the other journalist present, a tall shaggy-bearded Glaswegian almost twice her height, dressed in lumberjack chic shirt and skinny tie. They visibly knew each other. A couple?

But Noah's gaze strayed away from her revealing blouse and remained fixed on her hair. A thick ball of fuzzy curls in varying shades of orange and red under the club's somewhat nocturnal lighting. An uneasy feeling began to brew in his stomach.

Had he ever held such a fascination about red-haired women previously? Not that he remembered.

He tried to recall how many he had actually known. As acquaintances, friends or, more rarely, lovers.

He could count them on the fingers of one hand.

Vivacious schoolmates with freckled faces at an age when he was still more interested in his stamp collection than the other sex. The earthy scent of the ambassador's daughter who, in his teens, had smuggled him into the dormitory where she was sleeping with her class on a study trip to Avignon, who kissed with a savage hunger, aggressively biting his lips, allowing his hand to wander down below and experience the coarse texture and tightness of her pubic hair while she gave him a clumsy handjob. They'd been shopped the following morning by a classmate in a nearby bed and he'd been unceremoniously despatched back home in minor disgrace. Just over twenty years ago now, and he didn't remember either her name or her face, he uncomfortably realised.

The Scot had excused himself and headed for the toilets. Barbara had casually put her hand on his knee and was leaning forward, the tone in her voice shifting ever so slightly to confidential mode even though she was still singing the praises of her pet project.

His eyes moved closer to the explosion of her hair.

Which had now adopted an unnatural shade of sun under his near scrutiny.

He could smell her breath this close. A whiff of spearmint. The hint of a parting in the close-knit map of her scalp. A variation in colour. A thin line of darker hue.

Her hair was dyed.

Noah had felt a strong sense of deflation. And relief. Noting his lack of response to her less than subtle approach, Barbara had instinctively retreated and the conversation had continued, neither of them openly acknowledging that the moment had passed.

He checked his watch, a black round-faced Tissot model, and raised the small white cup to his lips, draining the last dregs of cold coffee, and waved his credit card at the bar attendant to settle his account. He was soon in the back of a cab travelling to North London. A sparse curtain of rain parted in front of them as the taxi cruised past the British Museum. The London lights flickered as if it was already Christmas, late-evening commuters running like clockwork mice in random directions as the storm opened up, hoods and umbrellas shielding them as best they could. Noah could still smell Barbara's scent breeze around him. More spearmint than redhead.

And he thought of Summer.

Wherever she was.

Desperate to know more about the woman behind the music and the dazzling, inviting images he had begun to collect in the madness of his obsession.

Mentally assembling a jigsaw of her life from all the often conflicting morsels of information he had succeeded in gathering so far in his casual investigations. His stalking?

He realised how, to any onlooker, his quest might even appear a touch creepy, unhealthy, but it was something he could no longer control. The elusive classical musician had taken over his thoughts by stealth.

He had never believed in love at first sight. Was too much of a realist for that.

But lust at first sight, well, that was a whole different kettle of fish!

His name was on the guest list and he checked what time the group he was keen on watching would be on stage. He still had an hour to spare. He was given a square pink voucher for a free drink but, not a great drinker, elected to pick up a bottle of San Pellegrino sparkling water. He noted the presence of a few familiar faces, A&R scouts for other labels grouped around the upstairs bar. He descended into the small, darkened auditorium, the strumming of a guitar luring him in, a rangy mid-length dark-blonde girl in a long peasant skirt, scuffed boots and a grey sweatshirt, straight from folk-singer casting central, the support act, her voice, almost masculine in its bass depths, at strong odds with her appearance. Sitting next to her, an earnest slide guitar player who looked like an under-age college student and was studiously caressing his strings and punctuating the singer's studied melodies with widescreen soaring notes. A pleasant overall sound but a pity about the repertory: Joan Baez and Buffy St Marie standards, and 'Greensleeves' on predictable hand for the finale. But, Noah noted, there was something there, a glimmer of originality, personality; the way her voice swooped in uncommon patterns, treading a delicate line between the melody. Did they also write their own material?

At the end of the opening act's set, he walked over and introduced himself. The girl's eyes widened when she realised he was genuinely from a record label and not just a passing bullshitter. Her name was Magdalena, she said, and her accompanist happened to be her younger brother.

'Do you write anything yourself or just stick to covers?' Noah asked.

'Yes, yes,' she said hurriedly, hoping to please. 'But it's not quite ready to be tried out in public,' she added.

She was raw but there was a kernel of untrained talent there, Noah felt. He advised her to keep in touch. Maybe in a year or so, if her own songs confirmed his instinct, she would be worth looking at again. In his job, he had to play the long game. Sow seeds. Hope. Wait.

A couple of roadies were now scrambling across the stage,

setting up the main act's equipment, checking connections, plugging the various instruments in, tuning them one final time, adjusting mike and drum stall heights and checking sound levels with the technician situated at the back of the room in charge of the control console.

Noah noticed that one of the sundry instruments they had left out on a chair by the wall of Marshall amps was a violin, a long cord leading from it to a smaller amplifier. He frowned. There had been no violin to be heard on the demo tapes he had been sent. Maybe it was only used on a song or two? From where he stood, the instrument looked battered and cheap, had nothing of the elegant angles and curves and burnished wood colour of the Bailly 'Christiansen' of Summer's he had seen auctioned.

'You've come to see them, I guess?'

It was Magdalena. He hadn't noticed she was still standing by his side. Her brother was nowhere to be seen.

'I have.'

'The bass player, Kristian, is a family friend,' the young woman said. 'That's how I got the support gig,' she explained.

'Have you watched them play before? What's the story about the violin?' he asked.

'It's just a gimmick. The rhythm guitarist plays it briefly during the finale. I saw them rehearse the number at the afternoon soundcheck.'

Noah looked round towards her. She appeared nervous, unsure of herself. On stage, she had appeared composed and serene. The secret life of musicians, he decided. Or actors. The moment they walked onto a stage, they changed, became someone else altogether.

She had a lovely mouth.

And she was, he couldn't help noticing, almost flat-chested under the shapeless sweatshirt.

'Is Magdalena your real name? Of Eastern European descent?'

'No. It's Tracey. Just a stage name. Tracey's not much of a folk singer name, is it?'

She grinned. Noah smiled back at her.

'Drink?' he suggested.

'Why not,' she said, a wry expression spreading across her face, as if a weight had been lifted from her shoulders, a decision she had been hesitant about had been taken for her.

He realised she reminded him a lot of Bridget, in both appearance, way of dressing and musically. Although she was patently more ambitious, the sort of musician who would do anything to succeed. She had that steel of determination in her eyes.

Magdalena stuck to him all evening, through the band's set. They were good but not enough in Noah's opinion. Would have made a perfectly adequate signing to the label five years earlier, but tastes had changed as had fashion, and he was seeking the next big thing and not an imitation of glories past. If only he knew what the next big thing would be; maybe he would know when he saw it, heard it. A fat chance.

The signs were there for all to see. The way she smiled or laughed just that inch too far when he made a moderately witty remark, moved closer to him in the crowd as if seeking out his heat, her fingers grazing his as the audience filed out of the club and onto the High Street, avoiding being separated from him in the rush for the last Tube.

The rain had stopped, but the pavements were still wet, shining, reflections of the street lights twinkling like will-o'-the-wisps on the surface of the road. Cars rushed by driving northwards.

'What about your guitar? Are you leaving it behind?'

'My brother took it home earlier. I didn't want to be saddled with it.'

An air of anxious expectancy on her face.

It took them a lengthy ten minutes to find a cab, standing in silence in the cold, looking out for a 'for hire' sign heading in their direction, unspoken words weighing on them.

Equally silently, Magdalena kissed him the moment he closed the flat's door behind them and chucked off his jacket and switched on the lights.

Noah wanted to say something but she quickly hushed him.

'I . . .' he protested. Yes, sex would be nice, he knew, but he wanted to make it clear it could have no bearing on his work, her career.

'I like you,' Magdalena said, to silence him, as if it was the only thing of importance right now. 'Take me to your bedroom.'

She pulled her sweatshirt off, revealing a diminutive bra that could have fitted a teenager whose buds had only just begun to grow. Her breasts were tiny, nipples dark and sharp. She pulled his hands to them and he abandoned himself to their comforting warmth. Closed his eyes. Magdalena shuddered. His hands were cold as he hadn't been wearing gloves outside.

He held her tight against him and they tumbled onto the bed. It was messy, the sheets untucked, as he usually left it. His cleaning lady only came twice a week to sort the flat out.

Her lips were cushioned against his, their bodies in close embrace and he could feel her skin shudder against his, every little vibration rushing through her betraying her lust and hunger.

Noah opened his eyes. She lay below him. She was topless, her wisp of a bra cast aside, fingers digging into his shoulders. Their lips separated and he caught his breath.

Looked down at her face.

Noticed, for the first time, the faint bridge of freckles dotted across her nose and the swell of her cheekbones.

The muddy green colour of her questing gaze.

Like a slap across his face, violent, immediate: a memory of a photograph of Summer. The same colour eyes, a similar landscape of freckles.

His throat felt tight.

But this wasn't Summer.

It was anyone but Summer.

He could feel his erection shrink by the second. Fast. His desire for Magdalena fade.

He pulled away from her.

She looked up at him, surprised. Bereft.

'I'm sorry,' Noah blurbed. 'I can't do it. Just can't . . .'

She lowered her eyes. Uncomprehending.

He called a cab for her. She lived in Croydon.

There was a sharp tap on the frosted glass that separated his office from the main suite of work stations occupied by other permanent staff in the lower echelons and freelancers hot-desking.

Rhonda. Everyone else just knocked on the door, but his judicious PA, who carried out even the most insignificant tasks with the utmost efficiency, always rapped sharply on the window-pane when anything out of the ordinary cropped up, to be certain of capturing his full attention, pronto.

As a rule, Noah operated an 'open office' policy, getting

on with his work while remaining visibly available to inter-ruptions and interactions with other staff. Although he was strictly an operations man and not a creative, he enjoyed being part of the hubbub that perpetually flowed around him. It had become something of a superstition now.

Too much of a realist to have any faith in some kind of ultra-developed second sight or intuition, he believed his instinct for spotting new talent didn't come from his gut but rather from little titbits of information that he absorbed from witnessing the comings and goings around him, and over-hearing the industry gossip spilled by his peers while he carried on with his regular work, apparently oblivious to his surroundings.

Lately, though, he hadn't so easily been able to retain his focus. A raft of difficult decisions awaited his sign-off. The Holy Criminals, sans Viggo. A new folk duo; sisters who wrote all their own material and were actually from Manchester but had the tall, blonde and robust good looks that typically arose from Scandinavian shores and who had amassed a decent level of popularity on the university pub scene, and who Noah was tempted to take a chance on. Whether or not their sex appeal was enough to carry them from underground clubs full of die-hard fans to commercial success was another question altogether. And that would depend on their readiness to allow the label to mould them into a more saleable band, which naturally meant changing matters of style to appeal to a wider, generic demographic. So many new bands turned down opportunities because they were too hung up on maintaining what they considered their artistic integrity. A handful of other hopefuls, none of whom he was ready to write off yet, but neither did he feel that familiar spark that lit up inside him when he was positive he had discovered a winner.

He looked at the pile of demo tapes in front of him, which he had already listened to half a dozen times each, searching for some nugget of difference, an infinitesimal sign of untapped fire that he had previously missed. The bands' websites and social media feeds which he had already scoured had proved disappointing – all perfectly competent but nothing that jumped out at him as any different from all of the other struggling musicians in the world, most of whom would never make it past maybe winning a couple of open mic nights in their local boozer, if that, before throwing in the towel to make some decent money in a run-of-the-mill office job.

Noah was well aware that even the luckiest talent scout did well to unearth one major hit in a lifetime. If he only managed to keep things ticking over he would still leave the London office assignment with a better reputation than his predecessor had built, but nonetheless he felt obliged to make his mark in some way, to prove himself. The feeling wasn't a new one, or particular to his current job. No matter what he achieved, professionally or otherwise, there was always something that drove him onward to seek out the next best thing. A faint shred of self-doubt that lurked in his subconscious which he was obliged to keep running away from.

His gaze alighted again on the Summer Zahova record. Classical and rock. A terribly unlikely combination to find commercial favour. Radio unfriendly. Even with his history of championing sounds that others glossed over and being proven right, he knew he would likely have to fight for it. And if he was wrong, his status would allow him some mistakes but he would have to endure gentle ribbing from the other execs at least. Then there was the possibility that a bad move would somehow affect his winning streak, knock his confidence, and he would lose his mojo for making the right decisions, for the constant gambling that his job required. And yet, and yet . . . there was something about that recording . . . surely others would feel it too?

He could not yet be certain that his feelings on the subject were strictly business, and therefore could be trusted. This strange attraction he felt towards the violinist whom he had never even set eyes on in the flesh was marring his professional judgement. Or was it? Damn it, if only he knew.

Another rap on the door. Sharper, this time. Rhonda did not appreciate tardiness.

'Yes?' he called out, the tone of his voice more acerbic than he had intended.

'There's someone here to see you,' she announced. 'A young woman. It's not in your calendar,' she added, when his brow furrowed in confusion and he glanced at his day planner to check if he had forgotten a meeting. Occasionally, hopefuls turned up on the record company's doorstep, desperately seeking a route to getting themselves noticed, but unless they managed to convince Rhonda that they were the next Madonna or Rolling Stones they were always turned away.

'A personal matter, apparently,' she continued, not bothering to mask her disapproval.

'Right,' he said, 'send her in then.' He hoped that Magdalena hadn't tracked him down here. If any rumours surfaced that he was allowing his professional life to be clouded by his personal interests, and sleeping with his potential new artists, he wouldn't be able to sign her.

Rhonda swept out of the room, giving the person waiting outside a curt nod and holding the door open so she could come through.

It was Lauralynn.

Dressed casually, totally unlike the last time he had seen her, in a pair of faded denim jeans, ballet pumps and a wide-neck maroon-coloured sweatshirt that had slipped to one side and revealed a pale pink bra strap. Not a colour that he would ever have thought she would choose for her under-clothes. He had imagined her in harsher hues of black and red, shades that registered danger and dominance.

'Hi,' she said. 'Sorry for barging in on you like this at work without calling first. I hope I'm not interrupting. I was just in the neighbourhood and . . .'

She was visibly flushing as she glanced around at the burnished hardwood of his desk, the glass expanse of his office and vertiginous view out over the gardens.

'It's no problem, really,' Noah assured her. 'Please come in, take a seat. Can I get you a coffee? Glass of water?'

'No, no, it's okay, I won't stay long.'

She showed none of her usual swagger, and her uncharacteristic bashfulness humanised her, in Noah's eyes. It wasn't that he hadn't liked Lauralynn before, but just that her egregious confidence had made her seem somewhat arrogant, and a little too perfect. People were more interesting when they possessed visible flaws, he felt. He kept his expression warm and passive, but hoped, desperately, that she had come to provide him with further information about Summer.

'How can I help?' he asked her, deliberately business-like. Noah recalled that he had jotted his number down on a white Post-it note that Viggo had provided while he was at their Belsize Park mansion, and which he suspected would be instantly tossed into the pile of unopened mail on their

189

counter to be forgotten about, but he had not given his office address. Of course, that information was readily available online, he knew, but the fact that Lauralynn had gone to the trouble of tracking him down indicated that she might have been completing some background checks of her own.

'It's about Summer.'

'You know where she is?' he asked, before he could stop himself.

'No, though I wish I did. Nothing that dramatic. I've been thinking about her since your visit, that's all, and I wanted to ask you if you could please tell her that I miss her, once you find her. Have her call me. Please.'

'Of course,' he said, 'though to be honest, I'm not sure I'm likely to stumble on her whereabouts, and if she's disappeared, as you suggested, to get away from her music career, then her location isn't of much use to me anyway. I can't sign an artist who won't play. Maybe it's better that she's left alone until she's ready to return? An intervention of sorts might just drive her further away.'

Lauralynn had moved forward and was gripping the back of the tall black leather chair that faced Noah's desk tightly.

'Maybe you're right,' she said. 'Then again, that girl can be so utterly frustrating, and half the time, she has no idea what's good for her. The other half of the time, she knows perfectly well and doesn't do it anyway. Believe me, if I had an inkling of where she was then I would be on her door-step first thing tomorrow to drag her home.'

'You're not selling her to me, you know,' he quipped.

'Don't pretend like you need any selling,' she replied. Her eyes had landed on the copy of Summer and Viggo's CD, still sitting within arm's reach on his desk. 'Besides, all the best artists are crazy, aren't they?'

'So they say,' he replied. 'Some are just good, and work hard, but that's not nearly so romantic, is it?'

'I suppose not. Look, I wanted to pass on an invitation. Viggo and I are attending a party tomorrow night. A gath-ering, if you will, of like-minded folk. I wondered if you would be interested. It's an exclusive sort of affair. Not the kind of thing you can turn up at without an invitation, someone to vouch for you.'

'You mean a sex party?' His eyes widened.

'Well, not exactly, though you might see a few people going at it, I suppose.'

She was so off-hand about the whole thing, that he nearly laughed.

'It's more of a kink thing. The two aren't necessarily related, you know. Sex and kink. Not for everyone.'

'Right,' he said, as if he understood.

He had a flashback to his night with Magdalena. The way that he had suddenly lost interest and gone soft. Come to think of it, the same had happened, before that, with Clarice, although she hadn't been aware of it, since he'd been able to slip into the bathroom and sort himself out before returning and finishing the deed. An unspoken benefit of having a woman tied to the bedpost. He hoped he wasn't losing his touch. It was too early for the little blue pills.

'Would I have to . . .'

'Get involved?' Lauralynn finished for him. A definite smirk lurked behind her mask of passivity. She was returning to her usual persona, enjoying his discomfort.

'Not if you don't want to,' she continued. 'Especially as you're new, and most of the attendees will be with their regular partners. It's not a free-for-all,' she explained. 'From our conversation the other day about Summer, I thought you seemed intrigued. And might be interested in seeing it for yourself. Understanding her better. Or the rumours around her, at least.'

He agreed.

Lauralynn promised to be in touch to arrange the details, and then left, refusing his offer to show her out of the building. He couldn't help but watch the way her jeans hugged her form as she turned away from him and walked out of the door. She was one of the few women that he had seen outside of occasional trips to LA or meet-ups with April's fashion-industry friends who managed to pull off low-riding denims without revealing an unfortunate muffin top. When modelled by a suitable figure, it was a style he always enjoyed. Casual, but with a not-so-subtle hint to what lay just a few inches below.

Enough thinking of women.

He gave his mouse a sharp wave across the mat to jolt his desktop back to life and get his mind back into work mode.

An email from April had popped into his inbox.

Frustratingly cheery, without even a mention of their parting in New York.

An assignment had come up in London that the magazine wanted her to cover. Their UK-based operative who would normally look after things had requested an extension on her maternity leave at the last minute, and they didn't have another staff member available locally. They were cutting costs and only prepared to put her up in a cheap hotel in zone three, and she couldn't bear it, for two whole weeks. She would be working most of the time, so would not be underfoot. She was looking forward to 'catching up' with him.

He read through her missive again, to check he hadn't missed anything. No, typically vague. April was the kind of woman who would find a way to kill a man without letting him know in advance that she was even the slightest bit upset. She had even signed off with a kiss.

Noah let out a loud sigh.

It had been one of those days.

★   ★   ★

Before tonight, Noah could not recall having ever felt the slightest concern over what he should wear. Perhaps he had weighed up options before attending job interviews or dates, sure, but he had always done so with a purely practical outlook and a strong feeling of certainty that he would reach the right decision.

In the end he gave up and called Viggo. Lauralynn had only advised that they would collect him at 9 p.m., without even telling him where they were going.

'Hi. It's Noah. No, no, I'm still coming – look – is there some kind of dress code?'

He hoped like hell that he wouldn't be required to put on some kind of all-over leather or rubber number. Too late for that, anyway, since the party started in a couple of hours.

Lauralynn was chortling loudly in the background.

'Tell him I'll pack something for him if he likes!' Noah heard her shout out.

Viggo's voice was calmer. Noah took a long slug of the bourbon and coke he had poured earlier. He didn't usually drink at home – the bourbon had been a welcoming present from his new London team that had sat on his side table for weeks, untouched, still with a ribbon wrapped around the bottle's neck – but tonight he had needed something to settle his nerves.

'Don't worry about it, mate. You'll be fine in your jeans.'

'You're sure?'

194

'Absolutely. We're nearly done here. We'll see you soon.'

As it turned out, Lauralynn was the only person among all the attendees at the modernist home in Holland Park hosting the event who was kitted out in the manner that Noah had anticipated, wearing a fire-engine-red latex cat-suit, polished to such a shine he could just about see his face reflected back at him every time he glanced at her.

The others were dressed in variations of what he imagined swinger's clubs would deem as sexy but kink chic. A look Noah found was usually anything but. Half a dozen women in tight micro dresses that threatened to reveal the twin moons of the wearer's butt cheeks the moment she bent forward, sky-high heels, long, ostentatious earrings that dangled from their lobes like the sort of thing fly fishermen use to lure trout with. The men were mostly dressed like he was, in designer jeans and shirt, with the exception of a good-looking duo whose short haircuts, carefully trimmed facial stubble and muscled physiques gave them the appearance of Bond villains, and were clad in mesh T-shirts that only half-covered their smooth, tanned chests. They wore matching leather belts with large, silver skull-shaped buckles, each the size of a fist, accessorising black denim trousers so tight they surely didn't need any help staying up.

Noah didn't smoke, but he wished that he did. Anything for a distraction. So far, besides the mesh shirts and the mul-titude of bare legs on display, it felt like any other ordinary gathering. A bunch of people standing around sipping from wine glasses and making small talk, filling up all the awkward silences with inane chatter. There was a lingering tension in the air though, as if everyone was waiting for something to happen, for a fuse to light. Noah had no wish to be there when that happened. The thought of seeing others bare their innermost selves in public made him uncomfortable. He asked the host, a bottle-blonde named Amanda, to direct him to the bathroom. Her husband was out of town, apparently attending a conference, 'and a girl's got to have a little fun, doesn't she?' she had said to him by way of introduction.

Noah had been informed by Viggo of at least half of the guest's proclivities in advance. The rocker loved to gossip. 'Manda and Tony only play away,' he was told, as they rolled to a stop at the traffic lights by White City and its monstrous mall, learning that each of them turned a blind eye to the other's conspicuous infidelity, while being fully aware of and even aroused by what they knew was happening in their absence, or at least their imagination's glamourised version of events.

Manda sported lime-green painted nails and conspicuously large fake breasts that bulged out of the tight lacy purple push-up bra strapped to her tiny body, the only garment she had on besides a matching mini-skirt that revealed her panti-less state and could have passed for a belt in other circumstances. Her voice quavered with high-pitched regularity when she spoke. She was already aroused, he realised, just by the circumstances of her transgression, her fantasy complete without any sex having even occurred.

The first lavatory was in use. He continued down the wide hall to the en suite in the master bedroom, towards which Amanda had pointed him.

As he approached, he heard a rumour of faint whimpers and low growls. He paused and peeked inside, wary of proving himself an unwelcome interruption if any of the guests had disappeared to seek some privacy. Then again, they had left the door wide open.

A young woman was lying spread-eagled and bound by her ankles and wrists to the four corners of the king size bed, the outline of her body severe against the stark black background of the protective plastic sheeting that had been spread over the bed covers. She was of average build, even a little plump, with a soft body, small, pointed breasts and large, rose-coloured nipples.

The man who loomed over her was fresh-faced – he might have been even younger than the interns who worked summers archiving records for the label. He was slim and pale, with the kind of heroin-chic physique that was popular in some men's fashion spreads these days in contrast to the usual bulked-up muscle-men of Noah's generation. A long, half-hard penis hung between his legs. His pubic area was totally smooth. Shaved. Black medical gloves covered his hands.

On the sheet alongside them lay a packet of condoms, lube, baby wipes, a small bottle of anti-bacterial cleansing gel and a variety of penetrative implements. Everything was carefully organised, with the lube and rubbers in easy reaching distance and the toys arranged with mathematical precision in order of size, from a small, silver butt plug with a jewelled end to a frighteningly large neon-orange coloured dildo that Noah would never have imagined could actually be slid inside anyone, if he hadn't seen women being invaded with similar objects within the context of pornography.

A long electrical extension cord ran from the socket beneath the bedside table up to the bed. Plugged into it was a device that Noah recalled finding hidden under the bed that he had briefly shared with Bridget when he first moved to New York. A tennis-ball-sized white sphere attached to a long handle, with a single blue switch giving the option of two settings. He had turned it on to high and held it against his balls and been shocked by the power of the apparatus and set it to low immediately.

Later online investigation had informed him that it was a Hitachi Magic Wand; a 'personal massager' that vibrated at 240 volts and apparently gave women earth shattering orgasms. The sex he and Bridget had shared had always been enjoyable, and adequate, Noah had felt, until that point.

After his discovery he hadn't been able to knock the lurking fear from his mind that he wasn't entirely satisfying her. On a handful of occasions he had masturbated using Bridget's Hitachi as an aid, and his orgasm had been all the stronger for knowing that she was unaware he knew her secret, which he never did have the courage to broach.

The woman on the bed emitted a deep groan in response to her partner's ministrations.

She had already been filled with two toys, one in her anus and the other in her cunt, and her partner was busily pumping each of them in and out of her as she tugged against her restraints.

'You know that the more you struggle, the more this is going to hurt,' he told her. 'Relax.'

Her body went limp.

She licked her lips.

'Thirsty?' he asked. She nodded briefly and he abandoned his assault on her openings, reached for the water bottle he had stationed near them and brought it to her lips. He had removed one glove so that he could use his bare hand to prop up her head as she drank. When she indicated that she was finished, he tenderly laid her back down again and pulled a fresh glove from a tissue-sized box full of them and tossed the other into a small plastic bag by the bed.

This was no spur-of-the-moment bondage scene like the one Noah had badly enacted in the hotel by the Strand with

– he struggled for an instant to recall her name – Clarice. These two sexual adventurers had come prepared.

'What do you say?' asked the woman's dominant, or top, Noah wasn't sure which. Lauralynn had given him a crash course in sex party and BDSM etiquette on the drive over but there was only so much a person could learn in thirty minutes.

'Thank you,' she replied.

'Thank you, what?' All tenderness had now left his expression and he was again a parody of menace, thin lips stretched into a scowl and his long body held straight, leaning over her as though he was about to strike out if she did not furnish him with the response he wanted.

'Thank you, Daddy,' she said in a small voice.

Noah inhaled sharply, and stepped backwards, away from the door. He had expected her to say 'Sir'; wasn't that the standard, albeit clichéd, expression in such circumstances? His cock had swelled to painful proportions in his trousers and yet his mind was reeling, unsure whether he ought to be aroused or disgusted by what he had overheard. Neither was he sure that he had any choice in the matter. He stepped forward again, this time concentrating on the woman's face. Full lips, wide eyes, mousey-brown hair spread out in untidy ringlets around her face. A picture of innocence.

Her partner turned directly to face Noah.

Caught in the act.

'No need to just stand there,' he said. 'You can come closer. This little slut loves being watched. Don't you, whore?'

She nodded.

'Say it,' he continued. 'Tell this nice man you're a dirty whore and you want him to touch you.'

She twitched and moaned, his words apparently a powerful stimulus.

'Say it,' he insisted.

She did.

Noah tentatively approached the couple and kneeled on the bed. He reached forward and placed a hand on the woman's breast and she jolted sharply in response to his touch.

'Make her come if you like,' her partner said, liberally spreading lubricant over the ball of the magic wand and then handing it to him. 'Press it down hard on her clit. She likes it on high.'

Noah followed his instructions.

'Harder,' he was told.

She began to convulse so strongly he feared that she might break the headboard.

'How do you like that, little whore, a total stranger toying with your cunt?'

He didn't wait for her to respond. Noah doubted she was capable of speaking. A blotchy shade of red crept over her skin and her mouth opened into a scream.

'Oh god,' she cried. 'Oh my fucking god . . .'

'I'm going to let him fuck you afterwards, as hard as he wants, whether you like it or not, slut.'

'I'm coming, oh god, I'm coming,' she whimpered.

Sweat pearled on her brow.

Her dom reached out and switched the wand off.

'Better give her a moment to breathe.'

Slowly, her taut limbs relaxed, and her previously contorted expression morphed into a wide smile.

'God gets a lot of credit for the work I do, you know,' he mused to Noah, a note of humour obvious in his tone.

The dom and his sub both laughed. Just another ordinary couple again.

'Well,' Noah interrupted, now feeling more than a little awkward. 'Thank you both. I should get back to the party.'

He stopped at the other bathroom on his return, having forgotten in the heat of the moment how badly he actually needed a pee.

When he returned to the main room, he discovered that a plate of cucumber sandwiches had been left out on the kitchen counter, a fact that struck him as singularly odd under the circumstances. He took one and munched on it, picked a bottle of beer from the ice bucket and went in search of Lauralynn and Viggo.

*   *   *

Out of the blue, Noah received a call from Nikolas Mieville. The older man revealed that he had managed to get hold of a hitherto unknown recording of Summer in concert. He sounded very ill. Probably an illegal capture of a concert she had given in Europe some years back when she had been briefly touring with the Holy Criminals, he stated. The pieces played were actually quite different from those that appeared on the later album, in all likelihood earlier still unpolished versions but also some new improvisations altogether. Would Noah care to listen to them?

He would.

The recording quality was poor, he was warned, as one would expect from sounds seized surreptitiously by inadequate equipment in an echoing concert hall, with the audience's coughs and whispers and even occasional conversation all too prominent and upfront. Technically speaking, Mieville suggested, the recordings might actually be the property of Noah's record label as Viggo's band were then under contract to the company, but as the tape's date of origin was unclear, possibly Summer was signed elsewhere or not yet a free agent at the time. Noah had to agree to come and listen to the music in a strictly private capacity. Conditions he was willing to agree to.

Mieville lived in Highgate. It felt to Noah as if he was becoming a captive of a small perimeter of North London sacred territory, where both the past and his obsession of

Summer unfolded as did the present. From the top-floor study where Mieville played the newly discovered tapes to Noah, the view looked out on the edges of Hampstead Heath in the distance, a rolling field of green like a becalmed sea under the grey autumn sky and its slow procession of clouds.

Noah peered out.

Seeking familiar pointers to the Heath's geography.

'Can it be seen from here?' he asked.

'The bandstand, you mean?' Mieville said.

'Yes.'

'No. It's further down on the other side of that hill.'

'Ah . . .' Another question was on the tip of his lips. Mieville guessed and cut him short.

'And, no . . . If the story of Summer playing there in the altogether is genuine, it would not have been possible to hear anything this far away. Anyway, I was living overseas, in Prague, at the time.'

The tape began to play.

The sound quality was indeed poor, but the recording proved fascinating. The idiosyncratic sound and rhythms of Viggo's band were instantly recognisable, jagged, in turns subtle and bone-crunching, but the counterpoint melodic lines of Summer's violin transformed the music, opening up new aural tides of fluid emotions and over-arching wide-screen panoramas of melancholy and rage that Viggo and his musicians had never been capable of raising to the surface. Sadly, there was not enough violin; some of the tracks only featured the Holy Criminals, and when they performed alone there was a sense of deflation, as if without Summer's violin they were incomplete. Noah estimated that the concert must have taken place towards the beginning of their fleeting collaboration, both parties still unaccustomed to each other, experimenting, moving one careful step at a time, stretching, flexing, still unsure how far they could take the music.

Noah tried to imagine how they had appeared onstage, Viggo and his acolytes in their rock 'n' roll gladrags and Summer – he was quite certain of it – in a short, tight black dress that espoused every shape of her body, her hair an explosion of red waves and curls, thrown one way and then the other as the music took hold of her, just as he had witnessed with terrible relish in all the infrequent YouTube clips he had managed to hunt down of Summer in performance.

'Rather beautiful, no?'

Mieville's voice interrupted his imaginings.

'Quite.'

The hiss and crackle of the tape was all that could now be heard. The recording had come to an end.

All Noah wanted was to listen to the tape again.

Immerse himself in this lost world of sensations that he

could feel fleeing with every passing second from the out-stretched tips of his questing fingers.

'Drink?'

Mieville handed him a glass, with a generous measure of Four Roses.

'I reckon you take it straight; none of that ice and on the rocks nonsense.'

Noah nodded.

'I can make a copy for you, if you wish . . .' Mieville suggested.

'That would be fantastic. I promise I'll keep it totally confidential.'

'I'm sure you will.'

The bourbon slipped down his throat, burning him, awakening him from all the dreams.

Mieville made a gesture to fill his glass again. Noah indicated he had no need for another yet.

'It's not just the music that affects you, is it?' the older man asked.

Noah nodded in agreement.

'I guessed. She has that effect. You're not the only one, if it's any consolation . . .' Mieville sighed, downing his second glass of Four Roses, his eyes distant, summoning the past.

Noah waited for the older man to continue.

Mieville sank back into his armchair, extended his legs as if to shake torpor out of them. 'From the moment I saw her playing, I was entranced,' he said. 'I was brought up from childhood on classical music. Always appreciated its beauty and certainties, its intellectual rigour. But Summer brought a strange new dimension to it. The notes were the same, obviously, but there was a gentle madness, an inner life that she communicated through her playing. I'd never come across the phenomenon so sharply before. She played as if her life depended on it. Put her soul into it. A rare quality.'

'I think I understand.'

'And you've never even seen her play, but still it has the same effect on you, Noah . . .'

'Uncanny.'

The two men fell into silence. Thoughts swirling. A ghost presiding over the room. Beyond the window, dusk fell over the North London fields and hills.

'She was damaged, you know . . . At least, I believe so.' Mieville finally burst the serenity of their private reflections.

'All those stories, the rumours?'

'Probably why she ended up disappearing from view. It all became too much. There's only so long you can play with fire and not get yourself burned. Badly.'

'But she's alive, surely. She allowed the violin to go up for auction. Though it's quite unlikely she'll surface, play in public again, is it?'

'I'm not so sure. You don't get rid of the demons so

easily, I've found. And if just a part of the stories are true, she lives for the danger. It consumes her. When she lived with that writer, I guess she managed to keep them at bay, but then he died and a new raft of stories emerged. She fell to pieces. Understandable. I heard terrible things.'

'I think I know,' Noah said.

The temperature in the room seemed to drop, the alcohol's fire raging in his throat and stomach keeping him on edge and warm.

'When I was younger, I met a young Italian piano player, Marirosa was her name . . . In a competition in Pescara. Technically proficient, but she had a fire inside that you could sense from the back row of the audience. It was difficult not to fall in love with her. I did. Even though I was married to another at the time. We ended up together, but I was helpless at protecting her from that fire. Eventually, it consumed her. Almost did me . . .' Mieville said with a note of regret. 'Coming across Summer Zahova had a similar effect. Fortunately by then the years had taken their obligatory toll on me, and I was able to just remain a spectator. Not get involved. Just sit back and admire, without getting my fingers burned.'

'It's not just the music,' Noah said. He found it difficult to explain.

'But would just the music on its own hold us in such a thrall?'

'I suppose not.'

'I've come across men,' Mieville said, 'who pretend they were present . . . That night . . .'

'You mean away from the stage?'

'Yes.'

'You believe them?'

'Some I do, some I don't . . . Tales of truth or tall tales?' Mieville expressed his doubts with a sad exhale.

'You?'

A soft sigh of resignation. 'No, only saw her just that time in the Spiegeltent. Sometimes I wish I hadn't, you know . . .'

'Because of the strength of the memories?'

As Noah conversed with the older impresario, he couldn't help but notice how his breath was halting and his frame frail and bent. The illness inside him spreading insidiously.

'Those images will persist, I know. As if the sight of her has marked me. But what good does it do me, a dream of madness that can't be repeated? A glimpse of the impossible.'

'I must confess that I often dream I will one day come across her,' Noah stated.

'And?'

'I don't know . . .'

'What would you do?'

'Not a clue.'

'Sometimes fiction is preferable to reality. She'd be too real.'

Noah shrugged.

'How did you meet the others, the men who say they've witnessed her in the throes of . . .' He searched for the right word.

'Her personal madness . . . "in flagrante", so to speak?'

Noah nodded.

'At random. A word here, a word there. Hints. On the web, reading between the lines, quiet conversations at the bar at concerts. Somehow the fans of the true Summer find each other even though they live in silence, like a small club of initiates, who appear ever so normal to the rest of the world. I suppose we're like a harmless bunch of crazies who recognise each other by sheer instinct. An invisible mark. Like you . . .' Mieville concluded.

Noah's throat was dry. Mieville filled his glass again.

'I've seen photographs . . .' Noah confessed.

'Tell me.' The other's eyes lit up.

'I'm almost certain it was Summer Zahova,' Noah said. 'A series of images of a woman in some sauna. Quite obscene, and troubling too. Bad quality. But haunting.'

'The Kentish Town series,' Mieville stated.

'You know them?' Noah asked, unsure of whether he wanted to hear the answer.

'I know of them. Never actually seen them, though. You're not the first to mention them. I thought it was apocryphal, something of an urban legend. Sounded too extreme to be true.'

'Oh.' Noah couldn't conceal his disappointment. He had somehow hoped that raising the subject might have enabled him to get access to the images again, although he feared that doing so might be a mistake.

'I once met a man – not a nice one, at all – who said he was present and actually claimed to have taken the photographs. He'd been summoned by another at short notice. Smuggled a mobile phone into the sauna and took the pics in secret.'

'So it was her?'

'Yes. The story's unclear but it seems she was a magnet of sorts for dominant men – not always the scrupulous majority – through her rumoured dalliances with BDSM, and a particularly persistent one tracked her down to the Hampstead bandstand. The locale we'd heard so much about and which was alluded to in the book. God only knows how he talked her into following him to the sauna and the reasons she finally did. He'd assembled a group . . .'

'Jesus . . .'

'It's all rather sordid, and the story changes in each successive retelling, but at core it seems the event did occur, and of course there were those photos. Which you've seen . . .'

'And lost any trace of,' Noah said.

'Maybe I prefer it that way. Not sure whether I would want to see them,' Mieville declared.

'All the men present involved, were "fans", aware of who she was?'

'Some. Probably not all.'

Noah felt exhausted by the conversation, fighting away disgust for the way the obscene images still lived so strongly in his mind but also exhilarated by the confirmation that it was indeed Summer at the dread centre of them. There was an eerie conjunction between her music and her life, a magnet he was drawn to in ways he failed to understand. And then the thought flashed through his mind that Summer too could not fully understand the compulsions that manipulated her musicianship and the lower depths of her mind. And her body.

He downed the bourbon, his thoughts now miles away.

If only he could meet up with her, somewhere, someday, somehow. Just to listen to the sound of her voice, see her play, look into her eyes and grasp at her inherent sadness, witness her hair shimmer in the breeze, mine her thoughts, perceive just the ghost of her natural fragrance. He sighed heavily.

Mieville observed him sympathetically.

'I once managed to identify one of the blindfolded musicians who played with her in the crypt for her lover, following the acquisition of the Bailly. Of course, he could see nothing of what was unfolding, but he affirmed that the music was simply divine, the notes she pulled from the strings, the way she managed to bend them to her will and add another dimension to the piece. And that was before her musical career even really began, when she was still something of an amateur. Nonetheless, he said it was electric.'

'I'm sure it was.'

One part of Noah wanted to stay here all evening and listen to any more stories the older man might retell, but he also felt that he had reached saturation point. He needed fresh air, time to think, absorb the new information. Anyway, the two glasses of bourbon were already clouding his mind.

He excused himself.

The following day felt hollow. It was a dull Sunday and he'd brought no work home, not that he would have been able to concentrate on listening to new demo tapes or discs, he realised.

As night fell, he took a long, rambling walk which led him to the edges of Hampstead Heath. He sought out the area where the legendary bandstand was situated but was unable to locate it, soon hopelessly losing himself among narrow paths beyond the ponds, venturing hesitantly into thick clusters of trees and seeking out clearings. The shadow of a half moon peered uncertainly through the high branches, casting a horror-movie curtain on the flickering night. Shadows peered between the trunks, shapeless forms, joggers, lovers in search of privacy. He turned back, following the sounds of traffic on the nearby roads for bearings until he was out of the woods. At the first opportunity he hailed a passing cab.

Back at the flat, he was briefly tempted to call up Magdalena and apologise for the other night and see if she would see him again, but then decided against it. April was coming tomorrow, and in case he got stuck at work and was unable to meet her flight, he had left a spare key for her with his neighbour in the basement flat, the dark-haired woman who had swept past him on the day he had moved in. Her name was Candy (not a stage name, she insisted), and along with proving much friendlier than Noah had first suspected, if still a little brusque, she had turned out to be a cookery-school student rather than a dominatrix, and told him that the receptacle she had carried on her back was a well-stocked kit of kitchen supplies that she took with her to classes.

It would be just his luck for April to arrive earlier than expected, let herself in, and find him in bed with another.

Not that they had ever insinuated they would remain faithful to each other long distance – it had been a mutually agreed clean break – but still, the less ammunition she had, the less awkward their time together would likely prove to be.

Sleep didn't come easily.

★ ★ ★

'Well, are you coming to bed?' she asked him.

He was in the living room hunched over his laptop, sending off some last-minute emails to his colleagues in the New York office, tidying up loose ends in preparation for a conference call the next morning during which they would discuss the marketing budget for the next quarter. Noah would have his chance to recommend which of the solo artists and bands that fell under his remit would benefit from a PR push, and argue for his slice of the pie.

April stood in front of him, clad in a short, pale peach satin slip and matching robe. He hadn't seen her wear either before. It was a clear invitation.

'Err, yes.' He closed his laptop and followed her to the bedroom.

She dropped her gown.

God, she was beautiful. Noah held his breath as he admired her form. April was like a model from a perfume commercial.

They kissed, and fell onto the bed together. Made love as they had a hundred times before.

There had been a moment of awkwardness, an obvious pause in their usual routine when he had been about to enter her and was momentarily too embarrassed to ask her if she had been with others, and used protection. April had handed him a condom and murmured, 'I don't expect that you have remained celibate, all this time,' and then lay there with her legs spread, waiting for him to roll it on and finish the job. He had almost gone soft.

It had felt like an accusation, not that he had anything to be ashamed of. Damn her. The rush of anger he felt had made him erect again, and he had fucked her harder than usual, though not so hard that she protested. He knew April didn't like it like that. More's the pity.

Afterwards, when she had rolled over and gone to sleep, he lay awake, unsatisfied. He had come. So had she. Predictably. But Noah wanted more. He just wasn't sure what exactly it was that he wanted.

He pulled back the sheet and padded quietly to the kitchen, without bothering to dress. His cock was still sticky, and had that horrible acrid smell from the condom's spermicide. He opened the fridge door and drank a few gulps of orange juice straight from the carton, knowing that April hated it when he did that. She would no doubt complain in the morning, when she discovered that he only had orange with bits, and she preferred it smooth.

He sighed. Had he always been this petty?

Visited the bathroom. Took a leak. Washed the rubber's residue from his hands.

Unbidden, images rose into his mind. The woman tied to the bed at the North London party, the way that the rope that bound her had bit into her skin as she pulled against it, unable to keep still in the heat of her arousal. Her full lips opening into a scream as Noah pressed the sex toy against her cunt, knowing that she could also feel the weight of the butt plug that her partner had pushed into her hole. The overtness of her responses.

Her orgasm hadn't been tidy. She had been driven beyond any normal expression of pleasure into a far more savage form, and, if pushed, Noah knew there would have been further screams, sweat, fluids gushing, even tears. Given the chance he would have made sure the bed really needed the protection of that black plastic sheet, despite its uncomfortable surface and irritating rustle.

He closed his eyes. Conjured up the scene again. But in his mind, the mop of hair that surrounded the woman's face as she arched her back and cried out wasn't mousey brown, it was flaming red.

Noah's cock was in his hand before he even thought of what he was doing. Not that he ever put a lot of thought into self-pleasure. It was an enjoyable biological release, no more.

His fantasy was vivid, and within minutes he felt himself edging that precipice, searching for just one more stimulus to make him explode.

He came. Shuddered. Looked down at his hand covered in his own ejaculate. Reached for the toilet roll.

The door creaked.

The Pleasure Quartet: Summer

April.

How long had she been standing there? Long enough.

'Well,' she said. 'I suppose it really is over between us.'

He spent the rest of the night on the couch.

6

Mistress and Lover

Joao had been away on his lands for a week and asked me if I could spend time at their villa with Astrid in his absence. He felt she was in need of company. He declared he had been wrong to have me followed and that I was free to conduct my life in any way I felt best. Begged me for forgiveness. It coincided with Raoul being busy with his tours, so I wasn't torn between alternatives. It was an uneasy status quo and left me with a deep sense of foreboding, but it suited me for now.

I tried to mend bridges with the young girl and was partly successful. When we were together, we bathed in playfulness and easy complicity, whether frolicking on the beach, messily cooking together or my pretending to be something of a martinet when instructing her in the ways of the violin, not that she ever took me too seriously when my patience snapped confronted by her frequent clumsiness.

It was also pleasant to have their lavish environment at my disposal, alongside all the domestic help. I had to admit my original awkwardness with being waited on had mostly passed, and now I just enjoyed never having to do laundry or vacuum. Alongside the glorious weather, there was something about Brazil that induced a guilt-free form of laziness and personal indolence that I was insidiously getting rather accustomed to. Morning lie-ins with no men around to distract me, fresh squeezed fruit juices and cool stone floors beneath my bare feet to greet the day. And, for now, I had no real need to dip into my shrinking funds.

I insisted that Astrid relentlessly practise her scales and whatever piece of music she was in the process of learning for at least ninety minutes every single day before she was allowed to go to the beach. She protested that the violin was just a hobby and she had no wish to become a professional musician – I had, in a rare moment of indiscretion, revealed that I had once been, and she took me more seriously following my confession, although I had insisted that she not mention the fact to either Joao or any of her friends. So long, my anonymity had held and I did not wish to endanger it further.

When Joao finally returned, he was delighted by the way his daughter's mood had improved.

'You're such a good influence on her, Summer,' he said, taking me by the waist, pulling me towards him and kissing me affectionately.

'She's a good kid.'

'She is. It's a long time since I've seen her so relaxed,' he declared.

We effortlessly fell back into our odd routine consisting of my staying a few nights a week in his bed and compensating by spending regular afternoons with Raoul, when I pretexted that I was working on some unknown project and unable to join Astrid at the beach which she invariably made a beeline for, cycling the five-kilometre distance around the lagoon to reach her favourite spot by Ipanema after she left school and completed her allotted time with her instrument. I'd had to inform Raoul that I was giving private violin lessons on occasion and he was full of questions, betraying his jealousy and possessiveness, trying to trip me up with details about Astrid once I had revealed I only had the one student, which he found bizarre. Maybe he intuited that there was more than violin lessons going on and that, of necessity, it was in some rich home and there was no way he could compete in terms of either money or comfort. And it didn't make him any easier to appease.

I had never experienced such controlling behaviour from men before outside of sexual games and I wasn't quite sure what to make of it. Often I wished that I had a real friend that I could talk to about the complicated web I had woven and now found myself trapped inside, but I did not yet feel ready to reach out to Lauralynn and admit where I was, and did not want to involve Aurelia. God knows what she might do if she believed that I was in some kind of danger, especially considering the mafia-like resources at her disposal within the Network.

There was to be a fundraising gala at Astrid's exclusive private school, the Escola Americana, to coincide with the end of term, and Joao, impressed by her recent progress, which he attributed solely to my efforts, had convinced his daughter to agree to perform. Together Astrid and I selected what she should play. Unlike me in my salad days, Astrid was a good technician but clearly lacking in emotions and sensibility, so we quickly settled on a classical Bach piece, his Sonata No. 1 in G Minor. It was an archetypal solo violin composition which I had never performed. Normally, one would also play the accompanying Partita, but I didn't feel Astrid was quite ready for such an extended exercise. I had always found Bach and his contemporaries and successors more like maths, perfect but cold, exquisitely crafted and mechanical, lacking a sense of life, and had always preferred the romantic composers or more modern music, with a soft spot for Eastern European tunes with a hint of folklore past; maybe it was the blood of my faraway origins, before my ancestors had moved down under, talking.

Although I was on one hand reluctant to attend the recital as it would mean being seen out in society with Joao again,

I was also curious to see Astrid play on stage, and her father insisted strongly that I come along.

'So you can show me off as your mistress?' I queried.

'Yes, and why not? You are beautiful. I am proud of you. Why shouldn't I?'

'You don't own me, you know,' I protested. I was wary of the idea of our fragile relationship being seen as a mere transaction with an older, wealthier man, displaying his younger 'property'.

For a rare occasion, Joao had joined Astrid and me at the beach, where he had looked on indulgently as we had played football on the sand with a bunch of small, excitable local kids, peering above the pages of the economics books he was reading and then joining us in the water when we needed to cool off.

I'd quickly run out of energy and Astrid had returned to play, volleyball this time, her lithe, tanned body in constant motion, like a free bird let loose, running, dancing, jumping. laughing her head off every time she missed the ball and splashed down ignominiously face first in the warm, grainy sand to the delight of the competitive, other players. Joao suggested we go have a coffee.

'Find some shade,' he explained.

There was a definite shortage of dedicated coffee shops or places to go to around Ipanema Beach, just an assembly of open-aired juice outlets, and sticky-floored bars that hadn't yet opened for trade. We made our way to Emporio 37 on Rua Maria Quiteria. The last time I had sat there was a couple of weeks earlier with Raoul. Was Joao aware of the fact? I certainly hoped not. I kept telling myself that having his driver tail me was a one-time thing, and that considering my infidelity I ought to cut him some slack for his reaction to it.

We were served. Joao's features were unusually drawn, a mask of severity spreading across his olive-skinned face.

'You're young; you have needs. I understand,' Joao said. 'And I'm away so much and older than you. In situation and responsibilities, not just years,' he continued. 'I realise it would be wrong to hold you down . . .'

I opened my mouth to comment in some way, wary of where his monologue was leading, but he raised his hand, indicating I should remain silent.

'What I'm suggesting is an arrangement,' he said.

Just like a businessman.

Clumsily, he tried to explain how, from personal experi-ence, monogamy was something of an awkward state of affairs for men, and coyly confessed he himself had not always been faithful when his own wife had still been alive, and conceded, to my surprise, that he realised that the same craving for new experiences equally applied to women. But he truly liked me, he said, felt we were so wonderfully com-patible. In addition to the fact that my presence was healthy

224

for Astrid. Unlike some of the air-headed young women it would be easy for him to bed and spoil. I was about to protest that I had no wish to become a substitute mother figure, but Joao was in full flow and developed his proposal.

He wanted me to keep on seeing him, sleep with him and be at his side for business and social occasions within reason. Beyond that he would want me to remain discreet on other fronts, take precautions of course, and he would choose to ignore what I was up to in my free time. In exchange, I would always have a roof to live under and he would see to my material comfort. I would have access to a car, his driver even, frequent opportunities for travel in Brazil and overseas should I wish to join him on trips, and would be generously rewarded in kind.

In other words he wanted me to become his official mistress. I was tempted to ask whether I would be the first, but refrained from doing so, as he kept on insisting how much he trusted me and the degree to which I displayed what he termed 'class', or as I mentally translated his words, was deemed suitable arm candy.

My initial reaction was that I had possibly been wrong to ask Susan to sell the Bailly to raise funds, until it dawned me how the whole matter felt like an impersonal transaction, both of us being granted rewards of a different kind in a compromise that banished emotions and feelings to the margins.

Observing my puzzlement, Joao hastily added that there was no need to provide an answer in the immediate, and that for the time being he was happy if we could continue as we were. Was he thinking of some written 'mistress contract', should I agree to his terms? His arrogance confounded me, although at the same time there were distinct attractions to his proposition.

It wasn't the first time I had given a spare thought over the years, albeit not in the recent past, to the idea of whoring myself for money, not so much for the actual proceeds of sin but for the thrill, the experience of selling something I had always given away for free, to know what it felt like. All this potential new situation would do would be to institutionalise the reality of it.

In the meantime, Joao's words continued to pour out, as my mind kept running through a labyrinth of tangents. He wanted me to be at my most charming for the fundraiser at Astrid's school and, with an expression of tender complicity quite at odds with his preceding exposition of the business arrangement he had so meticulously proposed, handed me over a small Bordeaux velvet pouch.

The clip-on earrings were stunning, exquisite minuscule amber ovals set in a sterling silver bed, probably antiques.

I had not worn amber for as long as I could recall, even when in full regalia at the Ball, and I was eager to try them on and see myself in a mirror. I just knew they would match my colouring.

'I've also got you a new dress. It's at home,' Joao said.

The American School of Rio de Janeiro, where Astrid was studying, was an architectural marvel. Set in the neighbourhood of Gávea on the edge of the Tijuca National Forest, on a steep hill overlooking the whole city and its expanse of natural wonders from the vast ocean below to Sugarloaf Mountain, it extended over eight towers, ascending in height towards the dark green curtain of the trees, that incongruously reminded me of medieval buildings and Alpine sanatoriums. In a city where land was at a terrible premium, its twelve-acre campus was as ostentatious as it was luxurious.

Joao's driver dropped us off and drove the metal grey bullet-proof 4×4 away, as one expensive car after another unloaded its human cargo and we trooped towards the school's main door in all our finery.

Astrid was sulking. She had wanted to wear some pale green eye make-up and possibly lipstick, but her father had put his foot down and forcefully stood his ground. I'd always studiously stayed out of arguments between father and daughter when present. Her white cotton dress was demure and fell to below her knees, highlighting the deep tan of her arms, face and delicate ankles. She had earlier given me a despairing glance hoping I would support her, but I agreed with Joao that she was beautiful enough and didn't require any artificial assistance. I later pointed out that neither was I wearing much in the way of make-up, but she had ignored me.

We followed the crowds into the large wooden-floored assembly hall which had been converted into an auditorium. I held onto Joao's arm as Astrid slipped off to join the other students lined up to perform tonight. His tuxedo wrapped around his broad shoulders to a tee, an Armani made-to-measure outfit with wide darker silk lapels and a crisp white dress shirt, the matching bow tie emphasising the firmness of his chin. I looked around.

All the other men present were similarly attired, shoes polished to untenable brilliance, expensive cufflinks peeking out of their sleeves, their wealth reflected in the way they stood upright and proudly, companions and partners hanging on to their arms as if they belonged there by divine right. Older wives in couture dresses that trailed along the ground, displaying ample cleavage and matronly curves, while thinner and younger 'friends' in body-clinging dresses, many slit at the side, in all degrees of voluptuous displaying a desert of leg and vertiginous heels, parading on the arms of their grizzled benefactors with all the arrogance of youth, eyeing the competition with a beady, calculating gaze, as if all along weighing the pros and cons of which protector they would next move on to.

The wives ignored the mistresses and escorts with a studied air of arrogance, while the younger women similarly pretended the legitimate spouses were not in any way different from them.

I immediately regretted having come along, as women in both camps began to look me over with a critical stare. I did not fit in by any measure. To emphasise this state of affairs, Joao had deliberately selected for me the type of dress no one else would be wearing tonight. It was a flowing floral dress which left my shoulders bare and emphasised my comparative lack of opulence. Compared to the other outfits, it was modest to extremes. As much as I applauded Joao's intentions, it just wasn't me. Never had been. It gave me the feeling he wanted me to stand out among the crowd and be talked about. To make matters worse, I knew the golden tones of the amber earrings did not at all match the crimson and violet hues of the fabric's flowered pattern.

We walked over to a group of parents standing by the improvised stage, most of whom were clad in more discreet attire and displayed a modicum of restrained elegance, although the breasts on partial display seemed to my untrained eye more obviously fake. These attendees were in the majority Americans, businessmen and women who worked for international corporations with offices in the Brazilian capital or diplomats from the embassy and consulate. At my earlier request, Joao never introduced me by name, merely as his friend. I took no note of their names. A silver-haired, tall and thin-as-a-rake man approached me while Joao was in deep conversation with others.

'You look familiar. Have we met before?' he enquired. 'You're not from here.'

'I don't think so.' I quickly moved on, without trying to appear rude. He was a cultural attaché. I hoped he didn't make a connection and identify me and my past, artistic activities, let alone the other less discreet matters I was hoping to have left behind. I had no wish for Joao, or anyone in Rio, to discover anything about my previous life.

The performances finally began, following a bunch of speeches in both languages, and we were invited to sit.

A parade of students took turns in front of the varied audience. A lanky crop-haired blonde with an atrocious West Coast accent declaiming a Shakespeare soliloquy, followed by quaint Brazilian twins in matching designer dungarees singing 'Greensleeves' to the accompaniment of a tape. Then came the first round of fundraising, with various gifts from the parents or friendly organisations being auctioned by the Headmistress, a buxom woman in her mid-forties in a frilly evening dress dripping with a thousand sequins too many. Joao occasionally bid, more out of obligation than enthusiasm, and paid over the odds for an electronic console which I knew Astrid already had a set of.

I felt relieved he did not raise his hand when jewellery items came up for auction.

It was finally Astrid's turn. She looked stiff on stage, visibly self-conscious, and her interpretation of the Bach composition was accurate but pedestrian. Even with the technique I had drilled into her, it was evident she didn't move with the music in her heart, played it mechanically and had no idea how to truly inhabit it. Perhaps the only sounds that truly moved her were the pop tunes that she had picked up from YouTube and been replicating when I first saw her swaying on the sidewalk. Classical music, and formal training, was not for everyone. Not that anyone present but me noticed, and the applause she received was cordial and warm, Joao leading the choir of praise by standing up the moment she set down her bow. We stayed on for a couple of further acts, a young boy who performed feeble magic tricks and a pseudo-operatic duo giving a pop spin on a Verdi aria.

Astrid had returned from the backstage area and suggested I join her outside. Joao nodded his approval.

The night air was humid. Small groups milled on the edge of the campus green, picked out by the pale moonlight, wrapped in furtive conversations, smoking and sipping drinks. Astrid pulled a cigarette from her pocket, cast a glance around to see if anyone close could help her light it. A classmate obliged.

'I didn't know you smoked . . .'

'Don't tell my father' she begged me, taking a rapid puff.

I felt I should say something to her, but also knew I had no wish to censure her, even though in tonight's environment it was obvious among her school friends that she stood out like a sore thumb, her personal loneliness visibly an open wound. It was no wonder she had attached herself to me after our initial encounter on the beach. It made me feel uneasy, as if Joao was passively manipulating me throughout the situation, like a puppeteer, just so I could befriend his daughter.

We left early. Joao had booked a large table at L'Etoile, an expensive French restaurant on the top floor of the Sheraton with a splendid view of the beach below and its fairy lights that shimmered in the darkness from the distance of the twenty-sixth floor. It had been Astrid's choice, but he had also invited a bunch of business colleagues including the unlikeable Matheus who, tonight, was accompanied by a floozy with more bare flesh on display than grey cells.

I switched off. Astrid was at the other end of the table and I sat wedged between Joao and an industrialist from the interior who spoke no English and occasionally looked over at me with an air of superiority, as if despising my presence and my person, judging me the lowest of the low, not just a younger escort but a foreign one at that. I half hoped he would put a hand on my knee under the table, make a pass or something, so I could protest loudly and make a scene and embarrass him in front of his dowdy wife and the rest of the guests, but he didn't even have the courage to do so. Throughout the meal, Joao ignored me totally, as if my decorative presence was all that was required of me.

As we were being driven home later, Astrid slumped on the back seat by my side, Joao sensed my unease.

'Did the evening bore you, my dear?' he asked.

'Somewhat,' I told him.

'I'm sorry.'

'Next time we have to go out in public, I would rather choose what to wear myself. I felt like a dress-up doll, Joao.'

I was about to suggest that I would prefer being dropped off at my apartment rather than spend the night with him at the villa, but he must have read my mind.

'Come back with us,' he said. 'Let me make it up to you.' His eyes were full of pleading. I gave in.

The driver carried a sleeping Astrid in past the front door, where a maid took over and supported her all the way to her own bedroom at the back of the house and she was quickly tucked in. The driver turned on his heels and the servants disappeared, leaving Joao and me alone in the echoing vastness of the high-ceilinged rooms.

He wasted no time in leading me to the master bedroom, where he lifted my skirt, pulled down my knickers and buried his face in my pussy. It was the first time in our relationship so far that he had actually gone down on me with any degree of focused enthusiasm, though god knows I had given him blow jobs a-plenty. Usually he returned the favour with a few obligatory laps of my slit, in part to ensure that I was well lubricated before he pulled himself up over my body and entered me, obviously eager to fuck.

His tongue felt good, but I could not quell the suspicion that his attentive worshipping at my clit was simply Joao throwing out all the stops by way of a sales pitch rather than any real dedication to my gratification. I took great pleasure from grabbing hold of his hair and grinding his face against me until I came, hoping that the residual ache in his jaw would serve as some slight reminder that I was not entirely satisfied with the arrangement he had roped me into.

I could barely sleep. At my side, Joao snored softly, his face buried into the deep pillow, his broad, hirsute shoulders emerging from the whiteness of the sheets, his close-cropped salt-and-pepper hair trimmed with uncanny precision. The random sounds of the house washed over me, a wall of deathly silence interrupted by slivers of creaks, a rustle here, an audible shiver there, as the building conducted its secret life, its materials shedding the heat of the day, relaxing into place, settling. I listened, seeking a pattern, the communication of a rhythm, but it was all a chaos of nothingness, my mind being teased.

I got out of bed. Walked nude and barefoot over the

stone floors to the kitchen on the lower level and took a carton of milk from the massive Whirlpool side-by-side fridge and poured myself a glass. Through the open window, the hill was a pool of thick darkness and the scent of the nearby gardens wafted along the gentle breeze.

I wandered aimlessly through the silent villa. Was even briefly tempted to brazenly call up for a taxi or one of Joao's drivers and be dropped off at the nearest expanse of beach and sand, although I knew it wasn't a good idea and a sure recipe for disaster. I wanted to feel the night air swirl across my bare skin, dip my inflamed flesh into the halting waves of the Atlantic.

My cunt throbbed. Unsatisfied, my clit still painful from Joao's attentive ministrations. I stood by the window, touching myself, daydreaming, craving I knew not what. I finally tiptoed back to the bedroom where Joao still lay, his position unchanged. I had somehow hoped he might have wakened and offered a cure for my restlessness, fucked me hard, harder than he usually did. But he failed to move even when I slipped between the sheets and barricaded myself next to him, hunting down the heat radiating from his body.

It took ages, but inevitably sleep finally overtook me.

It was already mid-morning when I shook myself awake. Joao had left for work and Astrid was nowhere to be seen. Probably at the beach. I took breakfast on the balcony, swam a few lengths in the pool under the unfazed gaze of the two maids who were busying themselves around the villa, cleaning and tidying up, professionally trained to ignore my nudity, no doubt judging me as just one more of Joao's walkway of conquests, soon to be replaced by a younger, more exotic model.

Finally I dressed. Willingly leaving the floral print dress I had worn for the school gala behind, reintegrating my uniform of short skirt, pastel-hued T-shirt and strappy sandals.

Back at my flat, I heard my mobile ringing as I turned the key in the lock but it had stopped by the time I had reached the desk on which I had set it down. I had entirely forgotten having left the phone behind. So few people knew my number. There were a score of missed calls listed. All from the same local number. I switched to the messages. Raoul sounded frantic. Insisting repeatedly I should call him back immediately. In turns angry, resigned and then angry again. I put the phone down, kicked my shoes off and ignored his demands.

Men.

Later that night there was a thunderous knock at my door. Initially I ignored the sound, thinking it must be some kind of mistake – I wasn't expecting anyone and the buzzer for the main security door hadn't gone off. I was luxuriously soaking in my apartment's small bathtub, shoulder-deep in hot water that I had perfumed with a whole packet of lavender bath salts, my legs stretched out and feet resting on the lip of the tub, drinking a glass of red wine and mulling over what to do next.

My limbs were utterly relaxed and the alcohol in combination with the water's warmth had made me quite drowsy. Music played through my laptop's tinny speakers. Hozier's 'Take Me to Church', a tune that I related to on multiple levels, having always sought redemption from sources more closely aligned to my personal brand of raw sexuality than any form of organised religion. I lay there letting the lyrics wash over me and surveying the events of the past few months with an almost hypnotic and objective gaze, half unconscious in my buzzed-out heat haze.

It had not escaped my attention that my departure from Aurelia's employ and abandoning my musical career in a laughable attempt to 'find myself' away from the world of sex had resulted in a life populated only by troubles with men. I had ended up achieving a situation the exact opposite of what I had been aiming for.

What a joke. I should have joined a convent instead.

I toyed with the idea of breaking up with them both and finding a proper job, or taking up formal Portuguese language lessons, perhaps enrolling in online university study and furthering my education. Even cookery lessons or signing up for a library card would do more for my self-development than spending every minute thinking about my love life.

The bathroom was fogged with steam. It clogged my lungs in a way that felt simultaneously cleansing and suffocating. And reminded me briefly of that night I had spent in the Kentish Town sauna with the bearded brute of a man who had found me playing the Bailly on Hampstead Heath in the altogether and led me there – whom I had knowingly followed – and the group of men he had assembled who delighted in taking every advantage of my willing degradation. No matter how complicated the tangled mess I was in now, at least I had managed to crawl out of that dark place, although the memories of it remained a familiar shadow I doubted I would ever be free from.

I dunked my head under the water, hoping to wash the unwelcome images from my mind.

There it was again, someone banging so loudly that I feared they would knock straight through the thin wood veneer and then let themselves in whether I wanted it or not.

I paused the music and eased myself out of the tub, head swimming as my over-heated body straightened to standing. The luxurious, thick white towelling robe that I often lazed around in after swimming in the pool of the Jardim Botânico villa, was not mine at all, but one of a pair that Joao owned, I realised, as I searched for something to cover myself with and finally snatched up a pair of relatively modest pink cotton panties and an old Holy Criminals T-shirt and pulled both on before peering through the door's security viewer. The violent hammering had reduced to a series of sharp raps punctuated by long pauses, as if the person on the other side had just about given up and decided that maybe I really wasn't in.

It was Raoul. His square jaw looming larger than usual through the artificial angle of the fishbowl-shaped peephole. He was holding his motorcycle helmet in one hand and a large bunch of roses in the other, blood-coloured blooms wrapped in clear cellophane bound tight with a black bow, the sort of bouquet that wouldn't have looked out of place in a vampire's lair.

I was sorely tempted to tell him to go to hell. And then get myself back into the now tepid bath.

But though he had been unbearably possessive of late, since I was sleeping with another man without his knowledge or permission I had to admit there was logic to his behaviour and the least I owed him was an explanation. We'd been dating each other long enough that I couldn't pretend even to myself I hadn't thought we were yet 'exclusive', or any other such cop-out. It was time to face the music.

I gritted my teeth and opened the door.

'Summer,' he said, his voice tinged with obvious relief.

'Raoul, I . . . I'm seeing someone else. Another man,' I told him, as soon as he stepped inside.

Better to just get it over with, I reasoned, before I changed my mind.

'I know,' he said.

'You do?'

'I'm not a complete fucking idiot, you know.'

'Oh.'

He waltzed past me to the breakfast counter, set the flowers down and began opening cupboards, pulling out kitchen equipment I didn't even realise I had. What on earth would I do with a rolling pin? I remained where I was and stared at him.

'Do you have a vase?' he asked. 'Something to put these in?'

His words spurred me to action. I was grateful for a reason to change the subject, though uncertain under the circumstances why he thought the occasion of my infidelity warranted a gesture of romance.

I fetched a plastic bucket from the shelf alongside the washing machine in my flat's wardrobe-sized laundry room and carried it towards him, stepping over discarded trainers and magazines on the way that still lay precisely where I had dropped them. A black lace bra and knicker set hung conspicuously from my bedroom door, across from the open-plan living area and visible from where Raoul stood, as if advertising my wanton nature. Tidiness wasn't one of my virtues.

There was a very definite gleam in Raoul's eyes. A look I recognised but couldn't quite identify right then. He stood too close to me as I turned on the tap and filled the bucket halfway, then extracted a pair of scissors from the cutlery drawer, removed the bow and protective film from the wrapped bunch of flowers and arranged the roses in the water.

'I used to be a florist, you know. A long time ago, just a casual job as a teenager . . .' I nattered on, filling the ominous silence that hovered between us.

Raoul just kept grinning at me manically with that look in his eyes, half lust and half malevolence. I looked away from him, tore a few more stray green leaves from the pointed stems, assiduously avoiding the sharp thorns. It occurred to me that I was afraid of him. Unlike Joao, Raoul was unpredictable. Always on edge. I wasn't yet sure that I could trust him.

He put his hands on my hips. Pulled me against him. His erection was prominent, bulging beneath the thin covering of his shorts and pressing against the small of my back. His fingers slipped inside the seam of my underwear and pressed against my slit.

'Hmm,' he said, 'not wet yet. Unlike you.'

I didn't know what to say in response so stayed mute.

'Nice and smooth though. I like that.'

I had shaved in the bath.

'Who are you keeping yourself smooth for?' he continued. 'Me or him?'

It evidently hadn't occurred to Raoul that my choices in matters of grooming were in fact personal and not related to the preferences of the men I dated, but it didn't seem like the time to give him a lecture on feminism.

He pushed me forward gently with one hand pressed between my shoulder blades. The fingers on his other hand maintained their pressure against my labia, now rubbing through the fabric of my knickers instead of against my bare skin.

'What's wrong?' he asked me. 'Can't speak? Don't tell me you're too ashamed to admit you're a whore, Summer. Nothing but a horny little bitch.'

'I'm not ashamed,' I fired back at him.

'Bullshit,' he snarled. 'If that were true, you wouldn't have been ignoring my calls. Hiding away here on your own, probably rubbing your cunt silly since you don't have a man here to fill your holes. Or has he just left, and I'm second? Tell me. I'm surprised I didn't find a queue outside your door.'

He pulled me up by the hair, bent his head close to my earlobe and hissed, 'Tell me. When was the last time you fucked him? This morning? This afternoon?'

As he spoke, he yanked the gusset of my panties to one side and slid two fingers inside me.

'Last night,' I replied. My voice came out in a high-pitched squeak.

'You had better not be lying to me.'

'I'm not lying.'

I wanted to say, *Or else, Raoul? I had better not be lying or else what?* His grasp on my hair was tight, but gentle. He hadn't hurt me. Yet. I wasn't sure whether I ought to be afraid if he would, or if this was all a bluff, the beginnings of a very realistic sex game. Did the oh-so-macho Raoul have a thing for cuckolding? I imagined how it would feel to be riding Joao on top of freshly laundered and probably ludicrously expensive Egyptian cotton sheets in the Jardim Botânico villa while Raoul, still sweaty from a day's work at the juice bar, looked on from a nearby chair, his muscular forearms restrained with two of Joao's Armani leather belts, his thick, dark cock hard and throbbing, his temper heating up to explosive proportions but totally unable to do anything about it, an unwilling slave to desires that he detested.

'Good.' I could no longer see his face, but I could tell by his tone that he was smirking. 'Now that's better,' he said. 'A nice wet pussy. Soaking. You like talking like this? Like a dirty bitch?'

My body had betrayed me. I could feel the humidity between my thighs, the throbbing need in my clit.

He withdrew his fingers and brought them to my lips.

'Open your mouth, whore. And don't pretend you don't like sex juices. I know you love it. You'll be eating my cock later so don't worry, I'll give you plenty more.'

He didn't wait for me to follow his instruction. Just smeared my own secretions over my face and forced his fingers halfway down my throat until I began to choke.

'You're out of practice,' he said. 'Your businessman isn't rough like this, is he? I bet you miss it. I bet you think about me when you fuck him.'

'Yes,' I admitted, 'I do.'

He grabbed me by the jaw and swivelled me around to face him and pushed his mouth against mine in a violent kiss. Our tongues pressed together, his teeth pulled at my lower lip. I ran my hand down the meaty firmness of his thigh and up between his legs and took hold of his cock through his shorts.

'And do you think about him when you fuck me?'

'Sometimes,' I told him.

He pulled away from me abruptly.

'I'll make you pay for that,' he said. His voice was low and soft, and frightened me more than his blustering did, which seemed to me more bark than bite. But with the pang of fear came a twist of further arousal. My nipples were stiff and pushed through the fabric of my T-shirt, I could

244

feel them aching, and I knew that Raoul could see it too. He pointedly stared at my chest.

'Go on then,' I mocked him. 'Make me pay.'

He pushed me down onto my knees. Slapped me across the face. Spat on me. Then rubbed his saliva over my cheeks and nose with the flat of his hand.

I inhaled sharply. Shocked.

Even in the depths of our darkest explorations, Dominik had never slapped my face. Would never have, I thought.

'Tell me I'm not turning you on, Summer,' he insisted. 'Dare to look me in the eyes and tell me that you're not enjoying everything I'm doing to you, and I'll leave, right now.'

I couldn't tell him that. It wasn't true.

I swallowed, hard.

'I thought so,' he said. 'But I want to hear it.'

'Want to hear what?'

'You know.'

'You're turning me on.'

'As if I can't tell, the way your tits are pressing through your shirt. Your nipples are harder than my dick. And your pussy is dribbling all over the floor, I can smell you from here. Get up.'

He placed a hand under my armpit, pulled me to my feet, and I stumbled against him.

'Fuck's sake,' he muttered, and picked me up in his arms

and carried me into the bedroom, where he unceremoniously dumped me on top of the bed, face down. It was only half made, the top sheet pulled messily across in the same position that I'd left it in when I got up after the last occasion I'd slept there. Raoul grabbed the bunched-up cover from under me, pulled it away and dropped it onto the floor.

'Lazy too, aren't you,' he remarked. 'Don't you ever clean up around here?'

It was a rhetorical question. He kept talking.

'Lazy, dirty slut, fucking a rich man for money and fucking me because he doesn't provide enough dick for you. Well, lucky for you, whore, I've got plenty of dick for you, exactly the way you like it. Turn over.'

I scrambled onto my back. Looked up at him. He was still standing at the end of the bed, watching me, his face a picture of savage lust. It was a terrible thing, and I knew it, but that didn't change the fact that I loved being looked at that way. Loved being the object of a man's uncontrolled desire.

'Take off your clothes. I want to watch you undress for me and spread your legs like the whore you are.'

I wriggled my knickers down to my feet and pulled my T-shirt over my head. Sat there proudly naked and defiant, silently daring him to make his next move.

His expression changed. As if a sudden thought had occurred to him.

'I was just going to fuck you,' he said, 'but I'm going to make you orgasm instead.'

I must have looked confused.

He explained.

'So that later, when you're trying to kid yourself into thinking that you didn't really want it like this, you can remember how hard you came.'

He undressed. Crawled on top of me. Kissed me again. And then carried on crawling up my body until he was sitting on my face, his cock deep inside my mouth, his balls smothering what little air I was able to gasp.

'Suck me, bitch.'

Just as I thought I might pass out if he didn't allow me to take a breath he pulled out. I gulped for air.

Raoul laughed. Grasped my chin and waggled my head.

'Don't worry princess,' he said. 'I'm not going to kill you.'

He turned around and began to lap at my clit. I squirmed under him and he grabbed one of my thighs in each of his hands and held me still. I heard him chuckle, a low, quiet laugh that birthed in the back of his throat.

'Enjoying it already, aren't you slut? And I've only just gotten started.'

It was true. Raoul was skilful. Unlike Joao, who had merely been average, Raoul knew exactly what he was doing, his tongue delving deftly within my folds, circling my clitoris with just the right degree of pressure.

I was half-crushed by the weight of his heavy body lying on top of me and still breathing in the musky scent of his groin. I wriggled in vain to adjust my position so that I could get his cock into my mouth again and suck him but it was no use, he was at totally the wrong angle for me to make any kind of proper job at it, the reason why I thought that 69 was a position best left to exploring teenagers. It just wasn't practical.

He paused. Lifted his head.

'Don't just lie there, slut,' he said. 'I want to feel your lips on my balls. And your tongue on my hole. I want you to come while you're licking my arse.'

I did as he asked.

And came harder than I had in as long as I could remember.

I woke before he did. It was becoming a habit, remaining sleepless while the man alongside me snored away peacefully, totally relaxed, a look of blissful innocence spread over his features.

We had both fallen asleep almost immediately after our exertions, spooning, his heavy arm draped over me and pinning me to his side. I eased my way out from under him, threw on a cotton beach dress and went out to pick up some fruit, juice and fresh bread for breakfast.

When I returned he was still lying on the bed naked, his

long, dark brown body spread out over the sheet, his head propped on one hand, long black hair swooped back and away from his face. I was relieved that his cock remained flaccid, curled up and soft within his nest of thick pubic hair. For once, I was not in the mood for sex. A sense of unease had shifted over me, which my morning walk had not dulled at all.

I leaned against the bedroom door frame and he looked up at me.

'Can I get you some juice?' I asked him.

'Sure,' he said, 'please.'

At least he hadn't forsaken his manners entirely.

I filled a couple of clean glasses with abacaxi juice from the carton and added ice. Dominik had hated ice in his drinks, but I preferred it, especially in Rio's heat. I didn't know Raoul's opinion on the subject, but dropped a couple of cubes into his tumbler anyway. He would have to live with it. A quick glance around the cupboards revealed that if I had a breakfast tray, I had no idea where it was, so I took a drink in each hand and then hooked my finger around the handle of the plastic bag filled with fruit and pastries and carried it all to the bed.

'No butter?' Raoul asked, as he delved into the carrier and extracted a bread roll.

'No butter,' I confirmed.

I picked at a few green grapes from the bunch I had

washed under the tap, scattering drops of water that still clung to the small fruits across the covers. I had lost my appetite.

'About last night,' I began.

'Yes?'

'Maybe we should talk about it.'

'Talk about it? What is there to talk about? We both had a good time, no?'

'You can't just turn up here and expect me to . . . to . . .'

I struggled for the right words.

'Expect you to be my whore?'

'Yes,' I said, although when he put it like that, it wasn't what I had intended to say at all.

'Okay then,' he said. 'Next time, return my calls and we won't have a problem.'

I turned to face him, furious.

He laughed, and reached a hand forward to touch my face.

'I'm just kidding,' he said. 'Teasing you. I know I was wrong. What can I say. I can't help it, when it comes to you. You bring out the devil in me . . .'

Bullshit . . . the word ran through my brain, a lone voice of reason. The more sensible part of me, maybe, the Summer who wouldn't stand for this crap.

'Forgive me?' he queried. He had shifted his expression into a pose of remorse, but his eyes still gleamed with humour, and a hint of something else. Considered evil, maybe.

'Okay, I guess,' I said. 'But I don't want you calling me over and over, or turning up unannounced again. Ever again.'

He brought both hands up to his face in a gesture of surrender.

'Woah, okay. You're the boss.'

I glanced out across the small living space to the kitchen counter and caught a glimpse of the red petals blooming in my laundry bucket from the bunch of roses that he had brought over.

'And no more flowers,' I told him.

'Really?' he said. 'I thought girls liked flowers.' It was the only remark he'd made that morning that had sounded really sincere.

'Not like that. As a nice gesture, sure, but not as a token of apology. Like you're trying to buy my goodwill with trinkets.'

'Perhaps a bigger trinket would have been more effective,' he replied, drily.

I nearly slapped him across the face. Took a deep breath and told myself that if I communicated my anger with violence, I'd be as bad as Raoul.

I wasn't even sure exactly what it was that I was angry about. Or who I was angry with – him or me.

He took both of my hands in his.

'Look,' he said. 'I really am sorry. I like you Summer. You're different. Give me a chance. That's all I ask.'

His grip was tight.

'A chance. Okay. I can do that,' I said.

One more chance.

'This might not be the best time to bring it up,' he continued.

'Yes?'

'In my bag, by the front door,' he said. I hadn't even noticed he'd been carrying a bag. 'There's two plane tickets, to Recife.'

'Recife?' It rang a vague bell but I wasn't even entirely sure where it was.

'In the north-east. Couple of hours' flight. My cousin lives there, he invited us to stay with him. For a few days, that's all. I thought we could get away, spend some time together. Just you and me. It's a popular city. Near the sea, nice restaurants, bars, all that.'

'And you didn't think to ask me first?'

'I wanted to treat you. To surprise you. Can't a man buy his girlfriend a holiday?'

'Okay. Thank you. It sounds nice.'

I agreed. I didn't have anything planned with Joao, and knew he wouldn't ask any questions. Astrid deserved a break from her violin lessons for a short period anyway, following the recital. I was beginning to get the distinct impression that the shine had worn off her hobby and she was growing to prefer other things. Music just wasn't Astrid's passion. At any rate, it meant that I didn't have any commitments for the foreseeable future.

Raoul had claimed that the tickets he had booked were flexible, when I had pointed out that it was presumptuous of him to assume that I could just drop everything according to his schedule. As we checked in, I noticed that our economy fares were non-refundable. He had lied to me. Again. I didn't bring it up. It seemed a petty thing to complain about, and I didn't want to spend the next four days stuck with him arguing.

His cousin, Lucas, was almost the spitting image of Raoul. They had the same wide mouth and slightly sardonic expression, as if every word they uttered was imbued with double meaning. Lucas's hair was also long, but his skull was shaved on one side in a punkish undercut and the rest of his dark locks pulled into a top knot. His hand was big and warm when I reached out to shake it. He pulled me into a hug, kissed me on both cheeks and laughed.

'She greets like a businesswoman,' he said to Raoul.

Raoul shrugged. 'She's foreign,' he replied. 'We Brazilians are friendlier than she's used to.' They met each other's eyes, sharing a personal joke.

'Hi,' I said awkwardly, unsure of how to include myself

in the conversation that they were having around me as though I were Raoul's pet.

'Come in, come in,' Lucas said. 'You two can have the big room. While you're here, I'll take the spare.'

He lived alone in a high-rise apartment block in Boa Viagem, a stone's throw from the sea. The place was not much larger than mine, and minimally kitted out with a long black leather sofa, mammoth-sized flat-screen TV, a fridge with a glass door packed with beer, and not a lot else. A surfboard leaned up against one wall. There were no pictures hanging on the cream-coloured walls, and I couldn't see any books or photographs either. Not even a dedicated sound system, or any magazines. Nothing that left me any clues to the type of person he was, besides that he liked to surf, and play computer games, judging by the console and stack of cases piled on the floor, all of them emblazoned with gangster types carrying machine guns and accompanied by large-breasted caricatural women wearing khaki-hot pants and crop-tops that would never feature in any real army. A world away from the cartoon car races that Astrid preferred.

We carried our cases into the master bedroom while Lucas pulled cold drinks from the bar fridge and searched for a bottle opener. I didn't usually drink beer in the middle of the afternoon, but today I decided to make an exception. I felt extraordinarily uptight.

A plain grey cotton cover was spread over the bed, with two pillows propped up at one end. There was a small set of matching drawers on either side, both made from cheap black wood veneer. A reading lamp with a cream shade was balanced on one set of drawers, alongside a digital alarm clock. There were no windows.

I had asked about Lucas on the flight. Where in Recife he was situated and what was his job, and whether or not he had a partner, children or housemates whom I would also be meeting, but Raoul had diverted all of my questions. Boa Viagem, like anywhere near the seaside, was an expensive part of town. Maybe it was better that I didn't know what Lucas did for a living.

'Why don't you have a shower, babe? Start getting ready.'

Tonight they had planned to check out the nightlife. Raoul had, to my dismay, overseen my packing, 'Just to make sure you have the right sort of things', he told me, and had insisted I bring along my short formal black dress. He seemed disappointed that I had few other options hanging in my closet as far as party wear went. Most of the stuff I wore to the expensive restaurants and society events was stored at Joao's villa.

I gathered up my cosmetic bag, took one of the towels that had been left folded at the end of the bed and began to head for the shower. Then stopped and collected my dress and underwear too. The bathroom that Lucas had pointed out when we arrived was on the other side of the living room and I didn't want to walk back past him and Raoul clad only in a short bath towel.

Lucas handed me an opened bottle of imported Japanese beer as I emerged.

'May as well get started now,' he said.

'Thanks.'

'You're looking forward to later?' he continued.

'Umm, yeah. I heard the nightlife is good here.'

He chortled.

I lingered in the shower. The bathroom was spotlessly clean, at least, and the water pressure blissfully strong. I had forgotten to bring any body wash, so soaped myself all over with Lucas's shower gel, a deep-blue-coloured substance labelled 'Ocean Crest' that smelled distinctly masculine.

By the time I had dried off, slipped into my dress and applied my make up and scrunched a little anti-frizz product through my hair, unfamiliar voices were audible through the bathroom door.

I came out.

'And here she is, the lovely lady,' Lucas said. He was still standing by the kitchenette counter, and raised his beer bottle into the air, toasting me.

I looked around.

Several more men had arrived. They were six now, including Raoul and Lucas, standing or lounged over the couch, beers in hand, long legs spread wide apart. Raoul was stationed by the bedroom door, sitting on the floor, wearing a distinctly smug smile. The men on the couch were speaking to each other in Portuguese, too quickly for me to follow their conversation, but I was certain that I was the subject.

I swallowed. Took a mouthful of beer.

'Hi.' They nodded at me, but didn't introduce themselves, and Raoul and Lucas stayed silent.

I felt like a deer in headlights as I walked across the flat's no-man's-land to the bedroom, convinced that all six pairs of eyes were focused on me.

I closed the door.

Heard further laughing.

Then it dawned on me that I was the only woman present. Lucas and his friends hadn't brought any female partners, girlfriends, with them but surely can't all have been gay. Neither was I about to tag along on a boy's night out, I knew.

My throat was dry, despite the beer.

Raoul's voice played over and again in my mind.

Whore

Slut

Animal

I'm surprised I didn't find a queue at your door

I want to watch you with other men

Maybe one day

I recalled and now recognised the expression that I had so often caught a glimpse of on Raoul's face when he thought that I wasn't looking. The same mask that I had seen on the men in the sauna. Arousal mixed with contempt. Just as I had known it then, I knew now that Raoul's attitude was not role play. Not a power-exchange scene where he would degrade and humiliate me while we fucked or he forced me to fuck others and then hold me against him tightly afterwards and tell me that he loved me, and we would both know that our words and actions meant nothing at all outside of the context of our mutual enjoyment of kinky sex.

Raoul didn't love me at all. He didn't even like me. This wasn't BDSM, it was real life, and he wasn't a dom, he was an arsehole.

I grabbed my passport, the small evening bag that held a handful of local banknotes and my mobile phone, and stuffed them down the front of my dress. The fabric was stretched tight enough to hold them there. Everything else I would have to leave behind, or Raoul would know as soon as I emerged from the bedroom exactly what I was intent on doing. He had our printed return boarding passes and I had no means to access or change the flight details. I would have to find another way home, but I would cross that bridge later. My ballet flats were stationed by the front door, I could grab them on the way out.

I bolted for the front door.

Once outside, I initially felt disoriented. The night was full of lights, burning bright and dazzling. The city was an unknown quantity. I knew the final flights back to Rio would have left the airport already and I had no wish to spend the night on a bench there. And then I realised, to my dismay, that I didn't have the means to purchase any such ticket anyway, having left my credit card back in Rio.

The bus station, then?

Or maybe an all-night bar or club could shelter me while I waited? Where I could sit and listen to music maybe, plug in to life. Although I also knew that, even more so in Brazil, as a lone woman I would become an inevitable target for men. Oh well, I had survived before. I would again.

7

On the Road Again

Noah drove April to Heathrow to catch her flight to New York. The journey took an eternity, or so it felt, as the morning rush-hour traffic built up around Hanger Lane and both of them grew increasingly concerned at one stage that she might miss her flight. Aside from that, it was a drive full of guilty silences, as they both knew this was in all likelihood the final occasion they would spend together and anyway had little to say to each other by now.

Noah was eager to return to his office, to get in touch with Viggo, who had called and left a voicemail on his phone that Noah hadn't yet been able to return, something to do with Summer, but the early morning slow procession of cars on the M4 was at a standstill. The music on the car radio kept getting on his nerves to the extent that he ended up well before the Chiswick roundabout switching over to

Classic FM. Which on this occasion didn't play any of Summer's recordings.

He arrived late and Rhonda had a handful of yellow slips for him, calls missed, calls to be returned, urgent matters to attend to, and he was unable until after the lunch hour to switch to private mode. By then, Viggo was bunkered up in his private basement studio, dabbling away at one thing or another and unable to be reached.

It wasn't until the following morning that they could speak.

'It's Noah.'

'Hi, mate.'

'You mentioned you had some news about Summer Zahova?'

'Hello would be nice, to begin with.'

'Sorry.'

He thought of telling Viggo that his interest was down to pressure from his board in New York, the need to come up with something new for the label, but he had the feeling that wouldn't fly. He was right.

'Something tells me your interest in our violin player might not be all business. Am I right or am I wrong?'

Noah mumbled some clumsy explanation, but he knew all too well that Viggo was increasingly aware of the obsession he was nurturing for Summer. He never had been particularly good at hiding either his thoughts or his emotions, a trait that had proved inconvenient in the past when

261

his motivations were spread plainly across his face for others to view.

'No need for apologies, mate. She has that effect on people. Or should I say men.'

From what Noah had gleaned over the months, he guessed men were far from the only gender affected and that Summer was not averse to experimentation. This was quickly confirmed by the amused tone in the singer's voice, and all the unsaid things it implied.

'You mentioned you'd thought she might be in South America . . .'

'Indeedy . . .'

He realised Viggo was now teasing him, enjoyed having him hanging on to every word and shard of information.

'And?'

'That's all.'

'What?'

'Not much to go on, I know.'

'You can say that again.'

'The thought first hit me when I noticed a photo of the three of us by the beach, taken a couple of years ago . . . then I was chatting to Susan – Summer and Lauralynn's agent – the other day. She popped over to catch up with Lauralynn on a new project she's working on, providing cello backing to some new experimental indie band . . . Anyway, she'd been in touch with Summer about the proceeds from the sale of the Bailly. Apparently, Summer didn't want the lump sum yet. Still hadn't found the right property, or had got cold feet about buying. Seems that was the principal reason for putting the violin up for auction, to purchase a place of some sort. She instructed Susan to park the cash in a bank. When I heard she was worrying about changing over pounds to real, things somehow fell into place.'

'What things?'

'We all once went to Brazil.'

'Brazil?'

'She was having problems at the time. I think the trip had a strong effect on Summer. Instinct tells me she might be found there. She loved the place. Rio maybe, where we stayed a few days. But knowing Summer, she's probably travelling around. Itchy feet, you know. Only time she ever stayed still long was when she was living with Dominik, before he passed.'

Noah fell silent, all sorts of thoughts spinning around in the fever dream taking root in his mind. And questions.

Viggo continued. 'Now I might be wrong, of course. It was just a thought.'

'Thanks.' Noah felt deflated. As if the trail leading to Summer had now branched out into a thousand dead-end lanes and cul-de-sacs. Brazil? It would be like seeking a needle in haystack.

Fortuitously, he had to move on soon after the call to

attend and chair the label's fortnightly A&R meeting, where he and his creative and marketing staff would listen to the bunch of tapes and demos submitted by management companies and artists. It was always a lively affair, with opinions flying in all directions and much passion at play. The distraction was welcome.

During the course of the following days, Noah hoped against hope for another phone call, a further random encounter, a stray piece of information innocently dropped into a conversation which might, illogically, bring him a further clue as to Summer's precise location, but the gods of obsession were no longer smiling down on him and nothing emerged. There was no way he could drop everything and set off on a fool's errand to South America in search of Summer Zahova with so little information at his disposal. It would make no sense.

It felt as if the trail was growing cold.

An improbable solution came up during the course of a global marketing meeting for which executives from all the label's international subsidiaries convened in Paris at the weekend to coordinate their plans and maximise promotional budgets. The company's compact building was situated by the Senate, the top-floor boardroom windows opening up on the Luxembourg Gardens and a glimpse of the distant fountains towards the Boulevard Saint-Michel and Panthéon intersection.

Michèle Becker, who ran their office in the French capital, mentioned in passing that The Handsomes, one of the main acts on her small roster, an electronic/deejaying duo with a strong and growing fan base beyond France, were planning to visit Central and South America on a month-long tour, and she wished to lobby for extra marketing support from both head office and local distributors. Michèle was a rail-thin woman in her forties, always clad in charcoal-grey designer business suits, and was one of the label's longest-lasting heads, having begun her career when punk was all the rage, and had survived through successive waves of easy listening, electronica and every passing fad to the present day, a cold-headed realist who ran a tight ship but attracted the respect of musicians and managers. Even though they were both French, she had discovered The Handsomes playing support at Webster Hall in Manhattan, had signed them for the French office and encouraged them to accentuate the dance and disco elements in their music and been proven spectacularly right with a couple of massive hits they still feasted on.

Noah's attention was wandering when she intervened. The Handsomes did well in the UK, but not on the same scale as in other territories where the rock scene was slower evolving. But the suggestion made sense, he knew. The duo were a low-cost outfit, and the injection of some added marketing cash could well provide their back catalogue as well as their latest album with a significant spike in sales.

He looked across the wide table at Michèle. Caught her eyes and nodded, hinting that she had his support should it come to an improvised vote. She held his gaze, her features severe, sharp cheekbones to the fore, an electronic cigarette dangling from her lips. For a brief moment, he imagined her in black leather and vertiginous heels with a whip in her hand, a daunting figure of a dominatrix. He smiled at the notion. She smiled back. He would have to ask Viggo if there were any interesting rumours about Michèle's sexual proclivities. Viggo knew all the dirt in the business and relished telling tales. Even if he wasn't quite as forthcoming when it came to Summer Zahova, for some reason.

A thought occurred.

'Do you have the tour's full itinerary, by any chance?' Noah asked.

'Of course.'

Michèle rummaged through her folders and pulled out a couple of sheets of A4 paper which she slid over to Noah.

The Handsomes' tour was scheduled to debut in Puerto Rico, before moving on to Panama, and a cluster of club dates arranged in Cancun to coincide with the riotous days of spring break when hordes of thirsty and heavy-money-spending American students swarmed over the Mexican coastal resort. There was a short break arranged and then the main part of the tour began with visits to Colombia, Venezuela, Brazil, Chile and, finally, Argentina. It was a gruelling schedule, and a testimony to the hardworking ethos of the duo and the reason they had not faded away, as so many groups did, after their initial success.

The Brazilian dates were to be in Rio and São Paulo in six weeks' time.

The conversations around the table continued but Noah's mind had by now drifted, unhealthily drawn like a magnet to the two lines on the band's itinerary. Should he? Could he?

Michèle had arranged to book a back room in one of the area's best Moroccan restaurants for the assembled executives to dine in after the meeting broke up. They walked over to the rue Monsieur Le Prince and walked down the steep hill towards it. Noah arranged to sit next to her.

'I've never seen them live,' he said, referring to The Handsomes. 'I was away on the West Coast on both occasions that they played New York.'

'You should,' Michèle remarked. 'They put on a spectacular show. Amazing stuff with the lighting.'

'Sounds great.'

'And they're also lovely guys. I really think you could do better with them in your territory.'

'Love their sound, but from the records I've always felt they were more of a club thing, maybe not big enough presence-wise for larger venues where the real money is and word of mouth originates.'

267

'Go and see them. You might change your mind.'

'Maybe I will.'

The heaving bowls of couscous, jugs of hot sauce and platters of mutton, brochettes and meat balls were delivered to the long table at which they were all sitting.

'When I get back to the office, I'll text you the telephone numbers for their management. Maybe you can set something up with them? See what can be arranged.'

'That would be good.'

It was all the excuse Noah needed. Back in London the next day, he made a beeline for his office straight from the St Pancras Eurostar terminal and arrived just in time to ask Rhonda to make all the arrangements for the trip. If she was surprised by his decision, she gave no sign of it, imperturbable as ever. It was some time since he had been on the road with a band.

A few weeks later, he arrived in Panama. As he walked out of the plane onto the ramp, the heat cloaked him in one gulp like a damp blanket rolling over his jetlagged body. By the time he reached the luggage carousel, after an interminable delay at passport control where just one official was processing two planeloads of arriving passengers, his pale blue shirt was sticking to his back.

There was no one to meet him and he caught a cab to the hotel where he knew The Handsomes and their managers and crew were staying. The cool gusts of the air-conditioning rushed towards him as the uniformed doorman held the wide glass doors open for him and a matching bellboy ran towards him to take his one piece of luggage and place it on a trolley while he checked in. He retained his computer case, which hung from his shoulders. It was frayed at the edges; he'd picked it up as a freebie on an old tour for which Bridget had provided second support and it held a strong sentimental value for him; he carried his papers, a couple of paperbacks, documents, assorted toiletries and odds and sods in it.

'Business or pleasure, sir?' the pretty receptionist asked with an artificial smile.

'Both.'

Entering the large, airy room, he could have been anywhere in the world – geometrical configuration, soft shag carpet, assembly-line top-of-the range functional furniture – until he pulled the curtains open after the bellboy, duly tipped, had left.

He was on the fifteenth floor and the view ranged across roofs and fields all the way to a bluer-than-blue ocean. The band was camped out in a set of luxury cabanas surrounding the outside pool, but since Noah was partly in holiday mode he had upgraded to a suite on the hotel's top floor. He always enjoyed having a view. He hadn't looked up anything about Panama before coming here. All he was aware of was its famed canal. But the light was white and flat and dazzling, the sky aquamarine, and a faint smell of spices lingered in the air, blending uncomfortably with some fragrance the room had been sprayed with by the hotel cleaner shortly before his arrival.

'What the fuck am I doing here?' Noah wondered aloud. It was mid-afternoon but his body was weary, still on European time. He would sleep. Meet up with the band tomorrow, he decided. He stripped.

Alain, Stéphane and the rest of the crew had risen hours before Noah, despite having apparently all spent the previous night out on the town. The two young musicians and their entourage had taken over a large round table in the hotel's dining area and were busily gorging themselves on the buffet breakfast, a cornucopia of tropical fruit platters, corn tortillas, meat dishes and the usual fare of miniature boxed cereals, containers of low-fat yoghurt and slices of countless varieties of bread that was always on hand in hotels around the world for unadventurous tourists.

Noah took a large plate up to the hot food counter and ordered the Panamanian breakfast: fresh fried beef flavoured with garlic and paprika, which came with a liberal serving of salty fried dough balls and a scoop of spicy scrambled eggs. He carried his mountain of food towards the table where a pot of fresh coffee and jugs of juice already awaited.

Sampling the local cuisine was invariably one of Noah's

favourite parts of travelling, and he did so with relish now that April was not eyeing his plate and tutting while she munched on wheat-free granola, egg-white omelette, or whatever her latest diet happened to entail. He had been blessed with one of those metabolisms that enabled him to eat whatever he liked and stay in moderately good shape, and he never gave a second thought to the state of his arteries or his cholesterol count.

There was one free seat, apparently saved for him, along-side a pixie-sized girl in her mid-twenties with hair cropped in varying short lengths that formed a bob-like helmet around her skull in a mess of dark roots and peroxide blonde ends. She had a sharp, pointed nose and a face shaped like an upside-down teardrop with a wide forehead, angular cheekbones and narrow, pointed chin. Her brows were thick and formed two animated dark streaks across her temples.

When she spotted Noah heading towards them she rose to her feet and waved, sending the jangling stack of silver bracelets that circled her wrist down her stick-thin arm where they were prevented from dropping all the way to her armpit only by the barrier of her elbow. Her cupid's-bow red lips opened into a round O as she called out to him.

'Hey, Noah,'

He racked his memory but didn't think they had met previously. Surely he would have remembered. Roadies were a dime a dozen and he had been vaguely introduced to hundreds over the years, but nearly all of them were men, and fewer still were slim young blondes.

She extended her hand and Noah took it. Her grip was firm, although he felt like a giant with her tiny palm within his grasp.

'I'm Dana,' she said. 'Michèle told us to expect you.' She had an unusual accent with a strong US twang. Later she told him that she had grown up in Serbia glued to American TV shows before moving Stateside and meeting The Handsomes at a Cinnabon store in Florida during one of their early club tours. She had ended up training on the sound crew before being promoted to PA and all-round assistant, with her ability to help out on the technical side an added bonus. She was now based in Paris and an indispensable part of the duo's team as principal troubleshooter and maid of all trades.

Dana introduced him to the others. Pete and Jerry, the senior technical guys on lighting and sound, who were both in their thirties and looked distinctly bored and tired in comparison with the exuberant expressions and unlined faces of their assistants, who were relatively new to life on the road.

Even if Noah hadn't already seen publicity pics of Alain and Stéphane, they would have been immediately recognisable as the actual stars of the band before they were pointed out to him. Oftentimes, off-duty rockstars and musicians were like actors away from camera or the stage and surprisingly meek and ordinary without an instrument or a microphone in hand. These two were the polar opposite of that. A blind hermit with a total ignorance of pop culture could have sensed the energy that they exuded and the chemistry that popped between the pair.

Alain was the more extroverted of the two, and jumped to his feet to greet Noah, embracing him in a particularly Eurocentric-style hug, complete with light kiss on each cheek. He wore tight skinny jeans in a coral red shade with a short-sleeved thin cotton shirt over the top, buttoned all the way up to the collar. Stéphane stayed seated, and reached across the table to shake Noah's hand. He had on a baggy black and grey Religion T-shirt that featured a woman's face with just one eye visible, the rest covered by a stylised hand with all its bones protruding like an X-ray skeleton, and an oversized, thin grey snood that he would surely have to abandon when they left the cool air-conditioned comfort of the hotel.

Noah was aware, from past press releases and many magazine articles, that the two French deejays had been childhood friends, but they could have easily passed for brothers, with their matching slim-line, medium-height figures and identical shaggy brown hair, cut and styled to achieve just the right degree of detached cool.

Noah suspected that the few thin blond streaks they both sported in their long fringes owed more to the bottle than any time spent in the sun; a sign of stylists getting involved to manufacture whatever they deemed to be a more commercial image. They'd come up through the scene at the same time as Daft Punk, but unlike their counterparts did not conceal their faces from their public.

'Good to meet you both at last,' Noah told them. 'I've heard great things. I've always been a fan of your sound.'

'It's our pleasure,' Alain responded. 'We're flattered you've come all the way out here.' He spoke fluent English with a mid-Atlantic accent.

They knew, no doubt, of his status at the label and the fact that a positive word from Noah could mean an injection of PR cash from their label's British arm and a chance to spread their wings further worldwide. Stéphane was appraising him curiously, probably wondering why an English record exec who had previously shown little interest in the two of them should bother to travel all the way to Central and South America out of the blue to watch them perform live.

Noah had no intention of explaining himself. They could think whatever they liked. He poured a strong black coffee from the cafetière – still piping hot, since the roving waitress attending to their table had noticed him join the party and brought a fresh pot – and bit into one of the fried dough balls. They were covered in powdered sugar and the flavour was at once sweet and savoury and took him by surprise.

'So, what are the plans for today?' he asked, between forkfuls.

'We're headlining at Next tomorrow night,' Alain told him. 'The place is pretty huge. We're going down there later on before doors open to run some soundchecks and liaise with their on site crew. Until then . . . sun, pool, while we can. Might take a trip into the city later, maybe the casinos. You're welcome to join us.'

They agreed to meet up in the lobby at 9 p.m. and then find somewhere for a late dinner, which would give the band and tech guys enough time to approve the set-up at Next for the following night's gig.

Noah remained at the breakfast table to finish off his coffee as the others trooped out. He declined to join in with their day-time activities, since strictly speaking he was not out here on vacation and had to go online and attend to the backlog of emails and messages that had no doubt reached his inbox over the course of his absence from the office so far.

He also hoped that during the flight over Viggo might have discovered some further nugget of information about Summer and mailed it to him. Fat chance of that, he mused, but it was the only vague hope he hung onto. Noah had told Viggo in advance about his impromptu trip with The

Handsomes, and prompted him to follow up again with Susan to check if there had been any developments on her side.

His room had wi-fi and, to his surprise, a pretty good connection. He pulled open the thick black-out curtains, letting bright shafts of light stream in through the wide French doors, and settled onto the white leather bucket-shaped swivel chair, angling his screen away from the sun's glare.

There was a whole raft of correspondence from Rhonda listing phone calls that he had missed and minutes from meetings that he had been due to attend. She had kindly sent him an abbreviated summary of all the urgent things he needed to do, letting him know that he could ignore most of the rest as office politics and waffle.

April had sent him a missive, which he opened and then quickly clicked away from after skim-reading a few expletive-ridden lines about how her recent stay with Noah had confirmed to her precisely how much of a pig he was, who she would warn all of her friends not to touch with a proverbial barge pole. He glanced at the time on the message and noticed she'd sent it in the early hours of the morning – probably a drunken rant that she would later regret and he could safely overlook.

Nothing from Viggo.

Noah racked his brains to come up with some reasonable

way to pin down the possible whereabouts of the red-haired violinist. He supposed he could Google private investigators, of the sort that populated B-grade Hollywood films, with run-down offices hidden behind nail salons and dubious taste in brown corduroy trousers, if such people really existed. Then wondered how he could possibly justify that cost on his expenses. Or try a more exhaustive Facebook search, beyond his one quick look to see if she had a website or fan page.

He was prevented from utilising such methods by an inner sense of right and wrong that told him reaching out to Summer through his industry connections, in view of his potentially signing her again, was perfectly legitimate, but that trying to find her through more personal means crossed the line from professional interest to possible creep. If the stories that Mieville had told him were true, then the poor woman had enough weird fans as it was, and certainly didn't need to think that another odd and potentially dangerous stalker had been added to the mix.

Noah didn't want to be that guy.

He had a few contacts in Brazil, from his freelancing days years ago when every single potential bit of industry gossip across the world had to be nurtured in case one of them might prove his big break. All of whom he hadn't spoken to in ages before he called and mailed them in the days prior to his flight out of Heathrow to drum up leads. He had received back a handful of mail server bounce-backs advising him of who had now moved on, and several replies that contained a warm greeting followed by an apology informing him that unfortunately they had not heard anything about a kiwi violinist performing in South America in any kind of show, either with an orchestra or something of a risqué or more private nature. They promised to let him know if any clues popped up.

There was a knock at the door, shaking Noah out of the fog of depression that had begun to settle over him.

He wasn't expecting anyone.

It was Dana.

She had changed out of the black stretch leggings and crop-sleeved button-up shirt that she had been wearing earlier into a pair of trainers, cut-off khaki-coloured shorts that reached only halfway down her thighs, and a white masculine-style muscle vest that featured a colourful print of a gorilla wearing sunglasses and was several sizes to large for her, with a low neck and baggy arm holes that made it clear she was not wearing a bra underneath, though since she was totally flat chested Noah supposed she didn't need one. A stone-wash denim backpack straight out of the eighties hung from one of her narrow shoulders, and in place of the silver bangles that he had noticed decorating her wrist at the breakfast table she now wore a Swatch watch with neon-yellow straps. On her left shoulder she had a badly drawn tattoo of a 3-D skull that sported a bright-red Mohawk. Noah longed to ask her if she had picked it up on a drunken night out that she now regretted, but he thought better of it.

In one hand she held a bottle of water, and in the other a Panama City fold-out map and guidebook.

'Hi,' she said. 'I'm not one for sitting by the pool. I have to be back by five to head down to Next with the guys, but before then thought I might take a Canal tour.'

Noah's expression must have been impassive.

'I know these organised things are cheesy,' she said, 'but if you want to see anything other than the inside of clubs and hotel rooms in this job, you soon learn to cram in what you can. I thought you might like to come along. Follow the band and see the world, and all that.'

He considered her invitation, and thought of how it would look; him, a decent-looking but obviously older man, wandering around town with Dana, a young punk whose slight frame and taste in fashion meant she could pass for a teenager. Not that he spent too much of his time worrying about what others thought of him, but Rhonda's emails wouldn't answer themselves and he knew that he was likely to have a few late nights and hangovers to recover from in the coming week that would make business matters even harder to get on with on another day. The older he got, the lower his tolerance for partying. He was grateful that the sound and lighting guys were older too, so at least he wouldn't feel like the band's chaperone hanging out with them all.

'That's kind of you, but I'm here on a sort of working holiday. More work than holiday, I'm afraid.' He opened the door wider and gestured his head towards the swivel chair by the French doors, his coffee pot and laptop resting nearby; a makeshift office.

Her eyes widened when she caught sight of the expanse of his view and de luxe-room mod cons.

'Wow,' she said. 'It's nice up here.'

'Yeah,' he said. 'Executive perks, I guess.'

'I guess I'll see you later then,' she said. 'If you get through your work and have any time tomorrow, I'm planning on an early start, to hike the Quetzal Trail. It's a day trip, by Volcán Barú. To see the rainforest. Not too taxing,' she added hastily, 'if you approach it from the right direction.'

Evidently Dana didn't think too much of his fitness levels.

'Don't you ever sleep?' he asked her. Noah might be able to sneak off early, but he doubted that the crew would be back before 3 a.m., by the time The Handsomes finished their last set and they packed up all the equipment.

She laughed, revealing a row of perfectly straight white teeth and the silver flash of a tongue piercing.

'Rarely,' she told him. 'You get used to it.'

She gave him an awkward wave goodbye, and turned to

go. Noah briefly observed her as she slung her other arm through her backpack's strap and walked towards the elevator.

Had she been hitting on him? Out of genuine attraction, or an attempt to further her band's career by sleeping with a label executive?

He didn't think so, unless he had totally lost his touch for sensing physical chemistry. She had seemed somewhat lonely, and eager for company. Noah recalled from his days of touring with musicians how you quickly grew bored of the people you spent every day with.

Noah took the seat next to her when they sat down for dinner. The concierge had suggested La Trona, a striking location with good food and a price list that wouldn't break the tour's careful budget, in the Bella Vista district. The building had formerly been the home of a famous Pollera dancer, Ramona Lefevre, he was advised.

'So how was the Canal?' he asked her.

'Industrial,' she said. 'But its history is truly fascinating.'

Over a main course of Sriracha mayonnaise with crab cakes, Noah found himself asking Dana if during the short course of her career on the road thus far she had ever stumbled across a red-haired musician by the name of Summer Zahova. As the words tripped out of his mouth, he blamed his indiscretion on the Chilean wine that the waiter kept liberally refilling his glass with, and the gaudy, wall-sized

Renaissance-style oil painting across the room that featured a giant bare-breasted woman and did nothing to take his mind off the opposite sex.

'The violinist, you mean?' she replied, after pausing for a moment, visibly mining her memories. Dana had ordered the spicy tuna and pistachio-crusted salmon and Noah deliberated over whether or not they were yet on good enough terms for him to ask her if he could try a mouthful.

'Yes,' he said, surprised she knew who he meant. 'That's her.'

'I actually saw her play live once, in a bar in Camden. Years ago, before she was even famous. I was only about sixteen at the time. Sneaking into whatever club or pub I could manage, you know how it was, all fun and games, not that anyone ever asked for ID.'

Noah nodded agreeably, although it had been many years since he had last needed ID.

'The only reason I remember,' she continued, 'is because she played with a band called Groucho Nights and I had a terrible crush on the lead singer at the time, Chris. He was my motivation for getting into music and ending up doing what I'm doing now. Just another groupie, I guess.' She threw him a dry smile. 'I know they played with the Holy Criminals for a bit, who are on your label, I think?'

'You've done your homework,' he told her.

'All part of my job.'

'Did you ever see Summer live again?'

'No. I know she went on to much bigger things. I was dead jealous of her then, since I guessed she was probably sleeping with the Groucho Nights frontman who I fancied, so her show posters always jumped out at me whenever I saw them, but I haven't seen her play since. I've never been much into classical music, reminds me too much about school days and homework somehow. Dance and electronica is my style these days, not just for work.'

Noah nodded.

'Why do you ask? Planning on signing her?'

'Hoping to,' he said. 'The label could do with a change, an infusion of new blood.'

He quickly changed the subject, asking her further details about the Canal tour and her leisure plans for the rest of the trip. She visibly didn't sense anything odd about his line of questioning, and continued talking animatedly about her love of travel and South America in particular. Listening to her was a darn sight more interesting than his earlier discussion with Pete and Jerry in the hotel lobby about the ins and outs of lighting gear, which Noah had only the vaguest clue about and no interest in, but her train of conversation highlighted exactly how vast Brazil was and how slim his chances were of stumbling across Summer without any further clue to her location. That was if she was in Brazil as Viggo had guessed, and hadn't stretched her wings to other parts of the continent. Or somewhere else in the world by now.

After the meal, they ignored the calls from the eager cab drivers lined up outside the restaurant and walked the short distance to Veneto Casino where the shimmering gold lights and potted palm trees reminded Noah of Las Vegas and encouraged him to squander a regrettable sum of US dollars at the blackjack table before returning to the hotel in the early hours of the morning.

He shared a taxi back with Stéphane and Alain, who sensibly wanted to get at least some sleep before the sun came up so that they could perform at their best the following night. The two deejays were both stone-cold sober and didn't seem to be under the influence of drugs either, Noah noted. He hadn't even seen either of them light a cigarette, and both had ordered the vegetarian courses at dinner. Noah was confident that neither he nor Dana would have to deal with the fall-out from any rock-star hotel room high jinks, televisions being thrown out of cabana windows into the nearby pool or other such nonsense.

Jet-lag and alcohol took over the moment that his head hit the pillow, and Noah was asleep without even resorting to a nightcap.

There was a break in the duo's touring schedule. Following two nights of gigging in Rio, it had been planned for the band and its staff to stay on for a week before moving on, an opportunity to relax, beach surf and recharge their batteries. Noah had been quite unsuccessful through his local music contacts in finding any trace of Summer or her passage through the Brazilian city. In the wake of either Alain or Stéphane or the nightbirds in their technical support crew, he had roamed through the city's clubs and bars, befriending barmen and other DJs and peppering them with questions, but no one knew anything about an English-speaking red-haired woman answering to Summer's description, let alone one who played the violin. The task was thankless, and Noah was convinced the whole enterprise was turning into a total waste of time.

The phone by the bed rang, strident, intrusive. He opened his eyes, feeling as if he had only drifted off an instant earlier, still hungry for the relief of sleep. He'd forgotten to pull the hotel room curtains when he returned from the bar trawl, but it was still a pale shade of dark outside. His free hand hunted for the handset.

'Hey!'

He recognised Alain's ever enthusiastic voice.

'Morning . . .' Noah mumbled.

'Want to join us? We're going up to Recife in an hour. We've a private jet. Some crazy rich guy's offering us a private birthday gig and wants to fly us there. Just one night. Want to come?'

'Where the fuck is Recife?'

'Up the coast in the north-east of the country. Everyone says it's a nice place. The Venice of Brazil, according to Google. Mucho rivers, bridges, islands.'

'I'm not sure.' He felt bone weary, tired of the whole affair.

'It'll be fun. We're only taking a small crew. All paid for. The two of us, Pete, Jerry and Dana, to run the sound and lights. The club we're hired to play is all kitted out, apparently. Top-of-the-range stuff. We've kept a seat on the plane for you. Just overnight. We should be back in Rio by noon tomorrow.'

'Hmm . . .'

'Come on. It'll cheer you up, Noah. You've been in a shitty mood since we landed.'

Noah packed an overnight bag.

A local businessman with more money than sense had hired one of the major hotspots, a nightclub called Nox, for his much-younger trophy wife's birthday celebrations. Getting hold of The Handsomes to deejay was the cherry on the cake, and knowing how tough a negotiator their manager was, Noah was certain they hadn't come cheap – in addition to the private jet that had brought them all here and the size of the rooms put at their disposal in the palatial hotel they were being put up at on the river front.

The club was crowded and the light show that

accompanied Alain and Stéphane's set was designed for a larger venue. Noah had the beginnings of a headache and retreated to the open bar on the riverside beach, where he was soon joined by other refugees from the party raging within. He knew the set The Handsomes would be playing inside out by now, and no one would notice his absence.

The scent of the nearby ocean was different here from in Rio, a subtle divergence in the marine atmosphere and its attendant balance of spices and rotting floral notes. It carried with it a remote hint of intoxication, of unknown danger.

'Enjoying the fresh air?'

Noah was nursing his beer, the cool glass of the bottle in the palm of his hand. It was Jerry, the sound guy. Once the equipment had been properly set up, he was free to roam. Dana had apparently hooked up with one of the local venue staff and probably wouldn't be joining them.

'Yes.'

'One of the barmen told me where the action is in town. A bunch of us are heading out. Fancy tagging along?'

It was either that or hanging around for hours, which Noah didn't feel like doing, so he agreed to go exploring the Recife night life more out of boredom than actual curiosity.

The evening soon became a blur of cabs, sharply lit strips bedecked by gaudy bar lights and palm trees, rooms full of shadows and repetitive background disco muzak, and the increasingly drunken behaviour of his companions, until the impromptu group Noah had joined reached the stage where it was made up of completely different folk than those he had set off with. He'd rapidly switched over to mineral water or apple juice, but even so felt as if he was already beginning to hear distinct words in Portuguese behind the shifting swarm of sounds following him from place to place.

The next club they hit saw them scrutinised by heavy-set doormen before they were allowed in. The long corridor was a haven of darkness, leading to a dance floor where shadows moved to the sound of music he couldn't recognise. A glitterball hung forlornly from the low ceiling but was unlit.

The melody playing was slow, melancholy, at times dissonant, the barely there silhouettes of the dancers on the floor ahead of him a murky low-key symphony of movements.

The others in his improvised group continued past, seeking out the bar which was in an adjoining room. Noah noticed a wooden bench against the far wall and sat himself down, captivated by the slow-motion swirl of the shadow-dancers. His eyes were not yet accustomed to the low light.

He was wondering what the hell he was doing here. He should have remained in London. He resolved to fly back and not follow the tour beyond Rio. Put this mistake behind him. A strong sense of lassitude began weighing on his shoulders, months of built-up adrenaline draining away and leaving a huge void.

The fog cloaking the activities on the dance floor began to clear, the shapes moving to the rhythm becoming sharper in the improving gloom, fuzzy silhouettes like puppets on strings more often than not out of sync with the classic seventies disco tunes being pumped from the speakers. Noah felt out of his element.

He dug a finger into the pocket of his jeans and pulled out a pack of mints and dropped a couple into his mouth, awakening his dry throat.

Lithe, tanned girls twirling in one corner, their colourful floral-print dresses shimmering in place, while their burly, equally tanned male partners guided them with hands on hips, creeping as close to the girls' respective arses as they were allowed. Nearer to the centre of the dance floor, an older couple, a mixture of spasmodic jerks and smoother patterns. Teenagers, would-be hipsters, locals and tourists. It was Recife, it was Brazil, but it could have been anywhere. Europe, the American Midwest. Just an old-fashioned club aimed at tourists, with old-fashioned music which meant nothing to him, didn't speak to his heart by a long distance.

The metronomic beat of the ersatz Giorgio Moroder tune came to a close. There was a brief aeon of silence and the next piece of music came streaming through. Which Noah recognised. David Bowie's *Cat People* song 'Putting Out Fire'. A song that always gave him the shivers.

Unsettled by the break in the beat, half of the dancers present retreated to the shadows, heading out of the room towards the bar or lingering aimlessly until a further frenetic track might be unleashed by the unseen deejay. Those who remained stood in place, shimmying quietly, adapting to the both sensuous and ominous tone of the song.

Further back, Noah caught a glimpse of movement that seemed to move along to the music with clockwork precision, espousing its shape with uncanny exactitude and drop-dead eroticism. He squinted.

Undulating like a horizontal wave. Not just one dancer, nor a couple. All in black and initially awkward to make out as they blended into the matt darkness of the background.

Three.

Two men, both in tight black T-shirts and jeans. Tall. Solidly built. Mountains of muscles. Brown arms rippling, spider-like, around their prey. Between them, the shape of a smaller woman, dwarfed by their mass, sandwiched betwixt their bodies, pressed, squeezed. The three-headed shivering beast sliding effortlessly across the dull shine of the dance floor, oblivious to the other dancers, onlookers, the world surrounding them, lost in the deep meanders of the music, dancing themselves into a trance.

Her face mostly shielded from his gaze by the consuming embrace of the men's powerful arms, the woman was also clad in black. It looked like a simple dress that ended high above her knees and also bared her shoulders. She wore flat ballet pumps and her tan was paler than her cohorts', betraying a more delicate shade of original skin. She appeared unsteady on her feet, supported by the men, guided by them, abdicating all control to her partners.

Noah kept on watching them intently, drawn to the hieratic quality of their movements and the animal sensuality emanating from their grouping.

One of the men's hands lingered on the woman's buttocks in a sign of ownership which she did not protest.

Her face was buried into the chest of the other dancer, his bulk enveloping her, concealing her face and hair, just a sliver of the soft cushion of her cheeks peering out from the composition that Noah kept on peering at with fascination. Flushed?

She swayed to the *Cat People* song.

The world retreated. Noah imagined he was in a cocoon, isolated from the club and its activities, miraculously linked to the vibrant bubble in which the three dancers he was contemplating were similarly held captive.

The trio, turning slowly in place, like a figurine in an antique music box.

The man's roving hand now alighted from her backside

and stealthily slid downwards, catching hold of the edge of the dress and pulled it upwards, revealing an expanse of thigh, and then dived up towards her crotch. She didn't appear to be wearing any underwear, or maybe just had on a wisp-thin thong, as the straight line bisecting her arse was briefly glimpsed before the dark material of her dress dropped down again, the man's hand still busy underneath its defenceless barrier. All the while, her other partner had grabbed her hair at the back of her neck and was now pulling her face towards his lips, mashing himself against her, his tongue no doubt now breaching the hill of her lips and sweeping across her mouth.

Her hair.

A blinding flash of red, as one of the dim disco lamps dotting the ceiling washed its weak light across the woman's head.

Noah felt a knot form in his stomach.

But the clarity faded as the lamp's thin cone of light moved to another corner of the floor, leaving a patch of darkness in its stead and the woman's mass of hair was again obscured from his view amid a blur of slow movement.

Noah was still glued to the bench but tempted to get up and move across the floor to get a better glimpse of the dancers. The woman. But there were too few people around and he would have stood out like a sore thumb, unveiled as too much of a voyeur as the trio's movements slowed almost

292

to a halt, and hands and mouths continued their frenzied covert activity.

Noah held his breath for a moment, feeling quite uncertain, vulnerable even.

The whispered electronic chords of the Bowie song faded into the distance, and a Daft Punk anthem took over. As other dancers rejoined the floor, the private trio had remained immobile, too busy in embrace, like a frozen statue of flesh, of bodies so close they could not be separated from each other.

The invidious sensation of dread and exhilaration washing over Noah persisted.

He was willing the dancers to part, move sideways, cease their increasingly fevered fumblings so he could see their features better, distinguish them individually. The men rapacious and predatory, cloaking the female equation of the trio in their grasp like an unresisting prey.

Was he the only one present captivated by them? The other couples on the dance floor shook to the repetitive beat and swirled around like clockwork figures, oblivious of the simmering sexual heat emanating in their midst, partly obscuring Noah's visibility. Some further tracks followed, an unrelenting succession of staccato beat box and electronic echoes. As the activity on the floor grew more animated, Noah's view was restricted further. He blinked and, suddenly, the self-absorbed trio was now standing all the way by the opposite wall, the woman's face mashed against the hard surface, the two men, towering above her, forcing themselves against her, their hands openly fingering her, her hair sweeping down to her shoulders, a mass of messy curls in flame-red shades punctured by the irregular attack of the flickering disco lights.

Noah rose.

Even if it meant embarrassing himself badly, he had to get closer, see her face.

As he did so, the burly men finally loosened their grip on the woman, stepped back and one of them, the taller, took her by the hand while his acolyte grasped her waist and they pulled her away in the opposite direction. She dragged her feet, as if unwilling to follow them, but they were stronger. Was she drunk? Fully conscious? Noah began to question what it was that he had witnessed, if the woman had consented to her captors' attentions. If he should intervene.

He dodged staggering dancers as he crossed the floor towards the departing trio who were making their way in the direction of one of the exits.

The door that they had walked through almost slammed back in his face. He turned the handle.

The alley at the back of the club was a maelstrom of darkness after the planetarium of flashing lights inside. The sounds reached him before his eyes could adjust and make anything out.

'No . . . please . . .'

Noah looked in the direction that the plaintive female voice was coming from.

The two men and the woman were standing against a pockmarked wall, towering rubbish bins and black plastic refuse bags piled up by their side. She appeared unsteady on her feet. Her short dress was pulled up to her waist, her midriff exposed. One of the men was holding her by her hair, attempting to push her down to her knees, and she was resisting. The other man was in the process of unthreading his belt.

Her knees buckled and as she resignedly lowered herself down. A flash of light from a nearby window illuminated her face before it was again drowned in the obscurity of the humid night air.

Noah's throat froze. He felt himself unable to breathe.

It was unmistakable.

The woman's face.

All the photos he had spent hours contemplating.

Summer Zahova.

It was her.

There was no doubt in his mind.

At the same time, he couldn't help himself staring at her bared middle, the pale shape of her thighs and the smooth revealed landscape of her private delta, and everything fell into place in his mind: superimposing the memory of the infamous photographs from the sauna on this new reality, matching images, body, the geometry of her curves, lines, the subtle cut of her slit . . .

He had found her.

But this was no mock porn scenario where the maiden in supposed distress would later get to her feet and assure the rolling cameras that it was all a game and how much she had enjoyed herself.

'Hey . . .' He hadn't even realised he had opened his mouth.

Both men looked round towards him, hostile, self-assured. Summer remained immobile, her eyes lowered, knees half bent, frozen in uncertain motion.

'What?'

For a moment, Noah briefly believed they were about to rush towards him and summarily beat him up on the spot for having interrupted their fun, when it occurred to him that the taller of the two men had actually responded in English. American-accented.

'Sorry, guys,' he continued. 'But I get the feeling the lady is not quite certain if this is all to her taste.'

'And what's it to you?'

Noah hadn't been in a fight since schooldays and knew he was in no shape to overcome the two brickhouse-like men facing him.

They stepped forward, leaving Summer, indifferent, where she half stood.

'Just saying . . .'

'You a friend of hers?'

'No . . .'

'She's been game from the outset,' the other man said. 'Just another cheap slut on the pull . . .'

'Maybe.' Noah was treading dangerous ground, he knew. Just one wrong word and he could well end up in a Brazilian hospital, or worse, and Summer would be left raped in this dubious alleyway.

Why wasn't she saying anything or attempting to flee while he engaged the men in conversation? Was she drugged?

Fortunately, the Americans appeared as uncertain as he as to where this confrontation might lead.

'Say,' one of them said. 'Care to join us? I'm pretty sure she won't object . . . Hasn't to anything so far . . . Not much, at any rate.' He grinned and looked back at Summer, who failed to respond. 'Maybe you have a room somewhere. We haven't a place of our own, just on shore leave . . .'

Noah was frantically trying to think on his feet.

'How much?'

The two men looked at him with surprise on their face.

'I'll pay you for her,' Noah continued. He knew how absurd it was, but he couldn't think of anything else. Maybe the allure of cash would overcome the certainty of a drunken fuck.

The American sailors turned towards each other, contemplating the possibility.

All the while, Summer looked on, silent. She'd pulled her black dress down to her thighs and was no longer as exposed. Observing them. The possible transaction.

Noah always carried a fair amount of cash. Whenever he was travelling, he always retained the currency he had been using in any particular country, though for safety's sake he kept it situated in various places over his person and had to pull a bunch of notes from a selection of pockets of both jacket and jeans as well as his wallet. Adding up his dollars, pounds and euros, he had enough to convince them to hand Summer over to him. They settled for much less than he had expected. Bills in hand and a wide smirk on their lips, the men faded down the dark corridor of the alley, leaving him with Summer.

She looked up at him, perplexed, faintly amused, he thought, as if it was not the first time she had been swapped for cash. He searched her face for some sign of upset emotion, but in that respect she was totally blank.

Noah's stomach was tied in tight knots.

'Hello, Summer,' he said to her. 'I'm Noah.'

'You know who I am?' For the first time this evening, her face was animated.

Noah looked into her eyes and was struck by that unmistakable fire and sadness burning in equal measure inside. He knew in an instant that all the anguish he had suffered in his lengthy quest for her had been worthwhile. And more.

8

Sense and Sensitivity

Who was this guy?

The departing American sailors were just pinpoints in the distance now and I stood uncertainly in the alley at the back of the club facing him, still trying to digest what had all happened.

In my brain, David Bowie was still singing that song about fire, its bittersweet melancholy call dragging me back to the dance floor where I had somehow disconnected from reality, found myself indifferent to the world, alien, both dreading the consequences and welcoming the total lack of responsibility for my actions.

I knew I had experienced those sorts of feelings before when despair had carried me to the edge and I just couldn't care any longer what was about to happen to me, and I resigned myself to the fact that I might not even emerge alive on the other side, let alone in one piece. An acceptance of oblivion as a way out, an escape. But from what?

Had this stranger just purchased me of all things? Or paid cash to stop me being used there and then by the men?

There was a sense of loss in his eyes which I couldn't understand.

'Hello, Summer,' he said to me. 'I'm Noah.'

My mind spun.

Was I no longer protected by the anonymity that Brazil had provided me with so far?

'You know who I am?' I was almost shouting.

And took a closer look at him.

It was night and the light was poor and flickering, a solitary bulb hanging across a drooping clothesline strung between the club's building and a nearby starving tree, barely illuminating the empty alley.

He was medium height and appeared to be in his late thirties, dark brown hair swept back from his forehead, thick and abundant, just a little too long for conventional respectability. His eyes were similarly dark, gazing at me with a terrible intensity, X-raying me on the spot with nervous fascination. He had sounded British but I couldn't place his accent regionally. His cheekbones were prominent and even in the surrounding shadows he clearly sported an untidy two- or three-day growth of beard, evenly darkening his features. He wore a pair of slim-fitting grey twill trousers, high-end trainers and a crumpled dark-blue short-sleeved shirt.

I searched my memory for where I might have come across him before. The Ball, or some place else?

'You're Summer Zahova, aren't you?' he said. And then as if he had guessed my thoughts. 'We haven't met before but I know who you are . . .'

It would have been creepy, had he not just saved me from a bad experience. He now gazed at me with an unsettling look both questioning and tinged with curiosity.

'I am . . .' I mumbled.

'Should we call the police?' he said. 'Or first go inside and report this to the club?'

I laughed, a distinct note of bitterness present in my voice.

'They won't care,' I told him. 'Thanks for your concern though.'

'But those guys . . .'

I shrugged. Scuffed the toe of my ballet flat on the ground. My feet were beginning to ache, from all the running, walking, and dancing I'd done that night already. At least I wasn't wearing heels.

'Really,' I said. 'I'm fine.'

'Would you like to go somewhere and sit down for a bit then? Talk? This isn't quite the right place for a conversation. Do you know anywhere?'

Was a mere conversation all he wanted from me?

I knew I couldn't return to Raoul's cousin's digs, seeing that I had ended up here after fleeing the place.

'Not really.'

'Hotel?'

'No. I was staying at a . . . friend's . . . But I . . . I can't go back there.'

'I'm at the Atlante Plaza,' Noah said. I liked his name. Sometimes a person's name fits just right with their face. This was one of those instances.

'Okay,' I said.

He glanced down at his watch. I always noticed men's watches now, as Dominik had always worn one.

'The bar stays open late, I think.'

Neither of us had realised how late it actually was and the bar was shuttered when the cab we finally flagged down dropped us off.

'Maybe the one by the rooftop pool is still operating?'

It wasn't either.

We ended up in his room.

He was checking through the mini-bar while I gave the large suite a look over. It seemed as if he hadn't been here long and wasn't planning on staying either. There was no clothing scattered around, or the sort of mess that usually clutters up hotel rooms. I couldn't even see a suitcase.

'You travel light,' I remarked.

'I'm just here for the night,' he explained. 'Flew in earlier with just a small carry-on bag, with a spare shirt and toothbrush. It's by the bed. I fly back tomorrow. Well, later today . . .'

'Where to?'

'Rio.'

'You live there?'

'No. Passing through for work. I'm from London.'

I nodded.

'What about you? Any plans to return to London?'

'I'm not sure. Some days I think about it. I've been in Rio for some time, now. But not sure how much longer. It's complicated . . .'

He passed over the small San Pellegrino bottle he had picked from the fridge and pulled the tab on the can of Cola he had taken for himself. He had picked up a bar of chocolate too, tore open the wrapper and handed a row of dark squares to me. We sat in facing armchairs sipping our drinks and nibbling.

I was finally beginning to relax, the flow of adrenaline running through my veins settling down, an impression of peace returning. There was no sense of menace about Noah, although I was well aware he was deliberately being very careful in trying to make me feel at ease here, in his presence.

'Care to tell me what happened at the club?'

'Just me being foolish, I suppose. I have a habit of getting myself into trouble.'

'From where I was standing, it didn't look like you were the one causing the trouble.'

'I'm gratified that you think that. But believe me, if we were in a court of law, yours would be the minority opinion.'

'Did you know the men well? Friends of yours?'

'No.' I think I blushed a little. 'Only met them earlier. I was feeling lost, maybe drank too much; I should have been more cautious.' I didn't tell him about Raoul and the situation that I had run from with only a small amount of cash and no immediate way to get home. At the time, the American sailors had seemed like a possible way out of an impossible bind, a safer bet than sleeping at the bus terminal.

I expected him to say something but he remained silent, his dark brown eyes scrutinising me and a thousand thoughts no doubt swirling inside his head.

He was visibly a man who knew the art of patience.

As Dominik had.

I sort of wished he would question me further, drag out my secrets, the layers of craving and shame that made me who I am, but he held back. Neither judging me nor blaming me.

'Where do you know me from?' I finally asked.

'Your music.'

'Oh.'

I had almost reached the point where I had forgotten my previous life on stage.

Had he been a face in an audience? At a legit classical gig, or a more dubious one, involving Antony or the Ball?

'I work for a record company. I came across one of your CDs and just loved it. Been stalking you ever since . . .' He smiled faintly. 'Musically speaking, that is.'

The mineral water, straight from the hotel room fridge, was freezing cold, momentarily numbing my throat.

'I even contacted Susan, your agent, to find out if you had any plans to come back to the recording or performing scene,' he added.

I felt a sense of relief wash over me.

'What a coincidence we should meet, then,' I said. 'In Brazil of all places.'

He hesitated.

'It isn't,' he replied. 'I knew you were somewhere around these parts. That's why I came.'

I mulled over his revelation. It didn't make sense.

'But until a few days ago I'd never set foot in Recife,' I protested. 'I've been based in Rio. How could you know to find me here?'

'I didn't,' Noah confessed. 'That's where the coincidence lies . . .'

Should I believe him?

The night was deepening and my lassitude along with it.

I was stranded in Recife with a man I didn't know what to make of. It was either that or risking a return to Raoul's. That was if I even had enough spare cash on me for the cab ride. I shuddered to think what kind of punishment Raoul might see fit to dole out in response to my running from him earlier.

'Can I sleep here?' I asked Noah.

'Of course. You take the bedroom; I'll make myself comfortable. He indicated the couch.

'I'll be okay here,' I said. 'You have the bed. It'll be morning soon anyway.'

He insisted.

All I had on was my G-string and the small black dress I had escaped from Raoul with. I kept both on and slid between the covers. The bed had not been slept in since Noah's arrival. The sheets still smelt faintly of starch and a green herbal note from whatever detergent they had been washed in. Part of me had hoped I would catch his scent, get a distant whiff of whatever masculine note defined him. Help me in my attempt to isolate what puzzled me about him.

I closed my eyes.

Listened to the almost imperceptible sounds filtering through the door from the lounge where he had remained.

He was restless, I could feel. Like me, unable to sleep properly.

I stayed in bed a couple of hours, tossing and turning, finding it impossible to switch off, a strong undercurrent of anxiety animating my heart and body. I rose, tiptoed to the en suite bathroom and wetted my eyes and face, in a vain attempt to wash away the last twenty-four hours. The door to the other room was not fully closed and I silently pushed it open. I cautiously made my way across, the deep pile of the carpet under my bare feet, towards the sofa where his shape was outlined beneath a formless blanket in the darkness.

Stood and looked down at him.

His eyes were open.

Watching me. Intently.

'You can't sleep either.'

It wasn't a question, just a statement of fact.

'No,' I said.

He didn't rise. The angle of his head against the edge of the sofa looked awkward and I felt a wave of guilt at having kept him away from the bed, seeing I hadn't even managed to get a minute's sleep in it myself.

'You should take the bed,' I suggested.

'What about you?' he asked.

'I don't know. Maybe I'll sit a bit here instead, gather my thoughts. Or I might leave. I don't want to impose on you.'

His eyes peered into mine.

'What is wrong, Summer?'

'Nothing. I'm fine now.'

'I don't mean now, I mean in general. Why did you come to Brazil, give up on everything?'

'It's a long story.'

'I'm willing to listen, you know.'

'It's just me. I'm a bit of a mess. Things are complex.'

Damn, why did he keep on looking at me like that? I was not ready for confession. I wasn't that sort of girl. Or was I? The sort that needs a kind and understanding shoulder to cry on, to exorcise the ghosts, the demons, the madness. Say something, Noah . . .

But he remained silent, didn't even appear to blink, as if expecting me to open up.

Which I knew I wouldn't. If only out of pride.

'I really should go.'

'Where?'

'Back to Rio eventually, I suppose.' Maybe he could loan me the money for the bus.

'I'm due to fly there around midday,' Noah pointed out. 'The guys I came up to Recife with . . . The Handsomes . . . you might have heard of them . . . They have a private plane ready to roll. There are a few available seats. You'd be most welcome . . .'

I felt torn.

He finally moved, threw his blanket aside. Like me, he hadn't undressed.

'Stay,' he asked.

The way he said it sprung like an arrow straight through my heart. As if that single word concealed a million others and his life depended on it. I couldn't remember another time when a man's voice had affected me so much.

'Okay,' I agreed.

The hint of a smile animated his features, one of terrible relief.

Silence dug in.

An aeon of silence that could have lasted well into the morning still hours away unless one of us moved or spoke first.

Noah gazed at me.

I looked back at him, allowing a sense of peace to wrap its arms around me, cauterise me.

'Come to bed, then,' I finally said. Put my hand out to him, and we walked to the bedroom.

I unzipped my dress and slipped out of it. He expressed no surprise at my wearing so little underneath; after all, he had no doubt known so from our encounter in the alley behind the club. I nodded to him and he undressed likewise, until we both stood lit by a pale silver shimmer from the sky outside the window and a crescent of faraway moon.

We pulled the sheets apart and slid in. His nose buried

itself in my hair. I could feel his warm breath against my ears.

I was surprised by how hot his body was as I squeezed against him, skin to skin, grinding my arse against his middle.

The animal hardness of his cock buried itself against the small of my back.

Aware of his arousal, I instinctively twisted my arm and extended it towards his midriff to take him in my hand, but before I could reach his penis, his own hand gently blocked me and pushed it back.

'We don't have to,' he said.

'Are you sure?'

'Yes, let's just sleep,' he whispered.

And then we did. Drifted away with childlike ease and naturalness.

No one batted an eyelid when Noah and I arrived by taxi at the small private airfield ten miles or so from the city to catch the private Lear plane hired to return The Handsomes and their small crew to the capital. Nor did anyone appear to recognise me, with the possible exception of the band's almost painfully thin young assistant, a spikey-haired blonde wearing a pair of black-studded ankle boots and a lime-green T-shirt dress that dwarfed her small frame, and who stared at me with a bemused look of curiosity on her face but didn't say a word, either to introduce herself to

310

me or point out that she knew who I was. The flight to Rio mostly took place in silence, the majority of the passengers dozing after a long night of deejaying and boozing. Noah and I sat together, but the proximity of so many others prevented any sort of proper conversation. We agreed to meet for lunch the following day. It seemed the group's tour was moving on down the coast to other South American countries, but Noah would not be accompanying them further and he informed me that he would only remain in Rio for a couple of days more before he was needed back in London.

There were three cars waiting for us at the small private Rio airfield. The other passengers and Noah were all staying in high-end hotels by the beach and it was arranged for me to be dropped off last in Leblon where my apartment was situated. Again, we were unable to talk much beyond banalities on the drive into Copacabana through Rio's teeming streets.

When I had woken up in his hotel room in Recife, the sheet had partly slipped away from my body and I was sprawled indecently across my side of the bed, my breasts fully uncovered, to find Noah with eyes wide open gazing at me, observing me and my body.

I could see the undisguised lust in his eyes and chose not to pull the sheet back to cover me, and allowed him a full view of my torso. It was too late to be shy, after all.

311

But it was already mid-morning, it appeared, and there was little time for anything before we had to rush to catch the flight to Rio which had been arranged. When he had again suggested I join him on it, I quickly accepted. It would have been foolish not to. Ever since, so many things had hung unsaid in the air between us. Room service had sent up a jug of freshly squeezed orange juice, some bagels with cream cheese spread and a few hardboiled eggs which we each feasted on separately while the other used the bathroom to clean up.

As my key turned in the lock, I experienced a strong sense of deflation, pushed the door open and trod into the familiar surroundings of the small flat where I had now been living for several months and which I'd been hoping to vacate as soon as I could find a decent property in the area, thanks to the proceeds from the Bailly.

Dust hung in the air, and the spartan furnishings of the room and my rare belongings scattered across it sang of loneliness.

I quickly slipped out of my knickers and black dress. I had been living in it for almost two days and it felt repulsive and dirty. I kicked it across the floor in a quiet rage, wondering whether any conceivable form of dry cleaning could possibly erase the memories now imprinted along its material. I didn't think I would ever wear it again. I needed a shower badly.

The building's water supply was patchy and the luke-warm stream from the showerhead was weak and halting. I scrubbed myself down as best I could.

I heard my mobile phone ring. Ignored it. By the door when entering I'd noticed a small pile of mail and not even glanced at the envelopes. All I wanted right now was to be alone. Unreachable.

The persistent ringtone of the phone was soon smothered by the sound of the water falling over my shoulders and hair. Eventually, whoever was calling me gave up.

I washed my sins away, until my skin felt raw.

By the time I left the comfort of the shower cubicle, the phone had rung several more times and I noticed a more recent envelope by the door, unstamped, handwritten.

It was from Joao.

He or one of his drivers had dropped me off here at the apartment block several times, but I'd never told him the actual number that I lived at. Obviously he had had me followed, right up to my door.

I checked my phone. Every single call had been from Raoul. It then occurred to me that I had not given Noah my number, nor had he asked for it. As if he implicitly trusted me to make an appearance at tomorrow's lunch date, or had no plans to chase me if I didn't show.

I neither opened Joao's note nor picked up Raoul's messages.

I browsed through the rest of the mail. Mostly property information sent by estate agents.

I was wandering naked through the small apartment and found myself facing the tall rectangular mirror by my dressing table, gazing at the reflected image of my own body.

The prolonged sojourn under the shower had not only cleaned me but had also sharpened my perception. I could see every single imperfection. The minor blemishes and nigh-invisible scars, an inappropriately placed mole, a dimple that annoyed me, the unequal distribution of my curves, the sometimes sickly pallor of my skin now held at bay by a tenuous Brazilian tan. What did men see in me? What was the flaw that attracted them, the wrong ones more often than not? Was I a map that could be so easily deciphered?

I badly needed to catch up on sleep. The time shared in the hotel bed with Noah in Recife had done anything but recharge my batteries.

The steady whoosh of the ceiling fan lullabied me away until my eyes closed and darkness welcomed me into a late afternoon of dreams, inaccurate memories, mild nightmares that made no sense whatsoever, only to awaken around three in the morning, unable to find solace again and emerging from the bed to an empty breakfast fridge, as physically and emotionally void as I had been at the beginning. Time flew by.

I felt I looked a fright as I walked through the lobby and followed the signs to the restaurant. Wearing anything that Joao had gifted me seemed wrong, and neither could I face the outfits that I had worn on dates with Raoul and which had inevitably ended up crumpled on the bedroom floor after we had quickly fallen into bed with each other. That had left me with few options, and in the end I'd opted for a pair of plain black stretch leggings that I usually kept for lazing around the house or for comfort when travelling, ballet flats and a short-sleeved blue silk top I'd forgotten I ever brought with me and which I hoped looked as if it was supposed to be crinkled and not as though it hadn't been pressed.

Noah, on the other hand, had taken the opportunity to shave and wore an immaculate white shirt with his jeans and appeared indecently refreshed when the hostess pointed me to his table.

'Hi,' I said, sliding down in the tall-backed black leather chair opposite him.

The waitress handed us a large laminated menu.

'Hi,' he replied.

The tension was palpable, as bread and a small plate of olives and sundry nibbles were delivered to our table.

I studied the fancy menu. Hotel fare at hotel prices.

'I'll have what you have,' I said, unwilling to peruse the menu in any detail. As he ordered, I observed him. I loved his dark hair, was even instinctively tempted to thread my fingers through it. His nose was not straight; had probably been broken once and clumsily reset. The heavily air-conditioned setting of the hotel's dining area carried no hint of deodorant or fragrance fading in from his direction, not even a faint whiff of soap, as if his personal scent was strictly neutral.

It was a particularly hot and sultry day and there were few diners in the restaurant. Most people had headed for the beaches.

Noah was nervous.

He was a fan of my violin playing and was hoping he could convince me to return to Europe and begin recording again. He was offering me an open-ended contract and happy to discuss terms with Susan if I proved willing. When I did not respond immediately, he added that although it would not be ideal – a shadow passed across his eyes as if this would be a thing of personal regret – it could even be set up so I could record here in Brazil if unwilling to travel back to London. Having completed his proposal, he looked away as if caught in a lie, or at any rate an important omission.

'I'm flattered, but couldn't you have made the offer directly to Susan? Coming all the way here was a bit much, no?'

'I happened to be accompanying The Handsomes on tour,' he said. 'They are also on my label.' There was no mention of the circumstances that had brought us both together in Recife.

Or the chemistry that undeniably flowed between the two of us.

He wanted to say more, I could sense it.

I wanted to say more.

But fear got the better of us.

As if we both knew that if we pursued that indefinable attraction, connection or however you wished to describe it, it could lead us down dangerous paths that we were at this stage reluctant to journey through. I was in no doubt that I was not the only one of us who carried personal baggage.

He quizzed me about the reasons I had given up music, both performing and recording, after I'd mentioned in passing that I didn't even have an instrument available to me here in Rio.

'It's a long story.'

The look he gave me was full of understanding, but it was also knowing, as if he was aware of some of the true reasons, or after seeing me in the clutches of the American sailors in Recife he could properly put one and one together. But he did not pursue the matter.

'There is no urgency,' he stated. 'Think about it. Take your time.'

He had to return to London very soon but he made me

promise I would carefully consider his proposal. We exchanged addresses and numbers this time, although I was unsure how long I might remain in Leblon in view of my plans to acquire my own place.

'Is there something or someone holding you back here?' he enquired, almost reluctantly.

I took my time to answer.

'No.'

I could sense the relief rush through his veins as I uttered the word, an incomparable weight visibly being lifted from his shoulders, betraying the undisguised attraction he nurtured towards me.

Part of me was ready, right there and then, to say Yes Yes Yes and damn the sweets selection and the coffee and scream out to the waitress to just put the bill on his room and run towards the block of elevators and go fuck him as if the world was coming to an end, tearing his clothes off on the ascent before we even reached his room, even if we were not alone in the lift.

But I knew I had unfinished business in Rio.

I had to be certain I was doing the right thing.

We parted at the end of the meal. He shook my hand and I was stung by his body heat. I pecked him on both cheeks.

Promises were made.

★   ★   ★

The last time I had seen Raoul was when I had stormed out of his cousin's room in Recife, the possessive gaze of the party of men looming over me. It felt as if centuries had passed since. He'd left countless messages. Initially expressing worry about my whereabouts, then being angry at my disappearance, then lacing his words with threats and later more conciliatory, informing me he was back in Rio and had my rucksack and the few clothes I had travelled with, asking when would I come and retrieve them.

I was unsure whether I was in a fit state to confront him again.

Then there was that note from Joao enquiring about my whereabouts and absence, ostensibly sweet, but pushed under the door of the apartment that I'd never given him the exact address of. I called him, and also spoke to Astrid first. He'd guessed that our brief fling had come to a natural end. Blamed it on himself, he stated, and the difference in our ages and cultural backgrounds. For politeness' sake and unwilling to get into a pointless argument I tried to reassure him partly that it wasn't his fault without truly knowing how sincere I sounded. We quickly ran out of conversation.

Astrid and I met up on the beach, at the exact same spot we had first come across each other. She knew from her father that I would no longer be coming to their home to help her out and was sad about it, but she was also excited to let me know that while I had been away she had found herself a boyfriend, it appeared. He played the guitar and his name was Edison. She had also succeeded in try-outs for her school's beach volleyball team. Sports were more of a natural talent and passion for her than playing music had ever been. I was happy for her, in the knowledge that she would soon forget me, as quickly as we had become friends. 'You will always be in my heart,' she informed me sweetly. She didn't even ask me what my own plans were. The insouciance of youth. Had I ever been that flighty, I wondered? Or had I been born wanton and darkly serious?

It had been ages since I had even given any thought to my own childhood in New Zealand. A world away, in distance and time.

When I returned to my small apartment, there was a bouquet of flowers and an accompanying gigantic box of chocolates waiting for me on the doorstep, with a note from Noah. He was flying back to London in two days' time. All the card pinned to the delivery said was 'Please'. How would florists survive without the lust of men? At least I knew he had my address because I had legitimately provided him with it.

The following day, I resolved to conclude matters with Raoul.

'How did you get back to Rio?' he asked me. 'I waited and waited for you, but you never returned or picked up your phone. I was hoping I'd see you at the airport, but you didn't turn up.'

'Someone gave me a lift in a car,' I lied.

'Bullshit,' Raoul stated. 'Nobody in their right mind would do that. It's an almost forty-hour drive at best . . .'

I nodded.

'Who?'

'No one you know.'

'Who?' he asked again, anger rising.

'I'm not going to tell you.' I had determined to stand my ground.

'You talked someone into it, didn't you? So how did you repay him, because I'm sure it was a man. With your body, no doubt. You're just a foreign whore, Summer. That's all you are.'

'And you're an arsehole,' I replied.

He huffed and puffed. But I had arranged for us to meet in a public place, in the food court of a large mall, where his temptation for violence would be tempered by reality and the buzz of the swarming crowds.

'You love being treated badly. Used. It's the way you are, the way your body responds, you know. You wear it like a sign over your head.' His expression was insufferably smug.

I knew it and he knew it but I refused to give him the satisfaction of an answer.

'Have you got my things?' I asked.

He threw the blue rucksack at me and stormed off. I waited a while to ensure that he was definitely not lurking around in wait for me and then made my way home.

He had shredded every single piece of underwear and the couple of skirts and tops I had left behind in the bag.

The next day it rained heavily, the beaches concealed from sight behind an impenetrable curtain of greyness. It reminded me of London somehow, despite its tropical aspects and sullen weight of humid heat.

I woke uncharacteristically early, went online and booked a one-way ticket on the first available flight to London with a vacant seat. Restless, I began already packing the few things I wished to take with me and made the necessary arrangements to transfer my few remaining funds to my UK bank account, where I had prudently left the proceeds of the Bailly. I would not be acquiring a property in Brazil after all. Neither would I be staying in town much longer. There was nothing in Rio for me anymore. My flight departed in just a few days from now.

By the time I had filled my suitcase and set aside a bag of things to discard or give to a charity shop – not that I knew where to find one here – it was barely 10 a.m. Packing had not been an arduous task. The bikinis I had worn almost daily for the past months were worn out, and I had little need for flimsy beach dresses in London, even on the hottest summer days in the capital. All of the things that Joao had given me that I had stored here – the handful of pairs of earrings, a silver chain with a single tear-shaped pearl pendant, a pair of strappy gold Manolo Blahnik heeled sandals that I detested – I set aside to have couriered back to him.

My eyes kept straying across to the flowers that Noah had sent to me, and then to my phone. I refreshed the display as I had every few minutes for the last hour, checking the time. Again. The minutes were passing interminably slowly. I had not yet had a bite to eat for breakfast. Wasn't hungry; my stomach a churning mess of butterflies.

Noah was flying out today, but I wasn't sure when. The early afternoon, I thought he had mentioned.

Was I hoping that he would ring, or that he wouldn't?

Somehow I knew that the bouquet had been his last move. The ball was now in my court and he was waiting to see what I would do with it.

I slipped on a pair of sandals and grabbed my purse from where it hung on my bedroom doorknob. Rain was pelting down, thundering against the apartment block and visible in great grey sheets through the kitchen window. There was a brolly hanging in the laundry room that I had never used; I took it. I didn't own any kind of rain jacket here. Not even a cardigan.

The umbrella sheltered my top half from the rain but could not prevent the horizontal spray from soaking my bare legs, feet and the bottom few inches of the red cotton T-shirt dress that I was wearing.

Cabs circled the streets at all hours in Leblon and they seemed to double in number at the first sight of bad weather, to whisk tourists who weren't prepared for a tropical storm back to the dry comfort of their hotel lobbies. I flagged one almost immediately and hopped in.

'The Windsor Atlantica, please. Hurry, if you can.'

The cab driver nodded and spun the vehicle sharply, taking a series of side streets that I hoped constituted a short cut. He kept glancing at me curiously in the rear view mirror. Probably wondering what I was doing heading to a hotel before noon, without any baggage. I knew the average Brazilian woman wouldn't be seen dead walking into five-star accommodation in what I was wearing, with hair unkempt and only the barest trace of make-up. All the women in Rio looked as though they fell out of bed dressed up to the nines. In fact, nearly all of the men were equally pristine, sometimes more so.

Along the Copacabana boardwalk, water pelted and swirled over the black and white tiles, giving a melancholy cast to the typically sanguine surrounds of the famous beach, today bereft of all but the hardiest locals insistent on taking their daily exercise, jogging along the roadside in soggy shorts with expressions of grim determination spread over their damp faces. The clouds overhead teemed with life and movement, slashes of black and grey battling against stark white streaks in a murky purple sky, a perfect witch's cauldron of bubbling vapour that made me feel as though the world was closing in, the heavens shutting down over the earth leaving me trapped in the middle and about to be swept away on the storm and wake up in Kansas.

I nearly asked the driver to turn around and take me back to my apartment. But somewhere in among the pounding of my blood in my ears and the pervading fear that raged inside me – fear of what? of moving forward? of turning back? – was an even stronger instinct which led me to Noah like a woman trapped on a sinking ship aims for a lighthouse. Was I running to him, or running from everything else? I didn't know yet.

We hit every red light and crawled behind every slow-moving vehicle all the way along the Avenida Atlantic. Each time a taxi passed travelling in the opposite direction, my heart fell through the floor, and I tried to catch a glimpse through the back window, convinced it must be Noah on his way to the airport, but none of the passengers were visible. All I saw was the flash of an anonymous shoulder or a profile in shadow.

When we finally pulled to a halt, I handed over a bunch of real and didn't even query the exaggerated fare or wait for my change.

'Keep it,' I yelled, as the driver waved the notes I had overpaid back at me.

The building was monstrous, a giant tinted glass and concrete brick of a thing, a few blocks down from the Belmond Palace, where I had once spent an evening with Joao and his business partners. There were fewer hotels at this end of the beach, and the Windsor towered over all of them.

I stood stock still for a moment, looking up, and swallowed hard. Water still hurtled from the sky and I realised too late that I had left my wet umbrella folded up on the cab's floor. The driver had already pulled away. I rushed into the lobby, escaping the rain, but couldn't move fast enough to avoid further dampening my hair and dress. The hem was soaking and glued to my thighs. I pulled at it in a futile attempt to encourage the fabric to hang correctly and succeeded only in producing a loud squelching sound, the suck of sodden-wet material peeling away from skin.

All eyes were on me as I strode to the reception desk, trailing wet footprints across the terracotta-coloured, patterned marble tiles.

I recalled Noah's room number from the receipt slip for our meal, which the waitress had left unfolded on our table momentarily before Noah had whisked it up, ignored my offer to split the bill and asked her to charge it direct to him. But the door number alone was no good to me. I knew that

I needed a security card to swipe through the elevator keypad and give me access to the upper floors.

The desk attendant, a young, handsome Brazilian man with a full head of dark hair, dimpled chin and smart suit jacket slightly too wide for his narrow shoulders, was all politeness despite my bedraggled state. His nametag read 'Victor'.

'Hi,' I said, plastering a broad fake smile across my face and keeping my arms pinned to my sides so he wouldn't see my hands shaking, 'I'm in room 2505, and I went out for a walk this morning and forgot my key. And my umbrella. Is there any way you could let me in? I think my partner is out enjoying breakfast, he's not answering the phone.'

'Sure,' Victor replied. 'What was the surname?'

'Ahh . . .' my mind drew a blank. 'Zahova. Summer Zahova. But the room isn't booked under my name,' I stalled.

He smiled at me sympathetically.

'I'll need to call through,' he said. 'For security. We need to verify all hotel guests and visitors, I'm sure you understand.'

'Yes, of course,' I replied. 'Hopefully he's back now.'

Damn. I hadn't wanted to explain my arrival to Noah. Just turn up at his door and think about what the hell I was there for when he opened it, but there was no backing out now, Victor had the telephone in his hand.

'Yes, Mr Ballard. Your partner is at reception. Yes, Miss Zahova. She's forgotten her room key. May we issue her another one?'

I breathed a sigh of relief. At least I knew now that he hadn't left yet.

Victor hung up the phone. Swiped a key card's magnetic strip through an electronic reader and handed it over to me.

'Here you go ma'am. I presume you know your way?'

I felt a flush of red sweep up my cheeks. Had he winked at me?

'Yes, yes,' I assured him, and then walked swiftly to the elevators, hoping that the same lift that I had taken to the restaurant on the fourth floor where we had met for lunch would carry me all the way to his accommodation on the twenty-fifth floor.

That was providing that I had remembered correctly where Noah was situated. Things could prove awkward if I'd mixed the door number up and walked in on the wrong man.

The journey upward took an age. The doors swooped open at half a dozen floors, collecting and depositing hotel guests.

A middle-aged couple with matching bobbed sandy-blond hair who held hands and might have been mature honeymooners.

A short, elderly Japanese man who wore an elegant silver

suit jacket with a thin white tie and a broad smile and was partnered up with a brunette woman who displayed the graceful poise and firm figure of a dancer, balanced on precarious hot-pink heels. She was at least a foot taller than he was and a quarter of his age, and when they departed on the fifteenth floor, he guided her forward with his hand on the small of her back. A freckle the size and colour of a misshapen copper coin marked the skin below his middle knuckle. The soles of her shoes were red.

At the level marked 'pool and gym', a woman who was likely in her fifties and carried a thick white towel under her arm stepped in and stood in front of me. She was dressed only in a Baywatch-red swimsuit with a low-cut back. Her broad arse was pale and dimpled, and deep blue veins trailed down the backs of her legs.

I wondered what kind of sex they each enjoyed. Did the Japanese man lie back in the bathtub while his younger lover balanced with her feet on the sides and peed on him? Did the woman in the red swimsuit like to masturbate to violent pornography? Did the bobbed-blond fuck silently, or did he whisper terrible things into her ear as he loomed over her in the missionary position? The secrets people held.

When the lift was finally empty and I only had two more floors to travel, I turned and peered in the mirrored panels and attempted to fix my hair which was still half damp and plastered to my skull, with a layer of frizz sitting

329

like a halo over it. My face was unnaturally pale and my eyes looked bright and dilated, as though I had just woken from an unusually vivid dream. Goose pimples had broken out on my arms and hands from the hotel's air-conditioning further cooling my already icy skin. Water continued to drip down my legs. The cold had hardened my nipples. I was not wearing a bra. Or underwear, for that matter, since I had left my apartment wearing just the dress I'd thrown on for comfort's sake while I worked on my packing.

Random thoughts and memories began to crowd into my mind. The feeling of the smooth slate tiles beneath my feet as I woke in the early hours of the morning at Joao's villa and paced his corridors, bored, lonely and restless. The rush of cool water on my skin on the nights that I dived naked and almost silent into his pool, wondering if any of his servants were awake and observing me. Raoul's heavy body over mine, pinning me down, and the fight in my mind as my internal sense of right, wrong and self-preservation battled with the desires of my wanton flesh, that part of me that wanted him even though I knew that he would hurt me – wanted him *because* he would hurt me.

Odd sensory recollections came hurtling back to me too. Memories that still lurked in my subconscious and crept out to surprise me at the most unwelcome times.

Like the burst of juices in my mouth as I bit into the

apple that I had bought the morning after I had been released from the Kentish Town sauna. The faces of the men who had used me that night remained a blur, but I would never forget the sharp taste of that piece of fruit, or the way my knees had ached as I was bent over on the tiles, or the clouds of steam that had clogged my throat.

Back in time further, to Dominik. The waxy sensation of the lipstick he had painted onto my nipples. His extraordinary tonal range as he moved through a series of moods in the course of our sex games; from good-humoured and seductive to commanding to insistent and severe. A streak of sunlight against silver; the flash of his Tag Heuer catching the glare from the window in his study as he typed, and I interrupted him to offer a coffee refill, or tempt him into taking a break to indulge in a daytime fantasy. The smell of his old books that had lined shelves of the house we shared on the hill in Hampstead.

So many other things about him were fading now. As if the Dominik that I had stored in my mind was becoming more ghost-like as the years passed. I could no longer recall the precise tilt of his features, or the exact shade of his hair, without looking at a photograph. Yet fragments from our time together that I would have preferred to forget still stayed with me. The everlasting silence as the Lana Del Rey record, that had been playing before I found him, ended. The red blinking light from his CD player. The particular shade of green that the uniformed paramedics who had collected his still-warm body wore.

I remembered the smell of the rubbish bags in the alleyway where the two American sailors had dragged me. The sweet scent of decaying fruit skins, the bitterness of rotten meat.

The look on Noah's face when he had found me there. Surprise and pleasure overwhelming any sense of fear, dread or disgust that another might have felt. And the sound of his voice when he called my name.

The elevator doors opened and I hurried up the hall, checking the digits on each room as I went, my soggy shoes sinking into the thick carpet with each step.

I reached 2505.

Lifted my newly acquired room card to swipe it through the security device by the handle, and then knocked instead.

The door opened. He was waiting for me.

Noah, standing there, in a pair of jeans that were too loose on his waist and a black T-shirt advertising a band I hadn't heard of.

'Summer?' he said.

I burst into tears.

He pulled me into his arms.

'Shh,' he said, 'it's okay.'

He smelled of hotel shampoo, a fresh scent tinged with

pine and cloves. His T-shirt was crisp and clean and freshly pressed as though it had just been returned by the laundry service.

I pulled away from him.

'I'm making you wet,' I said.

'I don't give a fuck,' he replied, and embraced me again.

He ran his thumb over my cheek and brushed a tear from my face.

Bent his head down, and kissed me.

His lips pressed against mine. The pressure firm, but gentle.

'Your flight,' I whispered, when our mouths broke away from each other.

'I don't give a fuck about that either.'

His smile was wide and tinged with warmth and humour. He glanced at the clock alongside the bed.

'It's not until two,' he said. 'We have an hour. Not nearly long enough.'

He kissed me again, this time so forcefully that the weight of his body pushed me backwards and up against the wall. Our tongues met. He tasted of fresh coffee and mouthwash. His hands landed on my hips and he held me tightly, his thumbs drawing a line beneath the ridge of my pelvis.

'Christ, Summer,' he said, stepping back. 'Have you been standing outside in the rain?'

I laughed. And grasped the hem of my dress, preparing to

pull it over my head but he prevented me, placing his palms on my forearms.

'No,' he said. 'Let me.'

Noah took my hand and led me to the bed. It was monstrous; an island of a thing that dominated the room, with a padded headboard covered in an oyster-coloured quilted fabric and a matching coverlet. To the left of the bed, opposite the door, the thick drapes were pulled back and revealed a view of the ocean, still murky after the recent downpour. The heavens had turned from grey to purple, the colour of an old bruise. Waves crashed against each other, stirring up a deep blue soup, white lines of froth billowing across the surface of the water halfway out to sea.

'I love the weather here,' I murmured. 'So alive.'

He had the air-conditioning switched off and there was no sound in the room besides the hush of our breathing and the whirr of the fan that turned slowly over the bed, washing a draught over my skin.

A fluffy bathrobe, in the same muted silvery tone that permeated the rest of the décor, lay across the coverlet. He sat down next to it and I stood in front of him. He looked up at me, my hands still in his, palms turned up. His skin was so warm the contrast between his temperature and mine made me shiver.

The three-day shadow that had lined his jaw and the top of his mouth when we first met had thickened and now formed the beginnings of a beard. He hadn't shaved for long enough that his stubble was soft to the touch, not prickly. His eyes were as dark as the sky outside had been, during the thick of the storm. He had a deep tan, much darker than mine although he hadn't spent anywhere near as much time beneath a South American sun as I had. His brows were the same deep chocolate brown as the rest of his hair, and animated when he spoke. He lit up when he smiled.

Noah wore his emotions across his face. Watching him was a joy, his moods visibly changing in the turn of his lips, the arch of an eyebrow, the sharp intelligence in his eyes, the intensity of his gaze. Age lines had worn gentle furrows across his forehead, but he didn't have that resigned, tired look of someone who has spent too long behind a computer. He could have passed for one of the whip-trim surfers who rose before the crowds did to dance across the breakers on Copacabana beach. A man of passions who saw the wisdom in indulging them.

The pads of his fingers traced a map along the skin of my inner wrist up to my elbow and down again.

He let go of my hands, took hold of the bottom of my dress and pulled it up. I wriggled, helping him shift the sodden fabric over my head.

Noah's eyes ranged over my body. There was no judgement in his scrutiny, only lust, curiosity and kindness. He seemed to be drinking me in, as if he intended to memorise all of my perfections and flaws and replay them again later.

He reached forward and brushed over my skin, the flat of his hand, knuckles, and sometimes his fingertips caressing my breasts, my torso and down to my slit where he grazed across my lips with a feather-light touch before moving away again.

'Oh,' I said, softly.

'You're cold.'

He picked up the robe that lay next to him and wrapped it around my shoulders.

'Now,' he said. 'Tell me why you were crying.'

How I wanted him to keep touching me. When he pulled his hand away, I felt bereft, as if my anchor had been cut and dropped into the sea.

'Lie down,' he told me, and tugged my wrist, motioning that I should join him on the bed.

Noah scooted backwards so his whole body was supported by the mattress and propped his head up onto his elbow. I did the same, and we lay facing each other, a few inches' gap separating our bodies.

He lifted the soft towelling fabric that had slipped over my waist to cover my legs as if he were pulling back a curtain. Continued to explore the surface map of my body. My nipples had stiffened again. This time, the room temperature was not to blame.

I searched for the right words to answer his question. How could I possibly explain all the events of a lifetime, try to tell him who I was and what secrets I carried inside me? As if he were my confessor and I his supplicant. Even if we'd had all night, I could not have helped him understand. How could he, when I so often didn't even understand myself?

'I've done so many things,' I answered him. 'Terrible things.'

'And so many terrible things have been done to you.'

His touch skittered across my jaw. He rested his index finger for a moment on my lower lip.

'Things that I wanted,' I insisted.

'I don't think that's always been true.'

'I suppose that depends on how you look at it. If you could see into my mind . . . my thoughts. The things that I dream about.'

I was convinced that if he really knew me, he would want me no longer.

'We all have our shadows, Summer,' he said. 'I'll show you mine, if you show me yours.' He smiled at his own joke. 'Besides, your shadows are what I want. I want all of you. The dark parts as well as the light. One day, you can tell me everything. Lay bare whatever it is that you think is so terrible.'

I closed my eyes. Tried to blank out the whirring of my

thoughts and concentrate on the pressure of his fingertips that now lingered on the curve of my buttocks. My body shifted on the mattress as he moved, redistributing his weight. His hair tickled my breasts. One of his hands moved down to my upper thigh, pushed it down onto the bed, rolling me onto my back. The firm denim of his jeans and crisp cotton of his T-shirt scraped over my torso as he crawled down my body. His lips followed the pattern of his retreat, pressing a path down to my groin.

I realised what he was doing and froze. Threaded my hands through his hair and tugged, gently pulling him back up towards me.

'I want to see you,' he said, 'all of you.'

He took hold of my other leg and pushed it down. I was spread open, my inner thighs trapped in the vice of his grip.

Dominik had done this to me, I recalled. In the dim shadow of his study, he had examined me beneath the fierce glare of his desk lamp.

At first, Noah didn't touch me. Just looked.

'You're beautiful,' he said.

I felt utterly bare. There was a transgression inherent in the act, the most intimate parts of me on display to him in the broad light of day, without the presence of any distraction at all in the form of music, alcohol, or the usual swift fumblings of lust. This was slow and deliberate.

He lowered his head to my delta and began to lick.

338

'Oh, god,' I breathed.

The flick of his tongue turned the desire that was slowly simmering inside me into a full tide of lust. My muscles tightened and I squirmed as he lapped at my clitoris. He pinned my legs down in response, ignoring my attempts to escape the sensitivity that the firm point of his tongue had aroused.

His explorations continued for an age. I was writhing, grabbing his head, the cushions, the coverlet, anything to try to quell the orgasm that I teetered on the brink of before it tore me apart.

I wanted to feel him.

He was on his haunches, bent over me. I wriggled my foot beneath him, brushing against his cock through his jeans. He was hard, and large. I shifted, trying to turn myself around so that I could unbuckle his trousers and take him into my mouth.

He lifted his head. Clamped his hands even tighter around my thighs.

'Don't move.'

I lay still, at least as still as I could, as he continued his explorations.

'I want you inside me,' I told him.

Had I brought any condoms? I tried to remember whether I still had some in my purse, still zipped into the pocket from the trip to Recife with Raoul. Would Noah have any nearby? I felt a piercing, and totally illogical, I knew, burst of jealousy, imagining him with another woman, and then an even more irrational burst of arousal at the image of him fucking someone else. It wasn't a fantasy that I was by any means certain I wanted to occur in real life, but right then the idea of it made my pulse quicken and my skin heat. I could feel a red-hot flush travelling from my chest up to my face, which had no doubt turned a blotched shade of pink.

'I don't care,' he said.

'Please,' I breathed.

'I like it when you beg. But the answer is still no. I want to taste you. And feel you come in my mouth.'

He drove his tongue through the valley of my slit, circled my nub, used the flat of his teeth to apply just the right degree of pressure to my folds. A low hum of pleasure emitted from his throat. Noah was groaning.

We were interrupted by the shrill ring of his room's phone. He ignored it. An automatic message played, and then the sound of the concierge. 'Mr Ballard, your taxi has arrived. Your driver is waiting at reception.'

Noah was immovable.

I tugged his hair.

'Noah, your flight.'

He slipped two fingers inside me.

'Ohhh, fuck . . .'

I drove my hips onto his hand.

He collected my juices.

Inserted a lubricated finger up my arse.

'Oh, fuck,' I cried out: 'I'm coming, Noah, I'm coming . . .' It felt right to call his name, to hear the word pass my lips.

Noah shuddered, his desire obvious in every taut muscle in his body as he continued to grip my legs and hold me in place. I bucked and writhed against him and he kept lapping, and lapping.

'Jesus Christ.'

I clutched the pillows, certain that I might tear through the silky fabric of the cases with my nails.

I came again. A smaller climax, the second time.

The spasms in my limbs gradually subsided. I lay there, spent. Utterly relaxed.

He lifted himself up, balancing his body over mine, and kissed me. His lips and tongue tasted of me, a sweet sea-salt tang.

'Summer Zahova,' he murmured, 'I think I love you.'

'I think I love you,' I replied.

I wasn't sure if we were joking.

'But I have to go,' he continued.

'Christ, yes!' I exclaimed. 'Your cab . . .'

He wiped his face on the corner of the robe. Smiled at me broadly. Then flew off the bed and grabbed his case that was sitting open on the floor, already packed. He pulled out a white-collared dress shirt and threw it over to me. 'So you have something dry to wear home,' he said. 'Room check-out is at two, so you can stay until then. Have a shower if you want to.'

He zipped his baggage shut and snapped the lock. A laptop bag was resting by the door, he slung it over his shoulder, then felt around in the side pocket and pulled out his passport, checking it was there.

I followed him to the door.

'You have my number in London?' he asked.

I nodded.

'Call me. When you're ready.'

He lifted my chin. Kissed me again.

And left.

9

Skin on Skin

Summer had been back in London for a fortnight before she finally decided to meet Noah again. She'd arrived at Heathrow in the early hours of a bleak, shadowy morning and called Lauralynn as she was waiting for her luggage to emerge on the carousel. Somehow Lauralynn had seemed anything but surprised to hear from her and greeted her with undisguised affection, immediately insisting that she take a cab to Belsize Park forthwith. Viggo was away recording in the south of France, where Lauralynn was due to join him in under forty-eight hours, but Summer was welcome to remain in their house for as long as she wished. Summer's own flat had been rented out while she was away travelling and the tenants had a three-month notice period so the choice was either finding a hotel or staying with acquaintances. She'd suggested the former but Lauralynn stood her ground, and it had actually been something of a relief to Summer who felt terribly uneasy at the prospect of residing yet again in a lonely hotel room, with all the consequences it might entail, knowing her character and past inclinations.

The spare bedroom on the top floor of the house became hers again. It hadn't changed much, bed piled high with cushions in every colour of the rainbow, high windows looking out over a panorama of red-tiled roofs and the taller branches of the sycamore trees outside fluttering in the directionless currents of the breeze.

Lauralynn was all ears, eager for news and more from Summer's sojourn in South America and was as ever anything but judgemental, listening with rapt attention and an indulgent look of amusement on her face. If anyone knew the quirks of Summer's nature by now it was Lauralynn, but she had never been one to take advantage of this knowledge, was a true friend and, when the occasion was right, an accomplished accomplice. The effects of the red-eye flight had soon taken a hold of Summer's body and energy and she had retreated upstairs for an early first night back in London. Lauralynn's embrace had been warm, almost motherly, and there was no hint of a suggestion that Summer come to her bed, as had sometimes happened on previous occasions.

'I have to start packing soon anyway,' Lauralynn had said. 'There are quite a few things Viggo has asked me to fetch, in addition to my own, and I'm going to have to do some foraging in his drawers to locate them all.'

Summer had carried herself up the stairs and, once in the bedroom, realised she had left her suitcase down by the front door. She stripped naked and, too lazy to take a shower and clean away the journey between continents, crawled under the duvet and was asleep in a wink.

Left to her own devices all too rapidly after Lauralynn was picked up by a minicab and driven to Heathrow for her flight to Nice, Summer had decided to renew her some-times complicated relationship with London before making contact with anyone else, even Susan and Noah. To seek peace in the exploration of a city that was as contradictory as she was, by turns barbaric and civilised, both elements sometimes operating together on the same street corner.

She walked down the hill, past Chalk Farm and the cir-cular mass of the Roundhouse to Camden Town where the weekend markets were in full flow, weaving through the crowds, navigating her way between the dozens of languages she could hear spoken, spotting a familiar New Zealand accent there and then a word or two of Portuguese until all the passing sounds merged into a swarm of buzzing voices, a soothing swirl of memories past. The smells of food from the Lock reached towards her and drew her in that direction past the hundreds of stalls selling heavy metal and sundry tasteless T-shirts, clothes she wouldn't be seen dead in, leather goods, bric-a-brac, amber and handcrafted jewellery and would-be antiques. As she emerged into the open area by the canal, she was amazed by how the place had changed since she had been here last, the food tents having spread and invaded the whole quayside, conflicting smells and scents lullabying her senses and causing her mouth to water out of control. And realise she was quite hungry. What to eat: Spanish, Creole, crêpes, rosti, Mexican, Eastern European kabanos, from steaming vats of African stews or boards laden with cheeses, fruit, dark Ethiopian stew or beef, turkey, chicken, pork, vegetarian or even kangaroo-meat burgers? Had her stomach been the right size, she would have gladly sampled everything.

Unable to even finish all the small portions of food she had then treated herself to and binned the abundant leftovers by the tube station where hordes rushed from the maw of the Undergound, she strolled south and reached Regent's Park and wandered beyond the Zoo and found herself in wide-open green spaces where families were picnicking and children in all sizes ran amok, rushing along the grass, hanging from the squared-off playground-area climbing frames, racing on scooters down the paths. She wasn't normally a great fan of small kids, but for the first time her heart warmed to their hustle and bustle and supreme indifference to the world's realities.

Then the chill in the air registered with her. Such a

contrast with Rio. She had goose bumps spreading across her skin. Had not dressed properly, just a thin summer blouse, denim skirt, ballet flats and not even a pair of tights. She turned back towards Haverstock Hill, and Viggo and Lauralynn's house.

The following day, still intent on continuing her awakened love affair with London, she walked the Thames embankment on the south side, following the muddy river from Waterloo to the Globe, beyond the concrete palaces of art past the Oxo Tower, the brutalistic bulk of Tate Modern and the parade of bridges that punctuated the journey, watching the barges and tourist embarkations drag themselves along the water, the eternal London skyline from the arch of Charing Cross Station to St Paul's carved against the grey sky on the other bank. Then she turned inland and reached the warrens of Southwark, and yet again the food choices of Borough Market where the fruit, meat, olive oil and cheese stalls were just about to pack up for the day and the crowds were thinning. On this occasion she had dressed more warmly, a padded parka and leggings partly shielding her from the autumn chill.

St Katharine Docks, where she had first met Dominik, a twist in her stomach.

Hoxton Square and its assembly of bars, once a starting point for drunken madness and the inevitable meaningless pick-ups she had so often indulged in.

The small market by the Cut near Waterloo.

The Isle of Dogs where she had spent time with Antony.

Portobello Road, Whitechapel in the tracks of Jack the Ripper, Wilton's music hall where she had always dreamed of playing in the days when she and the violin had still been an item, the fragrant curry corridor of Brick Lane.

The hidden enclave of Bleeding Heart Yard.

She had walked endlessly, without destination or intention until her calves had hurt, drinking the city back in, soaking herself in its smells and unmistakable atmosphere, until it felt she truly belonged here again.

The one place she carefully avoided was Hampstead Heath.

Finally, one morning, Summer knew she was ready.

She rang Noah.

'I'm back in London.'

'Great.'

'Let's meet.'

Noah had been hoping against hope ever since his return from Rio. Would she or would she not be in touch again?

He'd thrown himself into his work in a transparent attempt to banish Summer from his mind, but the task had proven impossible. The reality of her held him captive, now knowing the reality of how she looked in motion and no longer just a fixed image in a photograph, the way she sometimes avoided his eyes, the way she felt, smelled and tasted, walked and spoke, both open and closed, available and distant. It was a deadly combination and affected him badly.

She was more than he had expected.

At the same time, she was not what he had expected.

She was just . . . Summer.

They met for drinks at the Groucho. He felt shy in her presence, like a schoolboy on his first date. She appeared uncertain, as if a stranger in a strange land, a newcomer to London and the characteristic hustle and bustle of Soho, still in the process of reacquainting herself with the rhythms of the city's life after her prolonged South American sojourn.

'Anywhere special you'd like to eat?' Noah asked her.

'Somewhere simple.'

The cab dropped them on the edges of Clerkenwell.

'Are we here to talk business?' Summer enquired.

'If you wish.'

'You don't sound as keen as you did in Rio . . .'

'I am.'

He wanted to tell her that he would prefer they forget business and she let him taste her again, wallow in her juices right then and there at the table and damn what the other diners thought, but something stopped him. Fear? An unwillingness to appear overly keen and drive her away? A wall had appeared between them again, as if that morning in his hotel room had never happened. He waited for her to speak, to give him some clue to her feelings.

'I must be honest. I don't think I'm quite ready to pick up my violin yet.'

'That's fine by me. I want you to take your time. Only reach a decision when you're absolutely ready.'

'Good.'

There was a ghost of gentleness in his smile. He looked down at his menu and chose the Shrimp Burger and thick-cut fries. Summer opted for an unusual salad with a mix of ingredients that Noah felt did not go together, from feta cheese to pomegranate seeds, charred bacon pieces and pine nuts. They stuck to mineral water.

'So what are we going to talk about?' Summer said.

Noah held her gaze.

'You.'

Later, the bill settled and the restaurant almost empty, all the office workers with their laptops now returned to their nearby lairs, the conversation still felt unfinished. They had talked about Rio, her past concert tours, the studios where she had recorded her albums, Paris, New Orleans, Amsterdam, Berlin, the places they both knew well, occasional coincidences that littered their parallel trajectories, New Zealand, even Viggo and Lauralynn.

The remaining staff were willing them to leave.

'Are you returning to your office?' she asked him.

'I'm not sure. What are your plans?'

'I have none.'

There were no taxis cruising the area and they had to make a detour towards the Barbican Centre and Goswell Road where it might prove easier to catch some transport.

An alley. Northburgh Street.

Cobblestones and grey brick walls. Old warehouses converted into lofts and offices harbouring hi-tech start-ups with windows through which passers-by could peer and peruse open-plan spaces with white desks and naked walls scattered with cork boards and screens.

So neat and unlike the Recife back alleyway where she had first set eyes on Noah.

'Wait.'

The tone in Noah's voice was sharp and peremptory. He wanted to both dominate and please her, but still hadn't found his footing, the practical expression of her tastes and his desires.

Summer slowed down and came to a halt. She was right in the middle of the narrow road. She turned to Noah.

Even though he was of medium height, he seemed taller in the failing light of the afternoon.

She found herself staring up at him.

He leaned over and kissed her, holding her tight against him. She did not resist.

As she tasted his lips again at last, Summer wondered

what had taken him so long. The fear of combining business and pleasure? Or just fear?

They say the first time is never the best.

This time they both knew they were doing the right thing.

Instantly, Noah had her against the wall of his entrance hall, the door barely closed behind them, breathless from frantically kissing and caressing her while they haltingly walked the short length from the sidewalk to his flat, ascended the few steps to his front door, exploring each other's bodies like a pair of inexperienced teenagers. They were both panting, on edge. Switched on. Neither could have cared less who saw them.

He slammed the door shut behind them and pushed her hard against the blank wall. His hand still beneath her tight pencil skirt, pulling roughly on the elastic waistband of her lace thong, brutally dragging it down until it was held pooled between her ankles, barely maintained in place by the barrier of her shoes. Her sex now unprotected, hot and yearning, his hand swept across her smooth cunt, every fleeting contact against the silk of her skin exhilarating. As was her unabashed greed, the way that she lustfully surrendered to him.

His lips again rushed to kiss hers, his breath staccato, his heart pumping wildly in his chest, a shapeless knot forming in his stomach as he realised she really was now in his arms, no longer an obsession, an enigma, a distant fever dream. Their time together in Rio hadn't seemed real, the circumstances so removed from ordinary life. This felt hyper-real, as if they had been allowed to turn back the clock and experience their first time together over again.

With his free hand Noah quickly pulled her skirt up to her waist, baring her bottom half. She hadn't been wearing stockings or tights. He pressed against her, pinning her to the unwavering wall.

'Unzip me,' he said.

Summer, though lost in the kiss, heard his summons and inserted her hand between the closeness of their bodies and searched for the zip.

His penis was hard as rock already. She pulled it from his clothing and led it to her opening where it jutted against her mons, just a finger's breadth away from sliding straight into her, unprotected. She had wrapped her hands around his neck and was trailing her nails through his hair, gripping his locks between her fingers. Her lips brushed his throat, the line of his jaw; she pressed her cheek against his.

His cock edged closer to her opening and the rise and fall of her chest quickened. Her exhalations becoming more frantic with each millimetre that he bridged until they were almost joined. Her pupils dilated, every inhalation a gasp.

The strength of her desire multiplied Noah's until his

cock felt larger and harder than it had ever been before. He was overwhelmed by a brief moment of panic; he was not strong enough to withstand this. The hunger radiating from her. Her palpable need for him, so strong that she had relinquished all authority over her own body and almost collapsed in his arms.

Noah felt he was going to explode, to ejaculate all over her satin-smooth slit. She had shaved in preparation for their meeting, and the knowledge excited him. Ironically, so had the light covering of fine stubble that she had not removed before she arrived unannounced at his hotel room in Rio, as if her need then to see him had been so strong she had forgotten about any usual grooming routine that she might go through before a first date. Not that Noah gave a damn whether she was freshly shaved or not.

If he entered her now, he wouldn't last for more than ten seconds. But the thought – oh the thought of breaching her in one hard thrust and filling her with his seed filled him with violent, raging urgency. It was wrong – fucking without a condom – and he knew that she knew it, and he knew that the potential danger excited her further. As if she trusted him with her safety no matter what the circumstances. Noah wished he were certain what her line was, what rivers of desire and degradation he would have to cross before she would let him go no further. He wondered if she had a line at all.

The notion that there was nothing that Summer would not allow Noah to do to her, if he wanted it, caused a flood of emotions to sweep over him in waves that ranged from fear to lust to love to tenderness and threatened to overwhelm him before he worked out what it was that he wanted to do to her at all.

Summer longed for Noah to enter her more than anything else in the world. She ached. Every inch of her body throbbed with a desperate need to be filled. To be filled by Noah.

Part of her wished that he would just take her, use her; fuck her right now against this wall. Turn her face away from him and bend her over and grab her breasts in his hands and slide his cock straight inside her – her cunt, her arse, she didn't care which.

But she knew that he wouldn't.

She was right.

Noah groaned, a desperate animal's plea for release.

He dropped to his knees. The soft satin of his cock's head bumped against her as he fell. A bead of pre-come had pearled at the end of his prick and smeared a wet line down the inside of her thigh.

Summer bent her head down to look at him. She couldn't see his face, just the unruly mop of his curls level with her delta. He gripped her legs and she grabbed fistfuls of his hair. There was no need for her to hold him against her. Noah could not have buried his tongue any more forcefully inside her. She felt as though he was consuming her, trying to breach any gap that still remained between them by drowning in her most intimate parts. His hands kneaded her buttocks, spread her cheeks apart, his fingers traced the valley of her slit to her opening and pressed inside her.

Noah wanted to make her lose control of herself entirely, to feel her juices spray over his mouth and chin and face and hair. He was certain that Summer, given the right stimulation, would gush. He wanted to learn how to excite and tease her like nobody else ever had, to stimulate her in ways that she did not even know were possible, to give her stronger orgasms than she could give herself. He delved inside her with the firm tips of his fingers, searched for the rough, coin-sized pad of her g-spot.

He looked up at her, past the flat of her torso, the soft curve of her waist and breasts and her throat and the sharp line of her chin. She had her eyes closed now, and was leaning her head backwards slightly. He could not see the expression on her face, his view was blocked by other parts of her body that he could have happily stared at for an age.

Is this what she wanted? For him to please her, or to hurt her? Were they one and the same, to Summer? To him? Noah wished that he could make more sense of the language of their shared desires, find some way to navigate through the complex web of want that had made captives of them both.

Summer clung to his thick locks with one hand, her grip shifting frantically between loose and tight as she feared that she would hurt him, and then lost control of herself and tugged with all the clawing strength that she possessed. She couldn't help herself. She clutched at the wall behind her, snatched at thin air, hoped like hell that he would stop, she couldn't take it anymore, prayed that he would never stop, that he would carry on exploring her with his tongue forever. And his fingers . . . oh god, his fingers.

'Oh fuck, Noah . . . fuck . . . fuck!'

She loved to say his name. Two syllables that perfectly expressed everything that she felt about him in their intonation alone, like a magic spell.

Noah was doing things to her that Summer had never experienced before. Not quite like this.

Guilt twisted inside her. A momentary flash of Dominik in her mind – it was him, wasn't it, who made her feel this way? She shouldn't, couldn't compare them. Knew that if he could, Dominik would give his blessing. Another stab of her conscience; Summer ought to be pleasuring Noah, he had been licking her for so long now. No matter how skilled her explorations of his cock, she would never be able to stimulate in him the same responses that he was stimulating in her.

Why was her mind wandering . . .

And then another firm lap against her clit, and all of her buzzing thoughts and guilt and shame and worry washed away and there was nothing but her and Noah, making love by his front door.

Her orgasm began to build. It started as a blooming warmth that radiated through her from her core to her extremities, then grew to a violent, tearing flow, a tidal wave of sensations that surged from her cunt to her mind and out through her fingertips as she jerked and writhed against his mouth and he held her and ignored the ache in his jaw and the bucking of her body that threatened to dislodge her from his grasp. Summer caught hold of that feeling and rode it, the dizziness, the spasms, the oh so fleeting sense of pure, unadulterated life and pleasure.

She came into his mouth. Not in a gush, not yet, but in a glorious wet mess that drenched his beard and dripped from his chin.

His fingers clenched tighter on her thighs. A rush of satisfaction coursed through him. His cock was still hard.

He couldn't help noticing how much she glowed. As if the orgasm had allowed her access into another dimension, a world she had lost, where her inner light reigned supreme.

His heart tightened, unexpectedly moved by the way she had experienced her pleasure. Without shame or afterthought.

She leaned back against the wall, tried to prop herself up. Almost fell backwards and caught herself with one hand behind her and the other clutching his shoulder.

'Noah, your knees, your jaw . . . you must ache,' she said, laughing softly as he nearly lost his balance trying to hold her up.

He smiled at her. Helped her regain her footing and pushed himself up to standing.

'Believe me,' he replied, 'that's the last thing on my mind.' He brushed his hand over his face.

Summer stumbled, her mind still not back in total control of her body. He held her hand. Led her. They walked up the stairs to the bedroom.

They had still not had sex.

The first time, the night slowed, ground almost to a halt as Noah lifted his body over hers, naked except for the thin sheath that covered his cock, that he wished like hell was not a necessary precaution, craving as he did for a total lack of barriers between them, skin and flesh. She groaned as he entered her. Her cunt so slick that lubricant was not necessary. They were in the much-maligned missionary position, their bodies close, skin on skin as he rode her until he came and she grabbed his thighs to pull him deeper into her, held onto his back, tangled her fingers through his hair, brought his mouth down to hers and they kissed, and kissed again.

Afterwards, she told him that she wished that she could feel him inside her, all of him. The smooth silk of his cock, unprotected. That she wanted to feel him explode inside her; she wanted to feel his come dripping down her thighs. She wanted him to taste his own juices inside her and then kiss them into her mouth.

'You dirty bitch,' he replied, purposefully softening his tone, rolling the words in his mouth with a smile.

'Oh,' she whispered, 'I like it when you call me that.'

'What else do you like?'

She blushed, too ashamed to tell him all the things she liked at once. The filthy things, the wrong things. The things she had been told she shouldn't like at all.

He was hard again.

She brought his fingers to rest on her inner upper arm. He could feel something there, a hard ridge of a thing just beneath the surface of her soft skin. 'An implant?' he guessed. She nodded. 'But we should still . . .' he agreed. They would be safe, until they could both be checked, and then the next time, he would fuck her raw.

'I'll make you suck all of my come, and yours, from my cock . . .' he promised her. 'I'll paint your body with it. I'll use it to lubricate your arsehole and I'll fuck you there too.'

The second time, and all the times after that, were a lazy procession of touches, embraces, revelations, endless couplings slow and fast, sweat, fluids. A concert of sighs, and deep felt emotions.

There were parts of this night that Noah thought he would never forget.

Undressing her.

Unveiling every square inch of her body like a preordained ritual, taking mental photographs at regular intervals to fix the moment in his brain, capturing memories that might have to last a lifetime, fodder for his feelings and joys and regrets. Isolating the texture of a nipple until, up close, it resembled the ridge of a lunar crater, a microscopic recreation of rough crumbled rock and powdered earth, but surprisingly soft to the touch, a braille translation of her innate essence. The delicate angle of the valley between her breasts where pearl drops of perspiration gathered like the bed of a sweet river while her whole body shuddered under his touch.

The Escher-like layers and jewelled intricacies of her ear lobe as he lowered his lips towards her while they fucked wildly; the way it changed its shade of pink as the waves of her arousal rose, crested and faded again.

The deep distant seas at the back of her eyes as their lovemaking cut the faltering ties that still bound her to the present and he could watch her float away in that way she had of seemingly untethering herself from reality and going to some other place where he couldn't join her, where every word he spoke, every square inch of skin-to-skin contact provoked a chemical reaction hitherto unknown to science.

The sounds rising from her throat, animalistic, tender, savage, soft, loud, uncontrolled and grateful, a delicate blend of violence and joy animating her slender frame as he crushed her beneath him, almost afraid of his own rising strength but unable to restrain himself, her mere presence like a match to his ardour.

Feeling himself grow harder. And harder. Larger. And larger. Inside her mouth, lullabied by her tongue and lips. Inside her cunt, exploring her valley of heat and lust.

Groaning.

On the edge of screams.

Ascending.

Descending.

On that wonderful slope to nowhere, that inevitable destination that sex drew them towards. Naked. On the bed. Oblivious to the rest of the world. Struggling, fighting, loving as if nothing existed outside of his window.

Until the sounds became obscene, moans unrecognisable, the slap of wet skin against wet skin, groans turning to atonal music, cries becoming involuntary melodies, the pummelling of his cock in her holes drawing obscene rumblings in its animated and sudden displacement.

The uncensored beauty of sex.

The whisper of beautiful words in his ear.

A thumb drawing hieratic patterns through the invisible pale down in the small of her back.

The lingering raking of her nails against the skin of his shoulders, rousing lines of pain, torturing him sweetly to the rhythm of his own thrusts.

The way Summer ceased breathing for an instant when in the complicated geography of his movements his hands accidentally drew a path around her neck and an electric shiver ran across her, encouraging him to linger. Hold down against the delicate skin of her throat.

Feeling her, in furious mid fuck, suddenly insert a finger up his arse, instantly amplifying the wave of pleasure he was riding and almost bringing him to a rapid release until he somehow drew back from the edge and managed to delay the inevitable a little longer.

The sheets in the midst of which they scrambled growing increasingly humid, sticking to their fevered bodies.

A brief lull. Time to lie still, reflect, remain silent after their bodies and impulses had done all the talking.

Another kiss.

Tender at first, then quickly passionate and grasping.

Bodies coming together again, like magnets unable to remain apart.

Dawn outside.

A further coupling, an animalistic clash of bodies, the bed

a battlefield, sheets now crumpled across the floor, wet, stained, fragrant.

Night.

Now a slow fuck that could last until midday. Neither in any hurry, both teetering on the brink of consciousness, just fingertips, hands, mouths, genitals tired and swollen but sustaining their sated souls. His finger venturing unashamedly beyond the ring of her anus and drawing from her a squirm of delight. Licking the sweat now coating the underside of her breasts. Inside her but motionless, content to experience the feeling of peace now, his cock sensing the steady beat of her heart through the tight walls of her cunt.

Spent, unable to come again but still half hard and reluctant to withdraw from her sweet heat, Noah dozed off, vaguely aware that Summer, her legs wrapped tightly around him to accentuate the angle of his penetration, was likewise suspended between consciousness and dreams, fuck-drunk like him, exhausted and helpless.

Music.

In their dreams. At the conclusion of their journey towards each other.

Identical dreams?

Noah hoped so.

Lauralynn and Viggo were still in France, and Summer insisted on returning to their house most mornings after

Noah had to go, albeit reluctantly and physically drained, to his work at the label. He had quickly offered her to move in with him, but she was at this stage unwilling to do so. He didn't press her, still treading cautiously as he did through the quicksands of their budding relationship.

'I'm not ready, Noah. I need time on my own to think,' she pretexted.

But she was invariably there, waiting for him, every evening when he returned from the office. She kept hold of the spare key. Often had ordered takeaway food arranged to be delivered shortly after his own arrival when he invariably found the table was set. It became a welcome ritual in the first few weeks of their affair, an almost domestic routine.

'I should leave you my credit card number; you can't keep on paying for all the meals,' Noah protested.

'I can afford it.'

'But still . . .'

'Still what?'

Summer put her fingers to her lips, indicating the subject was closed, and they dug into the food. One evening Chinese, on others Indian, Italian, Thai, even vegetarian on occasion, Turkish, rustic French. Summer had quickly identified the best restaurants willing to make home deliveries in his area. On occasion she brought over bags of groceries and made seafood risotto with home-brewed stock, or flash-fried fillet steak – always cooked rare – and served it with salad or steamed vegetables and thick fries that she cut from sweet potatoes and rolled in spices.

Noah often wondered what she did during the day, but was too anxious to ask her. Right now, he still felt a sense of relief at seeing her again when he opened the door to his flat in the evening, always in fear that the bubble might have burst, the daydream shattered and his wanton princess flown in a burst of fairy smoke and Disney glitter, leaving him alone and bereft.

He also knew best not to harass her with questions about her plans. Nor her feelings. Summer's only desire appeared to be to live in a cocoon of sex and unreality right now.

Bending, leaning over to put the dirty dishes in the mouth of the dishwasher. Her hand on the back of his neck, her breath cruising across his cheek, a faint breeze of wine and sugar, her heat nearing.

Placing her carefully on all fours and spreading her.

The furnace of her wet mouth grasping his balls, her tongue darting in all forbidden directions, distilling his pleasure with every movement.

Her pliant nipples gripped between his teeth until she moaned, her eyes open question marks of unimaginable depth.

The way she insists on keeping all the lights on when they fuck.

Tongue wrapped around tongue.

Reaching that stage of intimacy where words become unnecessary or meaningless and all communication is through touch alone, or conveyed by sounds, guttural, muted, soft, endearing, rageful, primeval.

Where the mind becomes body.

Thoughts translate into pleasure.

Joy becomes sustenance.

Even though there was an untenable tension underlying their sex together, as if they were both walking a tightrope, novices still uncertain where the limits lay, tentatively pushing boundaries and barely noticing when they crossed yet another invisible borderline as they kept discovering, exploring each other, there was also a profound sense of comfort when they were not locked in fevered embraces. They felt at ease together.

At peace.

It was odd, Noah reflected, how easy it was to fall into habits so quickly with someone. Or was it a reflection of the seamless way they had connected? At weekends, they went for long walks each introducing the other to quirky parts of London the other was unfamiliar with, cautiously skirting areas which held awkward respective memories, dipping into street food and enjoying pit stops at random cafés and bars along the way.

'It feels odd,' Noah said. They were seated mid Sunday afternoon on a wooden bench facing the river by the

National Film Theatre, biting into overfilled piping-hot burrito wraps from the Wahaca van, warily trying to avoid spilling sour cream, guacamole or meat juices down onto their jeans.

'What does?'

'It's as if there are two of you . . .'

'How come? You can't be seeing double; you haven't even been drinking yet.'

'There's you and then there's the Summer I'd read about, the Summer from the book . . .'

Summer sighed.

'You've read the novel?'

'How could I not?'

'It was a long time ago now, another life,' she said.

'We all come with luggage.'

'I somehow think I carry more with me than most others,' Summer remarked. 'But then that's not news for you, is it?'

Noah told her about Bridget, and then about April.

He concluded his recollections.

'You know about Dominik,' Summer said. 'There have been others, too.'

'I realise that.'

'Too many.'

'It doesn't matter,' Noah insisted. Provided her health was not compromised – and he now knew that it hadn't been – he couldn't have given a monkey's toss if Summer had fucked half the population of London before they met. She did not seem to accept his opinion on the subject though, no matter how many times he tried to reassure her that her past history was none of his business unless she wanted to talk about it, and even then, he found that the vagaries of her sexual life and mind intrigued and aroused him. It was one of the very reasons that he had sought her out, that he found her so attractive now. Her unabashed taste for pleasure.

He remembered that brief but insistent glimpse of the sauna photos all those months back and how they had profoundly marked him. But dared not query Summer further. He wondered what she would think of him if she knew the full extent of his desires. If she suspected how her torment had aroused him. Would she want him more or less, if he revealed all of his inner secrets? He was not sure if he wanted to know the answer.

A few yards away the South Bank skateboarders rushed and ran and glided, a maelstrom of movement and agility, crowds gathered to observe and photograph them. The book-tables stallholders were packing up their stock as evening approached.

'I want you to fuck me,' Summer asked.

'Not an invitation it would be safe to turn down,' Noah remarked.

Her eyes stayed on him.

'Hard,' she continued.

'There will be cabs on Belvedere Road,' Noah said as they rose from the bench.

That night, Summer asked him to tie her down. He kept no rope in the flat, but they managed to improvise with some old neckties lying in the bottom of one of his drawers. He blindfolded her on his own initiative.

The sex was good. As if they had reached a new level, overcome a final obstacle.

She was alone in Noah's flat. They had shared a quick morning fuck less than thirty minutes ago and as a consequence he had been running late for a meeting and had darted out of bed, showered, dressed and rushed out of the door before he'd even had a chance to finish the coffee that she had brewed for him. He took it black, without any sugar.

Summer had finished her own and was now sipping his, thinking of his mouth touching the rim of the mug where hers now rested, and where his lips had earlier been as he expertly navigated the ever-shifting patterns of her arousal to bring her to climax. Noah rarely let a sexual encounter between them conclude without first making her orgasm. He seemed to take her satisfaction as a point of pride. Initially, Summer had found the attention strange to adjust to, and had reassured Noah that it wasn't necessary – he didn't need to make her come every time.

'I'll do what I like,' he had told her. The tone of his voice at once bemused and imperious. A threat and a promise in equal measure.

Now she revelled in it, let him spread her legs and go down on her when she was still half drunk with sleep and shaking off the previous night's dreams. Sometimes she came quickly, and on other occasions he lapped at her for an hour or longer as she mined the museum of pornography in her head until she found the fantasy that felt right for that particular moment from a library of scenarios that had been her companions for as long as she could remember. Her thoughts remained her own, too dark to share with anyone, even Noah, she feared.

The path of their relationship had followed a strange trajectory. Their bodies melded together so instinctively, it was as if they had always known each other. But the other things – the shared conversations, their histories, likes and dislikes and getting used to each other's habits and foibles – took time. Together they were like a tree with one solid root and an endless mass of new green shoots still finding their way to the sun.

She was wearing one of his shirts, a crisp white Hugo Boss that he saved for special occasions and important business meetings, with a shark collar and turn-back cuffs that flopped around her wrists without the obligatory links pinning them down. It hung loose at her narrow waist and skimmed her wide hips and barely covered the smooth valley of her slit and the firm curve of her rump.

Outside, the day was bright and crisp. She stood in the middle of the living room in front of the wide bay window with her feet bare on the smooth surface of the wooden flooring. She had pulled aside the net curtain to allow the sunlight to stream in. Not even a solitary puff of cloud scudded across the horizon. The sky was an uninterrupted slate of pale blue.

Noah's neighbour, Candy, the woman with the soft name that in Summer's view in no way matched the toughness of her exterior, surfaced from the door of her basement flat. Summer observed her as her silhouette came into view, her head first and the rest of her morphing into sight as she climbed higher on the stairs that led to road level. Today the dead-straight, shining ink-black length of her hair was loose around her shoulders and her ample frame encased all in black to match, her blouse buttoned tight over her breasts and cinched low with a patent leather belt that highlighted the turn of her broad hips and secured the denim leggings that made no attempt to conceal even an inch of her generous curves.

Summer had often wondered whether the ceiling that separated Candy and Noah's apartments was flimsy enough, or Summer's groans loud enough, that Candy could hear them making love. It was admittedly unlikely since Noah's bedroom was separated by another floor, but she still liked to think about it on the fleeting occasions that she bumped into the other woman when Summer was on her way out and Candy on her way in or vice versa.

Candy's full form disappeared from view as she turned up the street, and Summer quit staring out of the window, and turned back to the kitchen to put her mug down, seek out some breakfast from Noah's minimally furnished cupboards and start her day.

She poured some toasted granola into an earthenware bowl, cut a banana into pieces which she dropped in on top and added a few spoonsful of Greek yoghurt that yesterday evening had tempered the spice of the chilli con carne she had cooked for dinner. She mashed the ingredients together into a damp paste and took a bite. Since Noah didn't take milk in his coffee, Summer often found the fridge bereft of it and had learned to improvise with her cereal.

A problem had been niggling on her mind for weeks now. A weight that she just couldn't lift from her shoulders no matter how hard she tried. Its presence could no longer be ignored.

She called Aurelia.

She had thought of calling Lauralynn, but dismissed the idea. Her friend was too close to her and too invested in her happiness to help Summer initiate her plan. Lauralynn would provide her kind words of reassurance, try to convince her that she was being irrational. Ever-cool and curious, Aurelia would see the whole thing as a kind of sexual experiment. Considering Aurelia's history, which she had told Summer a little of, she might even empathise in her own, aloof way.

The Mistress of the Ball did not sound in the least surprised to hear from Summer, or to discover that she had now left Rio and was once again located permanently in London.

'I need your help.'

'Of course,' Aurelia assured her.

Later that evening, over a takeaway mushroom pizza that Summer had picked up from Le Cochonnet, off Lauderdale Road, and a couple of glasses of Fat Bastard Shiraz, she broached the topic with Noah. She waited until they had almost finished the bottle, her heart beating in her mouth all the while. Summer found talking about her feelings difficult. It would be so much easier to show him with her body. But she needed his permission to do that. She wished that she could somehow open a window into her mind, heart and soul for him to peer straight inside.

Noah had sensed that something was in the air. Bothering her mind. He could hear the brittleness in her voice. Had noticed her hands shaking as she topped up their glasses again, although it was unusual for them to drink during the week and even on weekends they rarely consumed more than a small glass of wine each. He feared that Summer might be about to tell him that she had decided the whole affair had happened too soon, was too intense, and call it off.

'There's something I need to show you,' she said.

'Anything,' he replied. His eyes reflected kindness.

The place that she took him to was light and airy, an artist's studio contained within an industrial-looking gated East London apartment complex near the Olympic village, with a wide open-plan living space, small bathroom and a bed-room that was more like a boudoir, kitted out in red and purple tones with luxurious, soft rugs warming the polished wooden floors and veils of chiffon hanging over the low futon bed. Bottles of lubricant, toy cleaner and a glass bowl full of condoms in brightly coloured wrappers sat on a side table.

In the main room, an assortment of beanbags and large soft pillows, wrapped in arabesque crimson and gold covers, had been pushed up against the wall. There was one sofa, as wide as a single mattress with sunken cushions, that looked as though it had borne the weight of many bodies. A series of black-and-white photographs hung at regular intervals displayed different sections of a man's body – the same man, Noah believed – undergoing various methods of what some might consider torture. In one image, hands that belonged to another were pulling on thick silver bars that had been pierced behind his nipples, stretching his skin from his chest. In another, thick hooks had been threaded through the flesh that covered his shoulder blades. The final shot displayed his face in profile and part of his mouth. His expression – passive, inscrutable – wore the shadow of neither a scream nor a smile.

Noah looked away.

Summer was nervous. He could see it in the twist of her hands, the rounded slope of her bare shoulders. She was wearing the short black dress that she'd had on when they met in the alleyway in Recife. The same pair of ballet flats. The exact same outfit, he realised.

He wished he knew what to say to soothe her, even as a sense of dread rushed through him, a dawn of anxiety he could barely control.

It was the middle of the day. Sunlight filtered through the thin curtains that had been pulled across the wide French doors, scattering dappled beams across the polished floor. He wondered who else lived in this block, what kind of secrets the neighbours were concealing.

Summer had introduced him to the other man and woman who were in the room with them. Vincent and Aurelia. He was young and buff and bronzed and half-naked in just a pair of baggy hemp trousers of the sort that Noah imagined yoga teachers wore. Aurelia was as beautiful as her name, a tall willow of a blonde who might have been just on or below thirty, dressed like an actress from the 1940s in an oddly modest, sky-blue tea dress that reached past her knees. They were both barefoot. She was covered in a tapestry of tattoos that Noah could have sworn shimmered and twisted when she moved. No matter how many times he looked at her and tried to capture in his mind the images she wore etched on her skin, when he looked again they had shifted or morphed into something else.

'Are you ready, Vincent?' Aurelia asked.

Vincent nodded.

'And you two?' she asked Noah and Summer together. Summer barely moved her head as an affirmation.

'Yes,' Noah replied, even though he was unaware of exactly what he was consenting to, just following in Summer's footsteps in the hope of keeping her happy.

'Then let's get started,' she said.

Beforehand, Aurelia had taken Noah aside and confirmed with him what he considered his limits to be, and what action he could take if he wanted things to slow down or to stop. Aurelia would be there to witness, to guide if needed and intervene if absolutely necessary, but would not strictly speaking be involved. Noah had told her that he wanted to see whatever it was that Summer – who had stayed mum on the subject – wanted to show him, and if that made him uncomfortable, then so be it.

Vincent had set up a length of red rope that hung down

from an iron loop fixed to a heavy beam that ran across the centre of the ceiling.

Summer approached Noah and kissed him softly on the lips.

His heart ached for her. She had the demeanour of a woman about to walk off the side of a precipice and he wanted to tell her that she didn't need to – whatever it was that she felt he must know – it didn't matter. It didn't matter at all to him, but he knew that there was no use in protesting. When she set her mind to something, she was immovable.

He watched as Summer walked over to Vincent, and the rope, and reached one arm behind her back to unzip her dress. The garment fell to the floor and down to her feet and she stepped out of it and tossed it to one side. She was nude underneath. He admired her body. The soft, now familiar lushness of her curves. Her breasts, full and ever so slightly uneven but perfect nonetheless. He couldn't look at them without thinking about how they felt cupped in his hands and the way that she responded when he gently sucked her nipples. The hollow of her tummy button, the smooth valley of her pudenda. That flaming, untameable burning bush of her hair and the way it flared out over her shoulders. The natural arch in her back that gave her an air of proud defiance. He loved the unapologetic way that she carried herself. Nudity suited Summer.

Aurelia followed suit, unbuttoning the fabric that covered her slender form and casting it over a nearby chair. She was wearing a bra and knicker set in black, a harsh tone against her white skin. She was even paler than Summer. The underwear was high-waisted and generously cut at the bottom, but the bra was a skimpy, half-cup affair that seemed almost pointless to Noah, since it underlined her small, pointed, breasts but left them and her rose-coloured nipples totally bare. When she turned and faced him, Noah realised that the pants were not as full as he had first thought. A triangle of sheer, wisp-thin nylon displayed Aurelia's slit and mons. He thought that he glimpsed a tattoo there too, but could not make it out.

He couldn't help it, wasn't sure if he ought to try. He was hard. His cock strained through his trousers, which he had opted to keep on, unless he was directly asked to undress at some stage.

Vincent was playing music through his laptop. A mix that Noah for once wasn't aware of, with a heavy drum beat and electronic chords that washed over the room with a strongly hypnotic allure.

Vincent had begun tying Summer with practised, deft movements that Noah could barely follow, never mind replicate. Noah was relieved to see the younger man slip his finger through the bonds around Summer's extremities, and periodically peer at the colour of her skin to check that she was not tied too tightly or turning blue. He seemed to know what he was doing.

Noah stopped paying attention to the specifics of the web that Vincent was weaving around her limbs and instead began to observe the changing seasons of Summer's expression.

She had relaxed totally. Her body now hanging limp from the loops that bound her, just below her wrists. Her eyes were closed and a beatific smile had begun to spread over her face.

A low moan escaped from her throat when Vincent placed a metal implement between her legs and buckled the leather cuffs that were attached to each end around her ankles. A spreader bar. Noah had seen them in pornography, knew their uses, but had never actually seen or used one during sex or other circumstances.

Vincent picked something up from the case that was laid down on the floor near him and touched his fingers to Summer's lips, indicating that she should open her mouth. He gagged her.

Noah's thoughts began to race. His cock was now so hard it was throbbing, his restrained balls heavy and painful. There was a lump in his throat. He swallowed. She was becoming the Summer of his other, darker fantasies, the images that still haunted him at night time when the real Summer, her body so trusting, seemingly fragile and precious, lay next to him.

A line of drool hung from her mouth. Sweat began to bead at her brow. Her skin was dappled with red blotches, a colour that he knew mapped the surface of her body when she was most aroused. Between her legs, her slit was slick with juices and her lips were beginning to puff as the blood rushed to the surface.

Noah groaned.

It took an almost inhuman force of effort to keep his hands to his sides and not reach out and caress her, pinch her nipples which were visibly stiff and swollen, slide his fingers inside her, taste the juices that he could see running from her cunt.

Aurelia was lying sideways on the sofa, watching. She had slid her hand into her knickers and was touching herself.

Vincent picked up a whip-like instrument with a burnished handle in dark wood, polished to gleaming, and a fall of multiple leather strands – later, Noah learned it was made from walnut and horse's hide and called a flogger – and began to hit her with it.

The sound of the first blow – a deep whump, like the beating of a heavy rug – made him jump.

The first few blows were relatively light, as Vincent gradually increased the intensity of his strokes. He was twisting the burnished handle back and forth in his hand like a tennis player switching from over- to under-hand grip, drubbing a rhythm onto the lower part of Summer's bare buttocks and the upper part of her back on either side of her spine. Vincent's eyes were glazed and every movement he made was in time with the beat of the ambient music; he seemed as hypnotised as she did. But his aim was true, each blow falling with total accuracy, avoiding the sensitive spaces around her organs and her spine.

Intermittently Vincent would pause his steady rhythm, pull his arm back and strike her with a mighty thud that made Noah wince and made Summer jump and grunt, but not once did she emit the sequence of sounds that Aurelia had told him was a signal she wanted to slow down, stop, or needed something. He longed to jump in and take the instrument away from Vincent, untie her and wipe away her sweat and tears and then hold her tight.

He also wanted to see her hit again, and again, and again. He was fascinated by the way the red marks bloomed over her white skin and faded and bloomed again, an animated map of lust. Noah wanted to create his own patterns over Summer's body, to raise in her the same responses that Vincent was stimulating now.

She was glowing. The same way that she did after he had made her come.

Noah wanted to make her glow. Now and forever.

Finally Vincent slowed and then stopped his assault.

Summer was visibly in a daze. She hung totally loose from her bonds, almost asleep and apparently unaware of what she had just undergone, were it not for the twitching of her limbs and the wetness that glistened between her thighs and betrayed her unmistakable arousal.

Vincent stepped back. Motioned to Noah.

'Fuck her,' he said simply.

Noah looked to Aurelia for approval. Summer was not in any state, right then, to consent to anything.

Aurelia nodded an affirmation.

He hurriedly removed his clothes. His prick needed no encouragement, it had not softened from the moment that he had watched Summer undress.

Noah slid inside her. Came almost immediately.

He pulled out, their mixed juices slick over his penis. Saw the stream of their joined secretions running down the inside of her thigh.

Unbuckled her gag and removed it.

Kissed her.

Vincent reached up to her wrists and loosened her bonds.

Summer fell into Noah's arms.

10

Journey's End

Ever since I had been a child, I was always being told I was prone to unpredictability. A teacher, or was it a friend, had told me that I walked to the beat of my own drum. Peremptory voices inside my head insisting I should conduct my life by personal standards that didn't rely on others.

I saw no reason not to continue down that path.

For several weeks I had reached a state of Zen-like acceptance with Noah, basking in the warmth of our relationship and its rhythms of blissful peaks of lust and necessary lows of holy silences.

Noah had gone up to Scotland for a couple of days to take a look at a band his A&R scouts on the ground had been monitoring for some time. The group were playing a club gig in Edinburgh and he would have to stay the night as it was unlikely to end before the opportunity to catch the last flight back to London.

As I wandered through the Maida Vale apartment, I realised this would be our first night apart in almost three months. Had I ever spent so long in such close proximity to the same man? Even when Dominik was alive, we were often apart due to my touring and his writing obligations.

Right now, Noah was probably still in his office by Notting Hill, just a stone's throw away past the canal and the Harrow Road, still hours to go until his departure for the Scottish capital, but I already felt a sense of loss. Of withdrawal, at the very thought of a whole night alone in our bed. The breakfast leftovers were still strewn across the kitchen table, a slice of toast orphaned and now cold and useless, the empty cereal bowls, dirty cutlery, the strawberry jam pot open, its lid nowhere to be seen. I ignored the mess and rose from the chair. I was once again wearing one of Noah's shirts, a blue linen short-sleeved one I had picked up from the bedroom floor, which he had worn for work the day before and that still smelled of him. My arse was uncovered, a morning sight I'd enjoyed teasing him with as I pottered around the kitchen earlier, fanning his libido and deliberately sending him off on his way with a hard on.

My phone was on the bedside table and I called for a minicab and rushed to dress.

An hour later, I was busy delving through the piles of

cardboard boxes scattered across a cold concrete floor in the storage unit by the North Circular Road where I had left most of my belongings before departing London for the Ball, setting aside items of clothing I had almost forgotten about, knick-knacks, books I had never read, pieces of jewellery I would probably never wear again. Motes of dust hung in the air of the narrow compartment. Wielding the Stanley knife I'd borrowed from the office, I slid open another box with a touch of anxiety; I should have labelled them, I knew, but had not done so originally.

I breathed a sigh of relief. It was the right one. Half a dozen violins, all carefully wrapped in double and triple layers of cloth. Not the Christiansen Bailly, of course, which I'd had auctioned to purchase a place in Rio, the proceeds still sitting virtually unused in my bank account.

I selected two of them, running my palm across the smoothness of the wood, wiping away the dust clinging to their sides, and set them down on the floor, and continued to make my way through the heavy boxes until I found the one in which I had packed all my sheet music. Rifled through them and selected a dozen or so scores almost at random. Shuffling the thin booklets I noticed one for Vivaldi's 'Four Seasons' and ignored it with a faint smile. If there was one piece of music I could play with my eyes closed it was that one, and I had no wish to ever play it again.

I had come unprepared and had to go back down to the storage centre's office and acquire an ugly jute shopping bag to pack the items I wished to take away.

At the flat, it took me several hours to tune the instruments properly until they almost sounded the way I wanted them again and I was then able to take a closer look at the bundle of scores, some of the music I was deeply familiar with and other compositions I'd never got round to tackling.

I settled on Saint-Saëns. Slowly reading through one of his sonatas and then the solo section of the third concerto.

Note by note, the melodies began moving from the page to my brain and then, instinctively, to my fingers, my whole body reading the music, absorbing it by osmosis. On the settee, the two violins sat, still mostly untouched, unplayed, defying me to pick up either of them.

I hesitated.

Made myself one cup of coffee and then another.

Gazed at the instruments, reminded myself of their respective sounds, how the one of darker wood, a violin I had acquired in a small music store in the backstreets of Genoa for a pittance, at the back end of short Italian tour, had sometimes to be coaxed into submission but then delivered a velvety richness of sound once tamed. The other, whose curves felt softer and whose shade of orange evoked a seductive warmth, had been the one I played when experimenting with Viggo and his band, I remembered, its lighter weight and suppleness encouraging improvisation.

I looked around.

Somehow Noah's rooms felt wrong for practising.

Maybe I should move back in to my own place once the lease expired and I could claim it again. Or buy somewhere else?

I moved to the bedroom and searched through the right-hand side of the cupboard which I had allocated myself for my clothes. Checked out a couple of outfits but finally opted for that little black dress. My performing uniform of sorts. Also the one I had been wearing in Recife but which I had since had dry-cleaned several times to erase both memories and stains. And then worn again for Noah, on the occasion that I had him witness me in full flight under the influence of Vincent's ministrations. Despite, or maybe because of, its history, it now felt the appropriate thing to wear.

The bus that would take me into the West End was just arriving at the stop, a few hundred yards from the apartment. The top floor was empty and I sat at the front, right above the driver's cabin, watching as the Edgware Road unrolled in front of me as the bus stuttered its way through the heavy traffic into the centre. I alighted near Oxford Circus and walked east down Oxford Street.

I was seeking the pitch at the bottom of the Northern

Line escalators, but to my dismay it no longer existed. Since my last time here, the CrossRail development had remodelled the station and I briefly wandered the corridors seeking out an area where I could busk. I hadn't applied for or been granted the appropriate licence from TFL so hoped to find a spot well away from the station's staff and wandering inspectors. It had been years since I let my previous permit lapse.

I finally found an area in a narrow alcove at the intersection of two wide, circular corridors connecting the Northern and Central lines. The light was harsh and a constant flow of commuters rushed by, with nary a look at the hirsute guitar player brutalising 'Blowing in the Wind'. I hung around a little, standing in a corner until he finished his set, picked up his case full of coins and walked off, then promptly occupied it and took out my violin, shed my coat which I spread across the floor and began to play. I hadn't brought the Saint-Saëns partition along with me and played from memory.

At first the sound was something of an echo-strewn screech, until I got a handle on the acoustics of the tunnels and modulated my fingering accordingly to extract a more harmonious flow, adjusting my angle of attack with the bow. It was still some degrees from perfection but at least the violin sounded more pleasant and acceptable as far as my demanding ears were concerned. Although I was also aware that the passing Tube users would generally not know the difference.

I wasn't playing for them though; I was playing for myself.

I shut my eyes. Immersing myself in the music. The notes on the page danced along my closed eyelids. My fingers flew over the strings and my wrist strained as my arm guided the bow through its necessary motions.

Then the notes disappeared and the fuzzy image transformed, morphing into a ballet of colours as the music began to overwhelm my consciousness and animate me, stealing me away from the draughty corner of the Tube junction of corridors and its cavernous acoustics, transporting me into that zone I now remembered so well. Where I flew through the spheres, where my whole body was just an extension of the music, of my instrument, where my will faded and I became insubstantial, a mere creature of emotion.

The sound of coins dropping onto my outstretched coat at regular intervals punctuated my reverie as the melody unrolled both in my mind and from the tips of my busy fingers. All too soon, it shivered to an end. The sound of a few hands clapping, and I opened my eyes. Two older women stood, watching me, gentle smiles drawn across their lips. As if expecting me to play something else. I returned their smile, bowed my head in response to their approval. The crowds of passengers came and went in waves, as trains on both lines drew onto the nearby platforms, disgorging their commuters. It was a weekday, so I knew I was not at risk from a horde of football fans as had happened on that first fateful occasion.

I briefly thought of what I could play next, but none of the prospects pleased me. I was badly out of practice, and in no state to improvise.

I returned home.

By the time Noah arrived back the following day, my fingers were raw and the strained muscles in my upper arm were groaning from all the hours I had put in playing, rehearsing, practising, failing time and time again until I was happy with my playing. I had barely slept.

'You look tired,' he said as he set down his overnight bag in the hall and kissed me. 'Are you feeling alright?'

I nodded. When he walked into the study, he caught sight of my violins, the music stand I had set up and the mess of partitions spread across the room on all possible surfaces.

'You're playing again,' he said. 'Wonderful.'

He took me in his arms.

'Yes,' I said. 'But early days.' I didn't want him to get too excited about it yet, make any sort of plans, but Noah was understanding and careful not to ask me any questions, which I was grateful to him for.

I felt so thankful for the delicacy of his intuition and a totally crazy thought ran through my mind.

'If you want,' I told him. 'I'll play for you tonight. Something special, somewhere special.'

'I would love that.'

'A surprise.'

All through the evening, I could sense his impatience, as we ate and then watched a Scandinavian thriller serial on the TV, slyly glancing at me throughout, wondering what I might have in my mind.

Towards midnight, I rose from the sofa.

'Now . . .'

'I thought you'd forgotten, or given up,' he remarked.

'Of course not.'

I changed back into my little black dress. Wearing it had become something of a ritual for me and I wondered whether he was aware of the fact. I chose the Italian violin.

The minicab I'd ordered earlier was waiting for us downstairs. The driver knew our destination, and I'd agreed to pay extra for his discretion.

As Noah opened the car door and held it for me, I handed him a black velvet blindfold.

He appeared surprised.

'For you.'

'Really?'

'To maintain the element of surprise,' I said.

He slipped it on, sat down next to me and slammed the door shut and the car drove off. The driver remained silent throughout the journey. The roads were empty. I held Noah's hands as we journeyed east, past Lord's Cricket Ground and along Regent's Park and then cut north on the Finchley Road towards Hampstead. The minicab dropped us off on the hill, close to the ponds. Still holding his hand as we exited the car, I could feel Noah's disorientation as he blindly tried to guess from the directions we'd driven where we might be.

'Hold on tight,' I said to him as I led him along onto the Heath. 'The ground is uneven.'

We passed the ponds. The darkness was overwhelming but I knew these paths like the back of my hand. The slope ascended and ten minutes later we reached the familiar clearing away from the canopy of trees. There was a thin sliver of moon, bathing us in an eerie glow. I pulled an often stumbling Noah along as we took the incline that led to the bandstand. He was remarkably restrained and unquestioning, considering the circumstances.

'Sit,' I told him.

He didn't mind the grass being damp, and did so.

He was facing the bandstand, looking upwards.

I slipped out of my clothes, climbed the half-dozen steps and placed the violin against my chin. It felt cold.

I had earlier given much consideration to what I should play.

'Fingal's Cave'.

393

The initial chill breathing across my body soon faded and I played for the hungry segment of the moon and for my new lover.

As I squeezed all the beauty and melancholy out of the wonderful piece of music, I kept my gaze firmly on Noah.

His face was serene. He knew exactly what my intentions were and sat absolutely still, accepting of the theatricality of the moment, not even tempted to pull his blindfold away, guessing I was bare and vulnerable and offered.

All too soon, carried along by the deep yearning of the melody I came to the end of the piece and knew I had no need for further improvisations.

'You can take off the blindfold,' I called out to Noah.

He took his time, savouring the tension in the air, the fading echo of each note and quaver, and delicately pulled the blindfold off, stretching the silk band across his ears, ruffling his hair.

Saw me.

His face showed no expression, confirming that he knew how he would find me.

Without a word he unbuttoned his shirt and stepped out of his trousers and walked towards me.

We made love on the stone floor of the bandstand.

Neither Summer nor Noah had ever been to Iceland, though she had always dreamed of visiting the stark landscapes of the far North, home to the legendary aurora borealis alien light show that she had only previously seen captured, still, in photographs. He had once thought of visiting the Holy Criminals' birthplace when Viggo and his then band had toured there, but another commitment had prevented him.

When Aurelia's invitation to the Ball arrived, they both joyfully accepted.

'So – what exactly is this Ball? Are you going to let me know this time what you're getting me into?' he teased her.

They were in Ping Pong by the Southbank Centre, sharing steaming baskets of dim sum. Summer was sipping from a boiling-hot glass of flowering hibiscus tea. He watched her with affection as she stared at the bud unfurling in the water that had now fully bloomed and appeared unfeasibly large and lifelike in all its three-dimensional, tentacular glory, like uncharted flora that belonged on the depths of the ocean floor.

She looked up. Met his gaze. Her chopsticks were resting on the olive-green, ceramic holder by her napkin as she waited for the next round of dumplings and wontons they had ordered to arrive. Summer was saving space for the seasonal special, a dish of crab shu mai – an open-top pastry with a filling of seafood, turnip and coriander. Noah was unconvinced by the advertised presence of goji berries, and instead filled up on another of his favourites, the sweet and salty char sui buns.

'Honestly,' she told him, 'I could try to tell you but I fear that I would only sound ridiculous. It's better if you rid your mind of expectations, and just appreciate the experience once we arrive. Besides,' she added, 'each occasion is different. I can barely believe some of the things that I have seen with my own eyes, let alone explain them.'

She had provided him with only sparse details of her employment with the Ball and the Network, of the theatre piece that Mieville had mentioned attending in the Spiegeltent, her later performance on the American desert plains of Nevada, and the circumstances that had led her to the Amazon region and then to Rio.

Noah was eager to learn and to see more but he knew better than to press Summer for details. She tended to close up when she felt harangued. In the course of their communication he learned that sometimes it was better just to leave her be and trust her to open up to him in her own time.

She continued speaking, as he thought she might.

'There's going to be a magician at this one, apparently,' she said. 'A famous illusionist.' She paused. 'I've agreed to provide musical accompaniment to one of his performances. Lauralynn too, on cello.'

'That's wonderful,' he said, and meant it. He was so glad to see her returning to the violin.

Her hand was resting on his thigh under the table, grasping him tightly through the denim of his jeans. His fly was a button-up rather than zip, and occasionally she wiggled her fingers through the gaps in the stiff fabric, managing to just brush the tip of a single digit against the bare skin of his shaft. She had insisted he go commando.

Earlier that evening, when they had dressed together in his Maida Vale flat before going out, he had told her to slip in the stainless steel butt plug with the jewelled end – a small, pretty toy he had gifted her with some weeks back – and he knew that she wore it now and was panty-less beneath her short black dress, the one he had noticed she now made a habit of wearing as a prequel to their particularly rough, wonderfully perverse sex sessions.

Her eyes were deep glowing pits of bright hazel. He had never been able to quite identify the precise shade. They shimmered across the colour chart, sometimes appearing paler and sometimes darker, the flecks of green tonight more pronounced than the flickering lines of amber or brown. Her pupils dilated in that glazed expression she wore when she was fantasising about what she knew would come later, and her gentle touches and gestures of endearment became more pronounced until the rest of the world receded entirely and she seemed totally oblivious to the diners that sat around them on the shared, hexagonal table as she groped his cock in full public view.

After they settled the bill, collected their coats and headed back into the crisp night air in the direction of Waterloo station, Noah intended to take Summer's hand and pull her under the relative privacy of the arches beneath the Hungerford and Golden Jubilee Bridges, press her against the damp wall, lift her dress and press the plug deeper into her arse or perhaps remove it and replace it with his fingers, or get down on his knees and make her come despite the presence of strangers walking by who would surely hear her moans. He was confident now of his ability to both tease and torment her. Had learned all of her quirks and limits and used them to his and her advantage.

Yet the infinite territory of her sexual landscape continued to intrigue him. He never grew tired of Summer.

Could not help but love the heart, the body and the soul of this flame-haired woman who had catapulted into his life when he had least expected it.

Summer did not bother to sling her jacket around her shoulders when she stepped onto the balcony of the small cabin that they were staying in for the night and stared out at the white and black expanse of the arctic ice fields spreading out in all directions around her beneath the inky sky, in which an endless array of bright stars shone their twinkling lanterns.

She had been unable to sleep, full of excitement and apprehension when she considered the events that the coming days would bring. It felt like the crossing of a final

Rubicon, introducing Noah to the Ball. The threads of their relationship were now woven over every part of her life. There was nothing that she kept from him anymore, not in the humdrum of her day-to-day environment or even the far richer tapestry of her inner thoughts, dreams and fantasies.

Her skin prickled in the frozen air, so cold that every infinitesimal puff of wind cut like a knife's blade. Summer thrived in the wintry depths of the North as much as she had loved Rio's humid air. The extremes made her feel alive, fed the opposing dichotomies of her contradictory personality.

The sliding door squeaked on its rollers. Noah had noticed the absence of her warm body between the covers next to him and woken. He stepped behind her and pressed his torso against her back, wrapping his arms around her shoulders and laying his hands over hers where they rested on the verandah's top rail. The heat of his body burned a sweet flame against her chilled skin.

'Brr . . .' he remarked. 'You're frozen.'

She burrowed back into the warmth of his welcoming arms.

His prick hardened against the small of her back and he shifted his weight and slid inside her, revelling in the sultry wetness of her slit, still slick from their earlier fuck.

She groaned and clung onto the wooden support for

balance as he thrust into her, hard. He shuddered and came quickly.

'Thought I'd better make it swift,' he murmured into her ear, mischievously catching the lobe and licking it gently. 'We'll catch our deaths out here. Come back to bed and I'll lullaby you to sleep with my tongue.' He took her hand.

She followed him gladly, this man who knew every inch of her inside and out and had captivated every morsel that was left of her untamed heart.

They had arrived earlier in the week, and spent three blissful days as tourists, based in Reykjavik, relaxing in the temperate milky waters of the Blue Lagoon, relishing tasting plates of lobster risotto, smoked fish selections and crème caramel made from skyr at Fridrik V, or feasting on shrimp tempura and sashimi at the Fish Market before stumbling back to their hotel on the bay in the dark after sampling too many of the exotic offerings from the cocktail list, and staying up late talking and making love throughout the night as the caffeine in the espresso martinis kept them both awake and terribly alert.

Summer fell head over heels for the shaggy beasts who carried them over a moonscape of pure soft white when they tried their hands at husky sledding, after first waking in the early hours of the morning to embark on a perilous drive across a volcanic dark mountain road where Noah could not even see two inches clear in front of the windshield but the driver managed to find his path through the falling snow. The sun's rising rays cast fingers of pale pink over the horizon, and standing behind the musher, rugged up in protective outer gear so thick they could barely move, they had felt as though they were speeding swiftly into a world imagined in a child's dream. Afterwards she made Noah promise to investigate the possibility of adopting a dog.

'An Alaskan Malamute?' he teased her.

'A mongrel,' Summer replied. 'One that's all mixed up and needs saving, like me.' She laughed, and Noah had embraced her and kissed her cheek, once he managed to locate it beneath the layer of her extensive fur-trimmed hood.

Noah got wind of an impromptu session by Vök, occurring at an underground bar that doubled as a café where they had earlier grimaced over a shared platter of Icelandic delicacies that included strong-smelling saltfiskur – salt fish – and harðfiskur, a dried fish served with butter. Noah had been surprised to find that he liked them both. They returned at midnight to hear the band play and were ushered downstairs and sipped expensive bottled beers while Noah compared the experimental electronica duo's sensual, dreamy sound to the more upbeat rhythms produced by the Handsomes and mulled over whether their act might work in the UK. Later he planned to follow up with the band's manager and find out the terms of their current contract. 'There's something about melancholy music and cold climates,' he told Summer, as they found their way back to their hotel in the dark after first taking a detour past Tjörnin, the pond in the centre of town, where Summer ventured slowly out onto the solid, iced-over surface and played at skating in her flat boots.

On their fourth day they hired a car and took turns driving on the dead-straight flat road to Geysir and Gullfoss. They stopped in Thingvellir to see Lögberg and the world's oldest parliament and both scoffed at the thought but could not shake the idea that they felt something there, as they stood by the rocky outcrop looking over at the wide plain ahead of them, surrounded by mountains rising in the distance like sleeping giants watching over the land. An indefinable sense of solemnity lingered over the place, the ghost of times past still intact despite the footfall of so many tourists disturbing the peace with their clicking cameras.

Summer delighted in the improbable rainbows leaping from the towering sheet of falling water at Skógafoss, and Noah stopped the car at Kerið to see the volcanic amphitheatre and its crater lake in the centre, on which Björk had once staged a concert from the safety of a floating raft.

They finally stopped and spent the night at an isolated

chalet in Vik, after first spending the afternoon exploring the moonscape of the black sand beach, listening to the waves crashing over the puzzle stacks and watching the tiny ink-feathered birds that might have been puffins flashing occasional glimpses of white bellies and bright beaks as they swooped over the basalt columns, hexagonal fingers of rock stacked up like a game of dominoes between the gods. 'Hours fly by like minutes in this no-man's-land,' Noah said, breaking the companionable silence they shared as the sun set and turned sky and sea into mirror images of glowing blue-black obsidian sheen and Summer thought this lonely ash-sanded coastline might be the most beautiful place she had ever set her eyes upon.

The nearby restaurants were closed and, too lazy to venture farther, they visited a service station that displayed bottles of motor oil and anti-freeze alongside a small grocery section. Noah selected a couple of large potatoes and a can of tuna from the minimally stocked shelves, pointing out the rack of ancient CDs on the counter and laughing at the cover of a dusty Elton John greatest hits album.

Summer turned the oven on, dug a roasting tray out from the cupboards and scrubbed the produce while Noah mixed the tinned fish with spring onions and lashings of thick mayonnaise and later stirred in the cooked vegetable's white flesh and spooned the filling back into the crisp skins. He set each overflowing baked spud onto a plate alongside a handful of limp iceberg lettuce leaves and sprinkled the tops with Cheddar cheese. Conversation was sparse as they shifted into quiet mode, both still awed by the view that stretched out in front of them beyond the glass windows of their log cabin, a blanket of nothingness that made them both feel like insignificant specks in a vast universe.

Later that night they finally witnessed the theatre show of the Northern Lights in all their splendour as a plethora of multi-coloured streaks collided in the heavens above them, while they reclined in the outdoor hot tub until their toes shrivelled up and avoided the inevitable rush of cold awaiting them when they trod barefoot across the iced-over porch to return to the bedroom.

'I don't want it to end,' Summer told Noah.

'There will be plenty more holidays,' he promised her, and they talked about all the other countries and cities they would visit, leaving ordinary life behind them and travelling to destinations they both already knew and loved or wanted to share with the other, and new places they could explore side by side too.

She threaded her fingers in his hair and he rested his face in her lap and thought of how he would pleasure her as soon as they got into bed, or better still, right now on the sofa as the clock on the wall ticked a merry meaningless rhythm and the field of snow still visible through the open curtains in front of them never seemed to darken, the moonlight reflecting on the white surface, making the world seem a little brighter.

Aurelia had arranged for them to leave their hire vehicle in Vik. One of the Network's drivers, a bearded, brusque man of Viking stature with a deep winter tan and a rich baritone voice, collected them in a sleek black 4WD and they drove for several hours through a wilderness of narrow roads. Barren peaks rose up all around them like the jagged back teeth of a humongous prehistoric animal. Two other attendants, each of them meek-mannered and half the size of the driver, had carried away their baggage which they were assured would be forwarded on and stored at the Ball to be returned to them before their transfer back to Keflavik International airport some days hence. They had each packed a small overnight case containing their outfits – an elegant tuxedo for Noah, who hadn't been able to face the thought of more traditional fetish wear – and a floor-length gown for Summer with an open back and halter neck, made in midnight-blue silk that flowed over her body like water, highlighting every curve and turning the copper red of her hair into a flame that glowed around her shoulders. She planned to wear it with a pair of small, opal studs in her ears that Noah had bought her to mark the occasion, which looked like miniature globes of the world in her lobes, reflecting every shade racing across her body.

A helicopter took them on the final leg of the journey. Conversation was impossible as the buzz of the blades was barely muted by the protective headsets the pilot handed to them as they navigated through grey skies in uncertain weather for miles, until the atmosphere seemed to shift around them and an array of tents, vehicles and microscopic people crawling like ants across the vast floor of the isolated valley beneath them came into view.

Lauralynn and Viggo were waiting at the landing pad for them to disembark.

'Christ, they must be hypothermic,' Noah remarked, as the chopper came to a standstill and their friends approached.

Viggo's lanky form was protected only by a pair of skimpy rubber briefs and a set of tall flat boots that flared out around his bony knees in a cloud of ermine trim.

Noah averted his eyes to Lauralynn, who looked like a Narnian Winter Witch in a striking latex catsuit and a flowing cape in the same faux fur that decorated Viggo's legs. Her boots were heeled, transparent, and appeared to be made of solid glass, revealing a row of blood-red painted toenails to match the streak of crimson lipstick that coloured her lips.

Latex, Summer had told him, tends to heighten whatever temperature surrounds the wearer, so although she was covered from head to toe Noah expected that Lauralynn must be freezing beneath.

Warm air swept over Noah's face as he exited the passenger seat and joined Summer in embracing their friends. Despite the season and the sheets of white that dominated the environment around them, the climate was as warm as a spring day.

He blinked. Overhead, he heard a rush of wind like the beating of enormous wings and looked up to see a group of women, nude apart from winged costumes that made them appear half bird, and apparently borne aloft only by invisible currents. One of them held a much younger man in her arms. They were copulating in mid-air. Noah squinted, scanning the sky for signs of hidden fly wires or some other mechanism that enabled the two to hover and wheel above them unsupported.

'Fuck me,' he muttered under his breath. His search had revealed nothing but an empty horizon.

'I know,' Viggo said. 'I haven't figured it out either.'

Noah shrugged. If Viggo, who had been renowned for his dazzling stagecraft during his time as the Holy Criminals front man, couldn't spot the wizardry responsible for this magic trick, he didn't have much hope. Not so long ago, Noah would have been shocked, if fascinated, by the spectacle of strangers coupling, but now the sight of others touching or even having sex in front of him seemed absolutely unremarkable.

Four sleds, which had evolved from black dots like

pinpricks in the distance, morphed into shape before them. Aurelia was driving one, pulled by a half-dozen husky dogs. She stood on the footboards with a crop in her hand, bare-foot and totally nude besides the blanket of tattoos that Noah saw covered every inch of her body and displayed a veritable kaleidoscope of colours and images, from Egyptian hieroglyphs to other unrecognisable runes and symbols, every kind of animal that might be found in the most exotic zoo, and a number of creatures that he believed were totally mythical but would now not have been surprised to see drop out of the sky directly in front of him.

'Thank god,' Lauralynn announced. 'I was worried I couldn't take another step in these shoes.'

'You didn't come by air?' Summer asked her.

'No,' she said, 'We walked along the mountain trail.' She pointed to a mighty obsidian crag in the distance. 'There's a section of tunnels that lead through the cliff face. And a half-dozen more routes in and out of here besides that, but you'd never spot them without proper guidance.'

Aurelia's hired mushers packed the group's luggage into the sled's cargo beds and they were carted at speed down towards the main concourse. Noah nearly shouted out as they drew frighteningly close to a formless blot that spread out on the ice field like a Rorschach ink splash on a blank canvas, thinking that they were about to hurtle directly into the path of a jagged rock, but the dogs veered away at the last moment and as they slowed to pass the obstacle he realised that it was nothing more than a jet-black fur coat that had been abandoned in the snow.

An invisible fog clouded the Ball's tents and pavilions, thick with the scent of toffee apples, a smell that reminded Noah of childhood fairs at Clapham Common. Multi-coloured bells were strung up on gold threads as thin as strands of hair, joining the circle of elaborate canvas structures. The bells tinkled with each fluttering breath of wind.

Aurelia disappeared to attend to her responsibilities as the Ball's Mistress and Viggo and Lauralynn strode off to explore the circus-like attractions of the daytime entertainment that was on display around them, leaving Noah and Summer to relax, eat and change out of their travelling clothes. They were ushered into a private yurt, a large teepee that contained a bubbling hot tub filled with mineral water that boiled up directly from the ground beneath them.

'How is all this possible?' he asked her, as he bit into a chocolate éclair as light and fluffy as any he had tasted in a Parisian patisserie. The room contained platters of refreshments; miniature cakes that were no more than a mouthful, cold cuts and cheese, slices of fresh tropical fruit, and towers of panna cotta and jellied berries. A series of jugs had been set up alongside the food and held sweet punch, bitingly sour fresh grapefruit juice, chilled white wine, red wine and champagne.

An ice-cold plunge pool stood next to the Jacuzzi, and two over-sized fluffy robes were warming on a towel rail within arm's reach.

'If I knew, I would tell you,' Summer promised him. 'But I genuinely don't have the faintest idea. Aurelia, and the Network, the organisation she works for which oversees all of this, are like the sex and sensuality mafia. They have unlimited resources when it comes to throwing these kinds of parties but I have no clue where it all comes from or how they do it.'

'Nothing for it but to enjoy ourselves then, I suppose,' he replied, joining her in the warm water. She was gazing at him with that fire he so loved to see in her eyes, submerged up to her waist and resting her elbows on the sides of the tub so that her breasts pointed out of the water, her nipples pink and hard, awaiting his attention.

It was twilight when they emerged, and instead of following the crowds of revellers who were marching towards the opera-size stage that formed the epicentre of their temporary surrounds, Noah led Summer into another tent marked 'the lair' where Viggo had informed him that a beehive of booths had been set up into temporary pleasure palaces, equipped with every implement that lovers could hope for with architectural options designed to suit those who sought isolation as well as to indulge those who preferred to enact their fantasies in public or view others in the guise of voyeurism.

The only sounds that later emanated from the private antechamber that Noah had selected was a chorus made up of the thudding flogger he beat against her skin, the slapping of their bodies, skin on skin, Summer's moans and cries as he manipulated all of her senses to crescendo and back down and up again, and finally the desperate groan that birthed from his throat when he came inside her and collapsed, utterly spent. They did not speak until they had left the tent and the shared experience of a fuck so wonderful it seemed like a sacred thing to them both, and Summer realised that she was almost late for her scheduled performance and had no time to bathe again or dress in the gown that she had planned to wear.

They had missed one of the main shows, a ballet beneath the ice floor that had been televised on giant screens set up on the stage and featured a woman of apparently Brobdingnagian proportions who danced on the points of knives and unsettingly took pleasure from her pain.

Noah could not have cared less.

Had an anonymous bystander observed the audience who were resting on tiered rows of gilded seats within the covered amphitheatre, they would have seen that among the hushed guests who were overwhelmed by the spectacle occurring on the circular dais directly in their centre, only one man's mind and gaze was fixed elsewhere.

The act began simply enough.

The magician, dressed all in black, stood to one side. His assistant was situated in the room's dead centre, a thin woman with medium-length, mouse-brown hair brushed to a shine who stood totally naked besides a rope of exquisite pearls that encircled her delicate throat. She looked afraid, and appeared to be totally unaware of the crowd that surrounded her. The magician's attention remained focused on the movement of his hands that played with invisible marionette strings in the air in front of him. It was no matter to him whether his assistant was afraid or not.

The audience emitted a single gasp in unison, as before their eyes a tiny bubble materialised, and floated, growing in dimension until it was the size of a fairy-tale Cinderella carriage large enough to fit four comfortably or six at a squash.

The woman shed a tear, wiped it onto the bubble's side, and disappeared from sight for a moment, shimmering into a hazy blur and reappearing within the sphere. It hovered just a few feet above the ground, seemingly controlled by the twitching fingers of the magician, whose severe features were now covered in a pronounced sheen of sweat.

She was joined by four others, three women and a man who were so achingly perfect in proportions they might have been sylphs rather than humans, oiled, buffed, sleek and nimble, creatures fashioned by the harsh and beautiful environment around them who would dissolve back into it once their task was complete.

They penetrated her. First with darting fingers and tongues and then with cocks so large she baulked at taking one, before being stretched to fit all three. Slowly her expression changed from fearful to beatific, a stream of emotions registering across her face for the hundreds of strangers in the tent to witness, until she was torn apart inside and assembled together again in a profile that illustrated a surreal form of peace.

Throughout it all, a brown-haired man in one of the front rows remained captivated by another. The red-haired musician standing in the orchestra pit whose nude body sheltered the curves of her violin as she immersed the whole crowd in a devilish pizzicato that peaked in a florid crescendo at the point where some of the audience feared that the woman in the bubble had been killed by her orgasm before the notes evolved into a sinuous melody, her fiddle now joined by the deeper tones of a cello as the two instruments together crafted a song that was both a torture and a delight to the souls of all those present.

The violinist played with her eyes closed, and the curve of a smile visible on her upturned lips. Her skin bore a map of red marks, some of them now fading and others that might bloom into bruises, the colour of the now violet sky presiding above the tent. When she shifted her position,

413

spreading her legs just slightly further apart, a line of moisture glimmered on the soft skin of her upper thigh.

He had eyes only for her.

That night their sleep was uninterrupted, the heavy dreamless slumber of lovers, equally spent and happy to be tangled in each other's arms.

They did not wait after Summer's performance, to watch the other shows or the couplings between the guests present that they knew would be inevitable as the early hours progressed to morning.

Neither did they wake to watch the traditional ceremony of Aurelia's re-confirmation as Mistress of the Ball at dawn.

When they finally arose, well rested, washed in the hot tub and then breakfasted on the leftovers of the extensive buffet that had greeted them on their arrival, it was close to midday and their transport was ready to return them via a long and complicated combination of air and road travel to the airport where they would catch their return flight to London.

Aurelia came to see them off.

Regal even in her casual wear of soft denim leggings, cashmere sweater and thick boots, Noah thought that she still bore the signs of the previous night's entertainment. Not in puffy eyes or lines around her face but in the same inner glow that suffused her features and which he often noticed in Summer after they had just made love.

'Hi,' she said to them both. 'Thank you for coming all this way.'

'No, Aurelia, thank you for having us. It's been . . . incredible,' Noah told her, struggling for the right words to describe his experience of the improbable wonderland they had been ferried to. 'The best show of my life,' he added.

She carried an instrument's case in her hand.

Noah saw that Summer's eyes were fixed on it, and her face had turned an even paler hue than her usual shade of white.

'Is that my . . .' she started.

'Yes,' Aurelia told her. 'Your Bailly. The Network bought it at auction, on my instruction. But Summer, the instrument belongs to you, and only you. You must keep it.'

She extended the case in her hand, where it stayed for several moments as Summer refused her offer.

'I can't . . . the cost . . .' she insisted. 'It's too much.'

'Your soul is entwined with whatever magic this violin holds,' Aurelia replied. Her voice was twinged with humour, as if even she wasn't entirely sure how true the myths were that surrounded the famed Christiansen. 'If you do not take it,' she added, 'I fear for the violin's next owner.'

Noah remembered from the tales at the auction house that the instrument had a tumultuous history and was aware that some saw ownership of it as a sure path to an uncertain fate.

Summer still refused. 'I've spent some of the proceeds already,' she told the Mistress, 'I can't pay you back.'

'We don't need or want your money,' Aurelia told her. 'Just your promise that you'll play it. And, at some stage, play it again for us. Consider it a down payment against future performances, a deposit that I'm sure even your agent would urge you to consider.'

Summer accepted.

'I have only one condition of my own,' she said, as she wrapped her hand around the handle of the instrument's jet-black case.

'Yes?'

'Don't ask me to play Vivaldi again.'

I could feel that fervent buzz of expectancy rumble through the Berlin Philharmonie building. Set in Tiergarten, in the heart of the Kulturforum, it had opened in the sixties and was one of the jewels in the crown of world classical music. I had never performed there before. The main auditorium, in which I would be playing today, was shaped like a pentagon, had over two thousand seats and had the dimensions of a pagan temple. During soundchecks and rehearsals I had felt awed by the sheer splendour of its beautiful acoustics and architectural lines, and knew all too well that my concentration, phrasing and sound were not yet at their optimum, fine-tuned enough for my own satisfaction. But Simon, my ex-lover from a time that now felt like another life, and the orchestra were also aware from experience that solo performers often held back their best for the actual concert, so there had been no sign of worry.

It had taken Noah weeks of negotiations with sundry commercial parties involved to arrange for Simon's youthful Venezuelan orchestra in full to make the journey. We had parted on good terms. Once approached, Simon had naturally been enthusiastic at the idea of conducting on the occasion of my return to the stage, but the finances had been complicated and had to be underwritten by the label against the future earnings of the live album which would be recorded on the evening. Adding to the pressure on all involved.

He turns and faces the wall, arms outstretched against it for support and allows me to undress him, steps out of the material I have loosened and unbuttoned, material falling away as in a dream. The solid bulk of his body, the sharpness of his hips, the meat of his strong thighs, the delicate curve of his neck and the untidy cascade of his hair flowing down towards his shoulders. I like the fact that his hair is always untidy, untamed. And its smell.

I pass my hand through his legs which he parts wider sensing my approach. Take his balls between my fingers, knead them, caress them, weigh them, careful not to touch his cock, although I can feel it throbbing already.

417

He backs into me.

His warmth, the gentle fire dancing across his bare skin, spreading its invisible tentacles around me.

I squeeze harder, testing his resolve.

He shudders.

Guttural sounds of pain and pleasure rise from his throat.

I was now alone in my dressing room.

I'd never suffered from stage fright earlier in my career, but today an uncertain feeling seized me, in the knowledge that Noah was putting his own job on the line by organising the concert. If I failed, I knew the awful pressure it could put on our relationship.

The bright bulbs illuminating the borders of the make-up mirror glared at me like tiny suns.

Every flat surface in the room was covered in goodwill cards and flowers: bouquets, vases, intricate confections in improbable shapes, wreaths.

The five-minute call boomed through the Tannoy. I was already dressed, though still shoeless. Make-up in place.

The single rose he'd given me was utter perfection, blood-red, carved with intricacy like a jewel, every petal a work of art, vibrant, electric. He had handed it to me with a soft farewell kiss on my forehead, elegant and forceful in his tuxedo, his dress shirt crisp and white, his eyes sparkling with pride.

Its long stem was festooned with fierce thorns and I took

it with care between my fingers and clipped it to my black dress with a gold piece of costume jewellery I had picked up while with the Ball. Slipped on my high-heeled, red-soled new pair of Louboutins, a present from Lauralynn and Viggo, and walked out of the dressing room.

The long corridor that ran parallel to the auditorium, leading to the stage, unfolded, the rumour of the awaiting audience growing with every step.

I get down on my knees.

He swivels round. His hard cock now standing at attention in front of my face. I keep on grasping on to his ball sack. He moans. A glistening pearl of pre-cum shines on the tip of his cock, forcing its way through the eyelet of his glans. I lick it. Taste it. Savour it. Suck savagely in an cruel attempt to pump him forcefully, extract his essence with every further drop I can raise to the surface. He stoically endures my perverse torture, his eyes both faraway and fixed on me.

His knees are unsteady and I allow him a respite.

I finally strip and we are both naked.

I get back on my knees, take his soft balls in my mouth, lick him clean, move my tongue further down, trailing over his perineum until I am forcing its tip inside him, his darkness, his most intimate part.

I can feel him resisting another surge of pleasure, holding back. I know how sensitive he is down there. He knows too.

We move to the bed.

419

Someone held a curtain aside for me, handed me the Bailly and I emerged onto the stage. The sound of applause was deafening but I was blinded by the light as I walked the short distance from the wings towards the centre, where Simon stood on the conducting podium. Lauralynn sat, legs wide open, her massive cello like a throne pushing back the folds of her long dress, leading the strings, a familiar face among the orchestra's players.

The light dimmed.

I bowed.

Caught a glimpse of Noah in the front row, amid a vast sea of faces.

I looked straight into his eyes.

Silently reminding him that I was here for him, that he was the only spectator I cared for. That the other two thousand plus members of the audience were superfluous, invisible.

He winked.

My throat felt dry. I evoked his unmistakable taste, and the way his whole body shuddered as if pierced by a sword of cold at the moment he would come in my mouth. Felt the heat rise from my core to my forehead.

I heard the pat-pat of Simon's baton across his lectern, bringing the orchestra to attention. The musicians scrutinising both the conductor, awaiting his signal to commence, and their unfolded leaves of sheet music.

There was a lengthy orchestral section before I was ushered in. I closed my eyes. Isolated myself. The soul of the Bailly poured through my fingers.

A weighty hush ran through the auditorium.

He takes me into his arms, tosses and turns me, uses hands, fingers, lips, tongue and toys on me, until I am begging for him to fuck me.

He cruelly and beatifically takes his time while I hover on the edge of a precipice.

I am hot inside and outside, a wreck, a supplicant begging for him to press his advantage and reduce me to pulp, ejaculate across my naked skin to mark me as his, like an animal, now that I have no shame left and am reduced to a brain imprisoned in cage of pure lust, striving for pleasure, a cage of flesh that he plays with, teases, insults, manipulates, pleases in ways I didn't know were possible. But I am greedy, always want more, more love, more lust, more pleasure until I finally reach that abominable wall against which I want to crash and explode into a trillion pieces. Filled by him, invaded by him, stretched and widened and pulled and torn. Until we are just one.

'Fuck me hard . . .'

'Yes, my love,' Noah says.

I shifted slightly, broadening the angle of my legs, imagining a soft, sweet breeze wafting upwards through the Philharmonie building and reaching my naked cunt lips beneath the tight black dress, soothing my inner fire. I wore no underwear. Noah had asked. A mighty secret only the two of us would share. Had he asked me, I would have performed naked even.

I raised the bow.

My music came to life. I came to life.

Acknowledgements

Three years ago, Vina met Jackson on a train between London and Bristol and the adventures of Vina Jackson in the land of pleasure were launched.

Ten books later, and it's been a wild, wonderful, erotic ride as the journey has come full circle and we bid farewell to Summer and all her fictional cohorts.

We've named names at the end of every volume of 80 DAYS, MISTRESS OF NIGHT AND DAWN and, now, THE PLEASURE QUARTET, so this time around discretion will remain the better part of valour. You know who you all are.

All we want to do is thank every single one of our publishers worldwide, our individual editors, copy-editors and translators: you've turned our naked words into gold and made them better.

The Pleasure Quartet: Summer

Without our literary agent Sarah Such who carried the flame all along, the journey wouldn't have taken us so far and wide both geographically and into the minds and hearts of our almost two million readers. Thank you.

And, of course, an immense vote of thanks to all those wonderful readers who made the mountain so much easier to climb, deadline after deadline.

Finally, there is no way to express how much friends and family, who stood by to support us beyond and above the call of duty, made the task worthwhile.

Until we meet again . . .